WINGS OF FIRE

THE LOST HEIR

THE GRAPHIC NOVEL

To Barry, Rachel, Mike, Maarta, and Phil —
thank you so much for understanding these dragons
and for all your graphic novel magic!
—T.T.S.

For Oscar — I can't wait to see how you draw.
—M.H.

Story and text copyright © 2019 by Tui T. Sutherland
Adaptation by Barry Deutsch
Map and border design © 2012 by Mike Schley
Art by Mike Holmes © 2019 by Scholastic Inc.

Library of Congress Control Number Available

ISBN 978-0-545-94221-8 (hardcover)
ISBN 978-0-545-94220-1 (paperback)

15 14 13 12 11 10   22 23

Printed in China   62
First edition, March 2019
Edited by Amanda Maciel
Lettering by John Green
Book design by Phil Falco
Creative Director: David Saylor

WINGS OF FIRE

THE LOST HEIR
THE GRAPHIC NOVEL

BY TUI T. SUTHERLAND

ADAPTED BY BARRY DEUTSCH
ART BY MIKE HOLMES
COLOR BY MAARTA LAIHO

AN IMPRINT OF
■ SCHOLASTIC

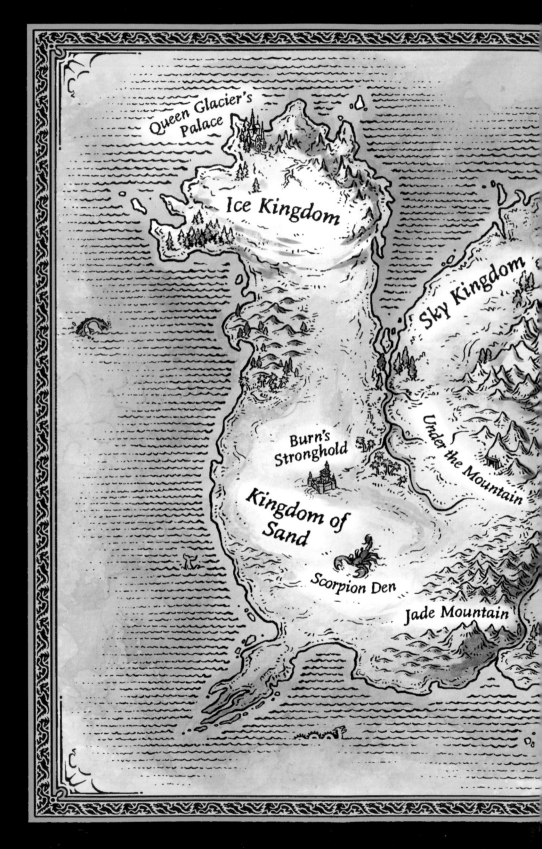

Queen Glacier's
Palace

Ice Kingdom

Sky Kingdom

Burn's
Stronghold

Under the Mountain

Kingdom of
Sand

Scorpion Den

Jade Mountain

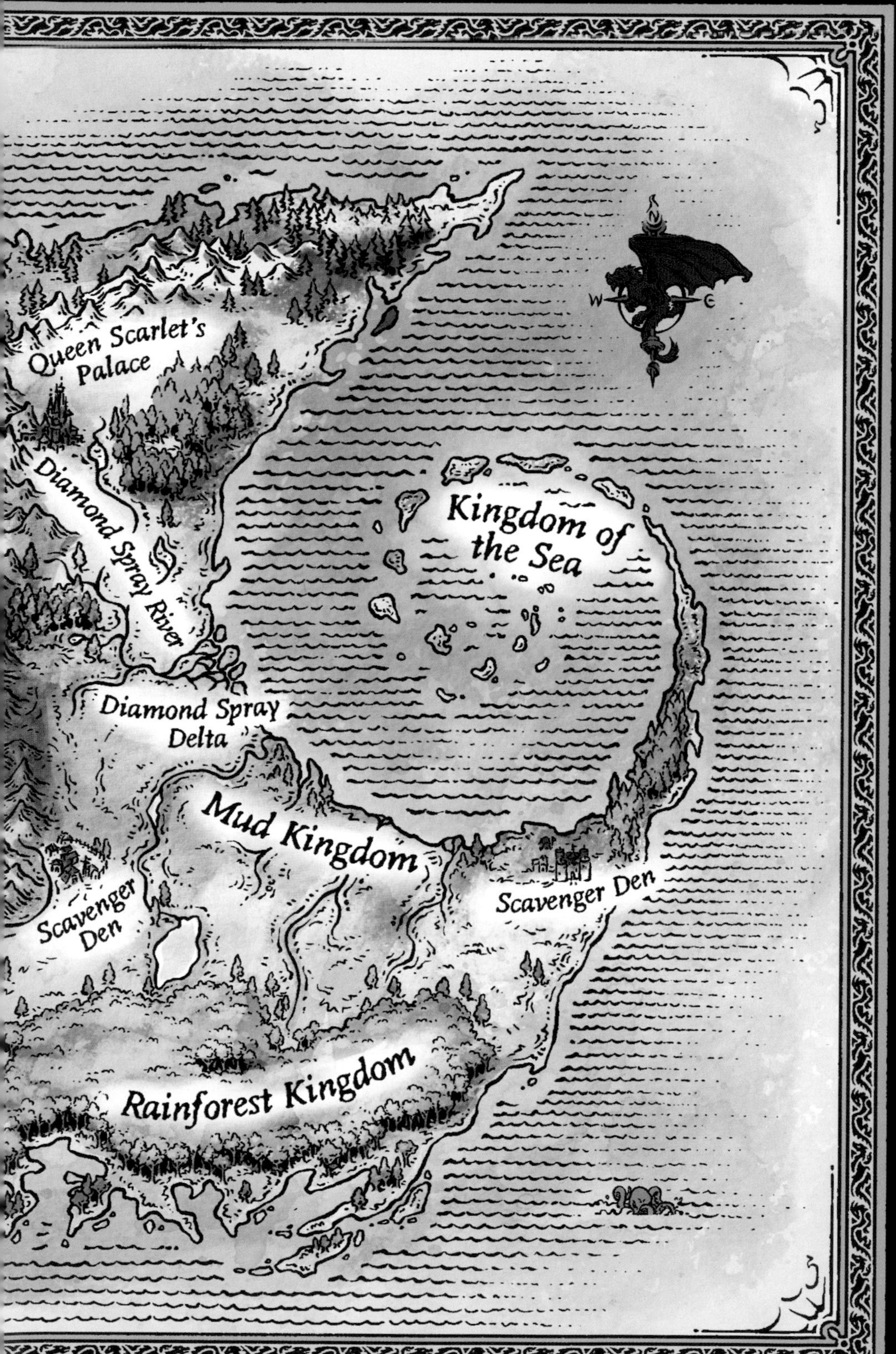

Queen Scarlet's Palace
Diamond Spray River
Kingdom of the Sea
Diamond Spray Delta
Mud Kingdom
Scavenger Den
Scavenger Den
Rainforest Kingdom
W

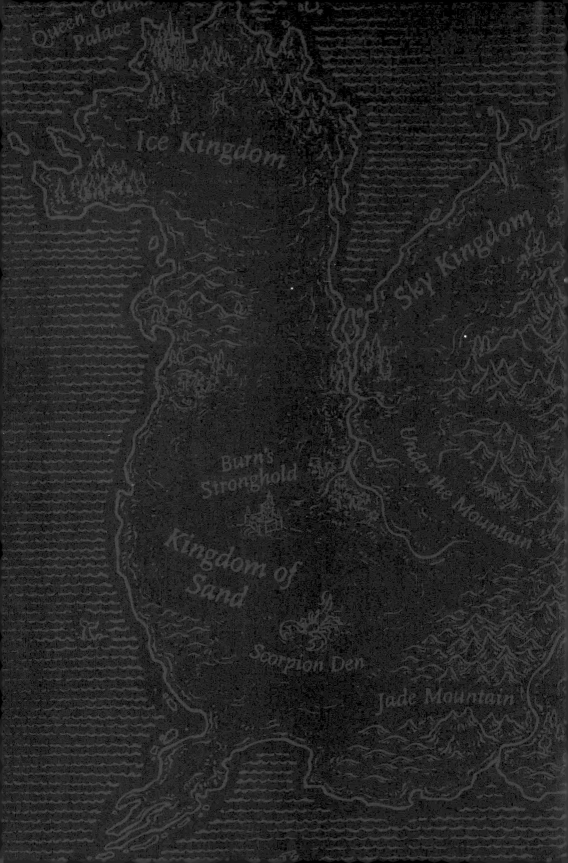

THE LOST HEIR

THE DRAGONET PROPHECY

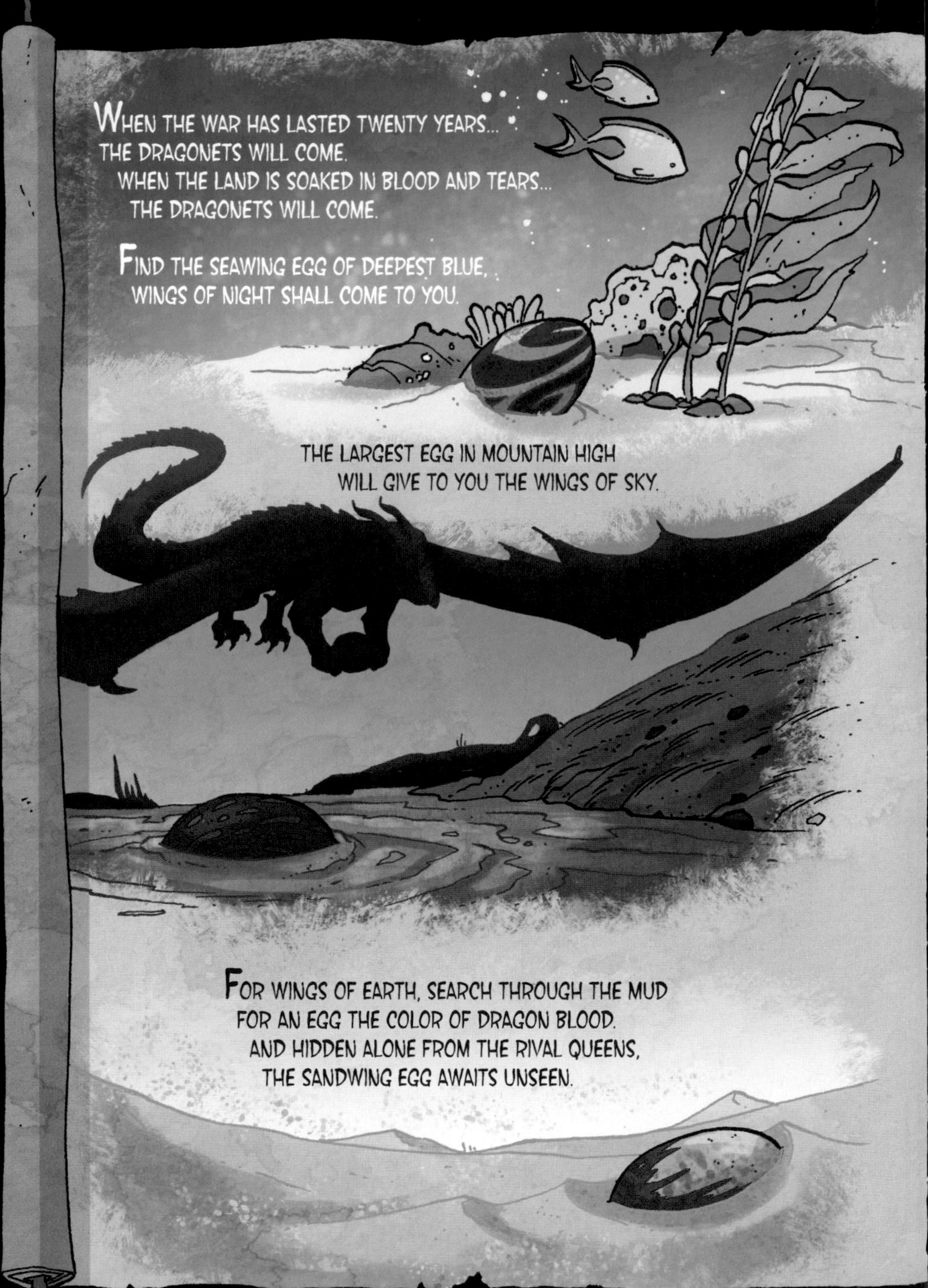
WHEN THE WAR HAS LASTED TWENTY YEARS...
THE DRAGONETS WILL COME.
WHEN THE LAND IS SOAKED IN BLOOD AND TEARS...
THE DRAGONETS WILL COME.
FIND THE SEAWING EGG OF DEEPEST BLUE,
WINGS OF NIGHT SHALL COME TO YOU.
THE LARGEST EGG IN MOUNTAIN HIGH
WILL GIVE TO YOU THE WINGS OF SKY.
FOR WINGS OF EARTH, SEARCH THROUGH THE MUD
FOR AN EGG THE COLOR OF DRAGON BLOOD.
AND HIDDEN ALONE FROM THE RIVAL QUEENS,
THE SANDWING EGG AWAITS UNSEEN.

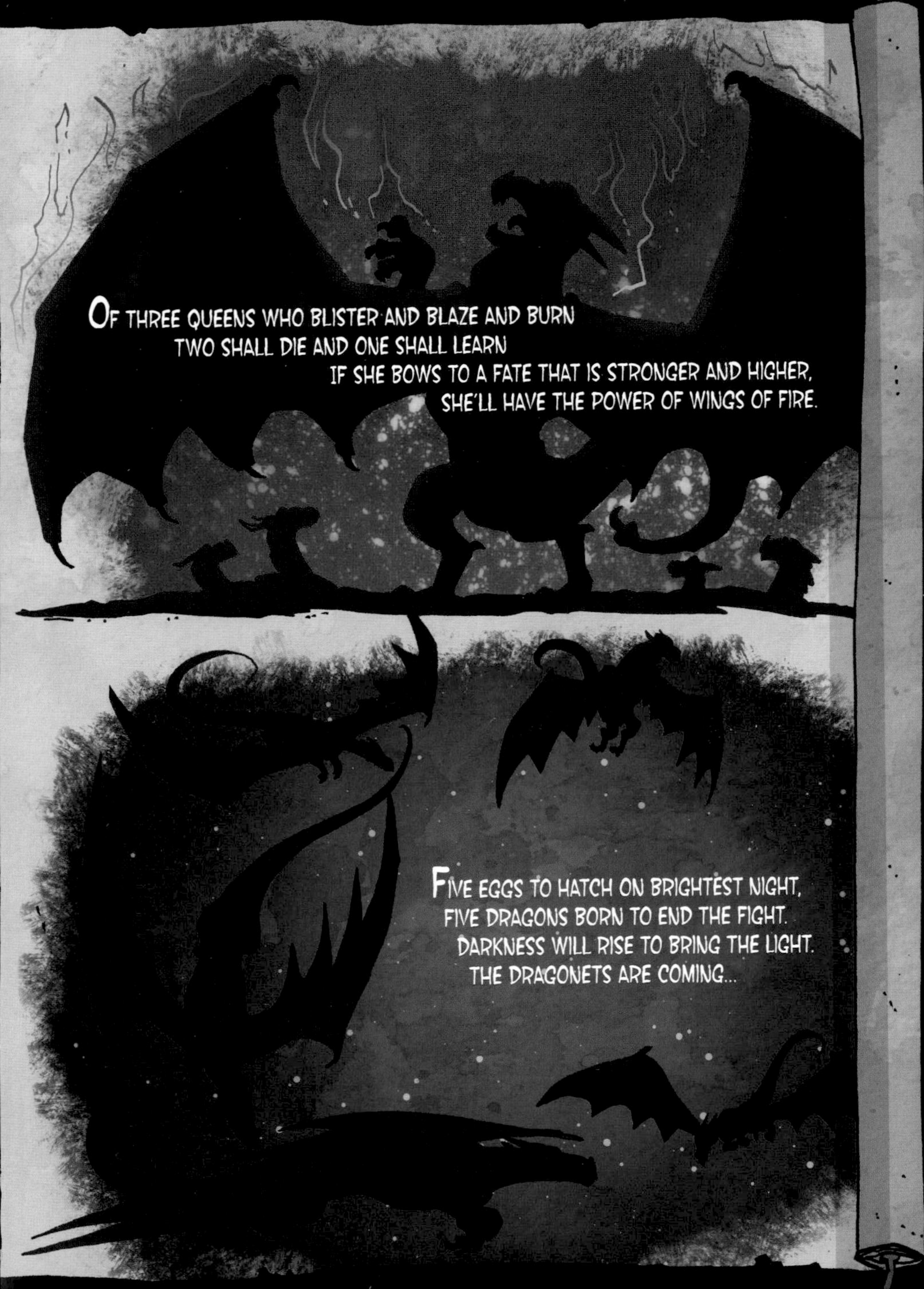
Of three queens who blister and blaze and burn
two shall die and one shall learn
if she bows to a fate that is stronger and higher,
she'll have the power of wings of fire.
Five eggs to hatch on brightest night,
five dragons born to end the fight.
Darkness will rise to bring the light.
The dragonets are coming...

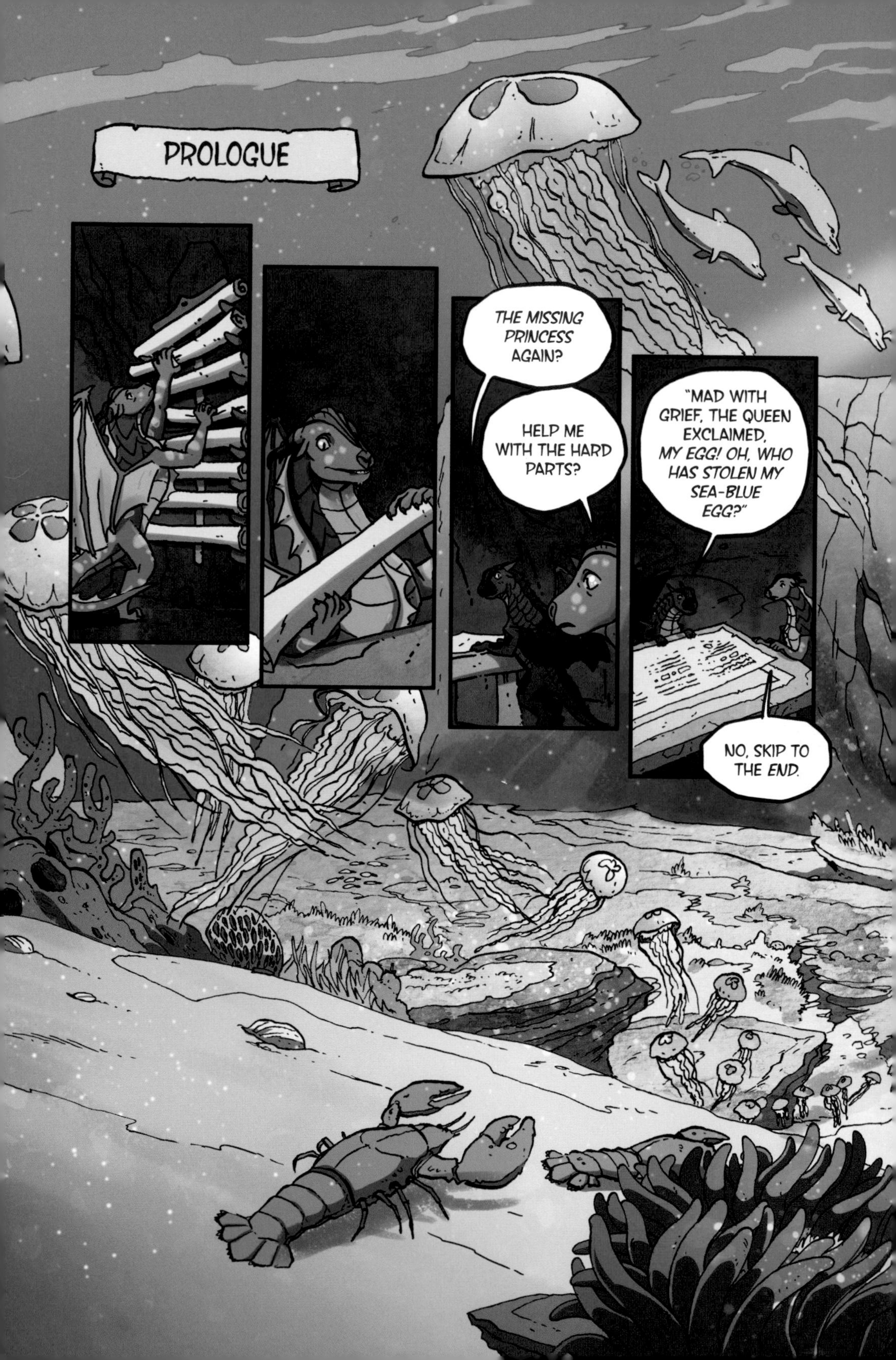
PROLOGUE
THE MISSING PRINCESS AGAIN?
HELP ME WITH THE HARD PARTS?
"MAD WITH GRIEF, THE QUEEN EXCLAIMED, MY EGG! OH, WHO HAS STOLEN MY SEA-BLUE EGG?"
NO, SKIP TO THE END.

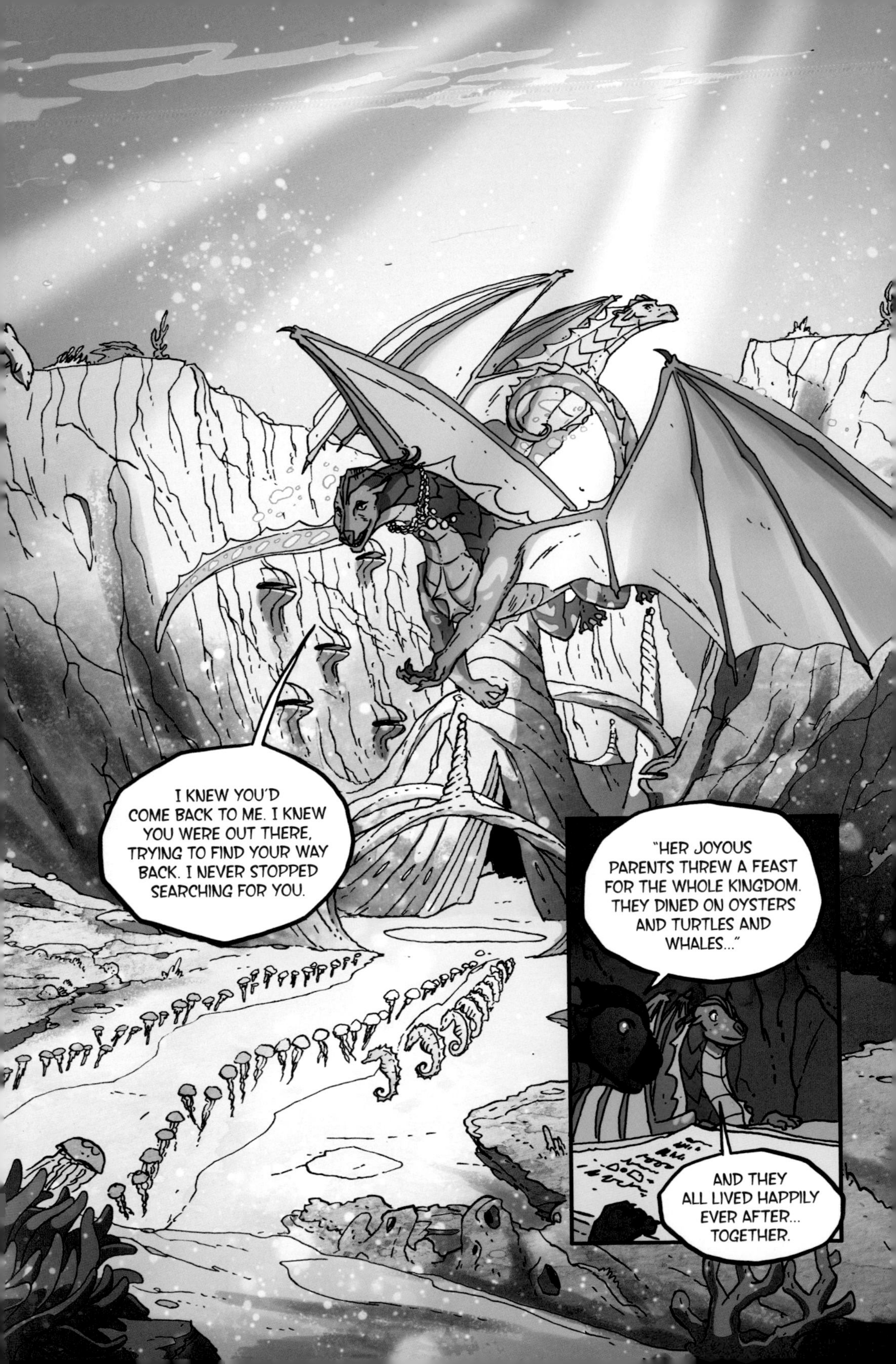
I KNEW YOU'D COME BACK TO ME. I KNEW YOU WERE OUT THERE, TRYING TO FIND YOUR WAY BACK. I NEVER STOPPED SEARCHING FOR YOU.
"HER JOYOUS PARENTS THREW A FEAST FOR THE WHOLE KINGDOM. THEY DINED ON OYSTERS AND TURTLES AND WHALES..."
AND THEY ALL LIVED HAPPILY EVER AFTER... TOGETHER.

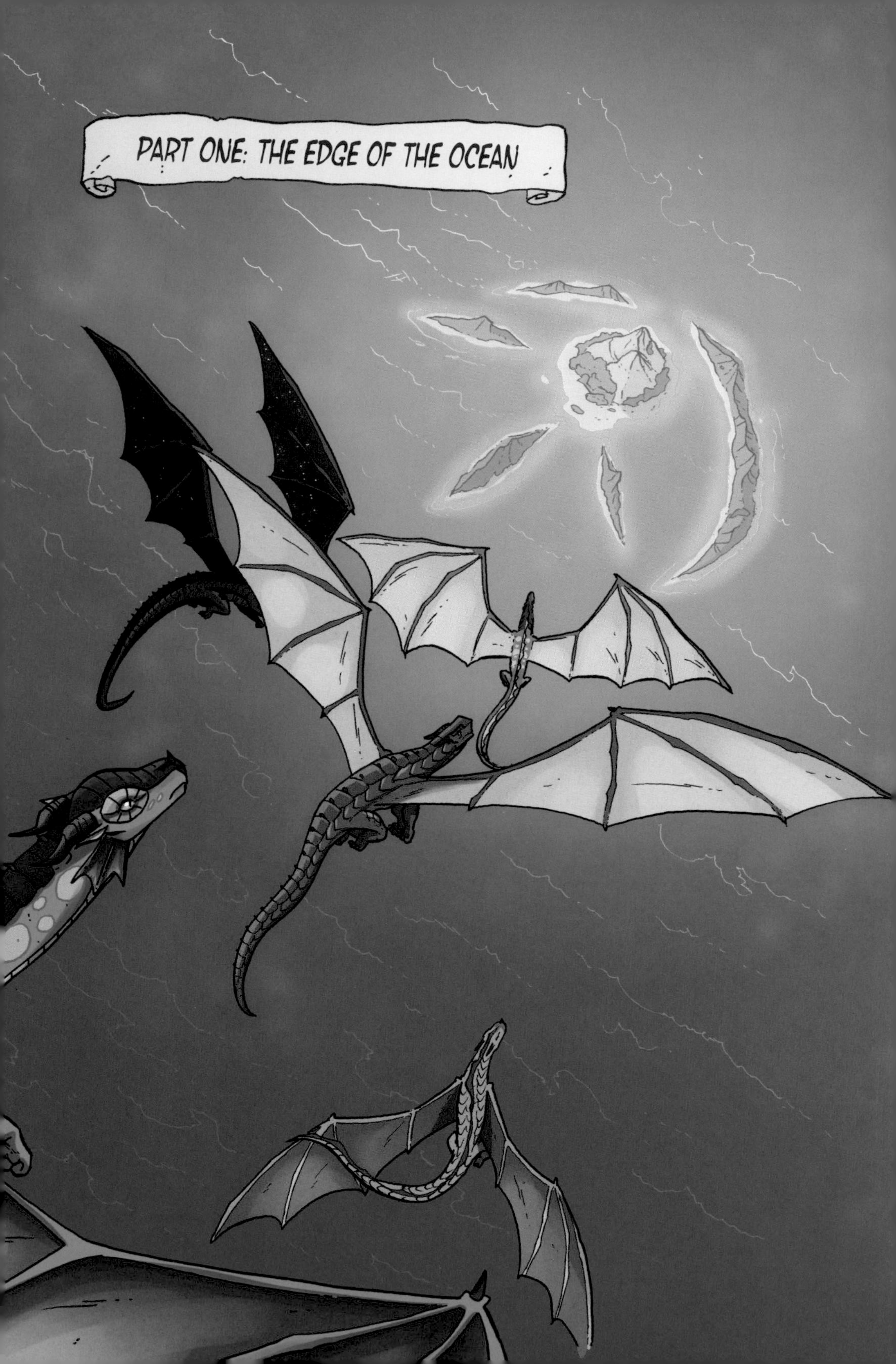
PART ONE: THE EDGE OF THE OCEAN

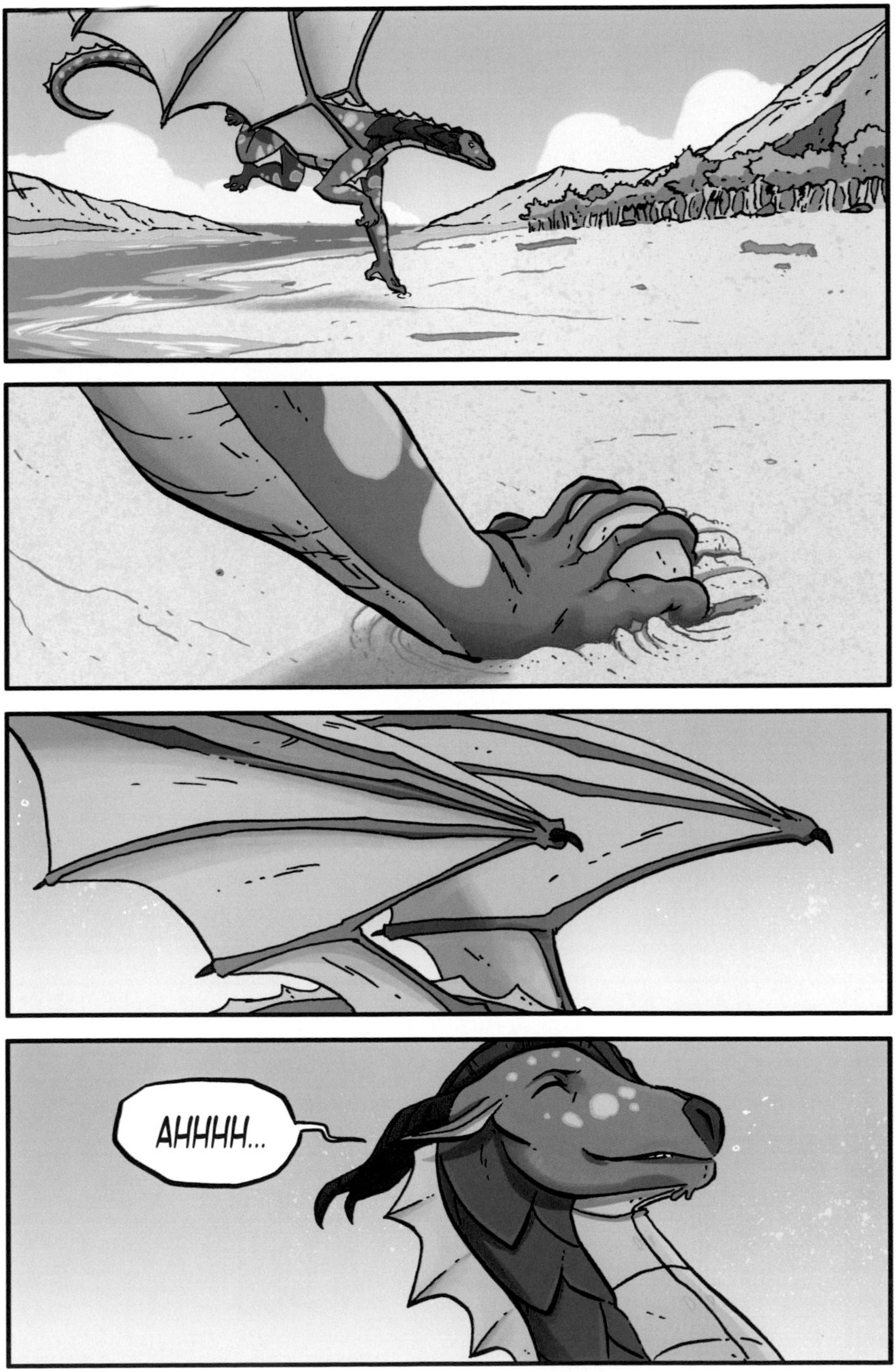
AHHHH...

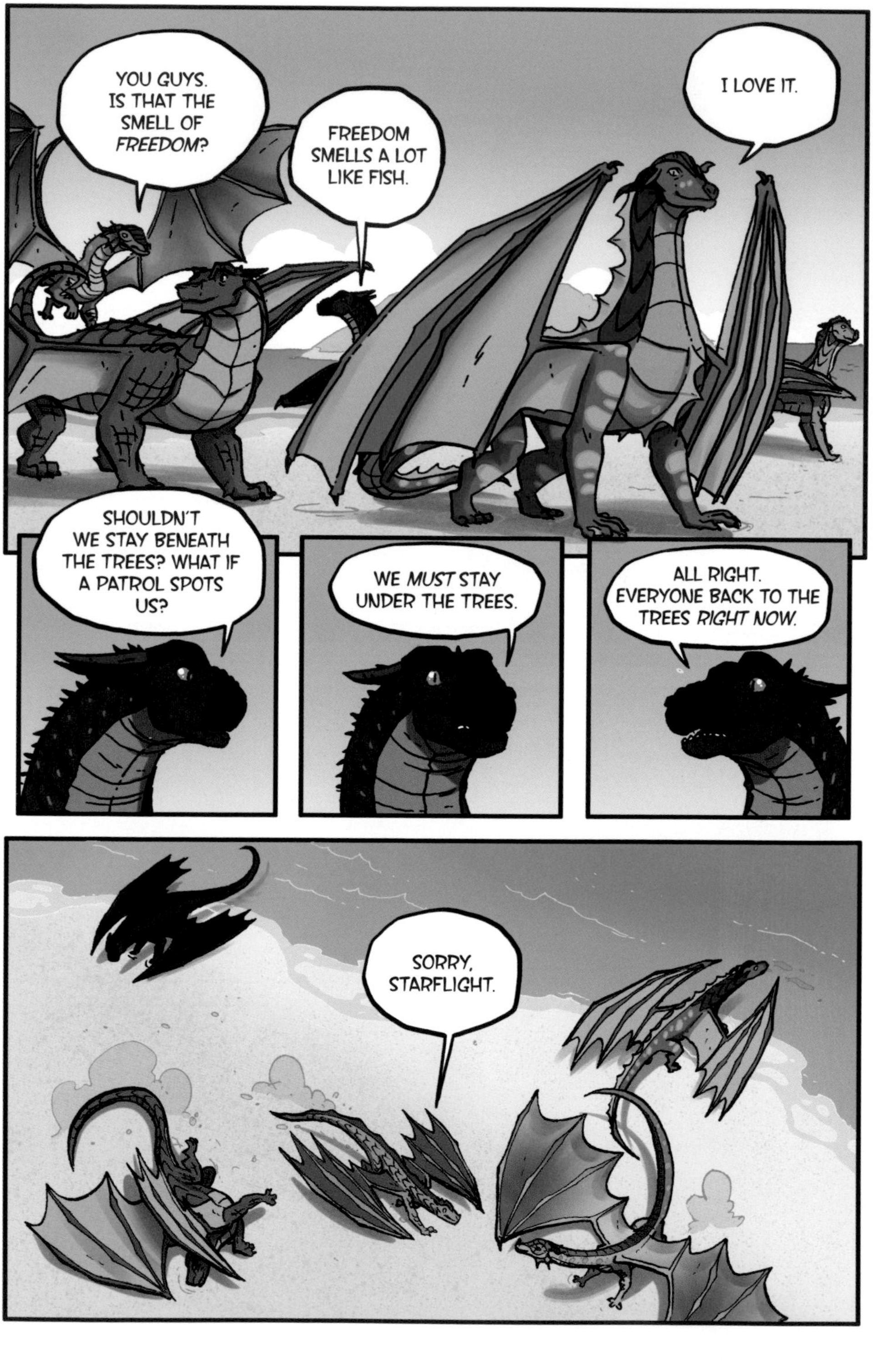
YOU GUYS. IS THAT THE SMELL OF *FREEDOM*?
FREEDOM SMELLS A LOT LIKE FISH.
I LOVE IT.
SHOULDN'T WE STAY BENEATH THE TREES? WHAT IF A PATROL SPOTS US?
WE *MUST* STAY UNDER THE TREES.
ALL RIGHT. EVERYONE BACK TO THE TREES *RIGHT NOW.*
SORRY, STARFLIGHT.

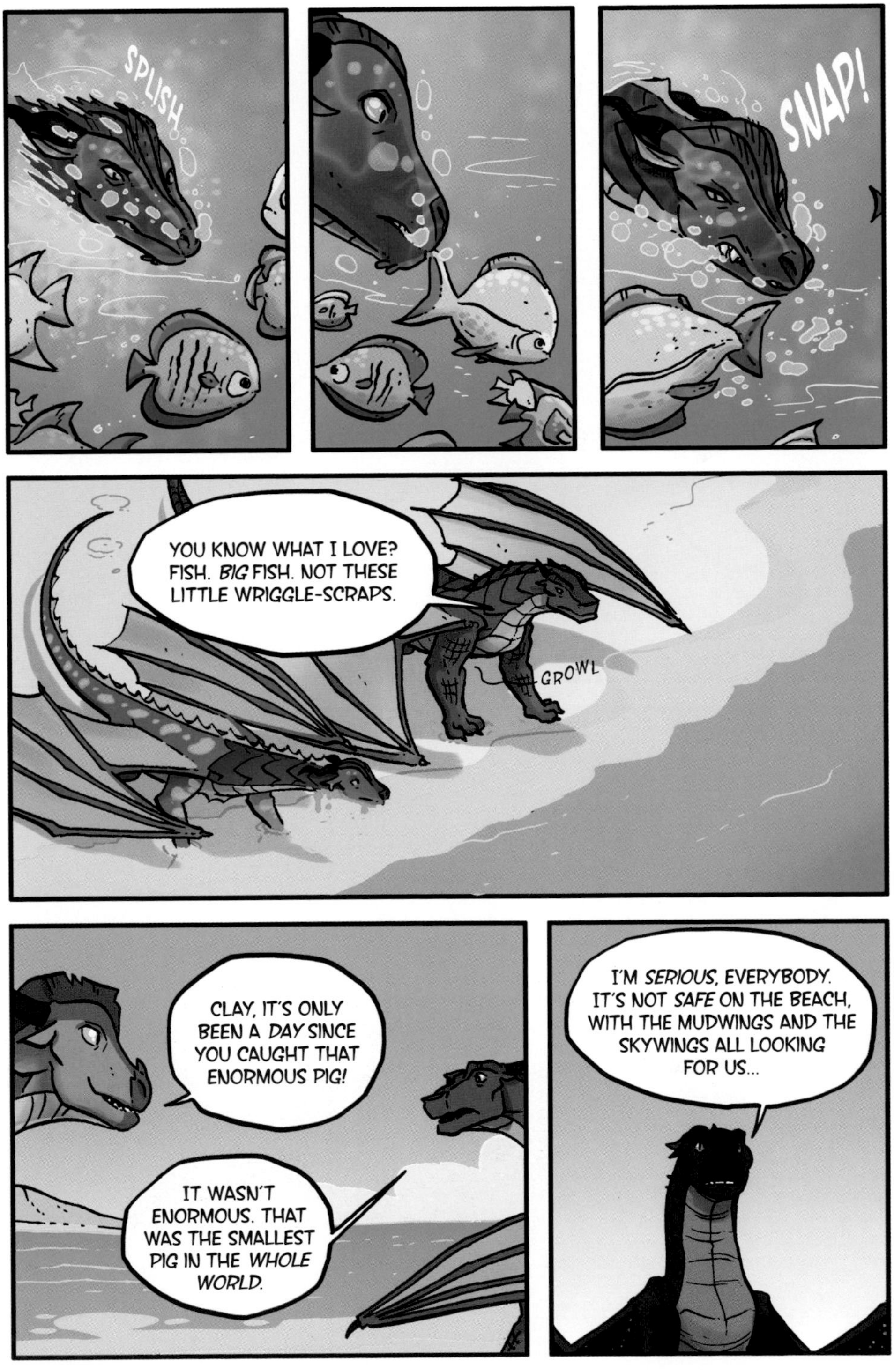
SPLISH
SNAP!
YOU KNOW WHAT I LOVE? FISH. *BIG* FISH. NOT THESE LITTLE WRIGGLE-SCRAPS.
GROWL
CLAY, IT'S ONLY BEEN A *DAY* SINCE YOU CAUGHT THAT ENORMOUS PIG!
IT WASN'T ENORMOUS. THAT WAS THE SMALLEST PIG IN THE *WHOLE WORLD*.
I'M *SERIOUS*, EVERYBODY. IT'S NOT *SAFE* ON THE BEACH, WITH THE MUDWINGS AND THE SKYWINGS ALL LOOKING FOR US...

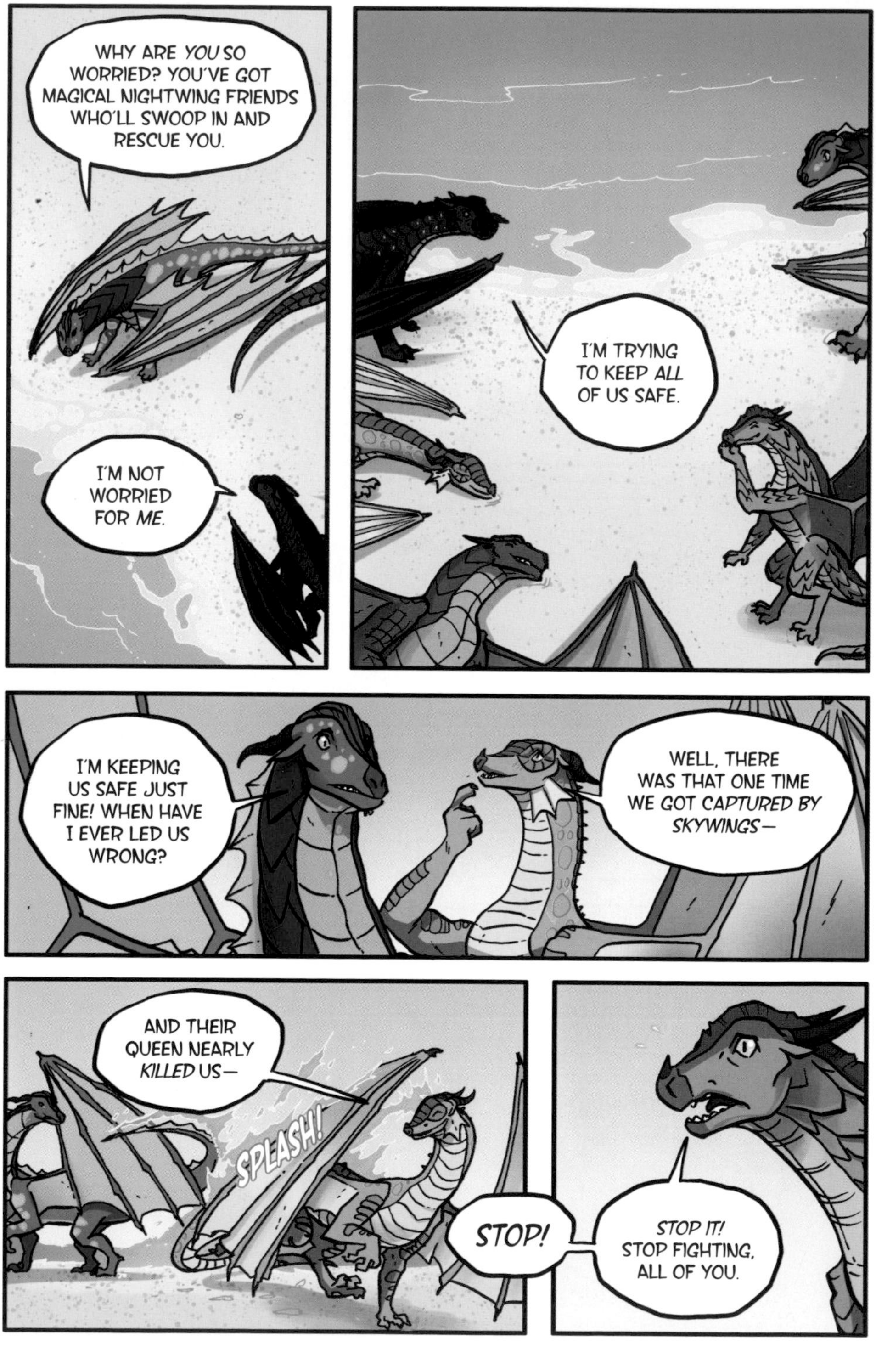
WHY ARE *YOU* SO WORRIED? YOU'VE GOT MAGICAL NIGHTWING FRIENDS WHO'LL SWOOP IN AND RESCUE YOU.
I'M NOT WORRIED FOR *ME*.
I'M TRYING TO KEEP *ALL* OF US SAFE.
I'M KEEPING US SAFE JUST FINE! WHEN HAVE I EVER LED US WRONG?
WELL, THERE WAS THAT ONE TIME WE GOT *CAPTURED* BY *SKYWINGS*—
AND THEIR QUEEN NEARLY *KILLED* US—
SPLASH!
STOP!
STOP IT! STOP FIGHTING, ALL OF YOU.

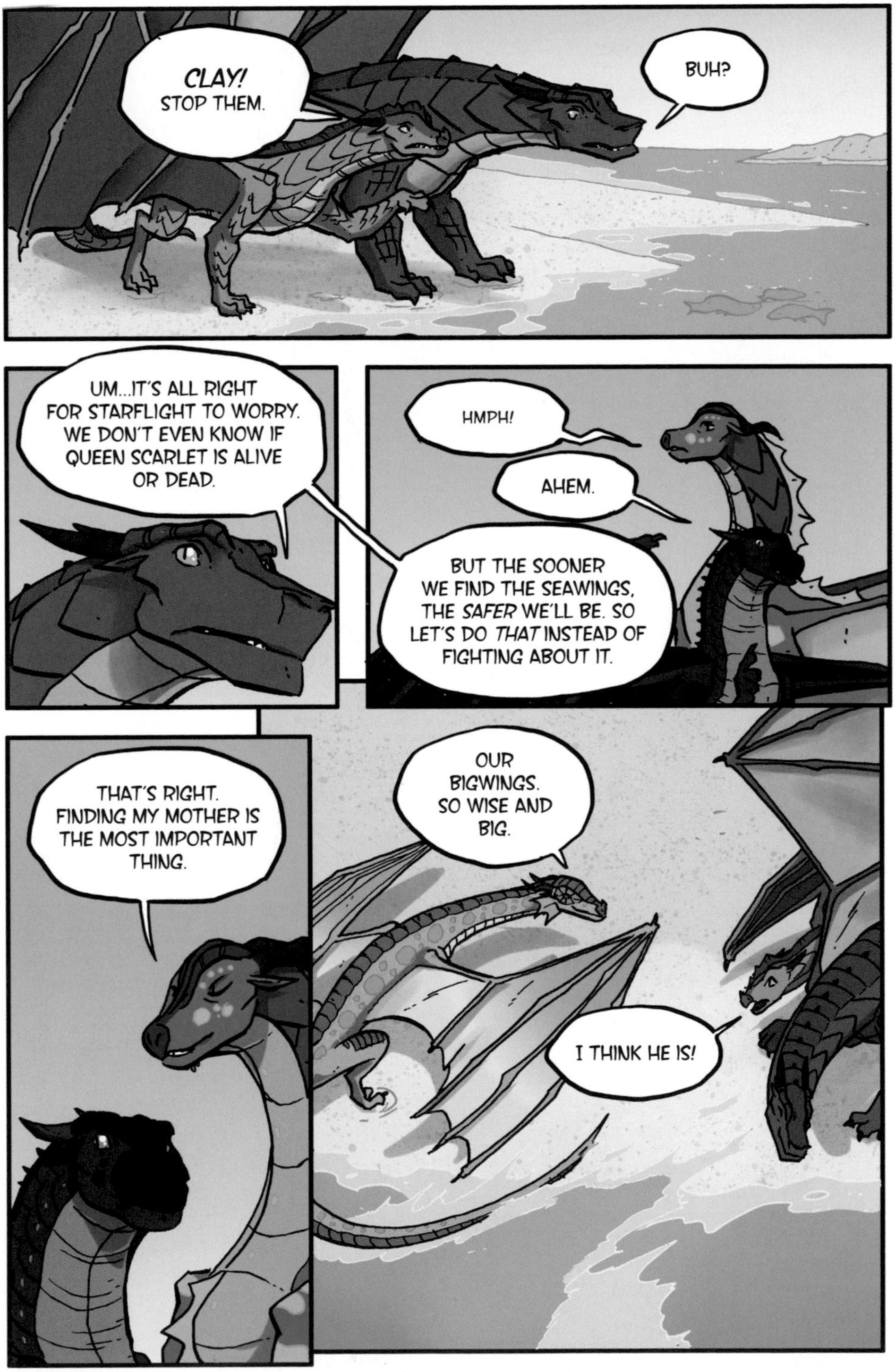
CLAY! STOP THEM.
BUH?
UM...IT'S ALL RIGHT FOR STARFLIGHT TO WORRY. WE DON'T EVEN KNOW IF QUEEN SCARLET IS ALIVE OR DEAD.
HMPH!
AHEM.
BUT THE SOONER WE FIND THE SEAWINGS, THE *SAFER* WE'LL BE. SO LET'S DO *THAT* INSTEAD OF FIGHTING ABOUT IT.
THAT'S RIGHT. FINDING MY MOTHER IS THE MOST IMPORTANT THING.
OUR BIGWINGS. SO WISE AND BIG.
I THINK HE IS!

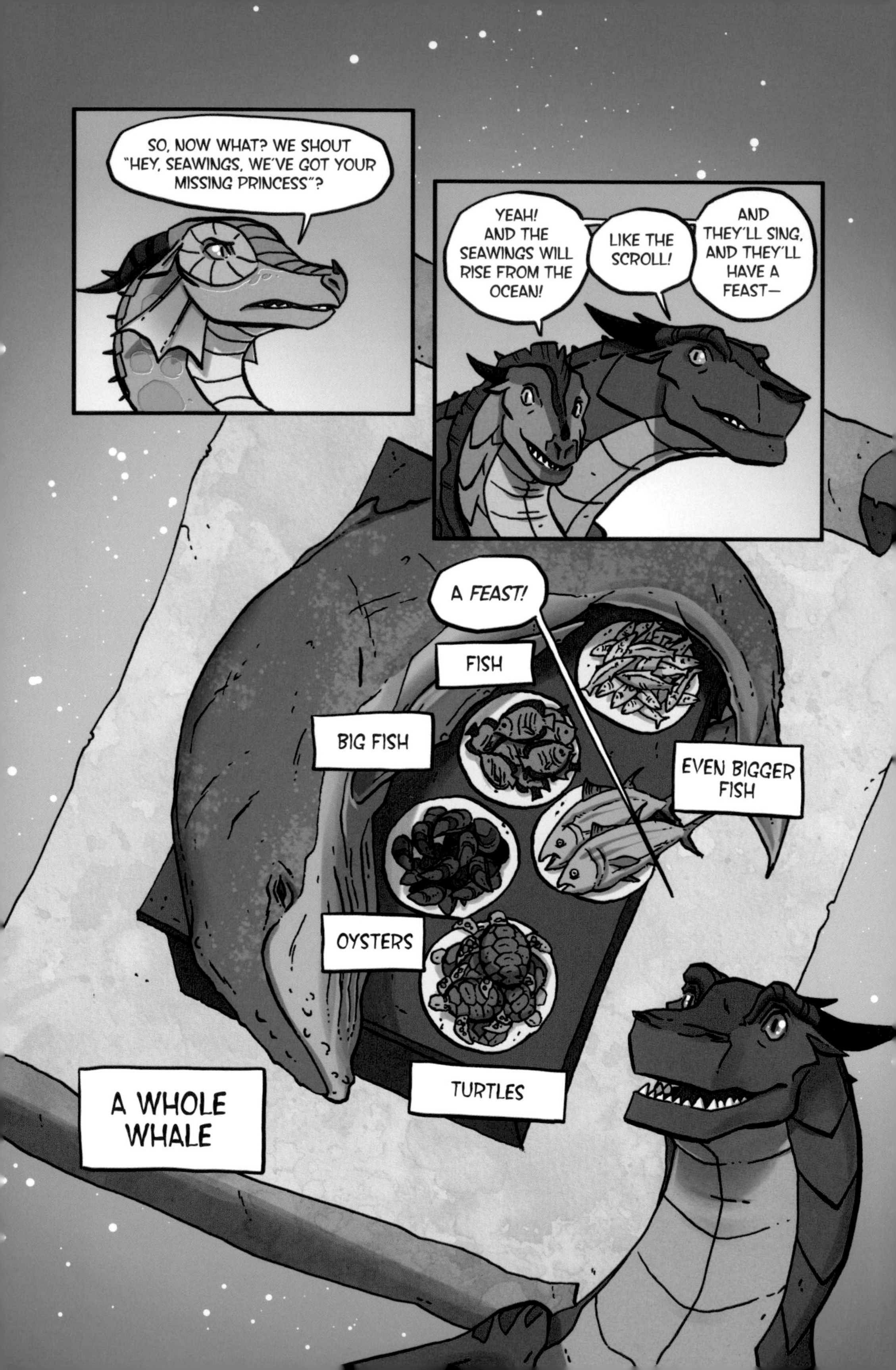
SO, NOW WHAT? WE SHOUT "HEY, SEAWINGS, WE'VE GOT YOUR MISSING PRINCESS"?
YEAH! AND THE SEAWINGS WILL RISE FROM THE OCEAN!
LIKE THE SCROLL!
AND THEY'LL SING, AND THEY'LL HAVE A FEAST—
A FEAST!
FISH
BIG FISH
EVEN BIGGER FISH
OYSTERS
TURTLES
A WHOLE WHALE

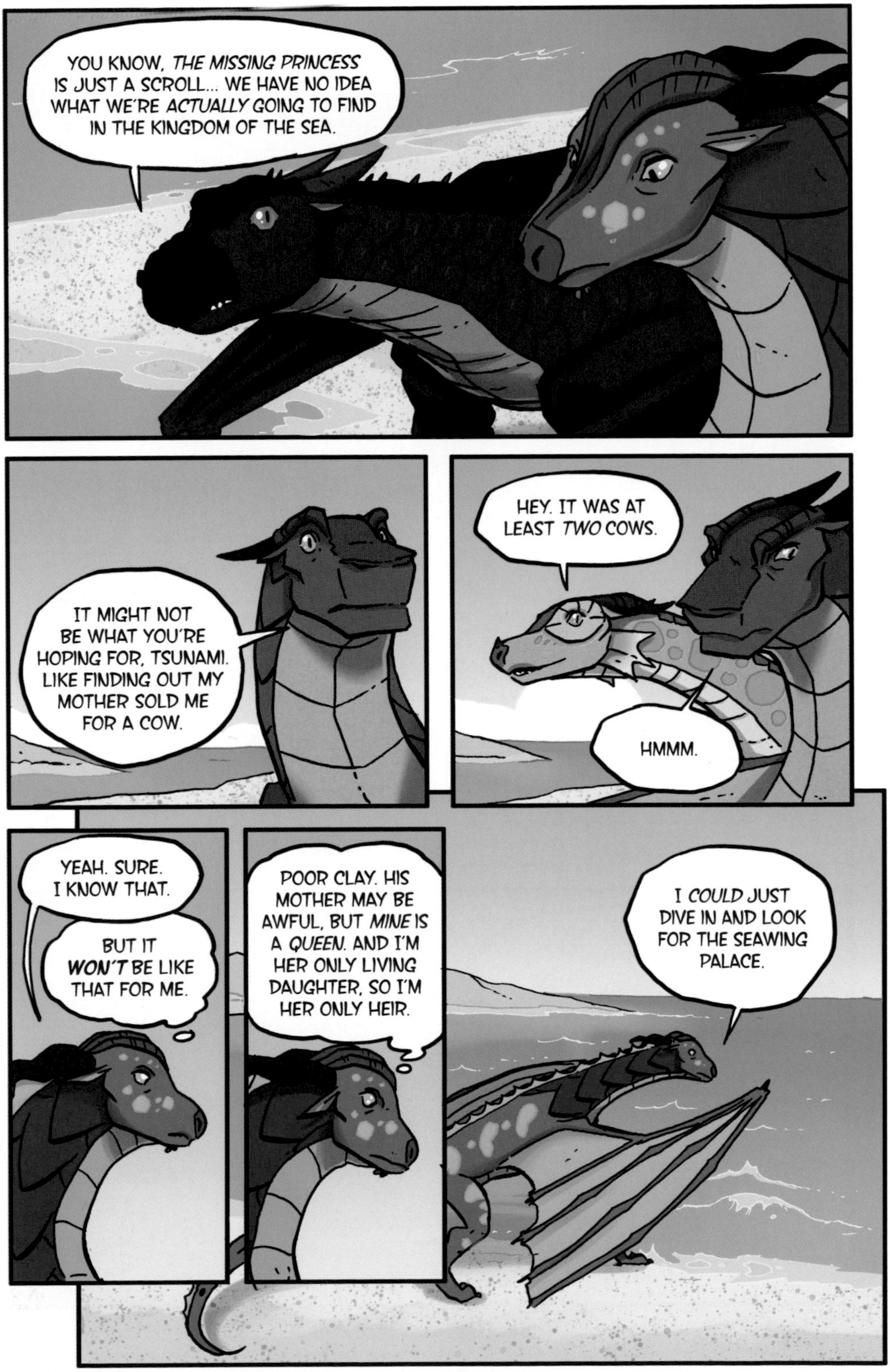
YOU KNOW, *THE MISSING PRINCESS* IS JUST A SCROLL... WE HAVE NO IDEA WHAT WE'RE *ACTUALLY* GOING TO FIND IN THE KINGDOM OF THE SEA.
IT MIGHT NOT BE WHAT YOU'RE HOPING FOR, TSUNAMI. LIKE FINDING OUT MY MOTHER SOLD ME FOR A COW.
HEY. IT WAS AT LEAST *TWO* COWS.
HMMM.
YEAH. SURE. I KNOW THAT.
BUT IT ***WON'T*** BE LIKE THAT FOR ME.
POOR CLAY. HIS MOTHER MAY BE AWFUL, BUT *MINE* IS A *QUEEN*. AND I'M HER ONLY LIVING DAUGHTER, SO I'M HER ONLY HEIR.
I *COULD* JUST DIVE IN AND LOOK FOR THE SEAWING PALACE.

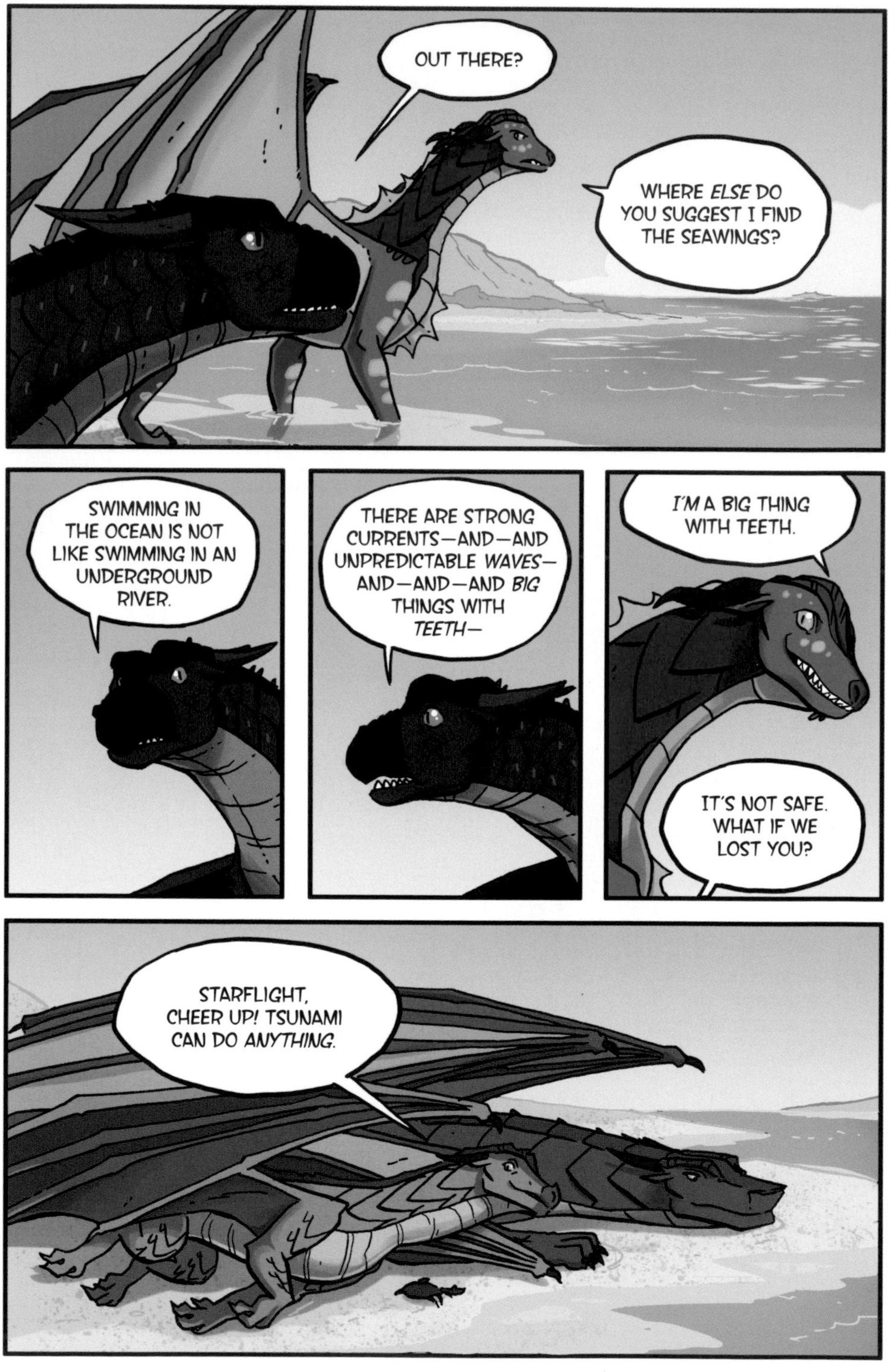
OUT THERE?
WHERE *ELSE* DO YOU SUGGEST I FIND THE SEAWINGS?
SWIMMING IN THE OCEAN IS NOT LIKE SWIMMING IN AN UNDERGROUND RIVER.
THERE ARE STRONG CURRENTS—AND—AND UNPREDICTABLE *WAVES*—AND—AND—AND *BIG* THINGS WITH *TEETH*—
I'M A BIG THING WITH TEETH.
IT'S NOT SAFE. WHAT IF WE LOST YOU?
STARFLIGHT, CHEER UP! TSUNAMI CAN DO *ANYTHING*.

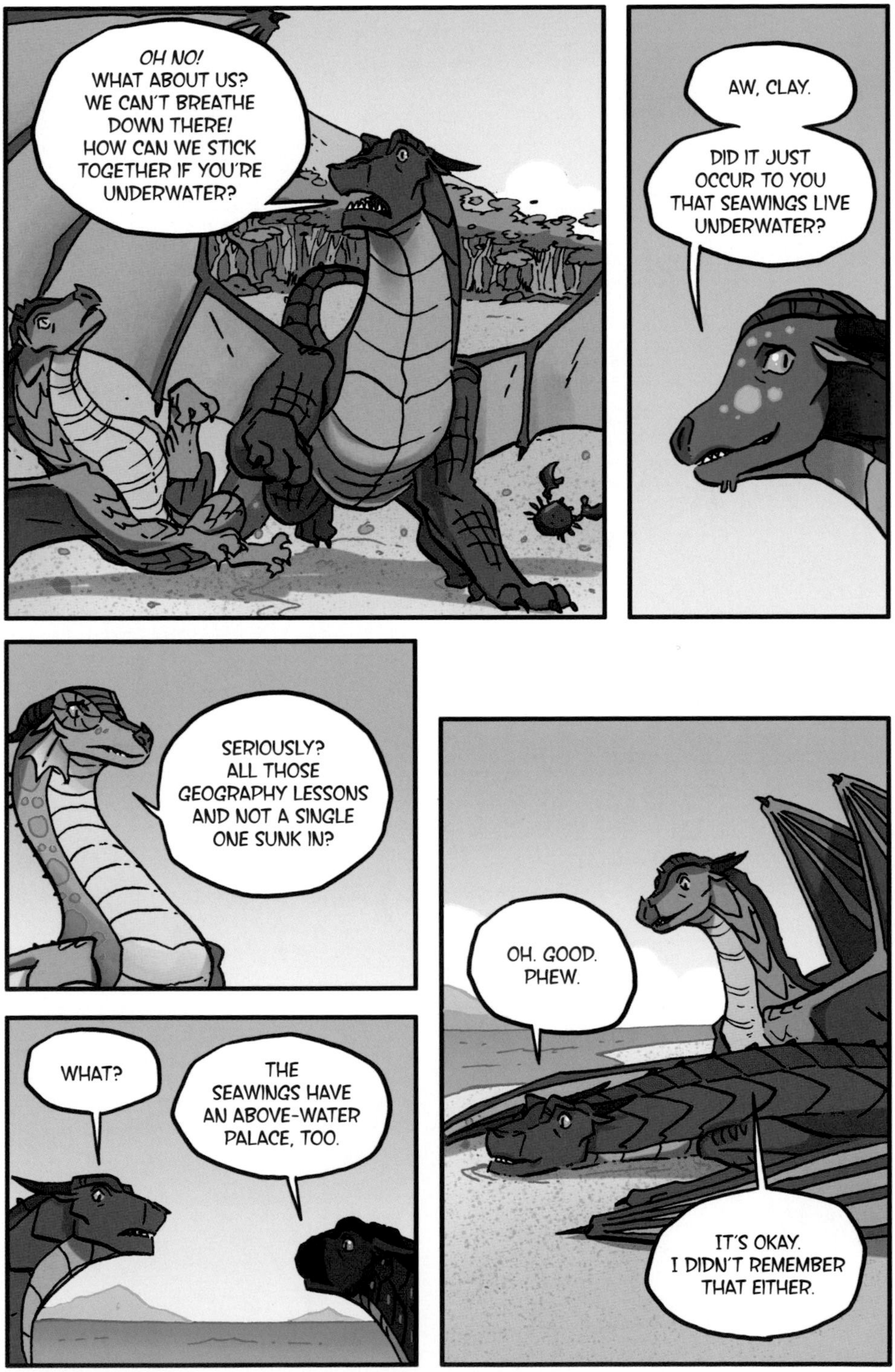
OH NO! WHAT ABOUT US? WE CAN'T BREATHE DOWN THERE! HOW CAN WE STICK TOGETHER IF YOU'RE UNDERWATER?
AW, CLAY.
DID IT JUST OCCUR TO YOU THAT SEAWINGS LIVE UNDERWATER?
SERIOUSLY? ALL THOSE GEOGRAPHY LESSONS AND NOT A SINGLE ONE SUNK IN?
WHAT?
THE SEAWINGS HAVE AN ABOVE-WATER PALACE, TOO.
OH. GOOD. PHEW.
IT'S OKAY. I DIDN'T REMEMBER THAT EITHER.

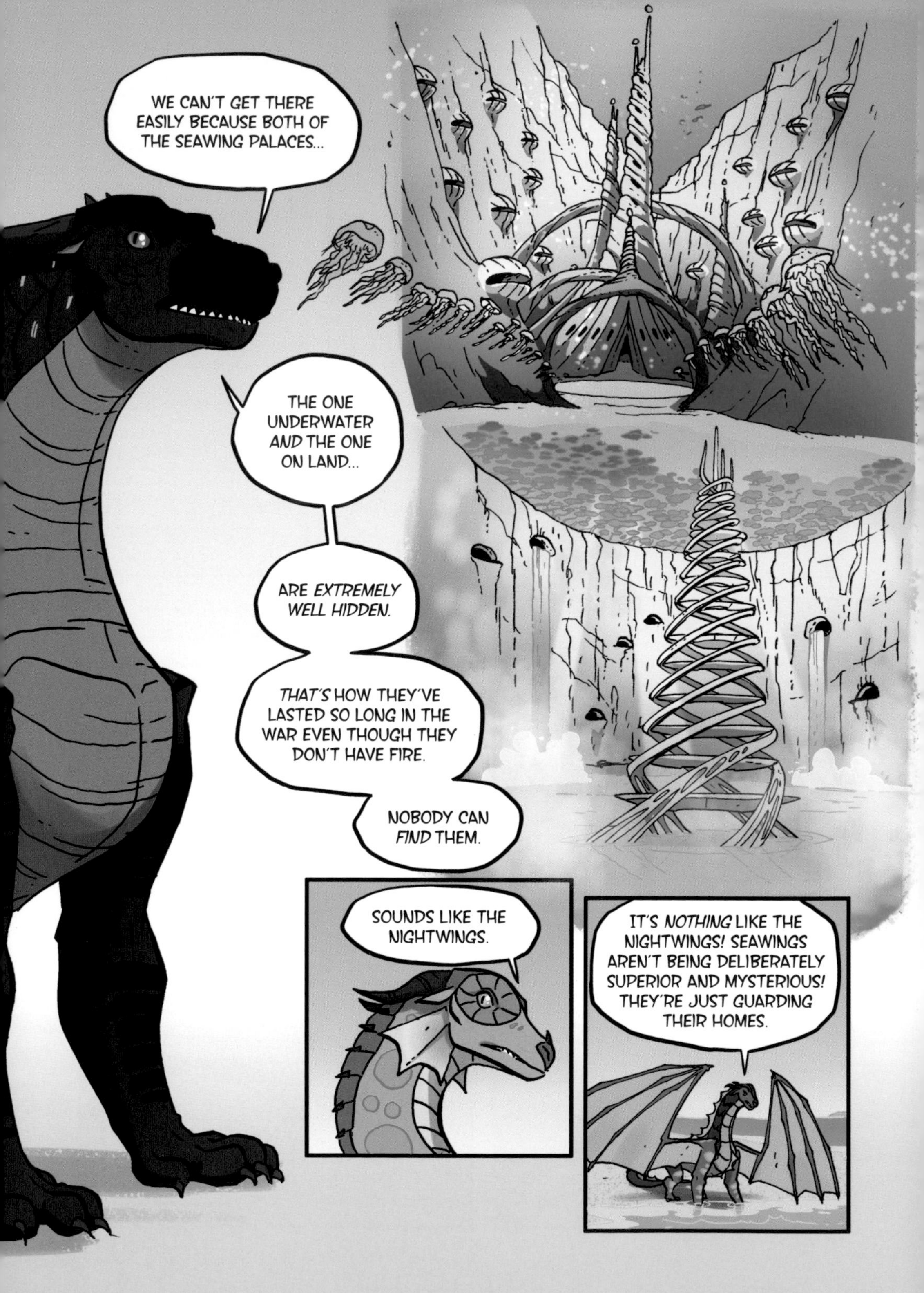
WE CAN'T GET THERE EASILY BECAUSE BOTH OF THE SEAWING PALACES...
THE ONE UNDERWATER AND THE ONE ON LAND...
ARE *EXTREMELY* WELL HIDDEN.
THAT'S HOW THEY'VE LASTED SO LONG IN THE WAR EVEN THOUGH THEY DON'T HAVE FIRE.
NOBODY CAN *FIND* THEM.
SOUNDS LIKE THE NIGHTWINGS.
IT'S *NOTHING* LIKE THE NIGHTWINGS! SEAWINGS AREN'T BEING DELIBERATELY SUPERIOR AND MYSTERIOUS! THEY'RE JUST GUARDING THEIR HOMES.

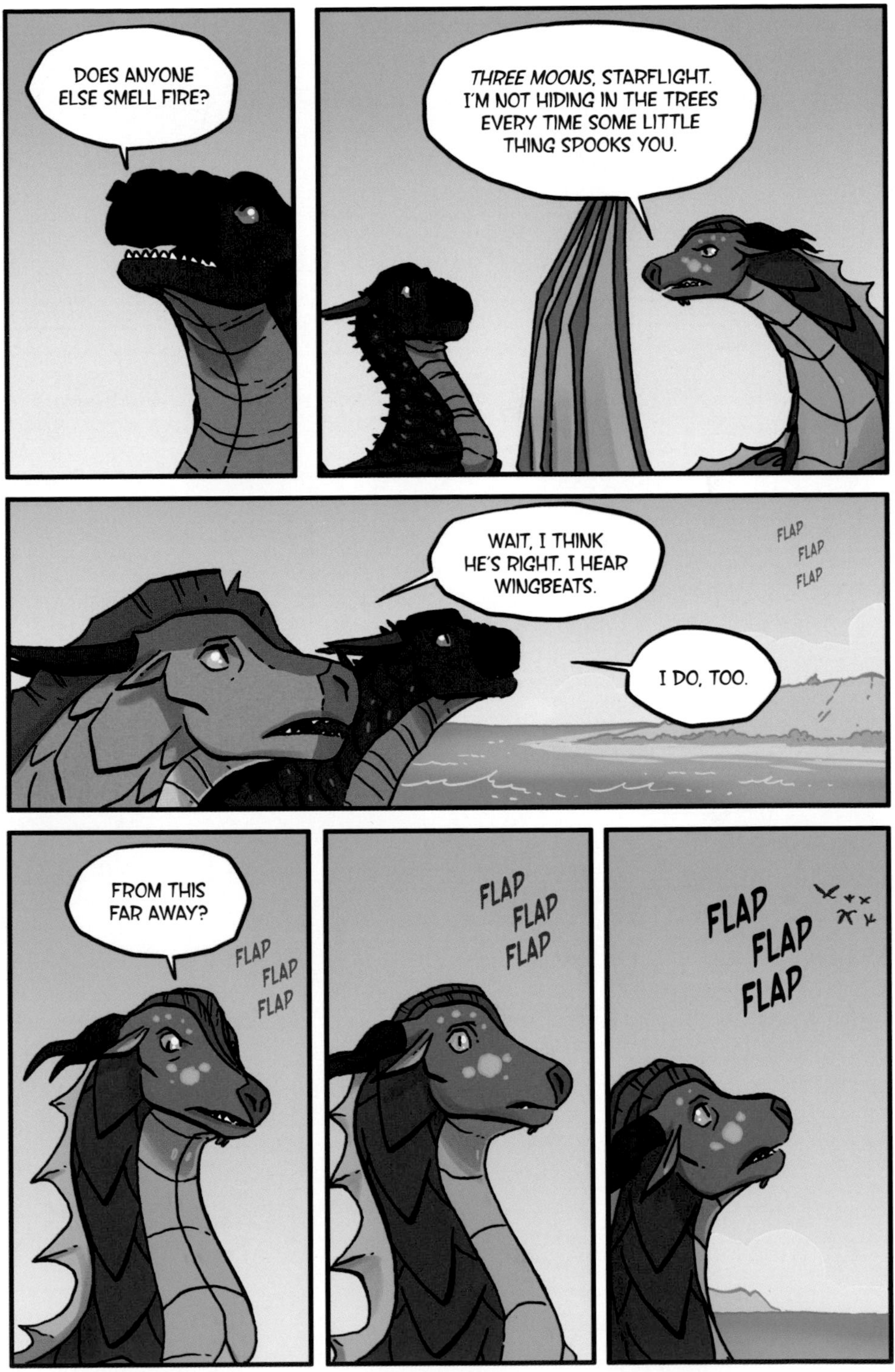
DOES ANYONE ELSE SMELL FIRE?
THREE MOONS, STARFLIGHT. I'M NOT HIDING IN THE TREES EVERY TIME SOME LITTLE THING SPOOKS YOU.
WAIT, I THINK HE'S RIGHT. I HEAR WINGBEATS.
FLAP FLAP FLAP
I DO, TOO.
FROM THIS FAR AWAY?
FLAP FLAP FLAP
FLAP FLAP FLAP
FLAP FLAP FLAP

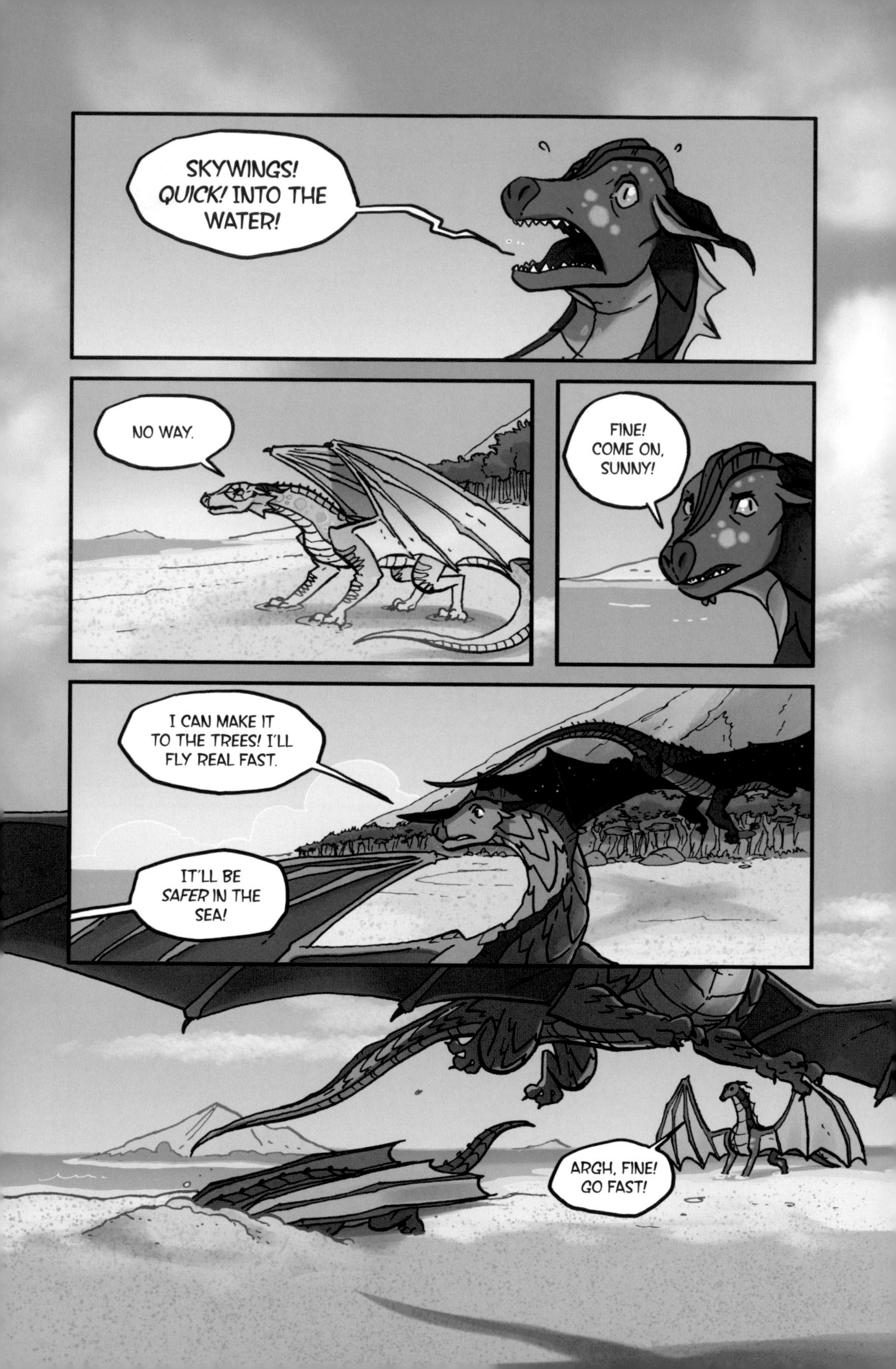
SKYWINGS! *QUICK!* INTO THE WATER!
NO WAY.
FINE! COME ON, SUNNY!
I CAN MAKE IT TO THE TREES! I'LL FLY REAL FAST.
IT'LL BE *SAFER* IN THE SEA!
ARGH, FINE! GO FAST!

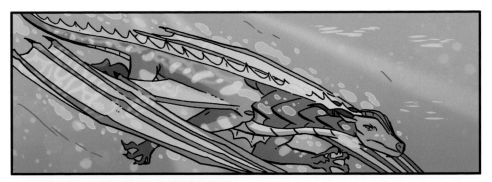

SUNNY MUST BE SAFELY HIDDEN BY NOW, RIGHT?

RIGHT?

I HAVE TO CHECK ON HER.

MAYBE IF I JUST SURFACE A *LITTLE* BIT...

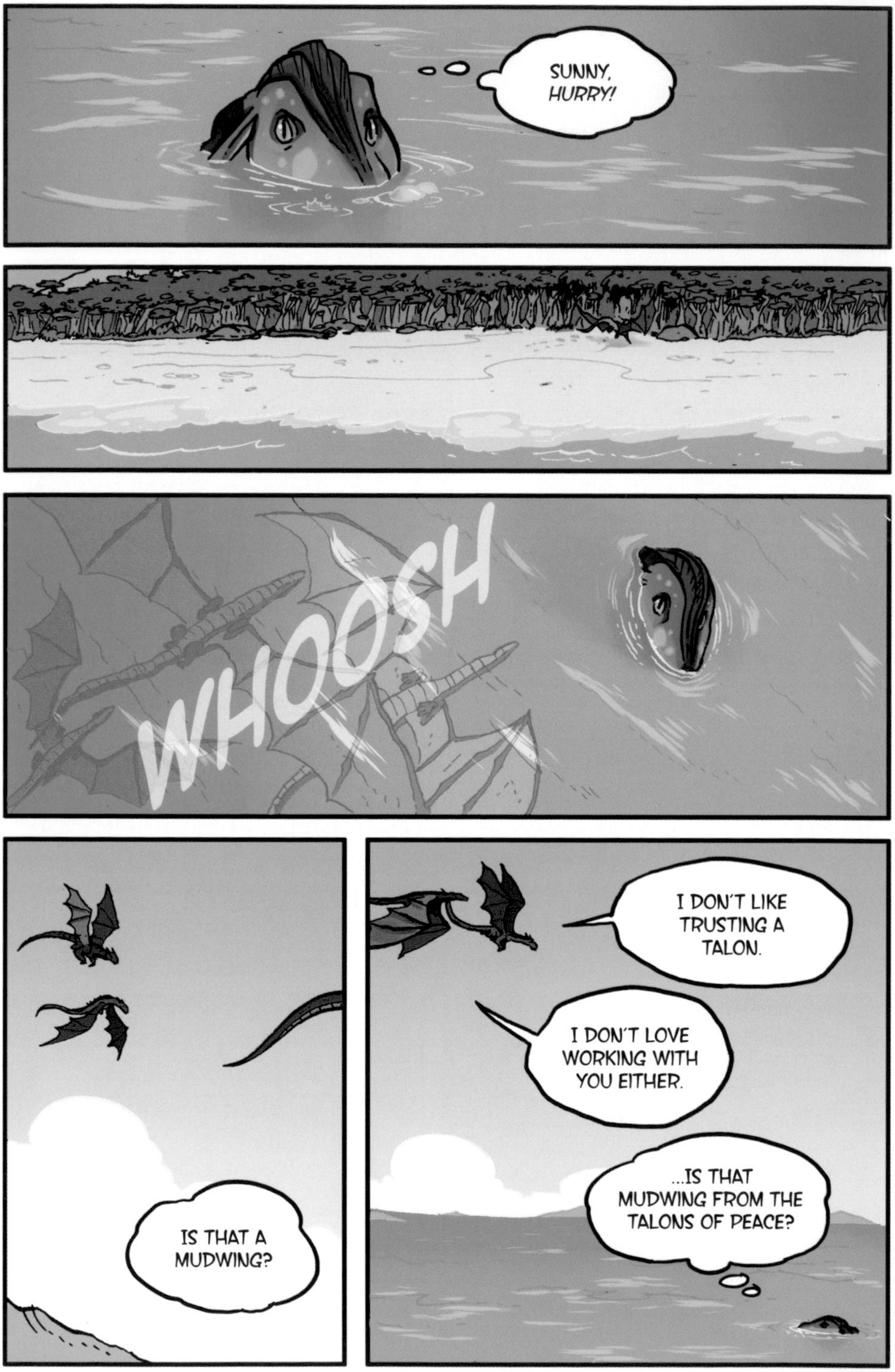
SUNNY, HURRY!
WHOOSH
IS THAT A MUDWING?
I DON'T LIKE TRUSTING A TALON.
I DON'T LOVE WORKING WITH YOU EITHER.
...IS THAT MUDWING FROM THE TALONS OF PEACE?

YOU'RE CERTAIN HE'LL LEAD US THERE.

POSITIVE.

HE'S A COWARDLY, SENTIMENTAL OLD SEAWING. HE MISSES HOME. I TOLD HIM QUEEN CORAL IS IN A FORGIVING MOOD.

AND HE BELIEVED YOU?

HE'S STILL GRIEVING...

WHAT ARE THE TALONS OF PEACE UP TO *NOW*?

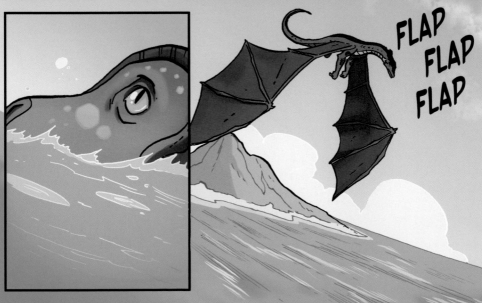

FLAP FLAP FLAP

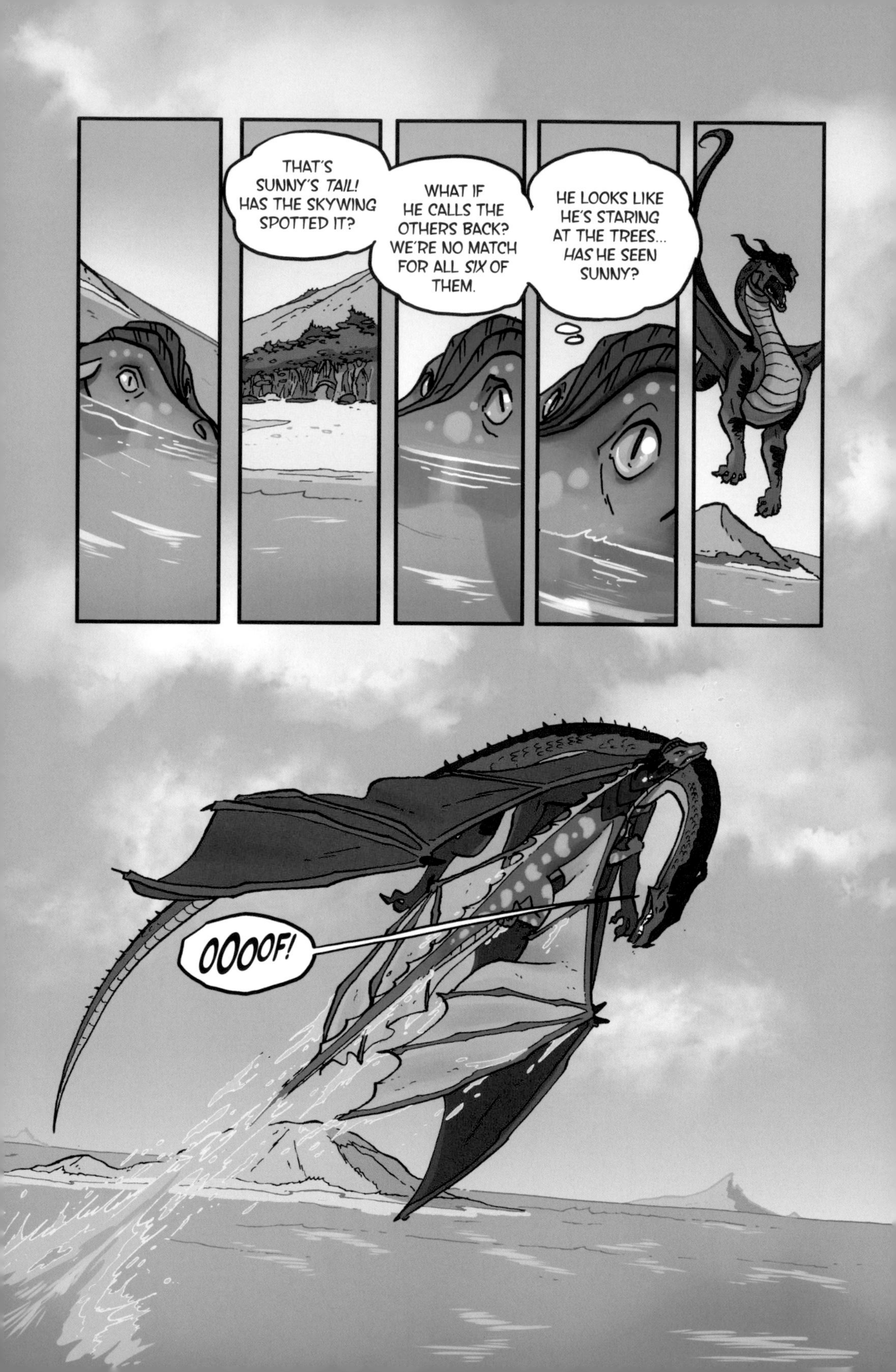
THAT'S SUNNY'S *TAIL!* HAS THE SKYWING SPOTTED IT?
WHAT IF HE CALLS THE OTHERS BACK? WE'RE NO MATCH FOR ALL *SIX* OF THEM.
HE LOOKS LIKE HE'S STARING AT THE TREES... *HAS* HE SEEN SUNNY?
OOOOF!

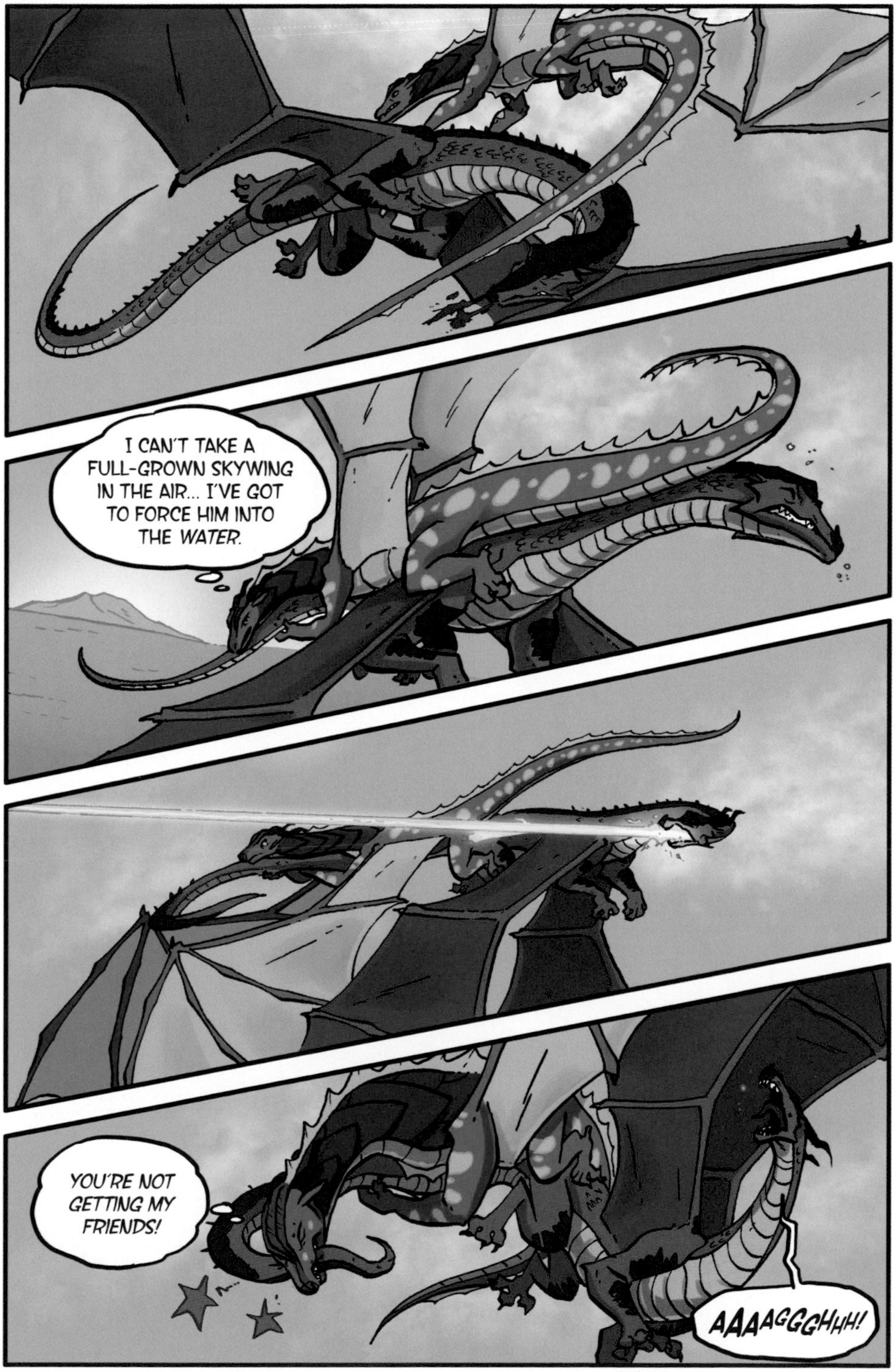
I CAN'T TAKE A FULL-GROWN SKYWING IN THE AIR... I'VE GOT TO FORCE HIM INTO THE *WATER*.
YOU'RE NOT GETTING MY FRIENDS!
AAAAGGGHHH!

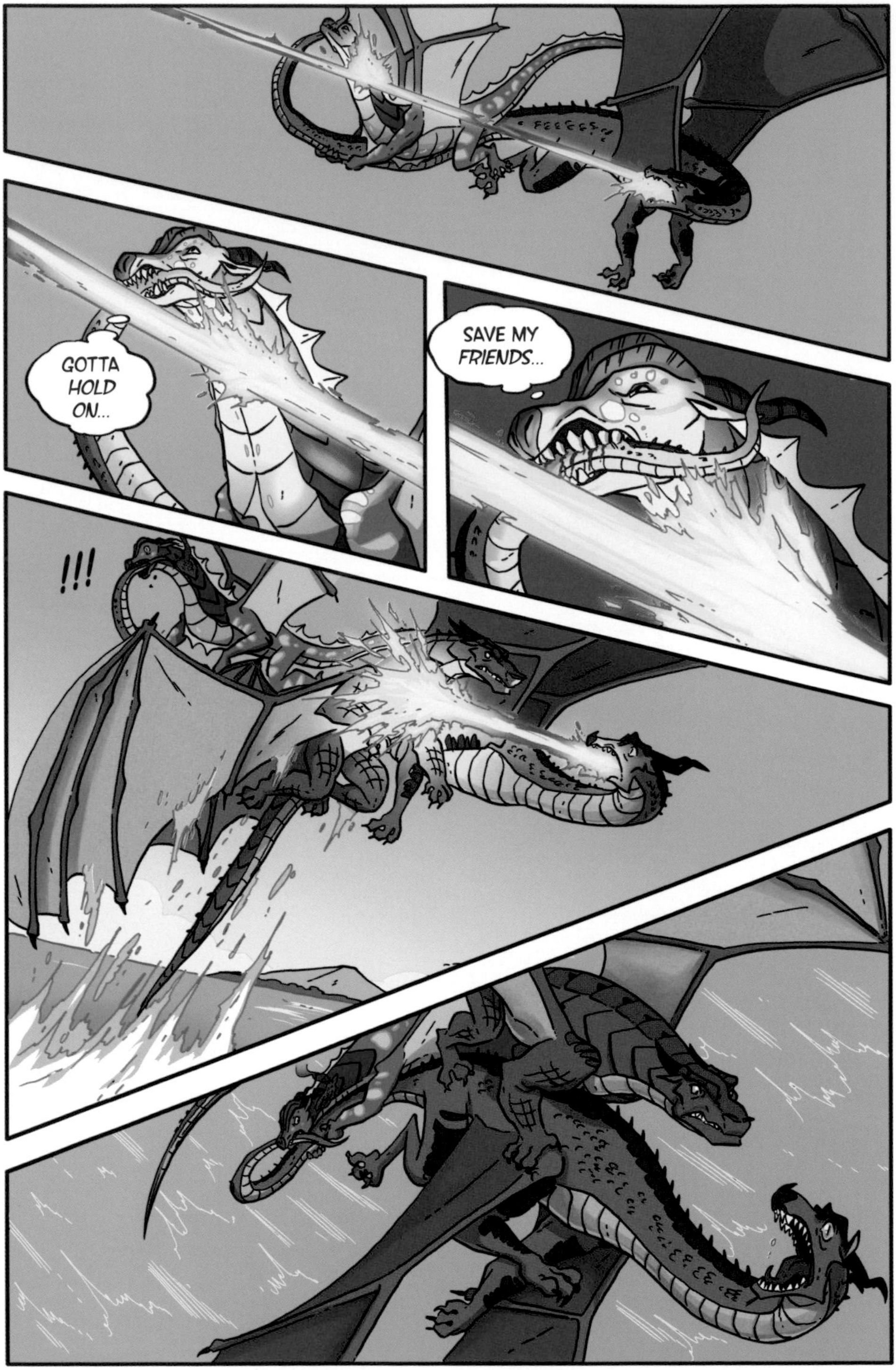
GOTTA HOLD ON...
SAVE MY FRIENDS...
!!!

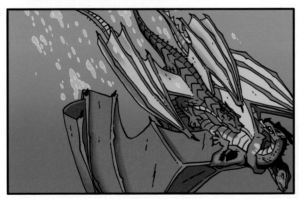

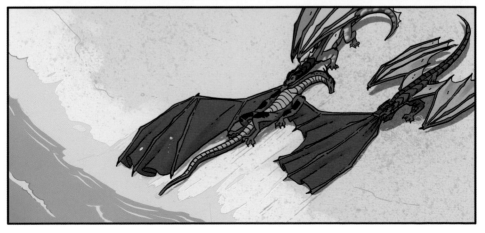

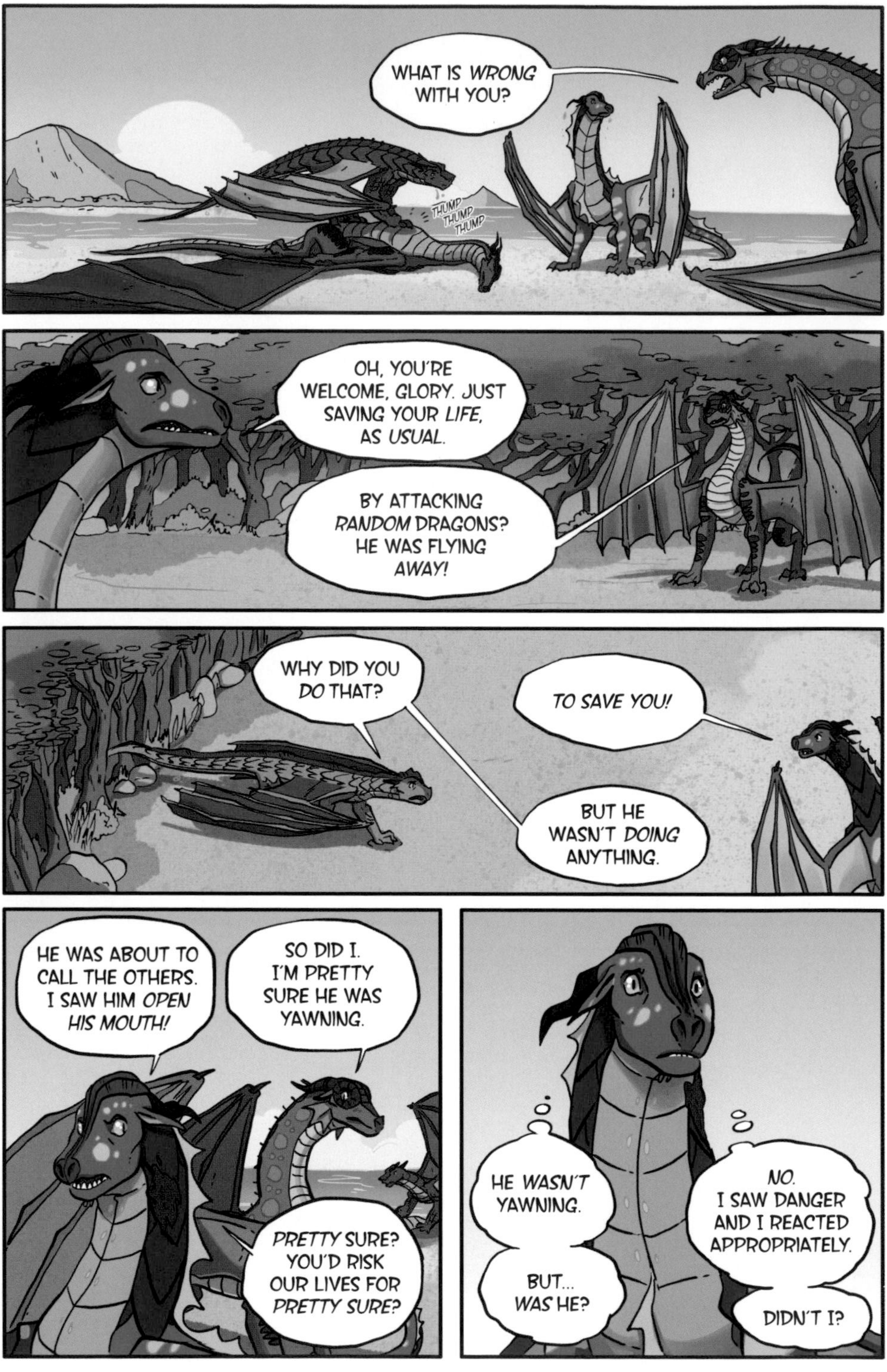

WHAT IS WRONG WITH YOU?
THUMP THUMP THUMP
OH, YOU'RE WELCOME, GLORY. JUST SAVING YOUR LIFE, AS USUAL.
BY ATTACKING RANDOM DRAGONS? HE WAS FLYING AWAY!
WHY DID YOU DO THAT?
TO SAVE YOU!
BUT HE WASN'T DOING ANYTHING.
HE WAS ABOUT TO CALL THE OTHERS. I SAW HIM OPEN HIS MOUTH!
SO DID I. I'M PRETTY SURE HE WAS YAWNING.
PRETTY SURE? YOU'D RISK OUR LIVES FOR PRETTY SURE?
HE WASN'T YAWNING.
BUT... WAS HE?
NO. I SAW DANGER AND I REACTED APPROPRIATELY.
DIDN'T I?

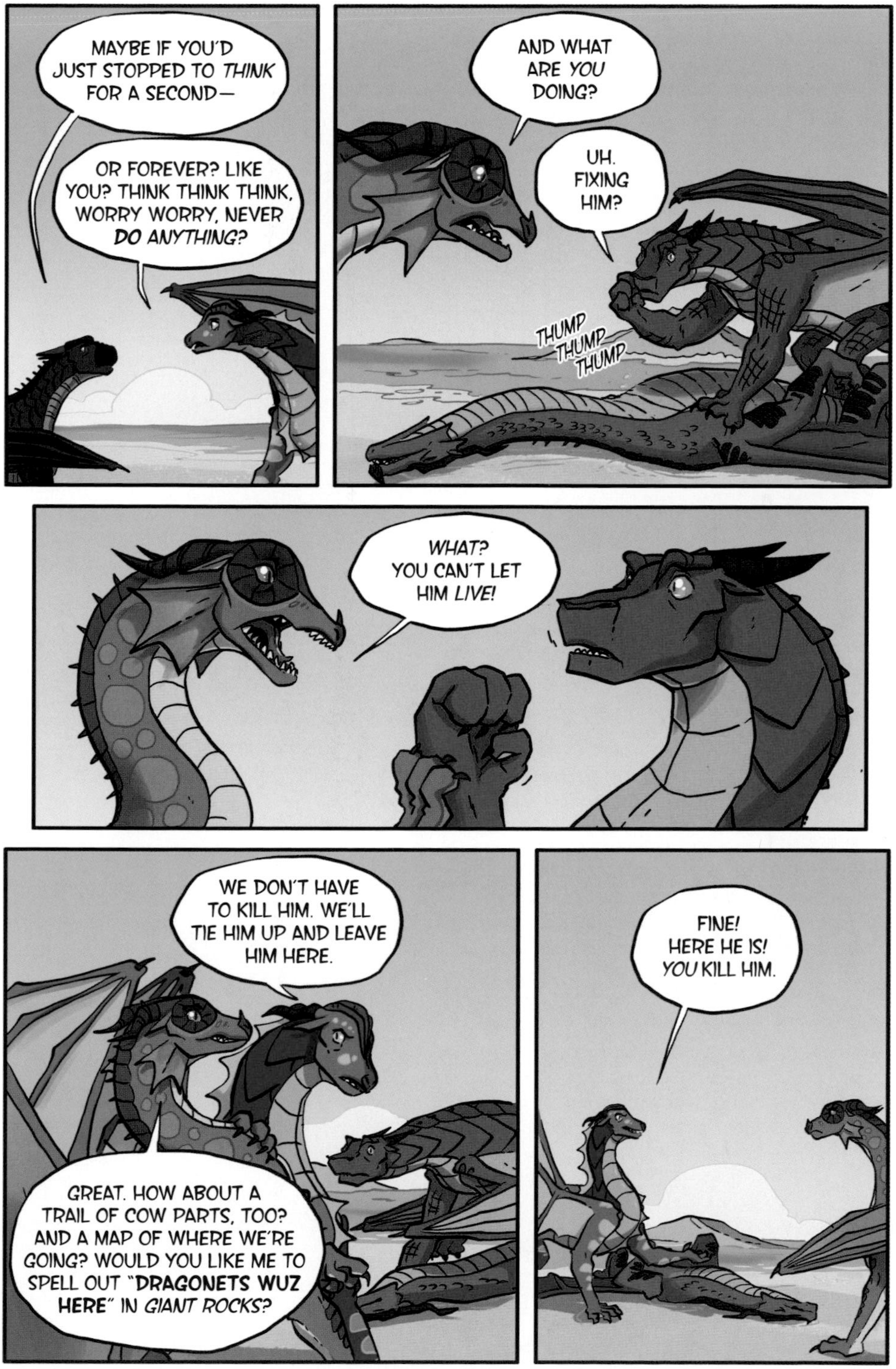
MAYBE IF YOU'D JUST STOPPED TO *THINK* FOR A SECOND—
OR FOREVER? LIKE YOU? THINK THINK THINK, WORRY WORRY, NEVER ***DO** ANYTHING?*
AND WHAT ARE *YOU* DOING?
UH. FIXING HIM?
THUMP THUMP THUMP
WHAT? YOU CAN'T LET HIM *LIVE!*
WE DON'T HAVE TO KILL HIM. WE'LL TIE HIM UP AND LEAVE HIM HERE.
GREAT. HOW ABOUT A TRAIL OF COW PARTS, TOO? AND A MAP OF WHERE WE'RE GOING? WOULD YOU LIKE ME TO SPELL OUT "**DRAGONETS WUZ HERE**" IN *GIANT ROCKS*?
FINE! HERE HE IS! *YOU* KILL HIM.

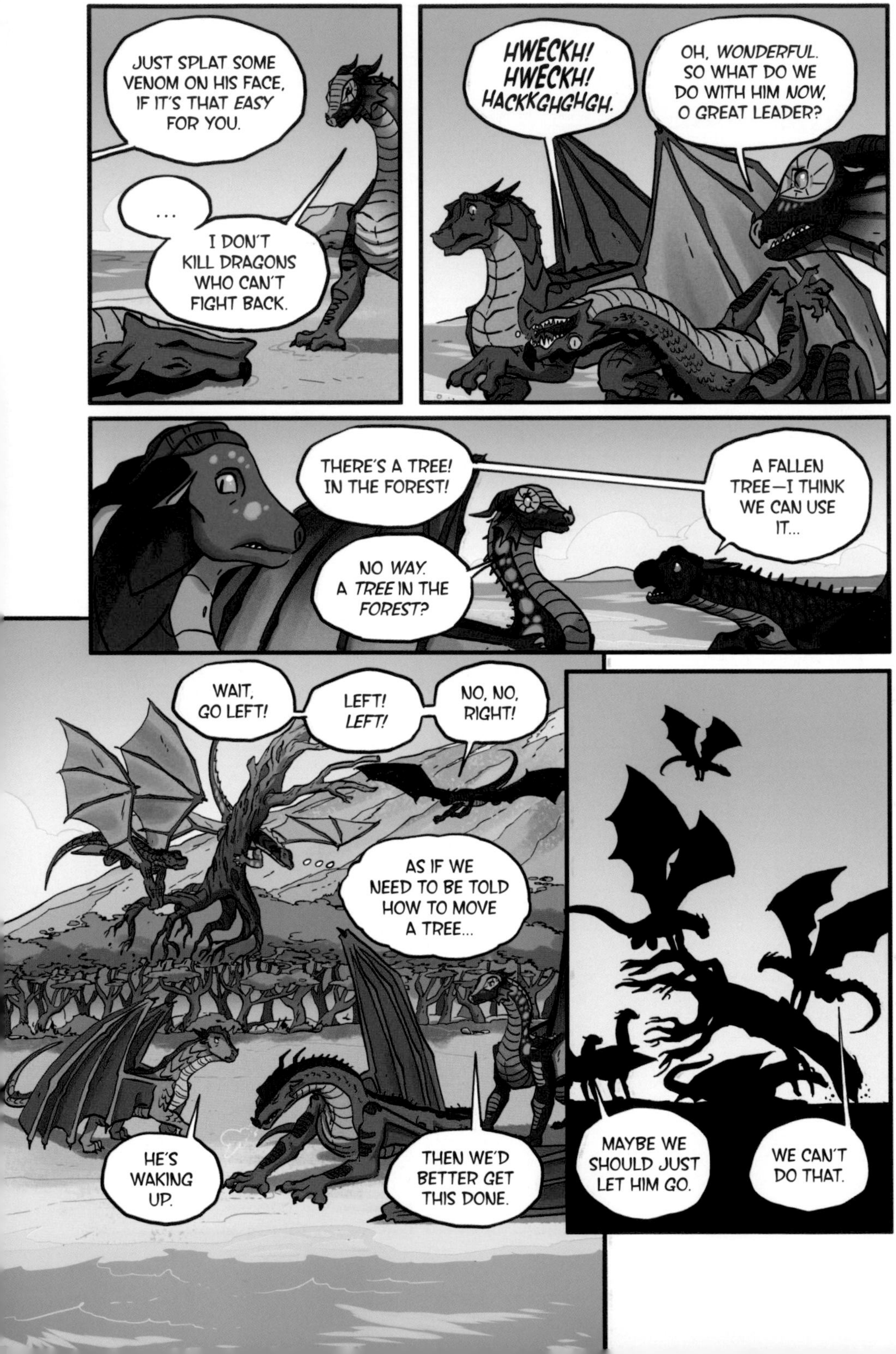
JUST SPLAT SOME VENOM ON HIS FACE, IF IT'S THAT *EASY* FOR YOU.
...
I DON'T KILL DRAGONS WHO CAN'T FIGHT BACK.
HWECKH! HWECKH! HACKKGHGHGH.
OH, *WONDERFUL.* SO WHAT DO WE DO WITH HIM *NOW,* O GREAT LEADER?
THERE'S A TREE! IN THE FOREST!
NO *WAY.* A *TREE* IN THE *FOREST?*
A FALLEN TREE—I THINK WE CAN USE IT...
WAIT, GO LEFT!
LEFT! *LEFT!*
NO, NO, RIGHT!
AS IF WE NEED TO BE TOLD HOW TO MOVE A TREE...
HE'S WAKING UP.
THEN WE'D BETTER GET THIS DONE.
MAYBE WE SHOULD JUST LET HIM GO.
WE CAN'T DO THAT.

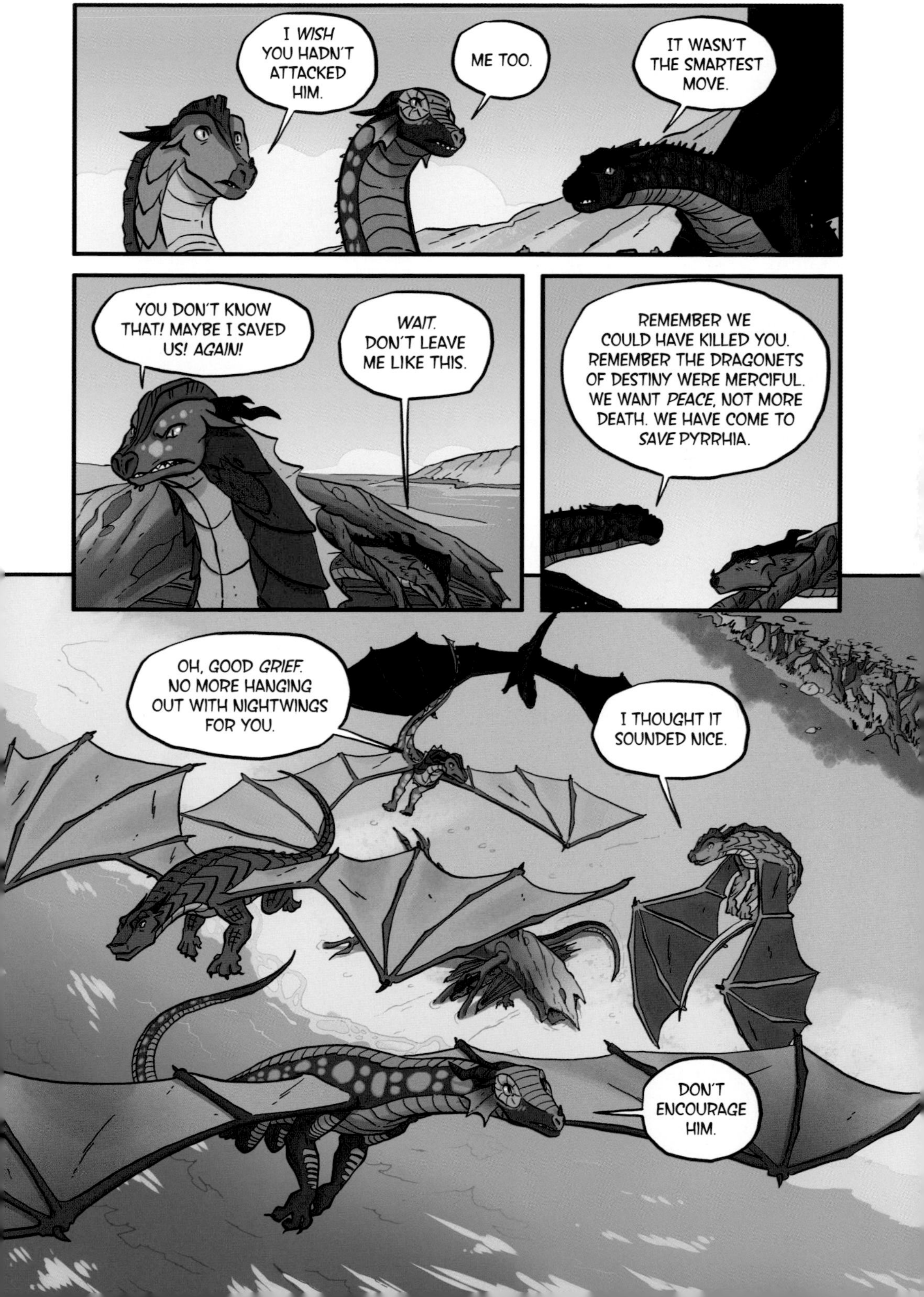
I *WISH* YOU HADN'T ATTACKED HIM.
ME TOO.
IT WASN'T THE SMARTEST MOVE.
YOU DON'T KNOW THAT! MAYBE I SAVED US! *AGAIN!*
WAIT. DON'T LEAVE ME LIKE THIS.
REMEMBER WE COULD HAVE KILLED YOU. REMEMBER THE DRAGONETS OF DESTINY WERE MERCIFUL. WE WANT *PEACE*, NOT MORE DEATH. WE HAVE COME TO *SAVE* PYRRHIA.
OH, *GOOD GRIEF.* NO MORE HANGING OUT WITH NIGHTWINGS FOR YOU.
I THOUGHT IT SOUNDED NICE.
DON'T ENCOURAGE HIM.

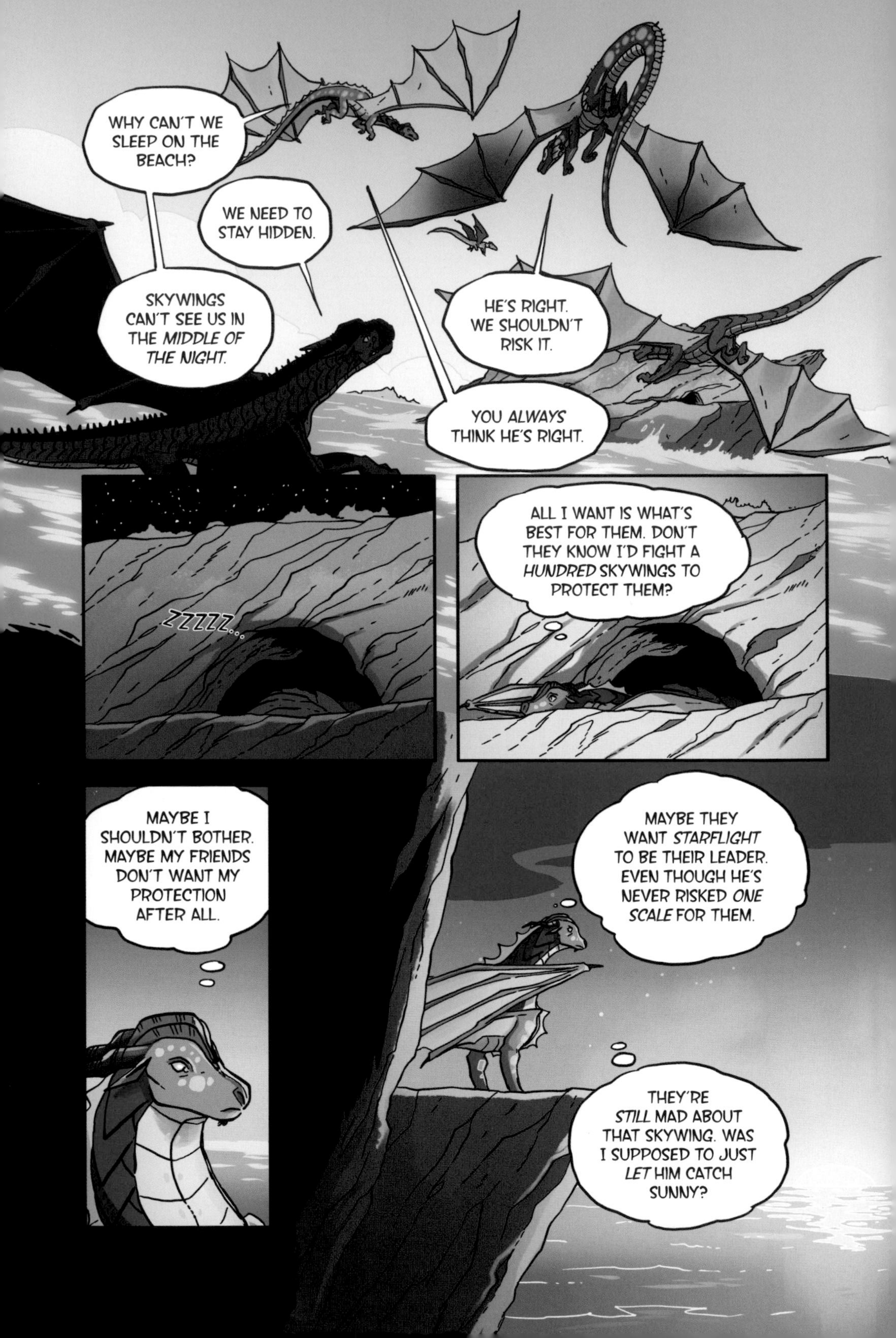
WHY CAN'T WE SLEEP ON THE BEACH?
WE NEED TO STAY HIDDEN.
SKYWINGS CAN'T SEE US IN THE *MIDDLE OF THE NIGHT.*
HE'S RIGHT. WE SHOULDN'T RISK IT.
YOU *ALWAYS* THINK HE'S RIGHT.
ZZZZZ...
ALL I WANT IS WHAT'S BEST FOR THEM. DON'T THEY KNOW I'D FIGHT A *HUNDRED* SKYWINGS TO PROTECT THEM?
MAYBE I SHOULDN'T BOTHER. MAYBE MY FRIENDS DON'T WANT MY PROTECTION AFTER ALL.
MAYBE THEY WANT *STARFLIGHT* TO BE THEIR LEADER. EVEN THOUGH HE'S NEVER RISKED *ONE SCALE* FOR THEM.
THEY'RE *STILL* MAD ABOUT THAT SKYWING. WAS I SUPPOSED TO JUST *LET* HIM CATCH SUNNY?

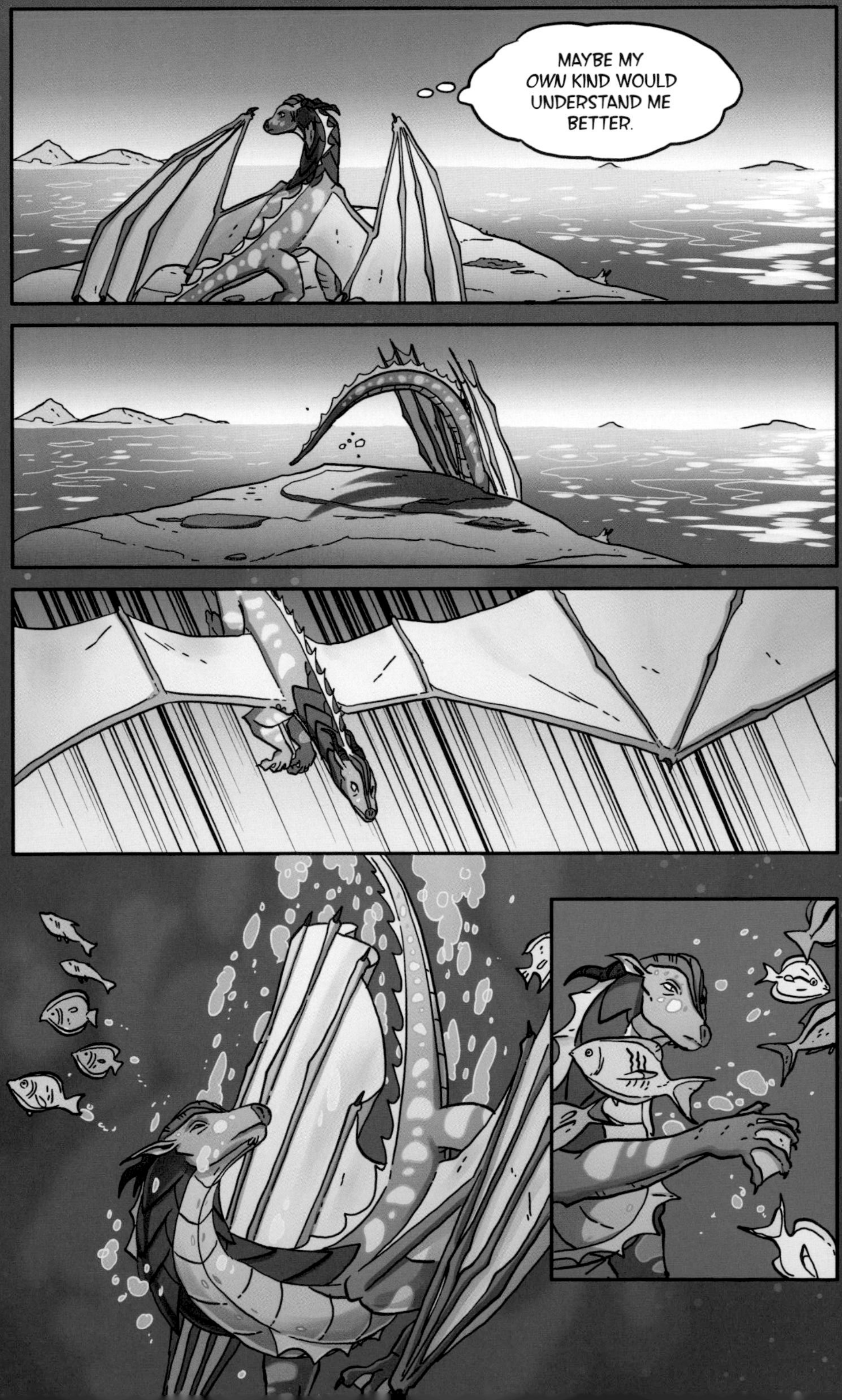
MAYBE MY OWN KIND WOULD UNDERSTAND ME BETTER.

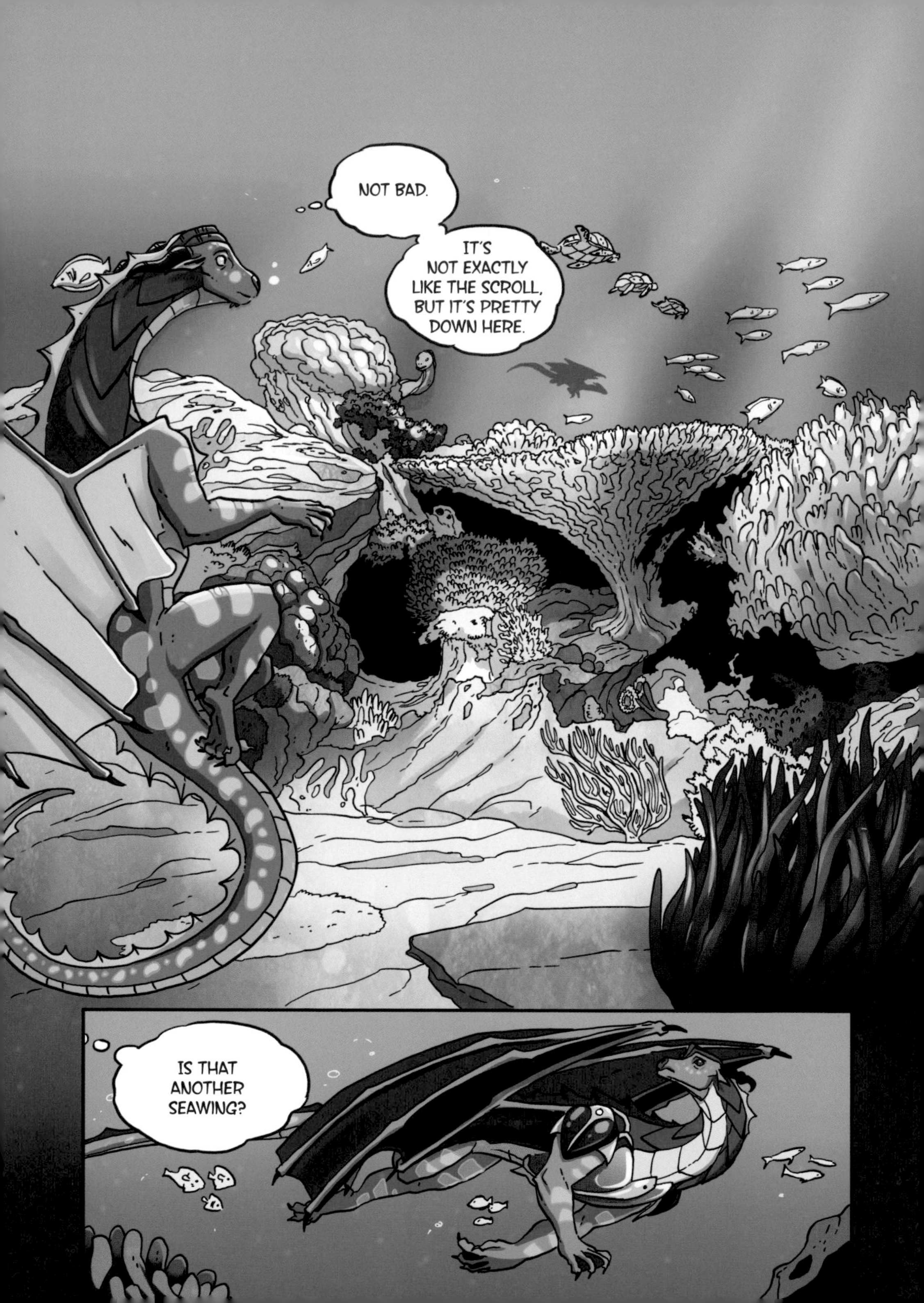
NOT BAD.
IT'S NOT EXACTLY LIKE THE SCROLL, BUT IT'S PRETTY DOWN HERE.
IS THAT ANOTHER SEAWING?

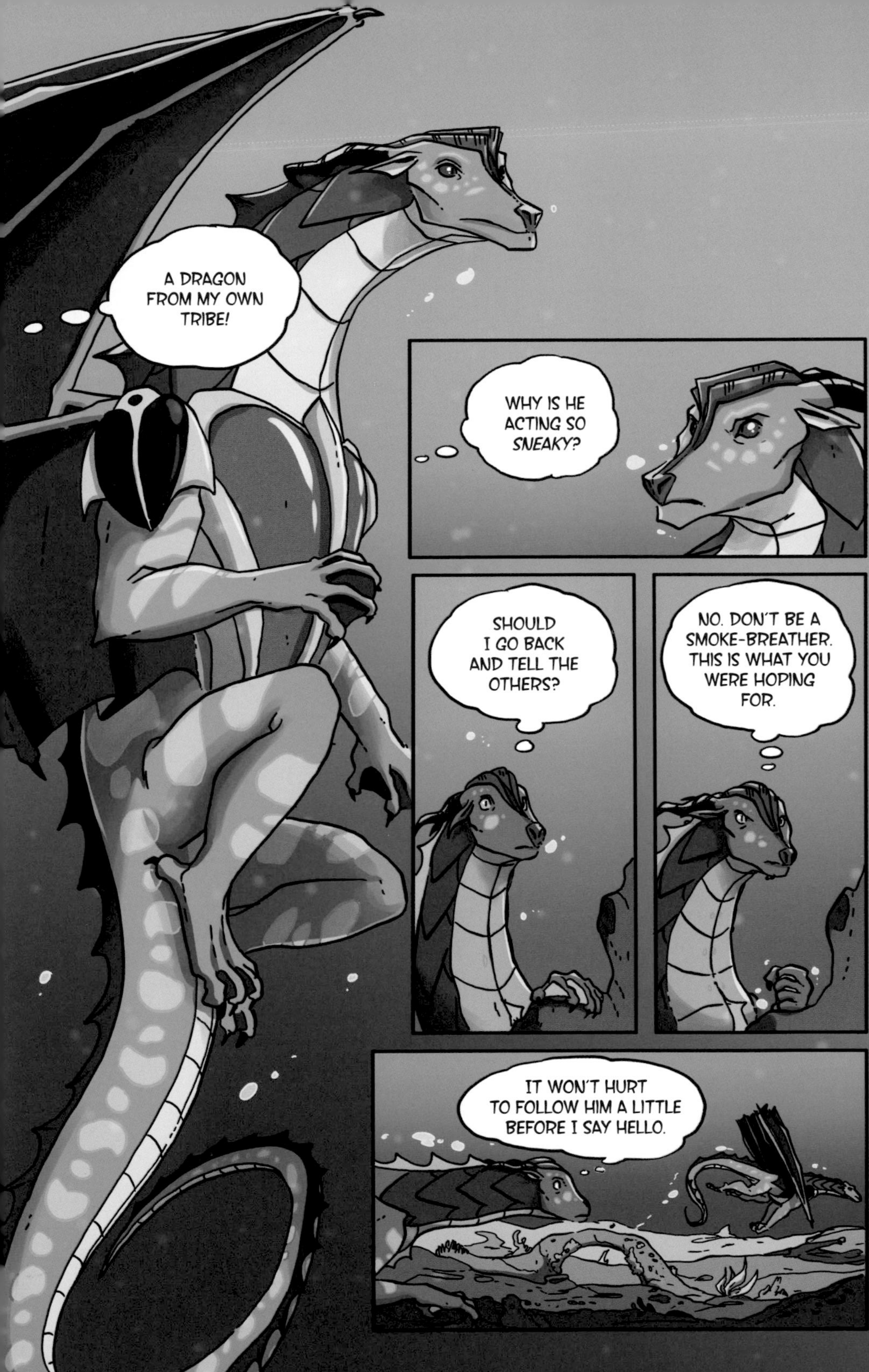
A DRAGON FROM MY OWN TRIBE!
WHY IS HE ACTING SO *SNEAKY*?
SHOULD I GO BACK AND TELL THE OTHERS?
NO. DON'T BE A SMOKE-BREATHER. THIS IS WHAT YOU WERE HOPING FOR.
IT WON'T HURT TO FOLLOW HIM A LITTLE BEFORE I SAY HELLO.

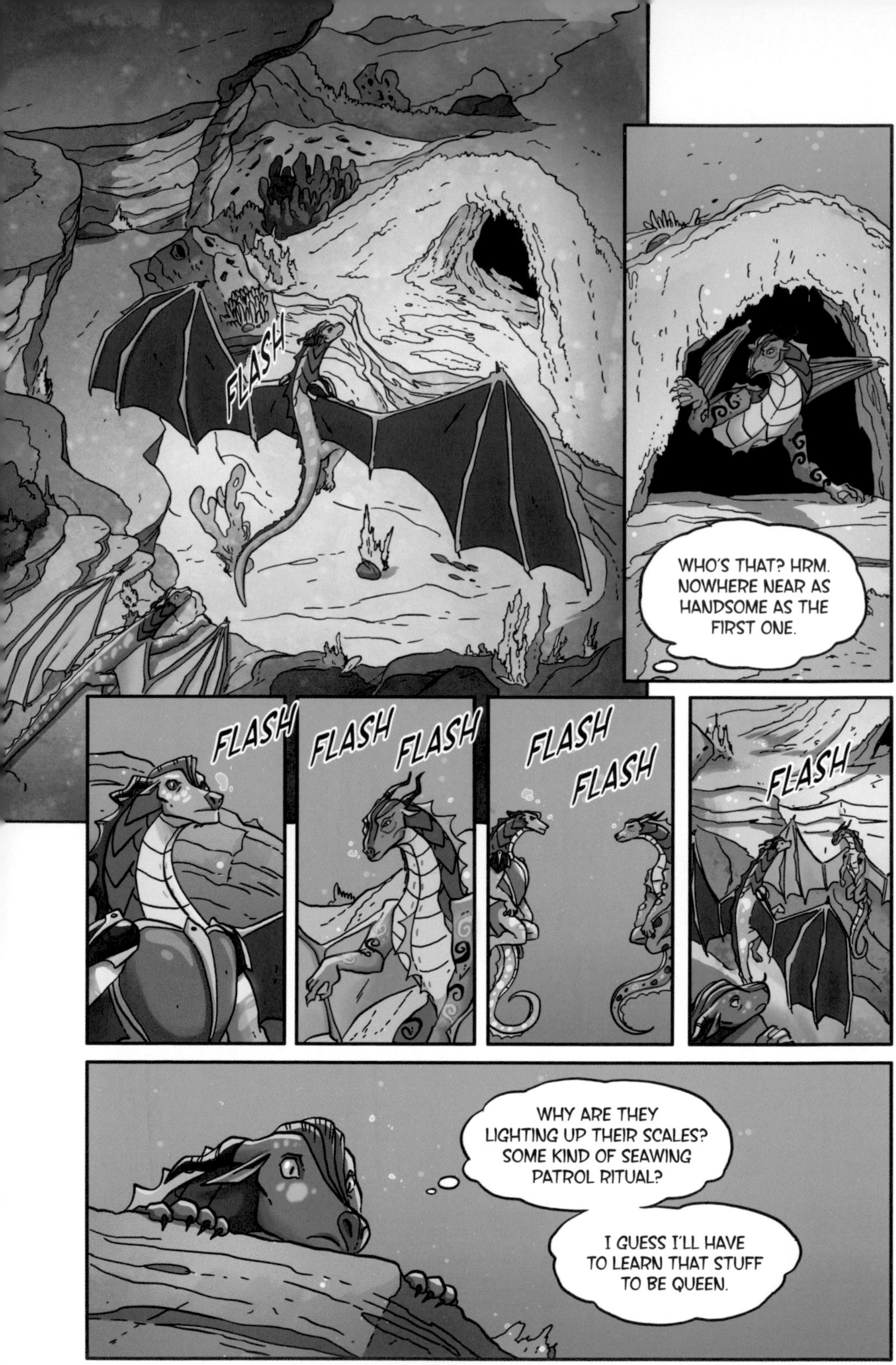
FLASH
WHO'S THAT? HRM. NOWHERE NEAR AS HANDSOME AS THE FIRST ONE.
FLASH
FLASH
FLASH
FLASH
FLASH
FLASH
WHY ARE THEY LIGHTING UP THEIR SCALES? SOME KIND OF SEAWING PATROL RITUAL?
I GUESS I'LL HAVE TO LEARN THAT STUFF TO BE QUEEN.

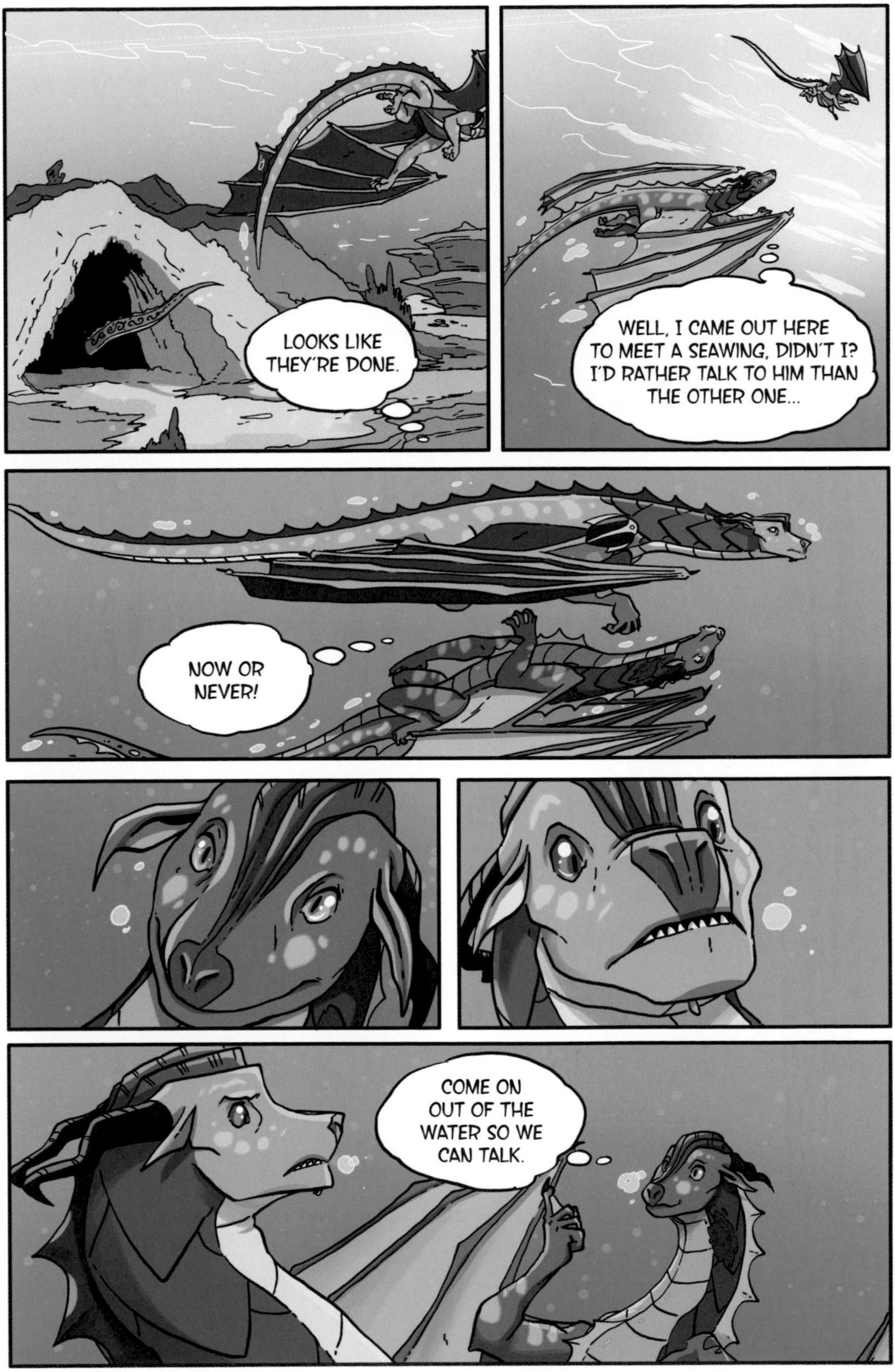
LOOKS LIKE THEY'RE DONE.
WELL, I CAME OUT HERE TO MEET A SEAWING, DIDN'T I? I'D RATHER TALK TO HIM THAN THE OTHER ONE...
NOW OR NEVER!
COME ON OUT OF THE WATER SO WE CAN TALK.

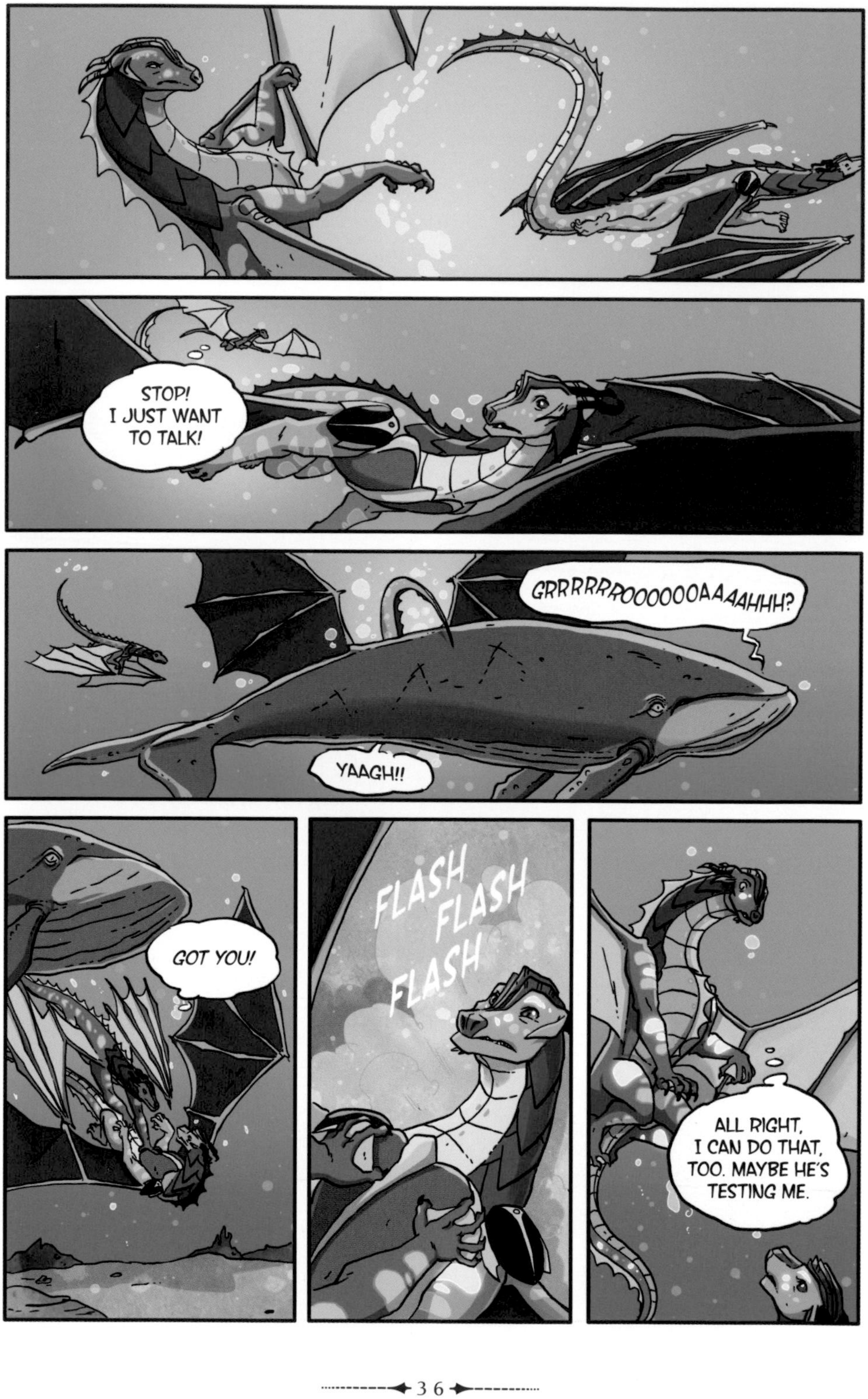
STOP!
I JUST WANT
TO TALK!
GRRRRRROOOOOOAAAAHHH?
YAAGH!!
GOT YOU!
FLASH
FLASH
FLASH
ALL RIGHT,
I CAN DO THAT,
TOO. MAYBE HE'S
TESTING ME.

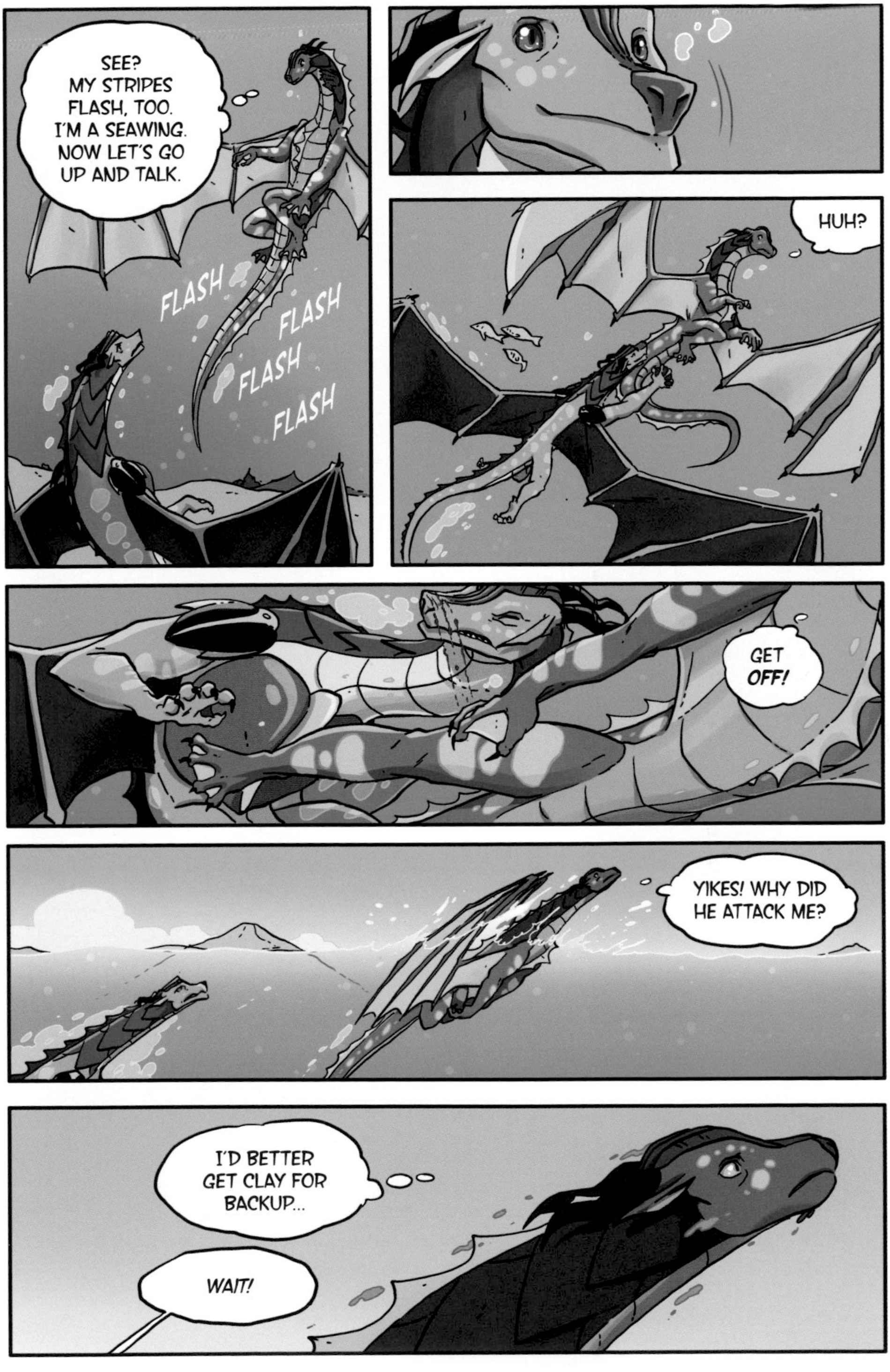
SEE? MY STRIPES FLASH, TOO. I'M A SEAWING. NOW LET'S GO UP AND TALK.
FLASH
FLASH
FLASH
FLASH
HUH?
GET OFF!
YIKES! WHY DID HE ATTACK ME?
I'D BETTER GET CLAY FOR BACKUP...
WAIT!

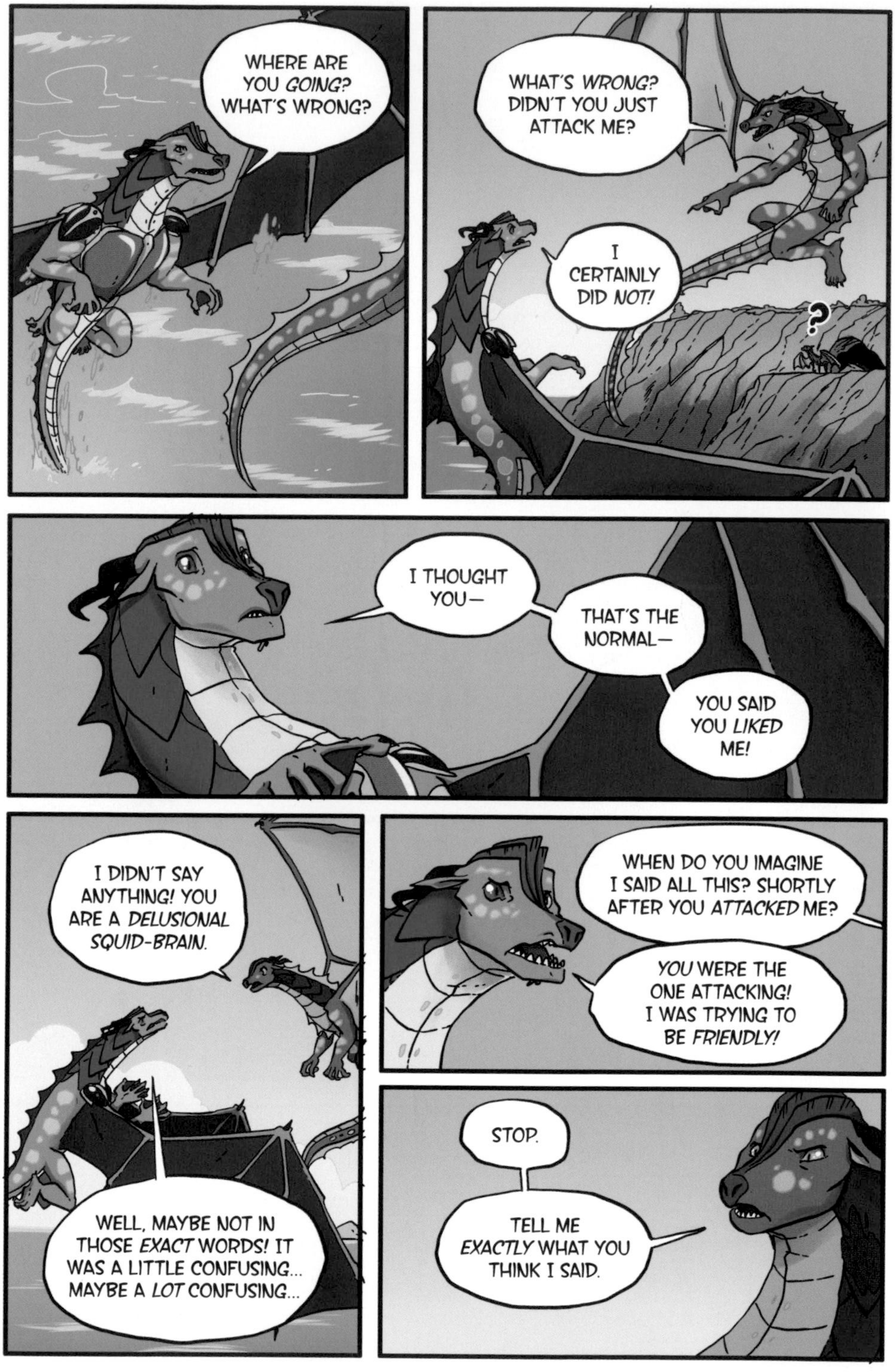
WHERE ARE YOU *GOING?* WHAT'S WRONG?
WHAT'S *WRONG?* DIDN'T YOU JUST ATTACK ME?
I CERTAINLY DID *NOT!*
?
I THOUGHT YOU—
THAT'S THE NORMAL—
YOU SAID YOU *LIKED* ME!
I DIDN'T SAY ANYTHING! YOU ARE A *DELUSIONAL SQUID-BRAIN.*
WELL, MAYBE NOT IN THOSE *EXACT* WORDS! IT WAS A LITTLE CONFUSING... MAYBE A *LOT* CONFUSING...
WHEN DO YOU IMAGINE I SAID ALL THIS? SHORTLY AFTER YOU *ATTACKED* ME?
YOU WERE THE ONE ATTACKING! I WAS TRYING TO BE *FRIENDLY!*
STOP.
TELL ME *EXACTLY* WHAT YOU THINK I SAID.

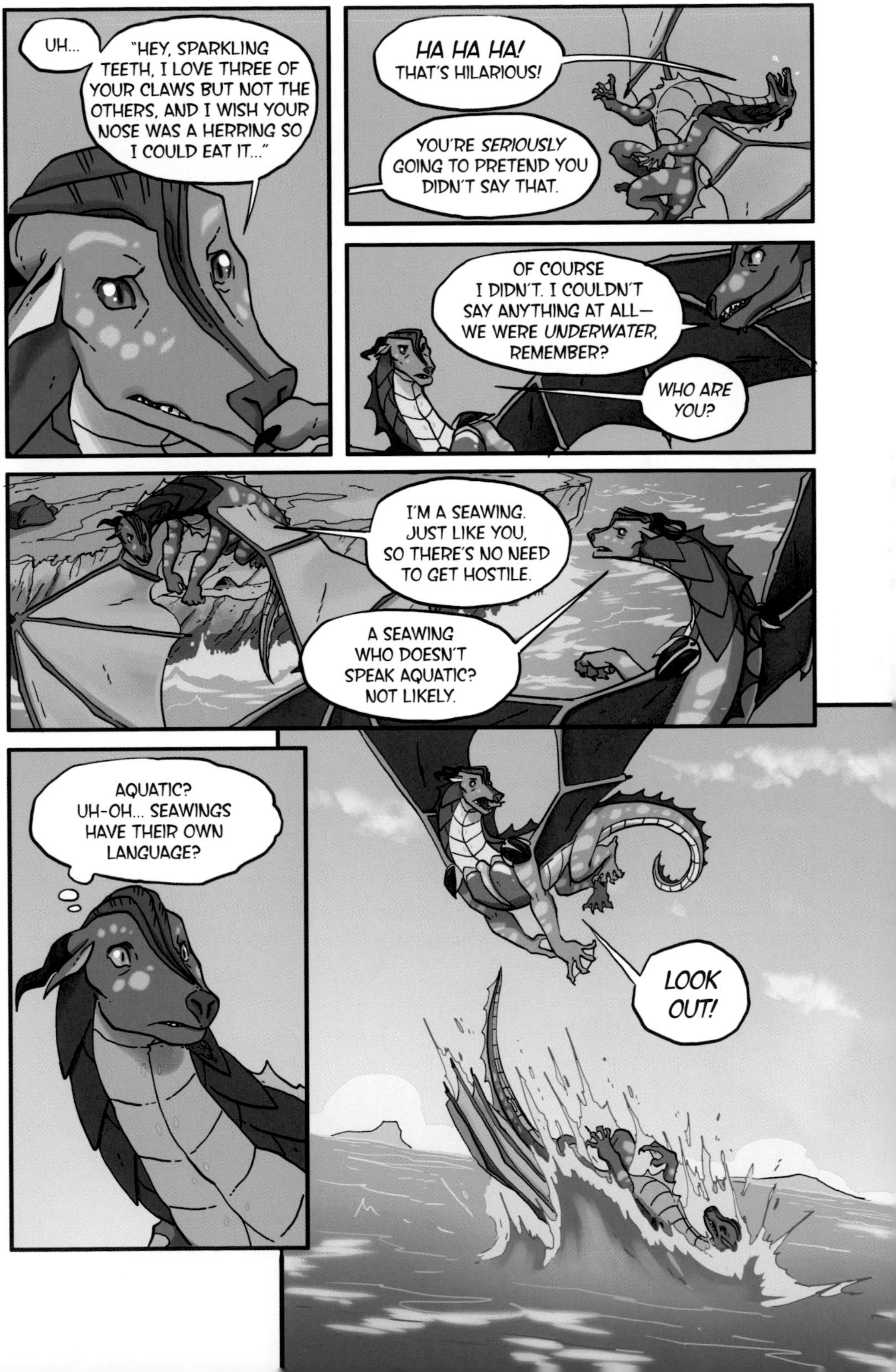
UH...
"HEY, SPARKLING TEETH, I LOVE THREE OF YOUR CLAWS BUT NOT THE OTHERS, AND I WISH YOUR NOSE WAS A HERRING SO I COULD EAT IT..."
HA HA HA! THAT'S HILARIOUS!
YOU'RE SERIOUSLY GOING TO PRETEND YOU DIDN'T SAY THAT.
OF COURSE I DIDN'T. I COULDN'T SAY ANYTHING AT ALL— WE WERE UNDERWATER, REMEMBER?
WHO ARE YOU?
I'M A SEAWING. JUST LIKE YOU, SO THERE'S NO NEED TO GET HOSTILE.
A SEAWING WHO DOESN'T SPEAK AQUATIC? NOT LIKELY.
AQUATIC? UH-OH... SEAWINGS HAVE THEIR OWN LANGUAGE?
LOOK OUT!

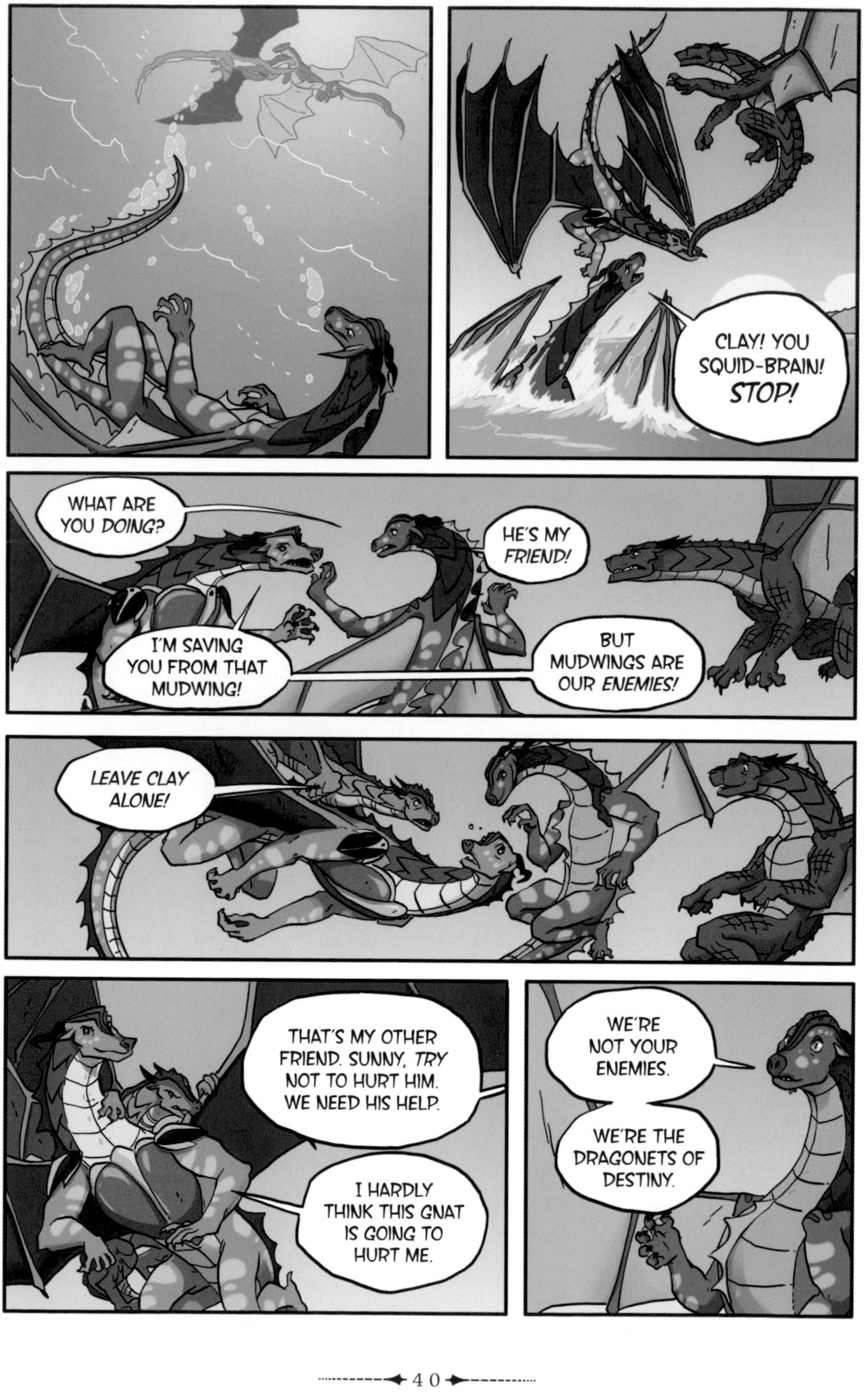
CLAY! YOU SQUID-BRAIN! STOP!
WHAT ARE YOU DOING?
HE'S MY FRIEND!
I'M SAVING YOU FROM THAT MUDWING!
BUT MUDWINGS ARE OUR ENEMIES!
LEAVE CLAY ALONE!
THAT'S MY OTHER FRIEND. SUNNY, TRY NOT TO HURT HIM. WE NEED HIS HELP.
I HARDLY THINK THIS GNAT IS GOING TO HURT ME.
WE'RE NOT YOUR ENEMIES.
WE'RE THE DRAGONETS OF DESTINY.

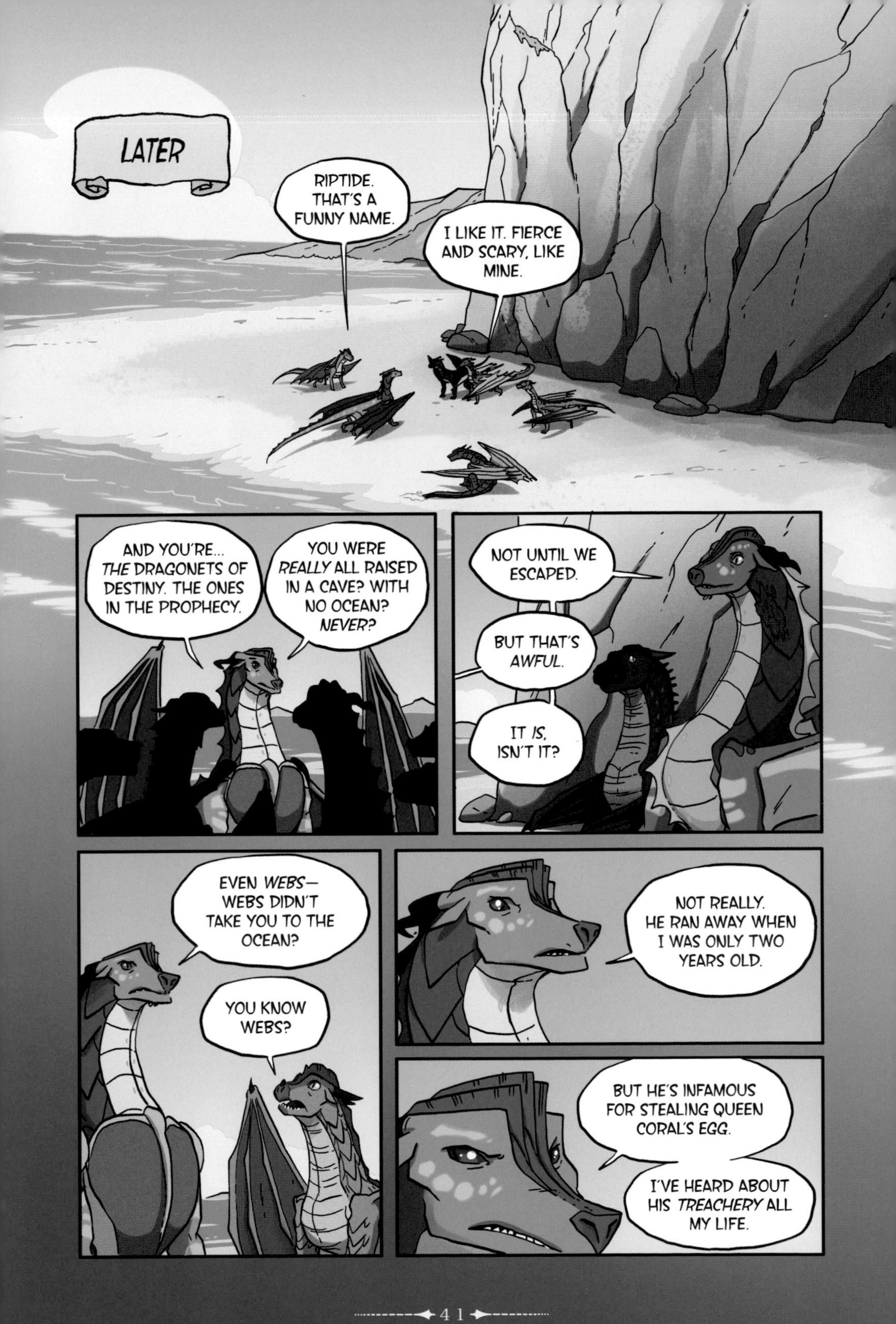
LATER
RIPTIDE. THAT'S A FUNNY NAME.
I LIKE IT. FIERCE AND SCARY, LIKE MINE.
AND YOU'RE... *THE* DRAGONETS OF DESTINY. THE ONES IN THE PROPHECY.
YOU WERE *REALLY* ALL RAISED IN A CAVE? WITH NO OCEAN? *NEVER*?
NOT UNTIL WE ESCAPED.
BUT THAT'S *AWFUL*.
IT *IS*, ISN'T IT?
EVEN *WEBS*—WEBS DIDN'T TAKE YOU TO THE OCEAN?
YOU KNOW WEBS?
NOT REALLY. HE RAN AWAY WHEN I WAS ONLY TWO YEARS OLD.
BUT HE'S INFAMOUS FOR STEALING QUEEN CORAL'S EGG.
I'VE HEARD ABOUT HIS *TREACHERY* ALL MY LIFE.

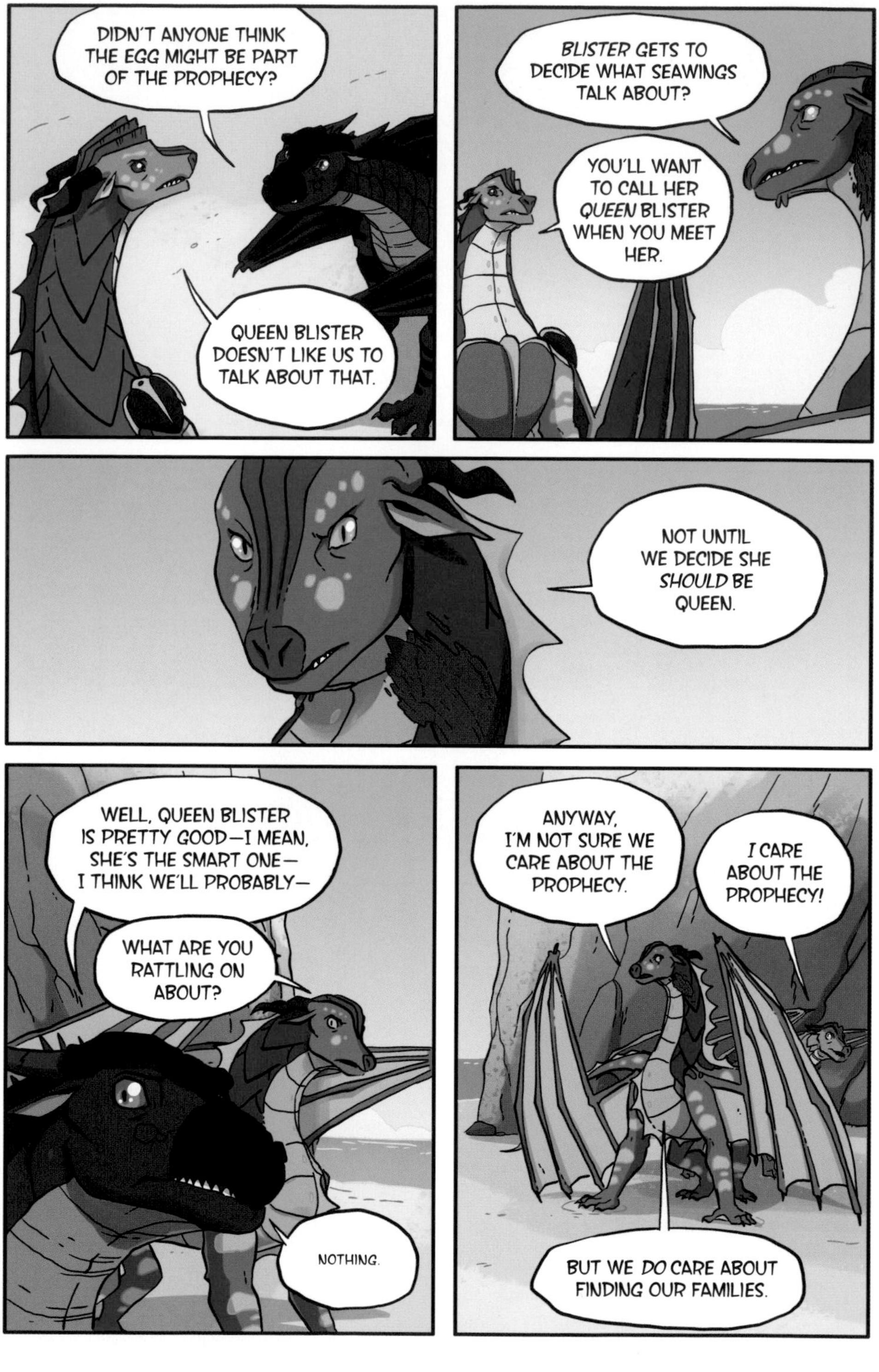
DIDN'T ANYONE THINK THE EGG MIGHT BE PART OF THE PROPHECY?
QUEEN BLISTER DOESN'T LIKE US TO TALK ABOUT THAT.
BLISTER GETS TO DECIDE WHAT SEAWINGS TALK ABOUT?
YOU'LL WANT TO CALL HER *QUEEN* BLISTER WHEN YOU MEET HER.
NOT UNTIL WE DECIDE SHE *SHOULD* BE QUEEN.
WELL, QUEEN BLISTER IS PRETTY GOOD—I MEAN, SHE'S THE SMART ONE— I THINK WE'LL PROBABLY—
WHAT ARE YOU RATTLING ON ABOUT?
NOTHING.
ANYWAY, I'M NOT SURE WE CARE ABOUT THE PROPHECY.
I CARE ABOUT THE PROPHECY!
BUT WE *DO* CARE ABOUT FINDING OUR FAMILIES.

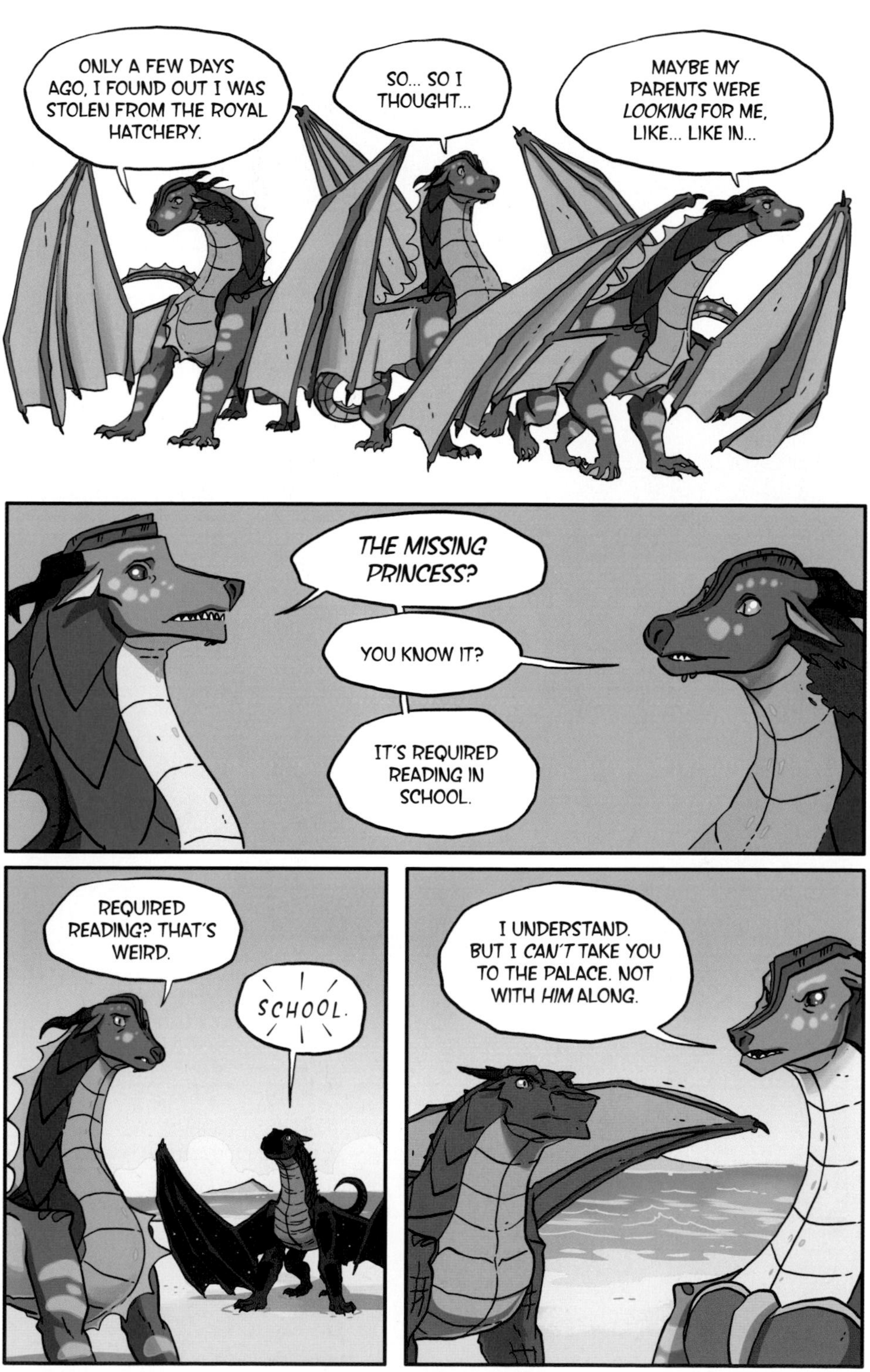
ONLY A FEW DAYS AGO, I FOUND OUT I WAS STOLEN FROM THE ROYAL HATCHERY.
SO... SO I THOUGHT...
MAYBE MY PARENTS WERE *LOOKING* FOR ME, LIKE... LIKE IN...
THE MISSING PRINCESS?
YOU KNOW IT?
IT'S REQUIRED READING IN SCHOOL.
REQUIRED READING? THAT'S WEIRD.
SCHOOL.
I UNDERSTAND. BUT I *CAN'T* TAKE YOU TO THE PALACE. NOT WITH *HIM* ALONG.

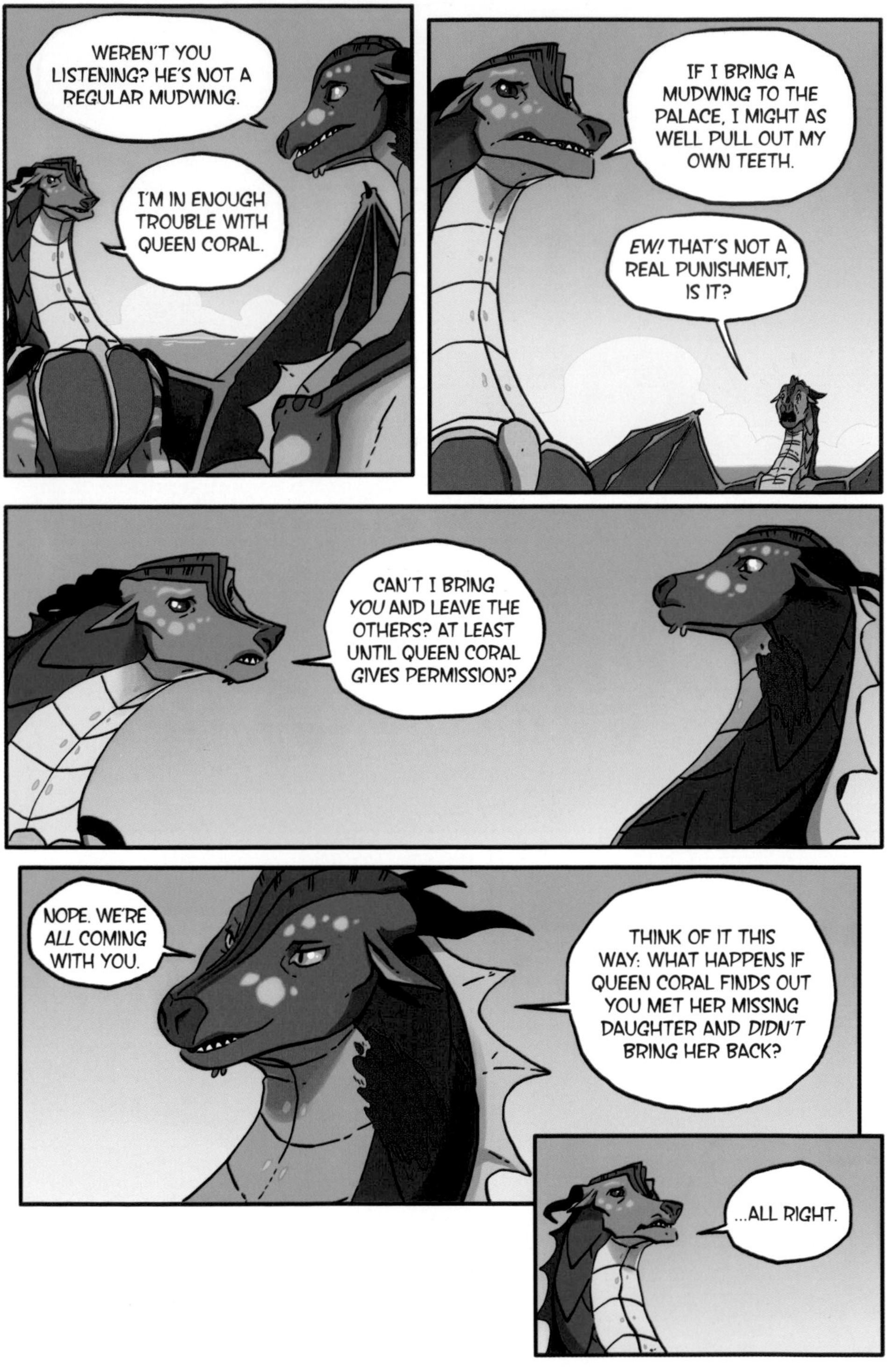
WEREN'T YOU LISTENING? HE'S NOT A REGULAR MUDWING.
I'M IN ENOUGH TROUBLE WITH QUEEN CORAL.
IF I BRING A MUDWING TO THE PALACE, I MIGHT AS WELL PULL OUT MY OWN TEETH.
EW! THAT'S NOT A REAL PUNISHMENT, IS IT?
CAN'T I BRING *YOU* AND LEAVE THE OTHERS? AT LEAST UNTIL QUEEN CORAL GIVES PERMISSION?
NOPE. WE'RE *ALL* COMING WITH YOU.
THINK OF IT THIS WAY: WHAT HAPPENS IF QUEEN CORAL FINDS OUT YOU MET HER MISSING DAUGHTER AND *DIDN'T* BRING HER BACK?
...ALL RIGHT.

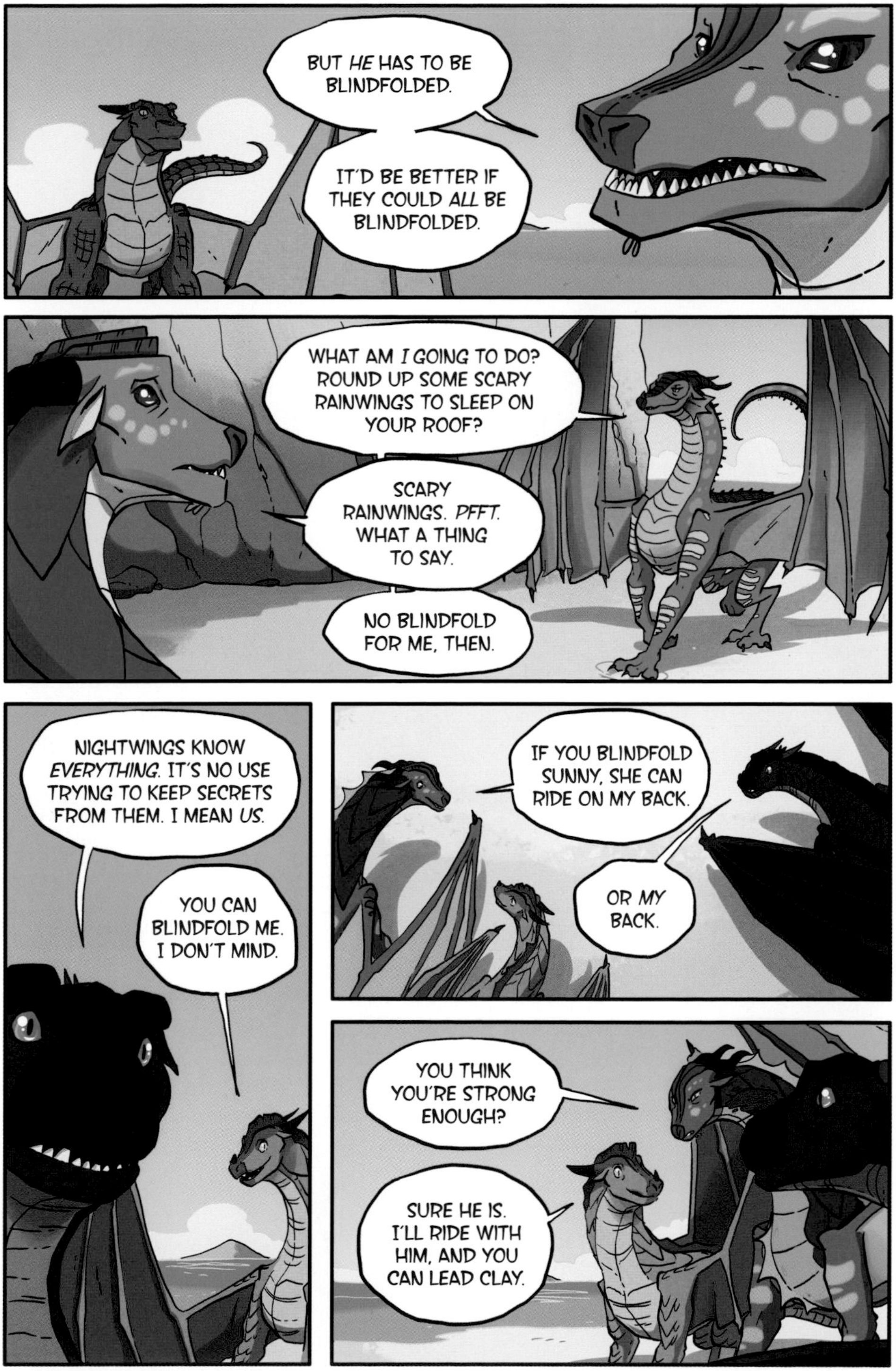
BUT *HE* HAS TO BE BLINDFOLDED.
IT'D BE BETTER IF THEY COULD *ALL* BE BLINDFOLDED.
WHAT AM *I* GOING TO DO? ROUND UP SOME SCARY RAINWINGS TO SLEEP ON YOUR ROOF?
SCARY RAINWINGS. *PFFT.* WHAT A THING TO SAY.
NO BLINDFOLD FOR ME, THEN.
NIGHTWINGS KNOW *EVERYTHING*. IT'S NO USE TRYING TO KEEP SECRETS FROM THEM. I MEAN *US*.
YOU CAN BLINDFOLD ME. I DON'T MIND.
IF YOU BLINDFOLD SUNNY, SHE CAN RIDE ON MY BACK.
OR *MY* BACK.
YOU THINK YOU'RE STRONG ENOUGH?
SURE HE IS. I'LL RIDE WITH HIM, AND YOU CAN LEAD CLAY.

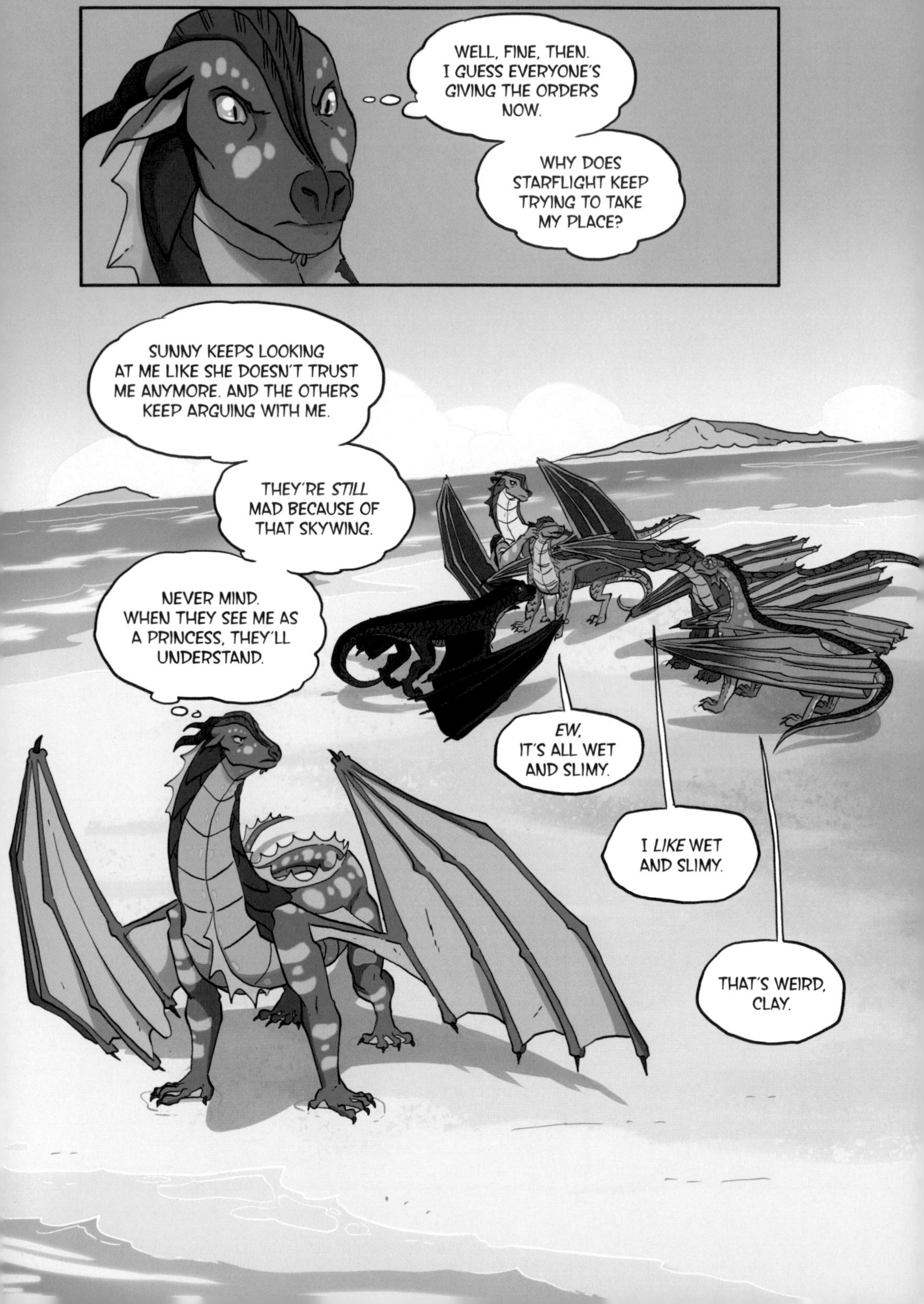
WELL, FINE, THEN. I GUESS EVERYONE'S GIVING THE ORDERS NOW.
WHY DOES STARFLIGHT KEEP TRYING TO TAKE MY PLACE?
SUNNY KEEPS LOOKING AT ME LIKE SHE DOESN'T TRUST ME ANYMORE. AND THE OTHERS KEEP ARGUING WITH ME.
THEY'RE *STILL* MAD BECAUSE OF THAT SKYWING.
NEVER MIND. WHEN THEY SEE ME AS A PRINCESS, THEY'LL UNDERSTAND.
EW, IT'S ALL WET AND SLIMY.
I *LIKE* WET AND SLIMY.
THAT'S WEIRD, CLAY.

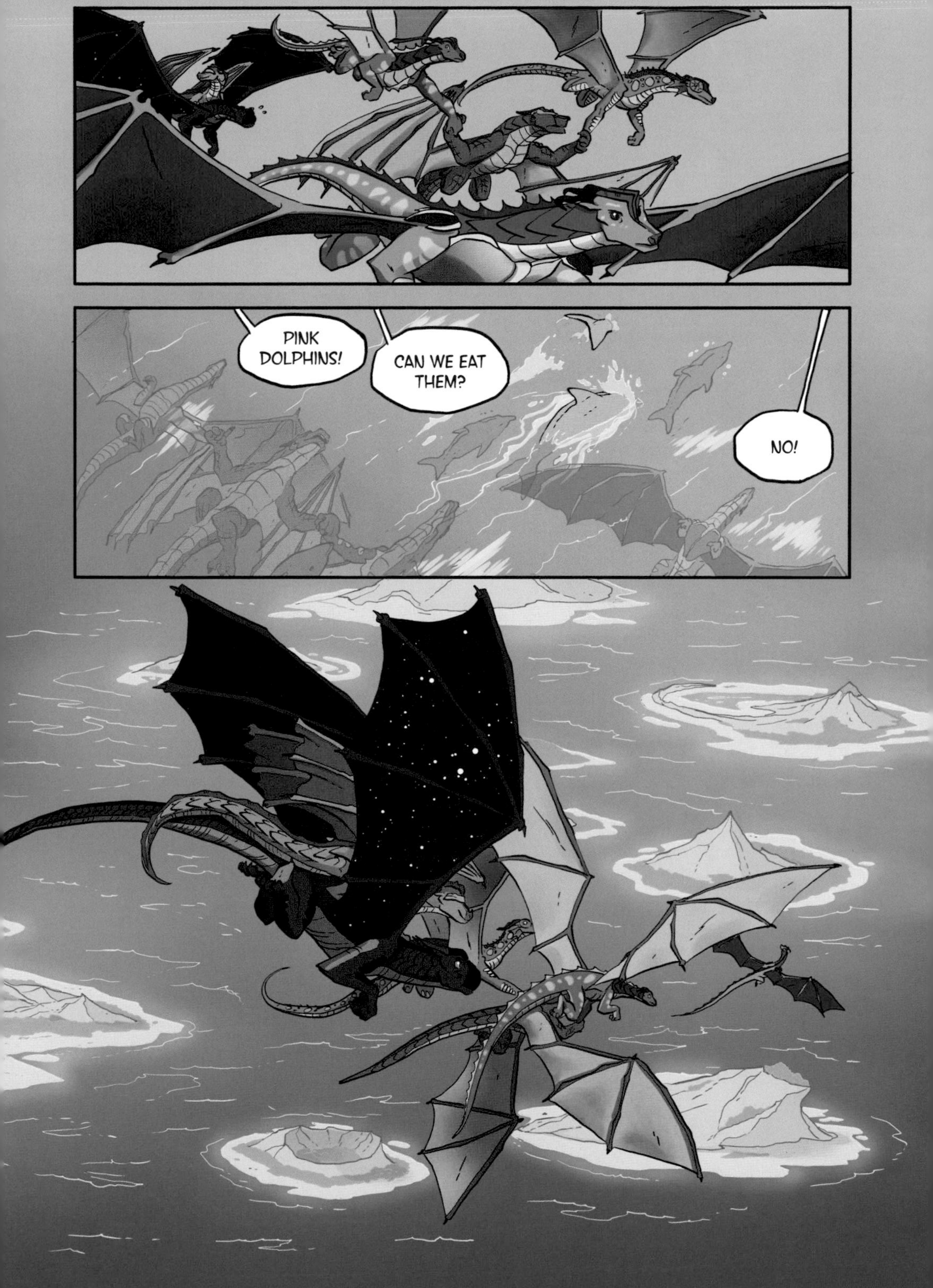
PINK DOLPHINS!
CAN WE EAT THEM?
NO!

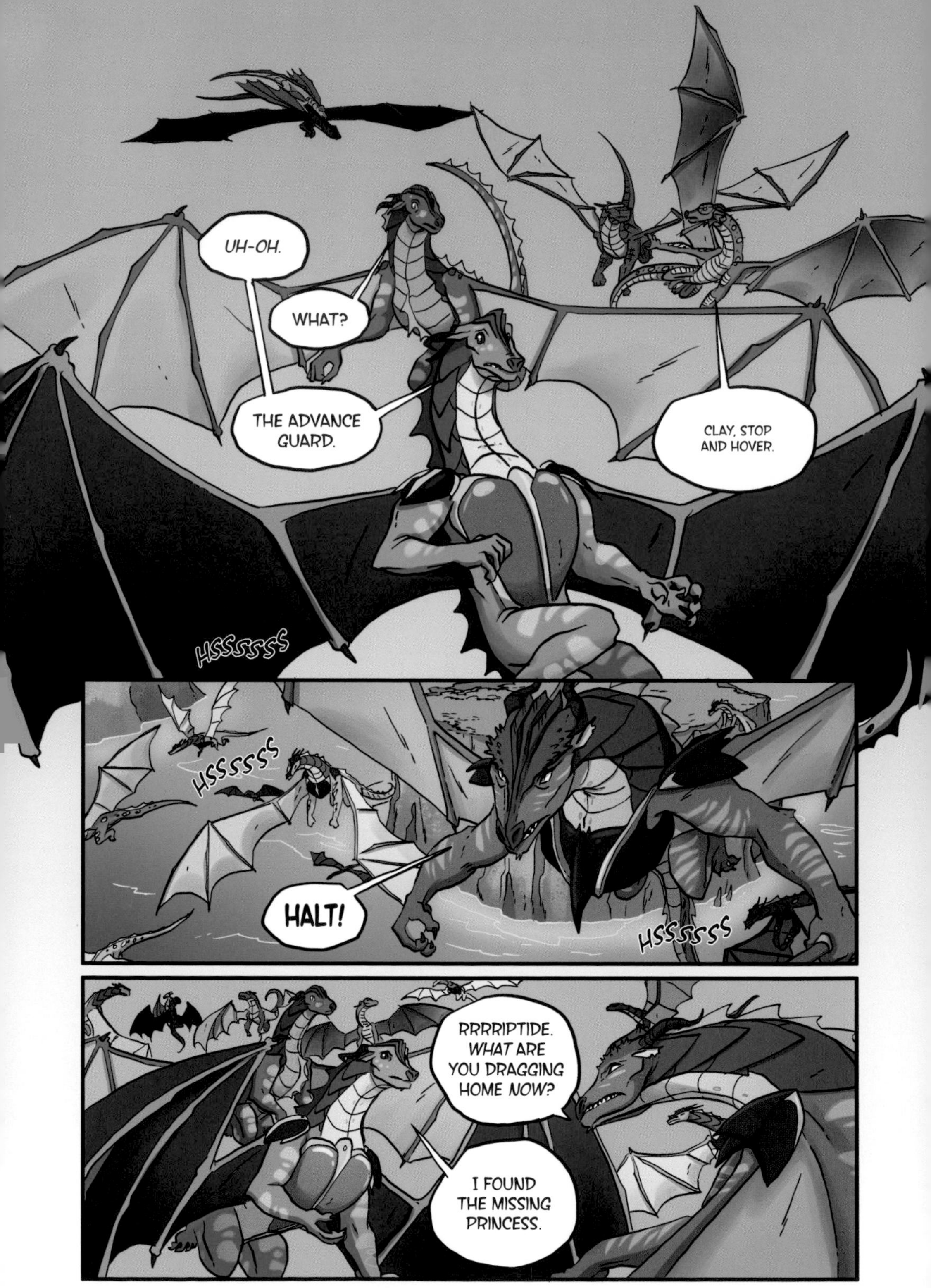
UH-OH.
WHAT?
THE ADVANCE GUARD.
CLAY, STOP AND HOVER.
HSSSSSS
HSSSSSS
HALT!
HSSSSSS
RRRRIPTIDE. WHAT ARE YOU DRAGGING HOME NOW?
I FOUND THE MISSING PRINCESS.

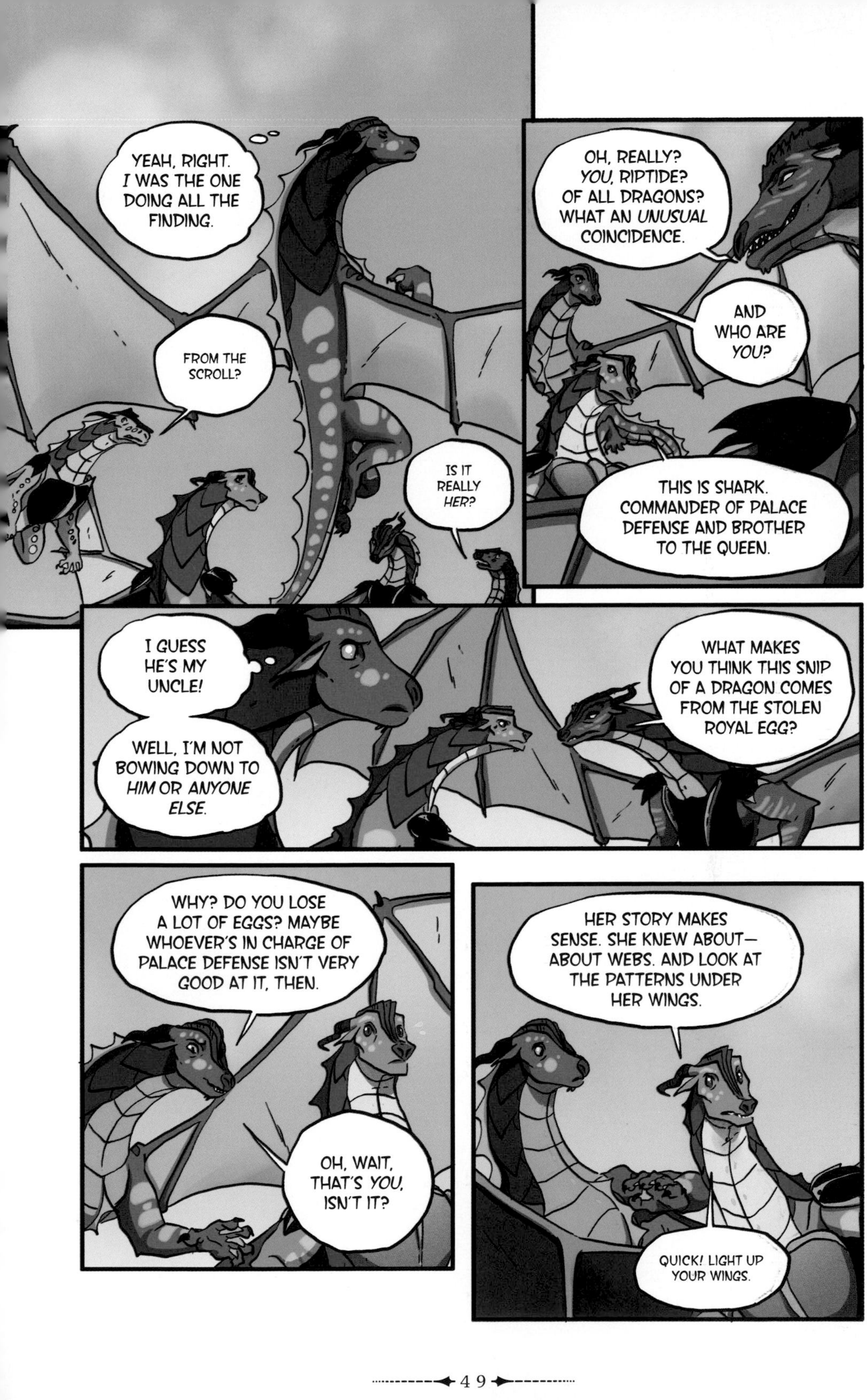
YEAH, RIGHT. I WAS THE ONE DOING ALL THE FINDING.
FROM THE SCROLL?
IS IT REALLY HER?
OH, REALLY? YOU, RIPTIDE? OF ALL DRAGONS? WHAT AN UNUSUAL COINCIDENCE.
AND WHO ARE YOU?
THIS IS SHARK. COMMANDER OF PALACE DEFENSE AND BROTHER TO THE QUEEN.
I GUESS HE'S MY UNCLE!
WELL, I'M NOT BOWING DOWN TO HIM OR ANYONE ELSE.
WHAT MAKES YOU THINK THIS SNIP OF A DRAGON COMES FROM THE STOLEN ROYAL EGG?
WHY? DO YOU LOSE A LOT OF EGGS? MAYBE WHOEVER'S IN CHARGE OF PALACE DEFENSE ISN'T VERY GOOD AT IT, THEN.
OH, WAIT, THAT'S YOU, ISN'T IT?
HER STORY MAKES SENSE. SHE KNEW ABOUT—ABOUT WEBS. AND LOOK AT THE PATTERNS UNDER HER WINGS.
QUICK! LIGHT UP YOUR WINGS.

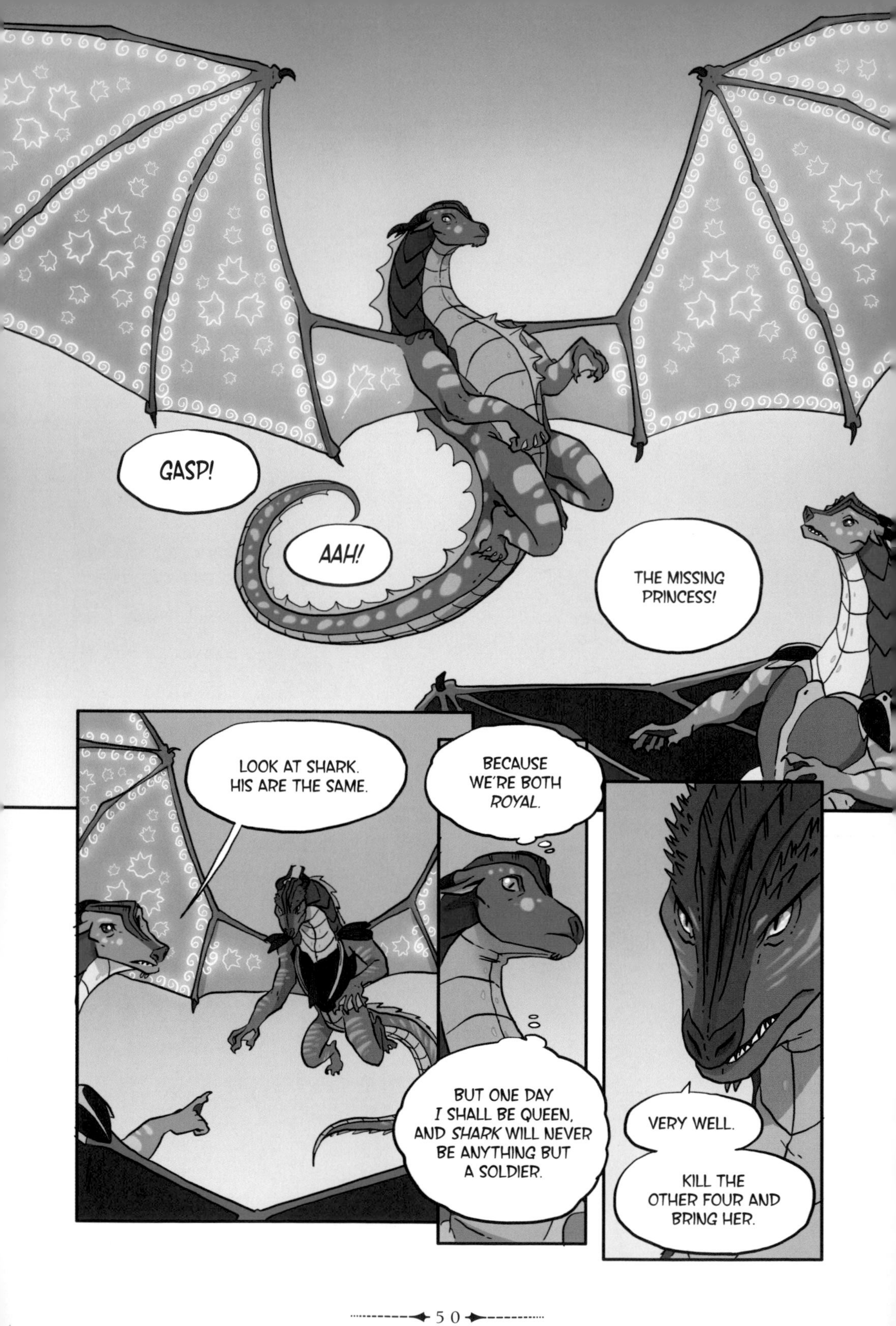
GASP!
AAH!
THE MISSING PRINCESS!
LOOK AT SHARK. HIS ARE THE SAME.
BECAUSE WE'RE BOTH *ROYAL*.
BUT ONE DAY *I* SHALL BE QUEEN, AND *SHARK* WILL NEVER BE ANYTHING BUT A SOLDIER.
VERY WELL.
KILL THE OTHER FOUR AND BRING HER.

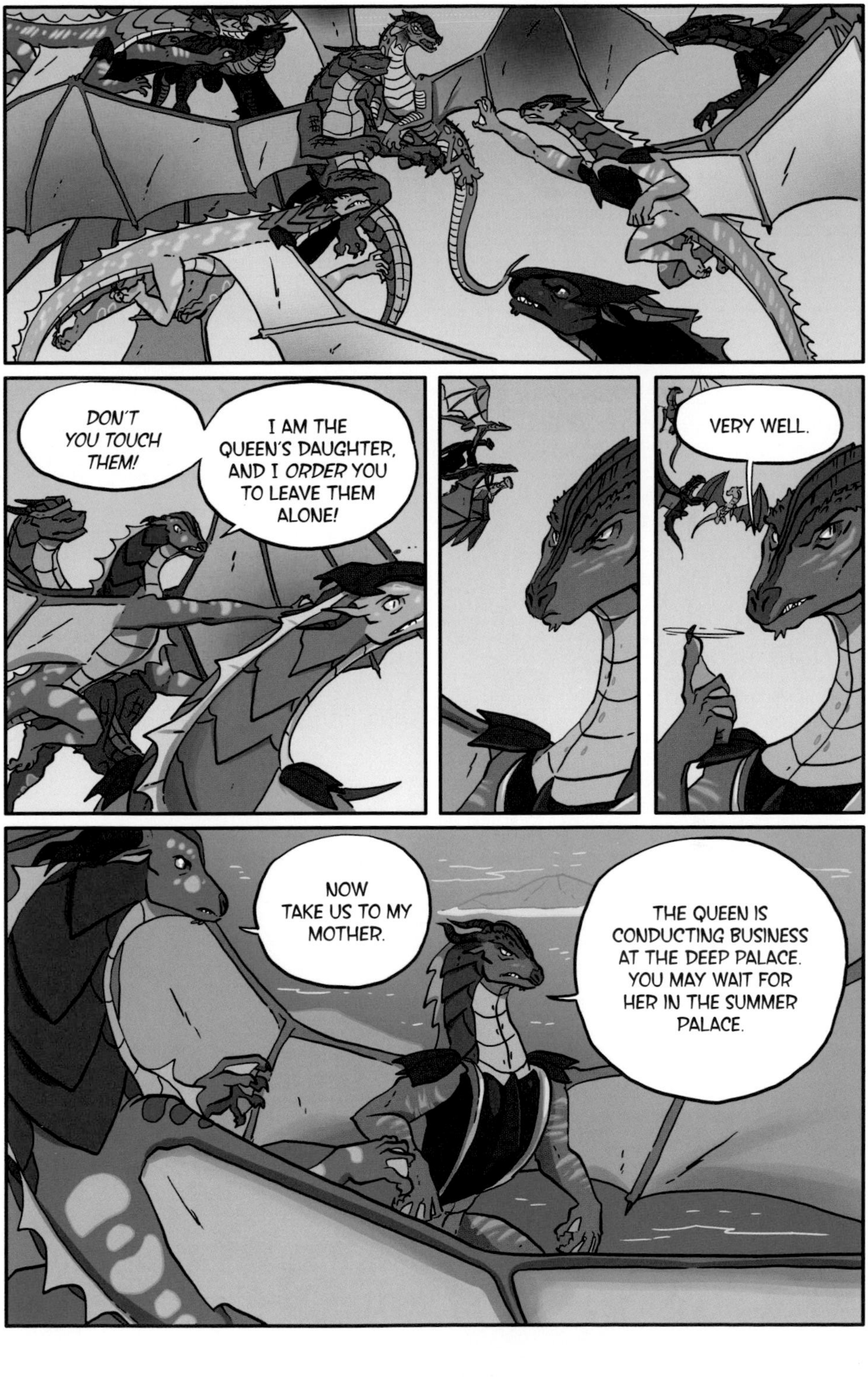

DON'T YOU TOUCH THEM!
I AM THE QUEEN'S DAUGHTER, AND I *ORDER* YOU TO LEAVE THEM ALONE!
VERY WELL.
NOW TAKE US TO MY MOTHER.
THE QUEEN IS CONDUCTING BUSINESS AT THE DEEP PALACE. YOU MAY WAIT FOR HER IN THE SUMMER PALACE.

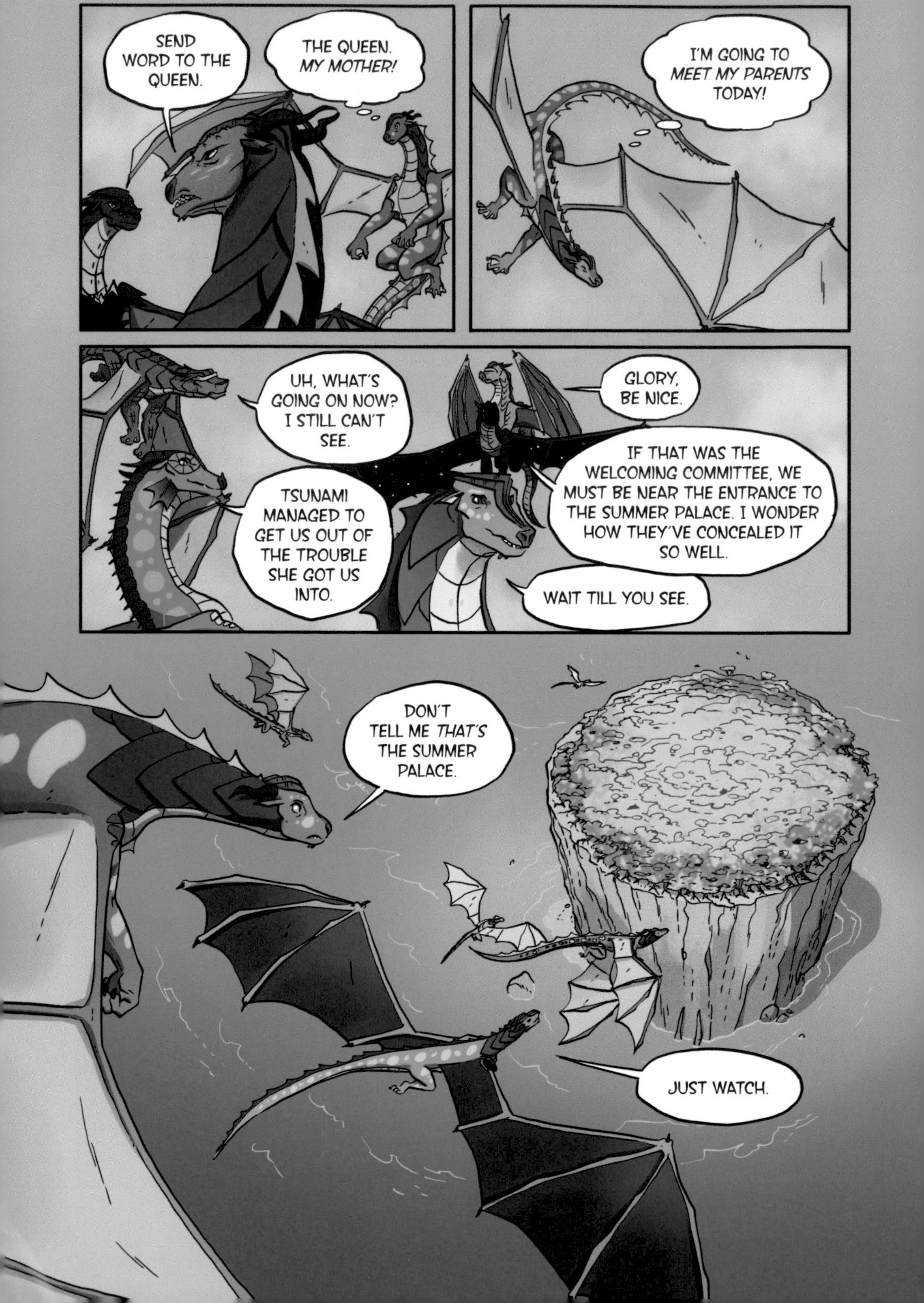
SEND WORD TO THE QUEEN.
THE QUEEN. *MY MOTHER!*
I'M GOING TO *MEET MY PARENTS* TODAY!
UH, WHAT'S GOING ON NOW? I STILL CAN'T SEE.
GLORY, BE NICE.
TSUNAMI MANAGED TO GET US OUT OF THE TROUBLE SHE GOT US INTO.
IF THAT WAS THE WELCOMING COMMITTEE, WE MUST BE NEAR THE ENTRANCE TO THE SUMMER PALACE. I WONDER HOW THEY'VE CONCEALED IT SO WELL.
WAIT TILL YOU SEE.
DON'T TELL ME *THAT'S* THE SUMMER PALACE.
JUST WATCH.

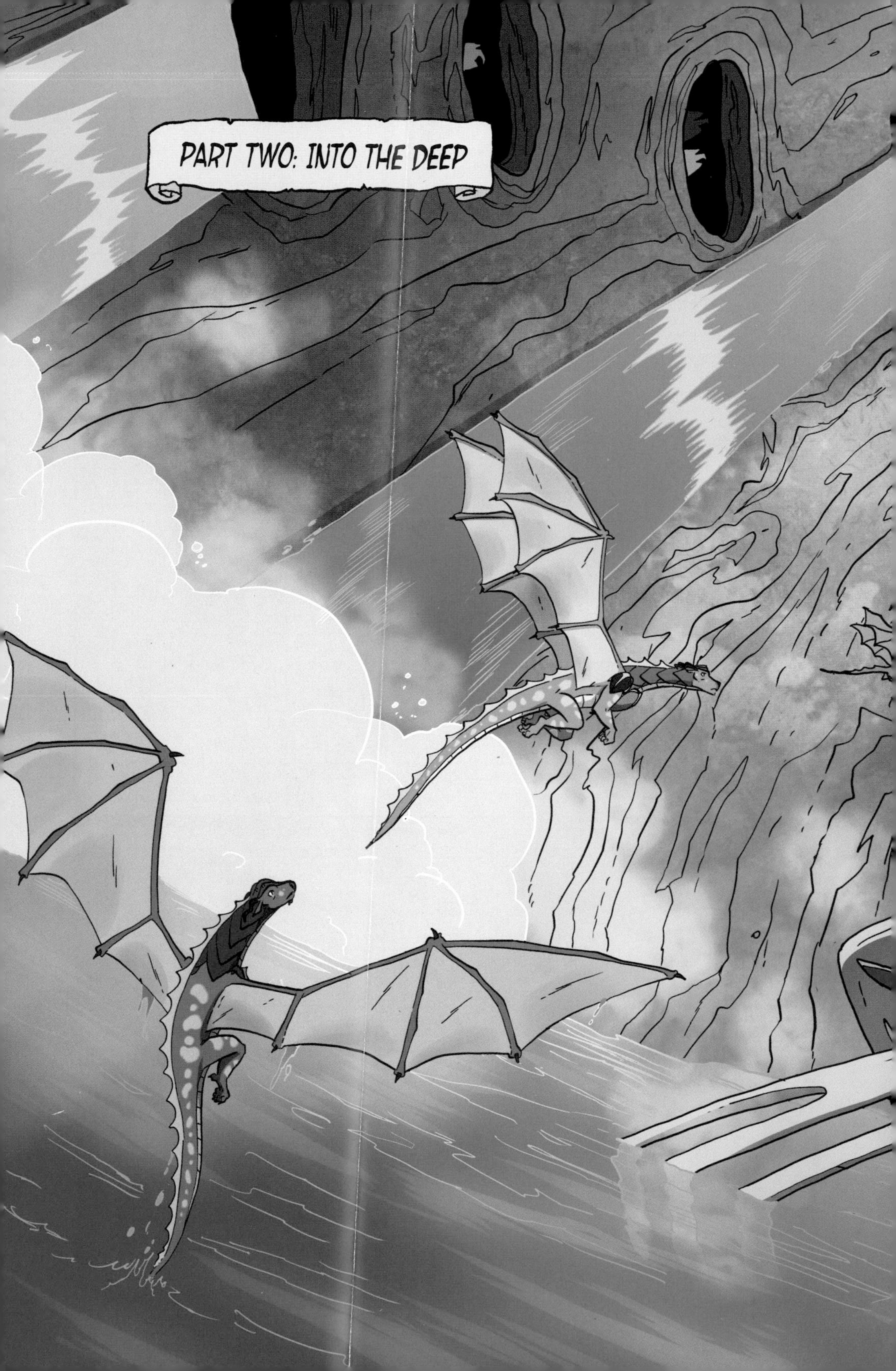
PART TWO: INTO THE DEEP

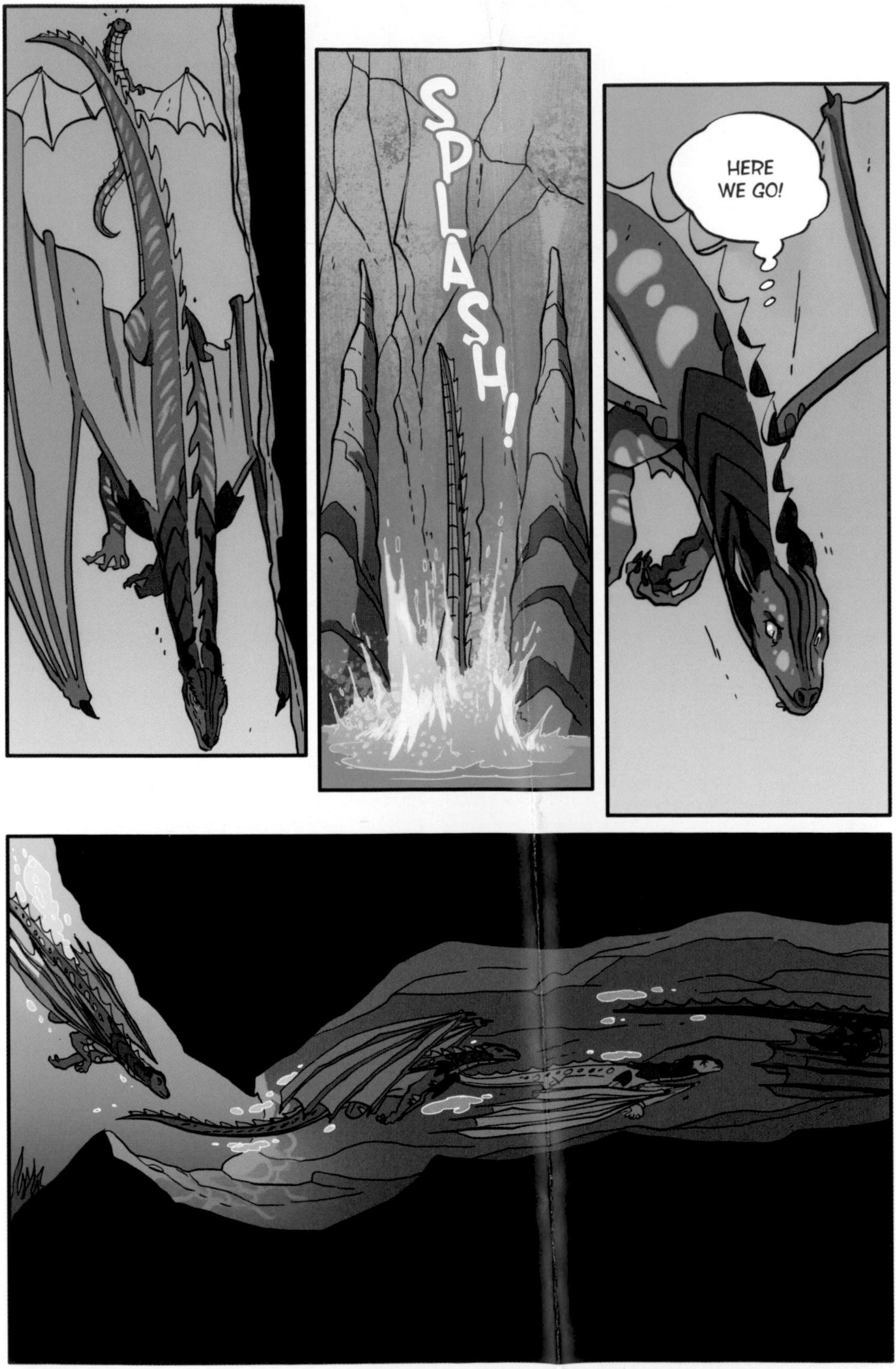
SPLASH!
HERE WE GO!

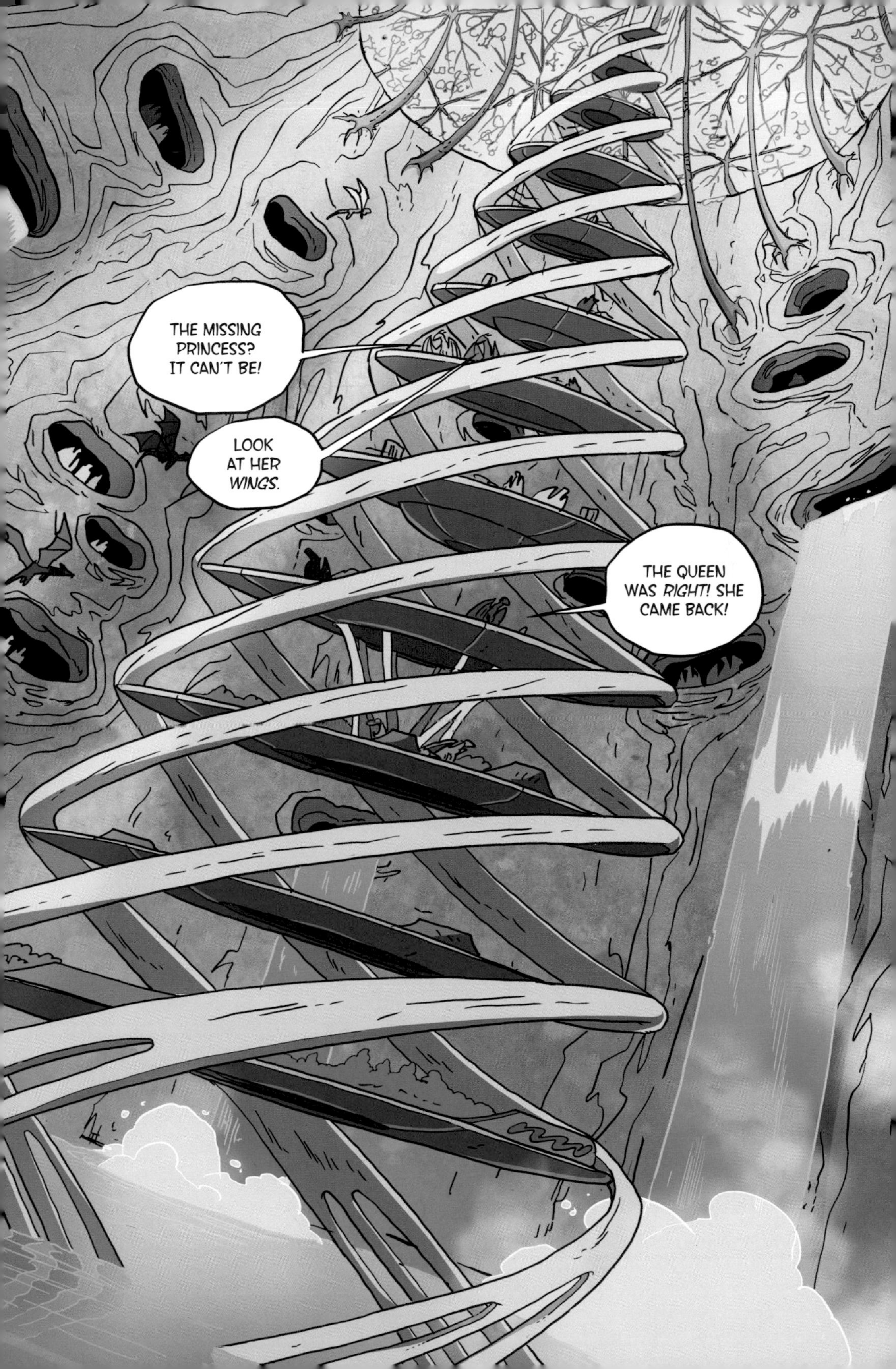
THE MISSING PRINCESS? IT CAN'T BE!
LOOK AT HER *WINGS*.
THE QUEEN WAS *RIGHT*! SHE CAME BACK!

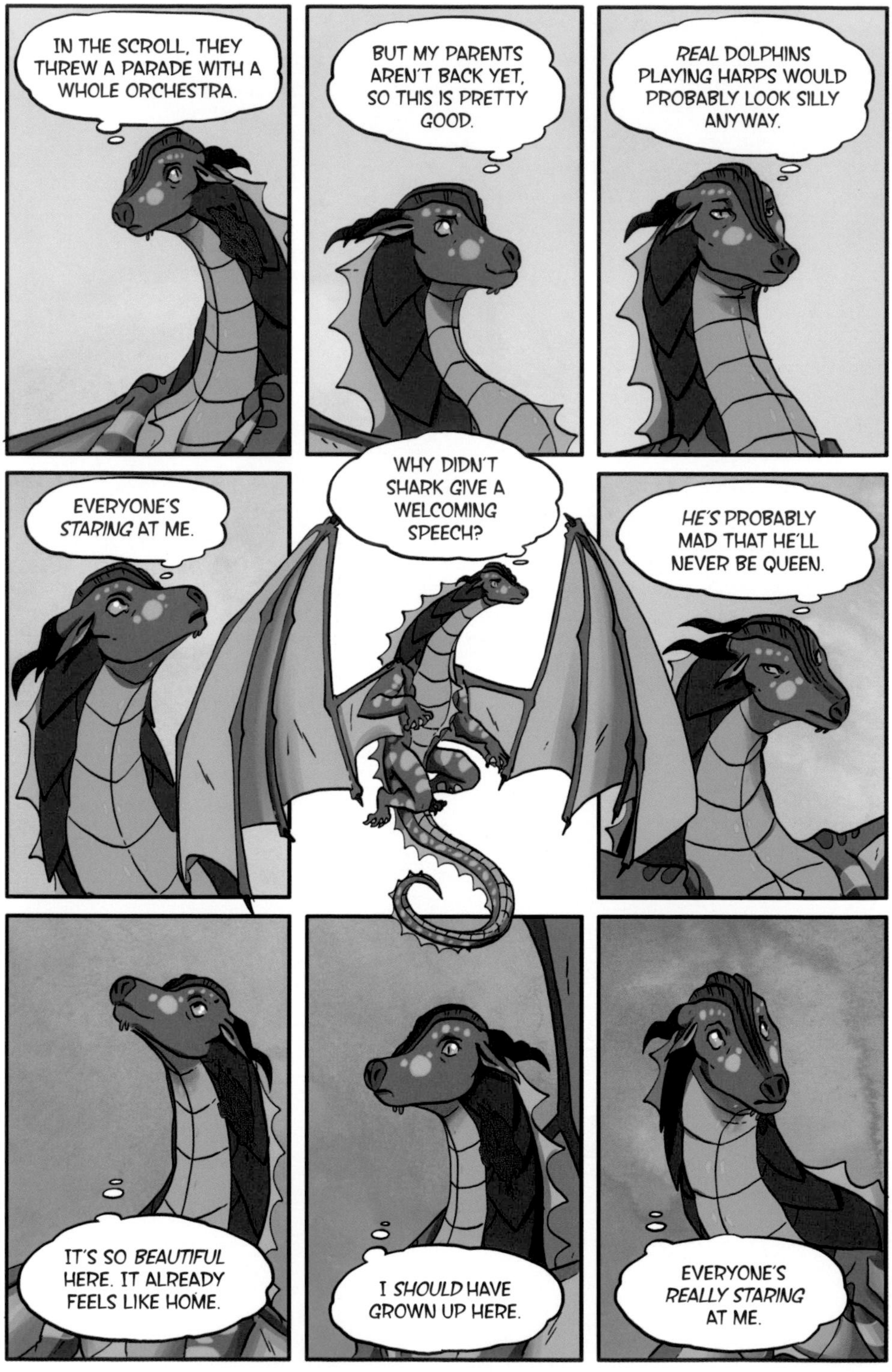
IN THE SCROLL, THEY THREW A PARADE WITH A WHOLE ORCHESTRA.
BUT MY PARENTS AREN'T BACK YET, SO THIS IS PRETTY GOOD.
REAL DOLPHINS PLAYING HARPS WOULD PROBABLY LOOK SILLY ANYWAY.
EVERYONE'S *STARING* AT ME.
WHY DIDN'T SHARK GIVE A WELCOMING SPEECH?
HE'S PROBABLY MAD THAT HE'LL NEVER BE QUEEN.
IT'S SO *BEAUTIFUL* HERE. IT ALREADY FEELS LIKE HOME.
I *SHOULD* HAVE GROWN UP HERE.
EVERYONE'S *REALLY STARING* AT ME.

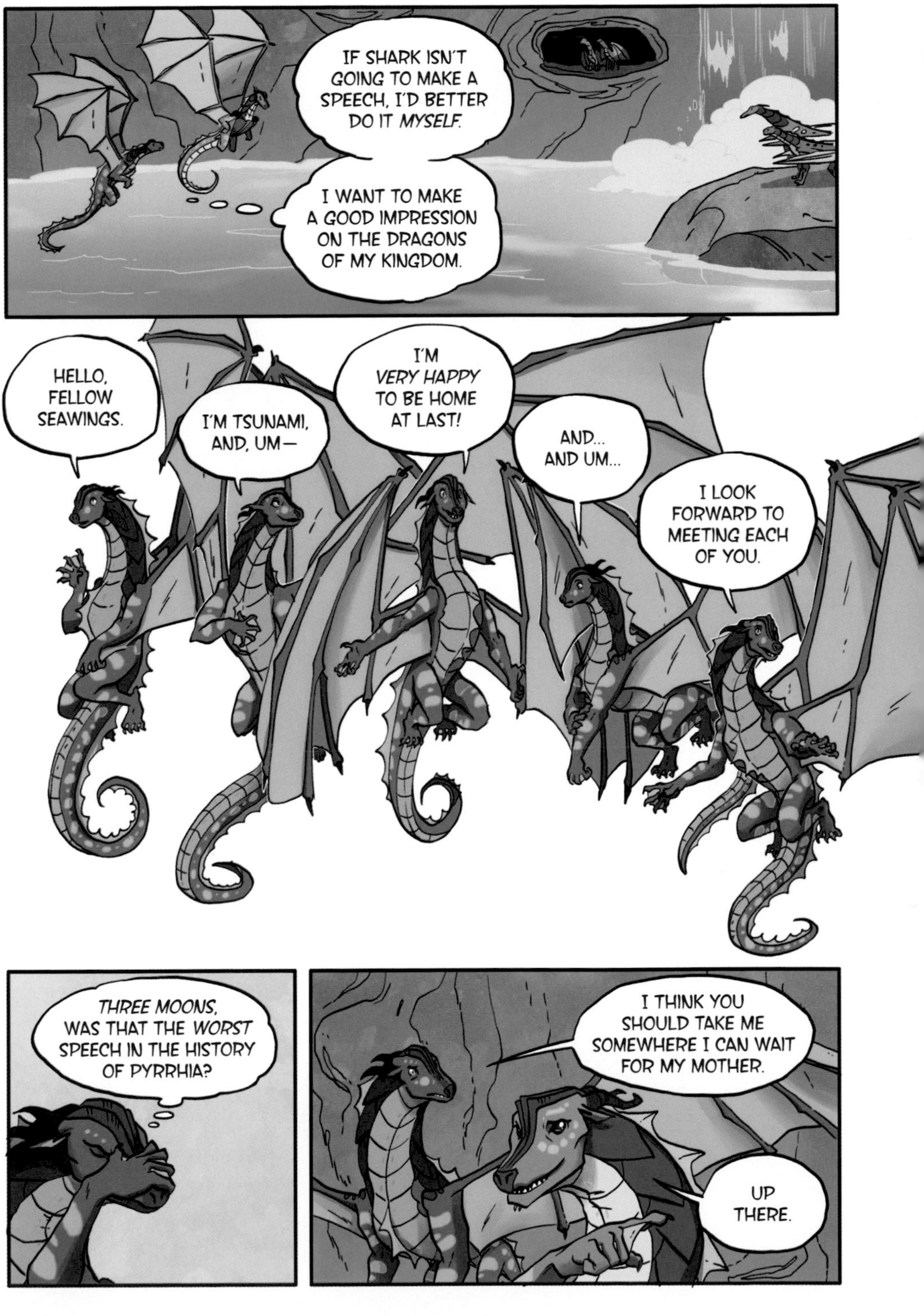
IF SHARK ISN'T GOING TO MAKE A SPEECH, I'D BETTER DO IT *MYSELF*.
I WANT TO MAKE A GOOD IMPRESSION ON THE DRAGONS OF MY KINGDOM.
HELLO, FELLOW SEAWINGS.
I'M TSUNAMI, AND, UM—
I'M *VERY HAPPY* TO BE HOME AT LAST!
AND... AND UM...
I LOOK FORWARD TO MEETING EACH OF YOU.
THREE MOONS, WAS THAT THE *WORST* SPEECH IN THE HISTORY OF PYRRHIA?
I THINK YOU SHOULD TAKE ME SOMEWHERE I CAN WAIT FOR MY MOTHER.
UP THERE.

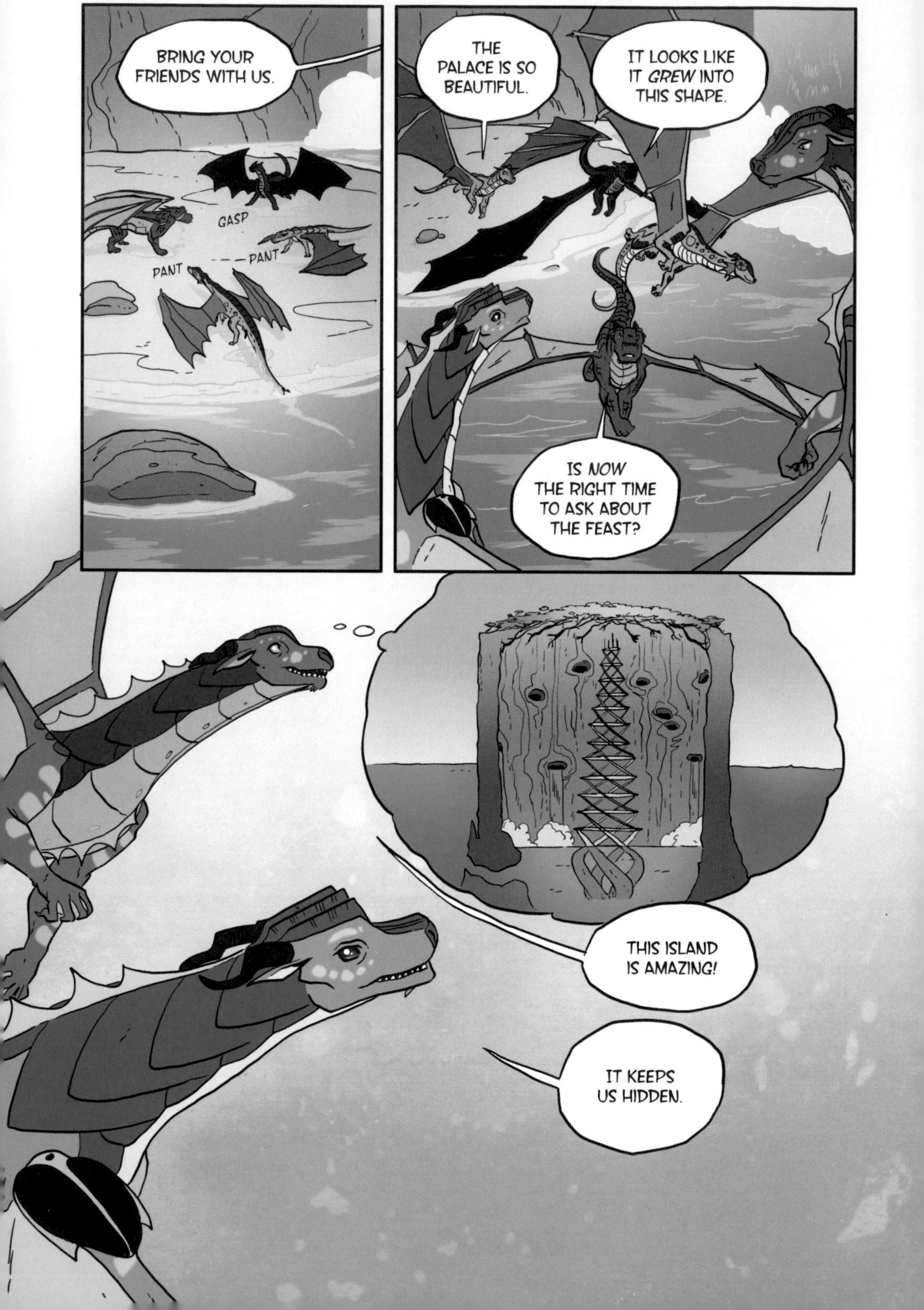
BRING YOUR FRIENDS WITH US.
GASP
PANT
PANT
THE PALACE IS SO BEAUTIFUL.
IT LOOKS LIKE IT *GREW* INTO THIS SHAPE.
IS *NOW* THE RIGHT TIME TO ASK ABOUT THE FEAST?
THIS ISLAND IS AMAZING!
IT KEEPS US HIDDEN.

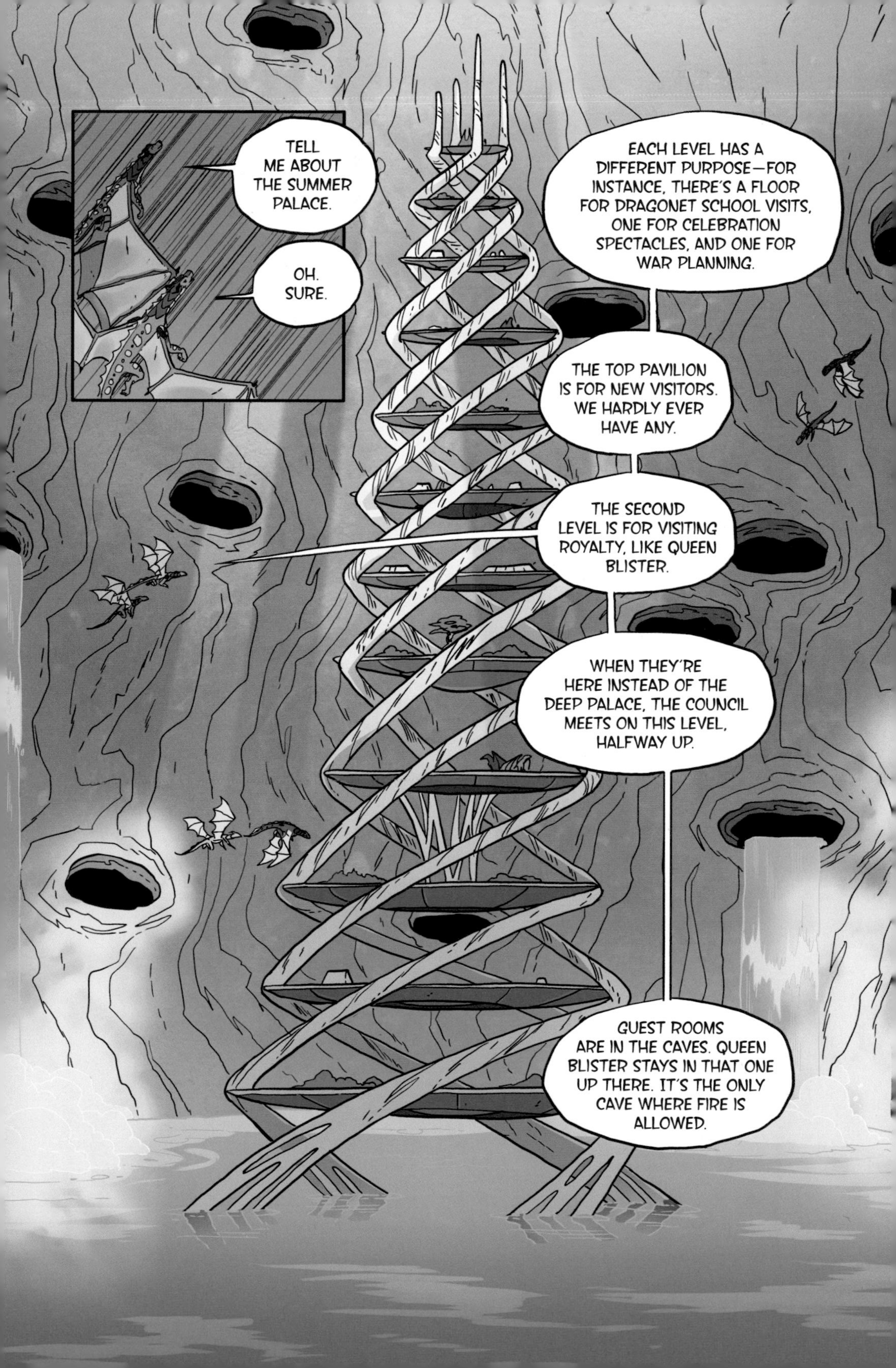
TELL ME ABOUT THE SUMMER PALACE.
OH. SURE.
EACH LEVEL HAS A DIFFERENT PURPOSE—FOR INSTANCE, THERE'S A FLOOR FOR DRAGONET SCHOOL VISITS, ONE FOR CELEBRATION SPECTACLES, AND ONE FOR WAR PLANNING.
THE TOP PAVILION IS FOR NEW VISITORS. WE HARDLY EVER HAVE ANY.
THE SECOND LEVEL IS FOR VISITING ROYALTY, LIKE QUEEN BLISTER.
WHEN THEY'RE HERE INSTEAD OF THE DEEP PALACE, THE COUNCIL MEETS ON THIS LEVEL, HALFWAY UP.
GUEST ROOMS ARE IN THE CAVES. QUEEN BLISTER STAYS IN THAT ONE UP THERE. IT'S THE ONLY CAVE WHERE FIRE IS ALLOWED.

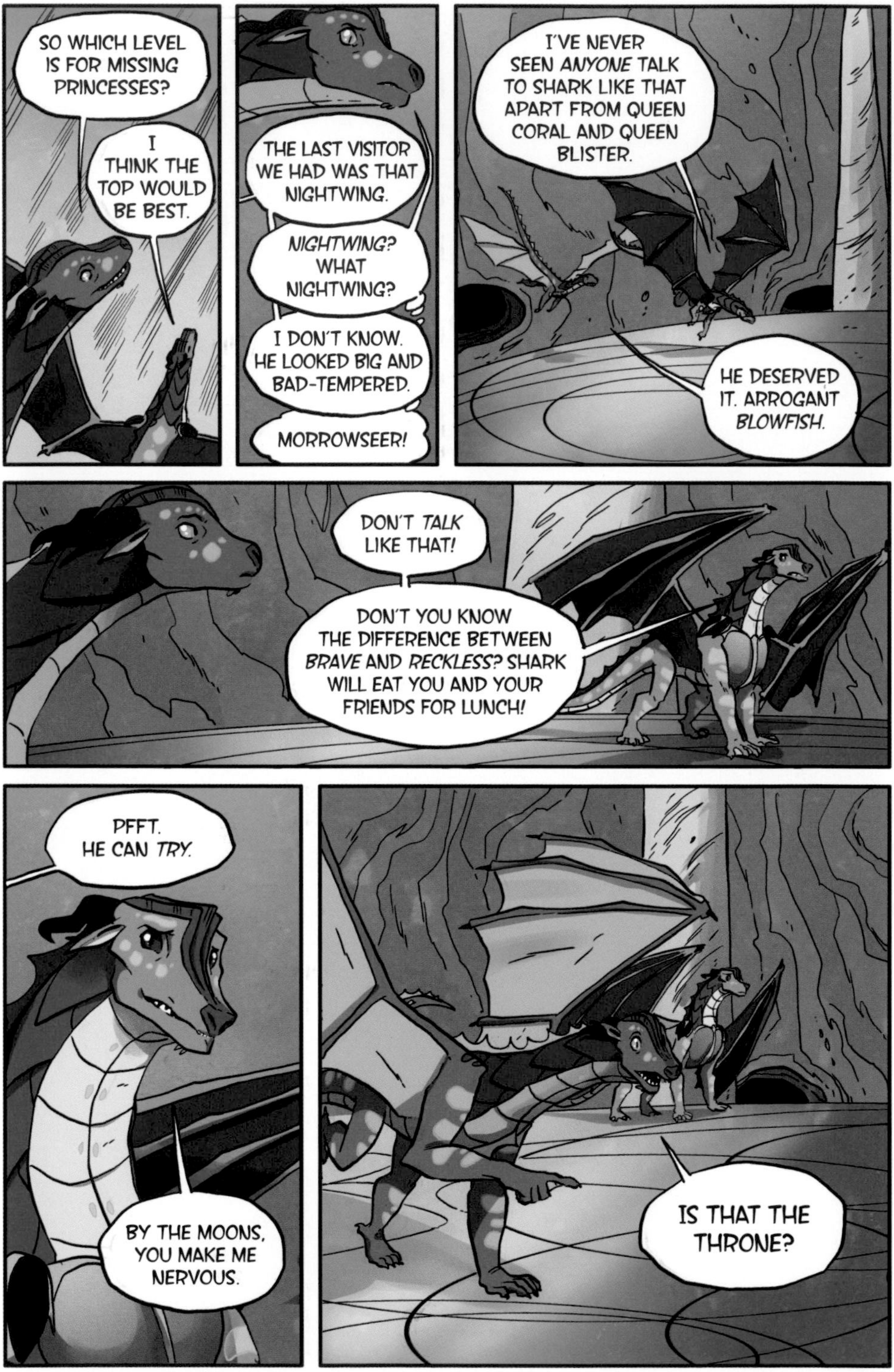
SO WHICH LEVEL IS FOR MISSING PRINCESSES?
I THINK THE TOP WOULD BE BEST.
THE LAST VISITOR WE HAD WAS THAT NIGHTWING.
NIGHTWING? WHAT NIGHTWING?
I DON'T KNOW. HE LOOKED BIG AND BAD-TEMPERED.
MORROWSEER!
I'VE NEVER SEEN *ANYONE* TALK TO SHARK LIKE THAT APART FROM QUEEN CORAL AND QUEEN BLISTER.
HE DESERVED IT. ARROGANT *BLOWFISH.*
DON'T *TALK* LIKE THAT!
DON'T YOU KNOW THE DIFFERENCE BETWEEN *BRAVE* AND *RECKLESS?* SHARK WILL EAT YOU AND YOUR FRIENDS FOR LUNCH!
PFFT. HE CAN *TRY.*
BY THE MOONS, YOU MAKE ME NERVOUS.
IS THAT THE THRONE?

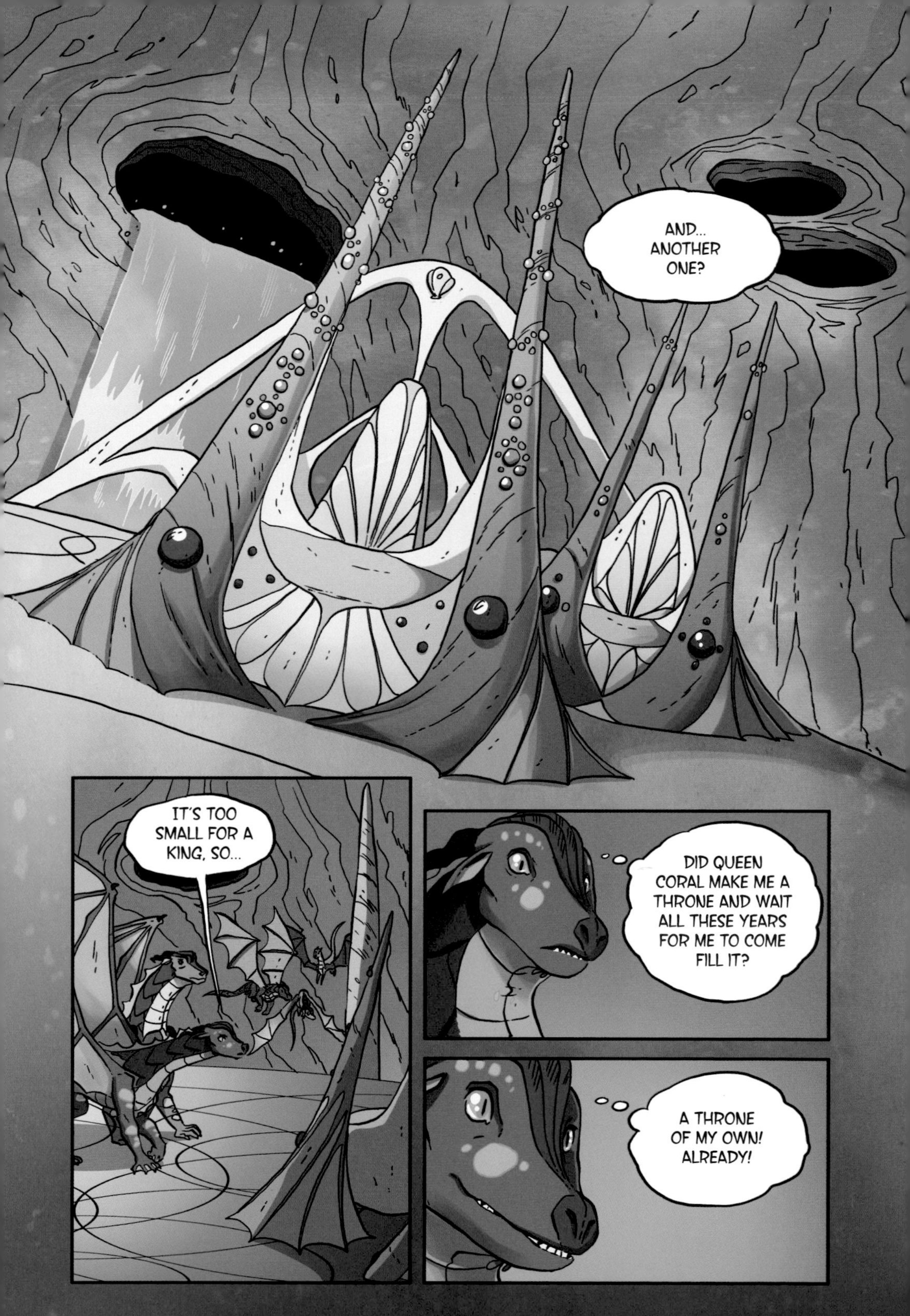
AND... ANOTHER ONE?
IT'S TOO SMALL FOR A KING, SO...
DID QUEEN CORAL MAKE ME A THRONE AND WAIT ALL THESE YEARS FOR ME TO COME FILL IT?
A THRONE OF MY OWN! ALREADY!

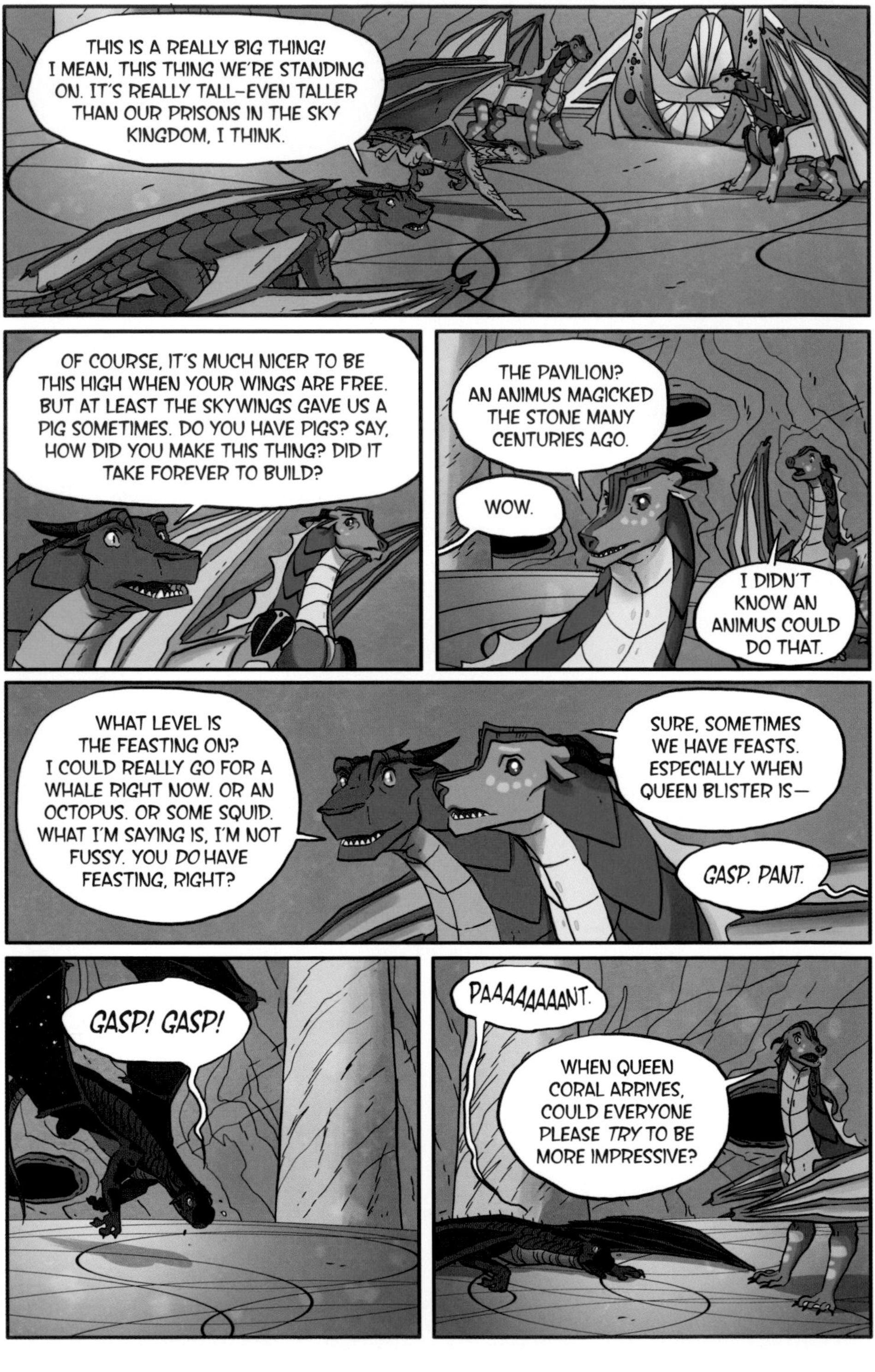
THIS IS A REALLY BIG THING! I MEAN, THIS THING WE'RE STANDING ON. IT'S REALLY TALL—EVEN TALLER THAN OUR PRISONS IN THE SKY KINGDOM, I THINK.
OF COURSE, IT'S MUCH NICER TO BE THIS HIGH WHEN YOUR WINGS ARE FREE. BUT AT LEAST THE SKYWINGS GAVE US A PIG SOMETIMES. DO YOU HAVE PIGS? SAY, HOW DID YOU MAKE THIS THING? DID IT TAKE FOREVER TO BUILD?
THE PAVILION? AN ANIMUS MAGICKED THE STONE MANY CENTURIES AGO.
WOW.
I DIDN'T KNOW AN ANIMUS COULD DO THAT.
WHAT LEVEL IS THE FEASTING ON? I COULD REALLY GO FOR A WHALE RIGHT NOW. OR AN OCTOPUS. OR SOME SQUID. WHAT I'M SAYING IS, I'M NOT FUSSY. YOU *DO* HAVE FEASTING, RIGHT?
SURE, SOMETIMES WE HAVE FEASTS. ESPECIALLY WHEN QUEEN BLISTER IS—
GASP. PANT.
GASP! GASP!
PAAAAAAAANT.
WHEN QUEEN CORAL ARRIVES, COULD EVERYONE PLEASE *TRY* TO BE MORE IMPRESSIVE?

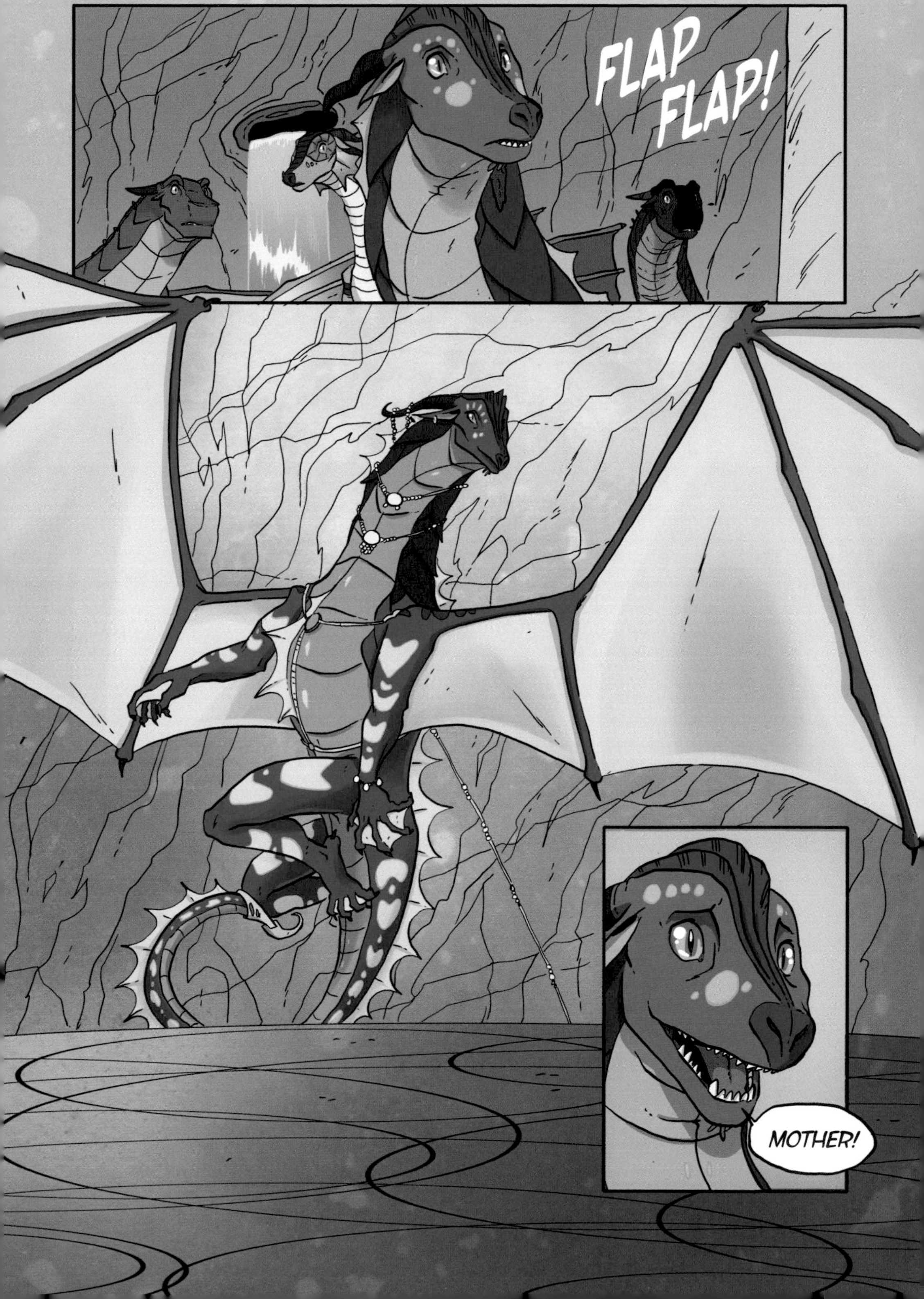
FLAP
FLAP!
MOTHER!

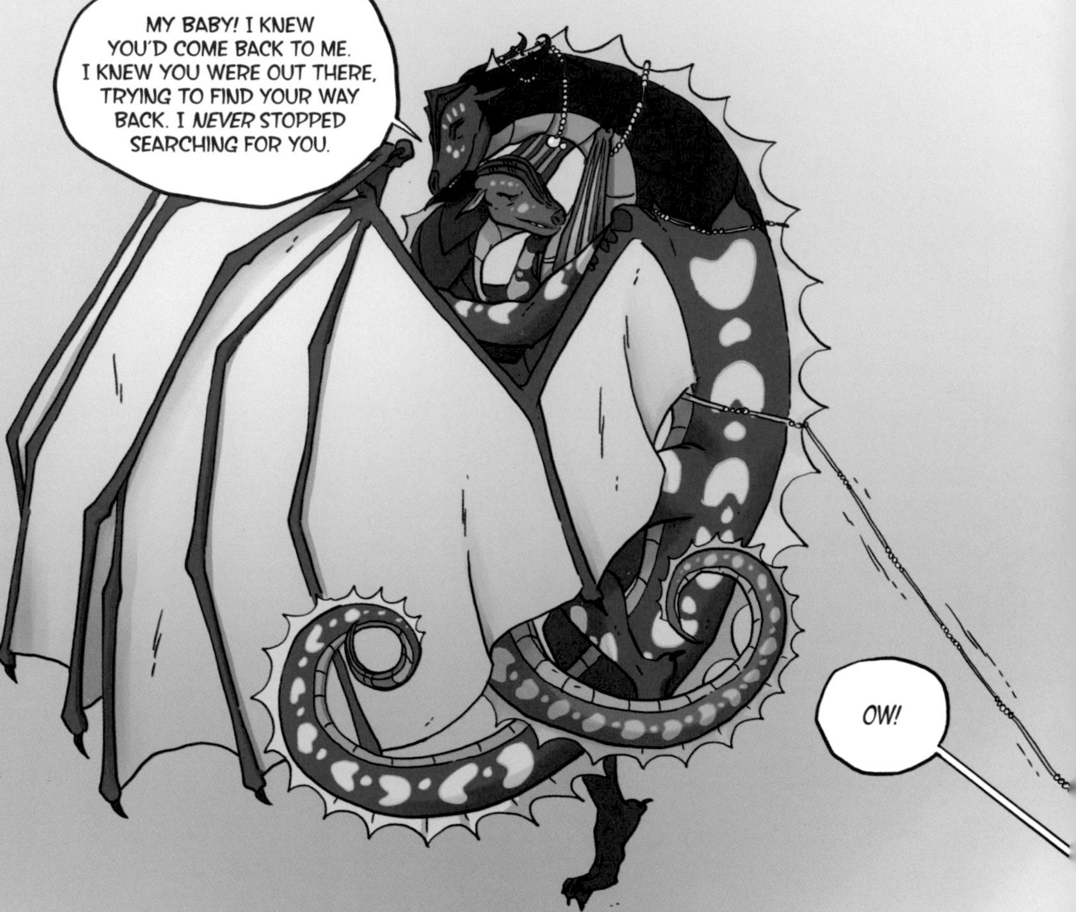
MY BABY! I KNEW YOU'D COME BACK TO ME. I KNEW YOU WERE OUT THERE, TRYING TO FIND YOUR WAY BACK. I *NEVER* STOPPED SEARCHING FOR YOU.
OW!

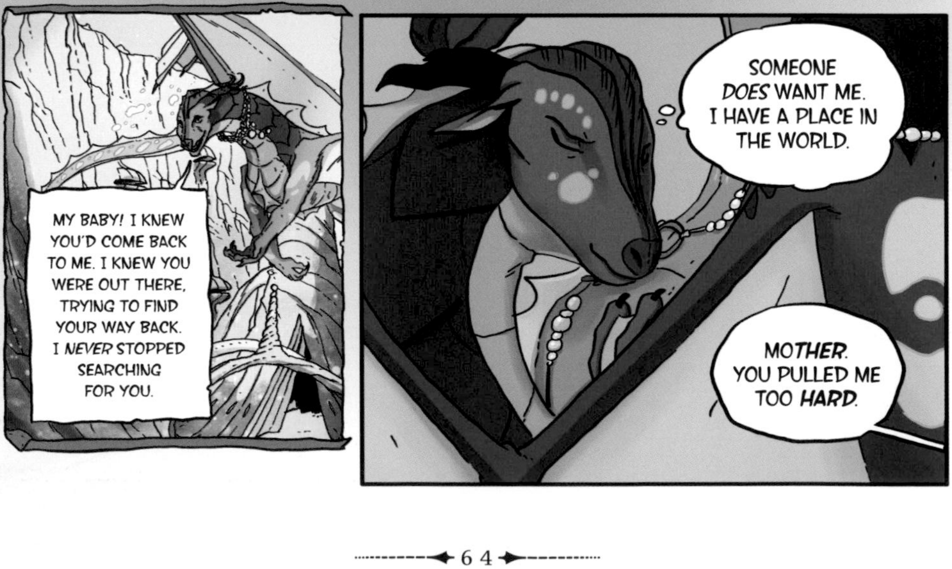
MY BABY! I KNEW YOU'D COME BACK TO ME. I KNEW YOU WERE OUT THERE, TRYING TO FIND YOUR WAY BACK. I *NEVER* STOPPED SEARCHING FOR YOU.
SOMEONE *DOES* WANT ME. I HAVE A PLACE IN THE WORLD.
MO*THER*. YOU PULLED ME TOO ***HARD***.

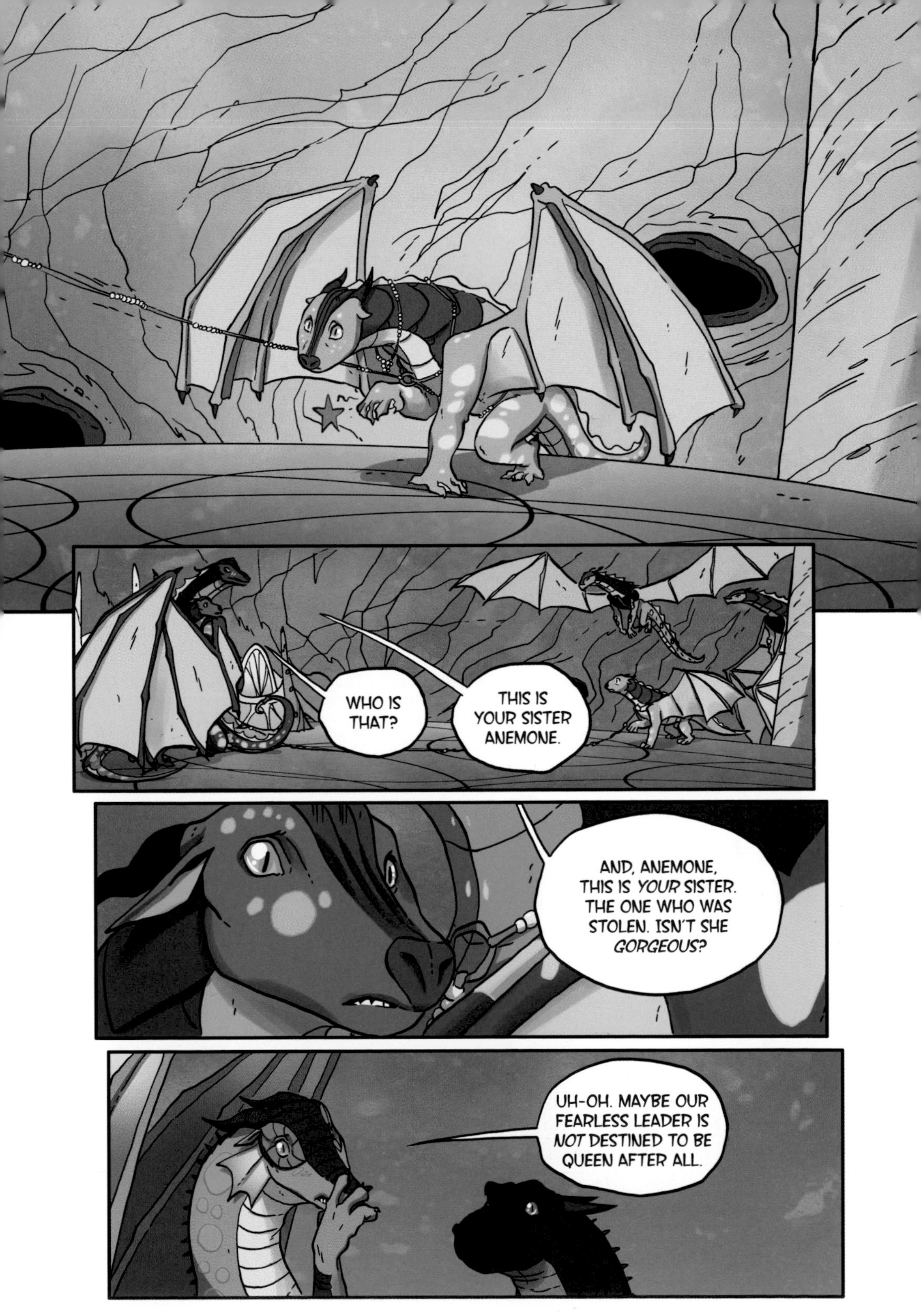
WHO IS THAT?
THIS IS YOUR SISTER ANEMONE.
AND, ANEMONE, THIS IS *YOUR* SISTER. THE ONE WHO WAS STOLEN. ISN'T SHE *GORGEOUS*?
UH-OH. MAYBE OUR FEARLESS LEADER IS *NOT* DESTINED TO BE QUEEN AFTER ALL.

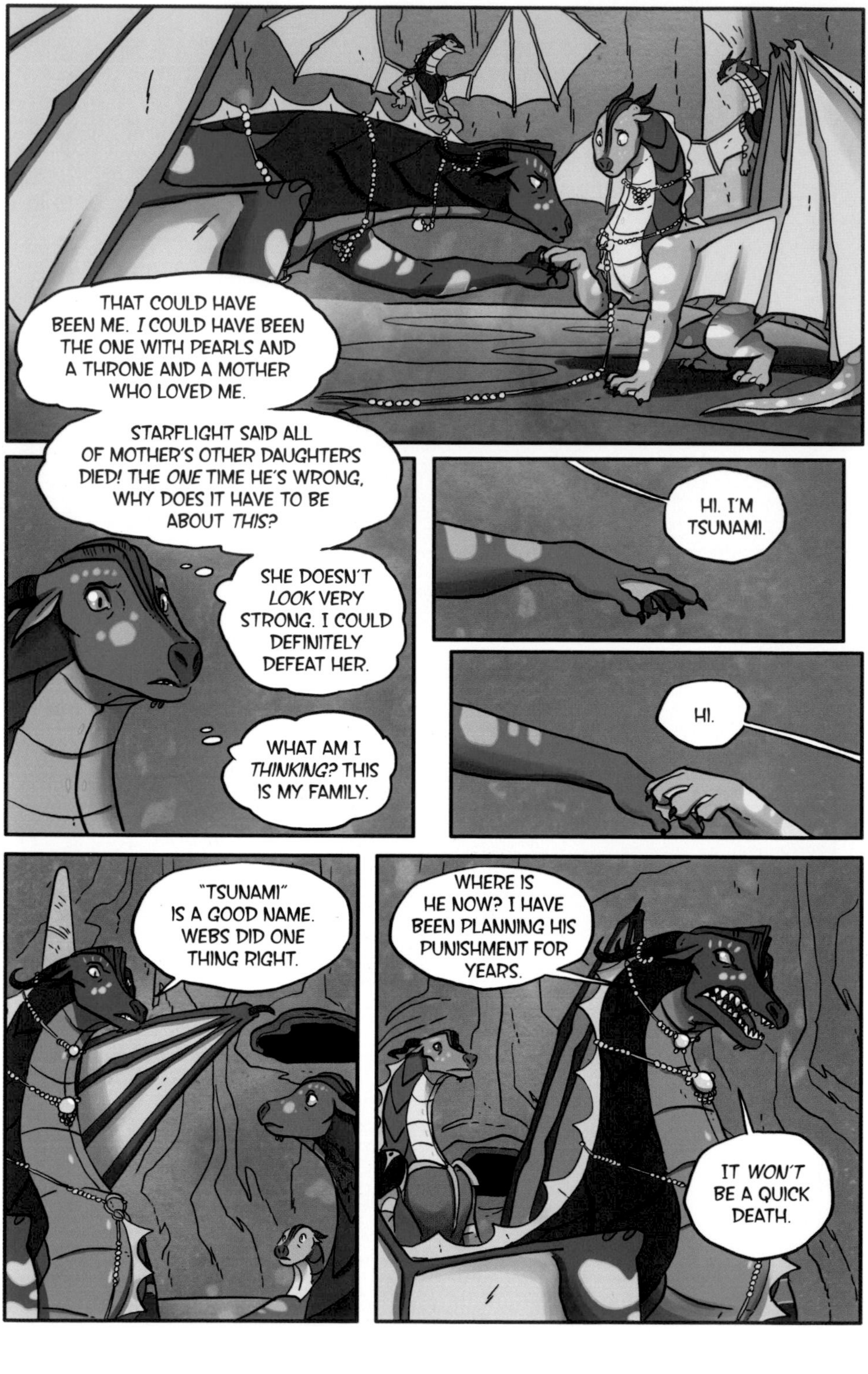
THAT COULD HAVE BEEN ME. *I* COULD HAVE BEEN THE ONE WITH PEARLS AND A THRONE AND A MOTHER WHO LOVED ME.
STARFLIGHT SAID ALL OF MOTHER'S OTHER DAUGHTERS DIED! THE *ONE* TIME HE'S WRONG, WHY DOES IT HAVE TO BE ABOUT *THIS*?
SHE DOESN'T *LOOK* VERY STRONG. I COULD DEFINITELY DEFEAT HER.
WHAT AM I *THINKING?* THIS IS MY FAMILY.
HI. I'M TSUNAMI.
HI.
"TSUNAMI" IS A GOOD NAME. WEBS DID ONE THING RIGHT.
WHERE IS HE NOW? I HAVE BEEN PLANNING HIS PUNISHMENT FOR YEARS.
IT *WON'T* BE A QUICK DEATH.

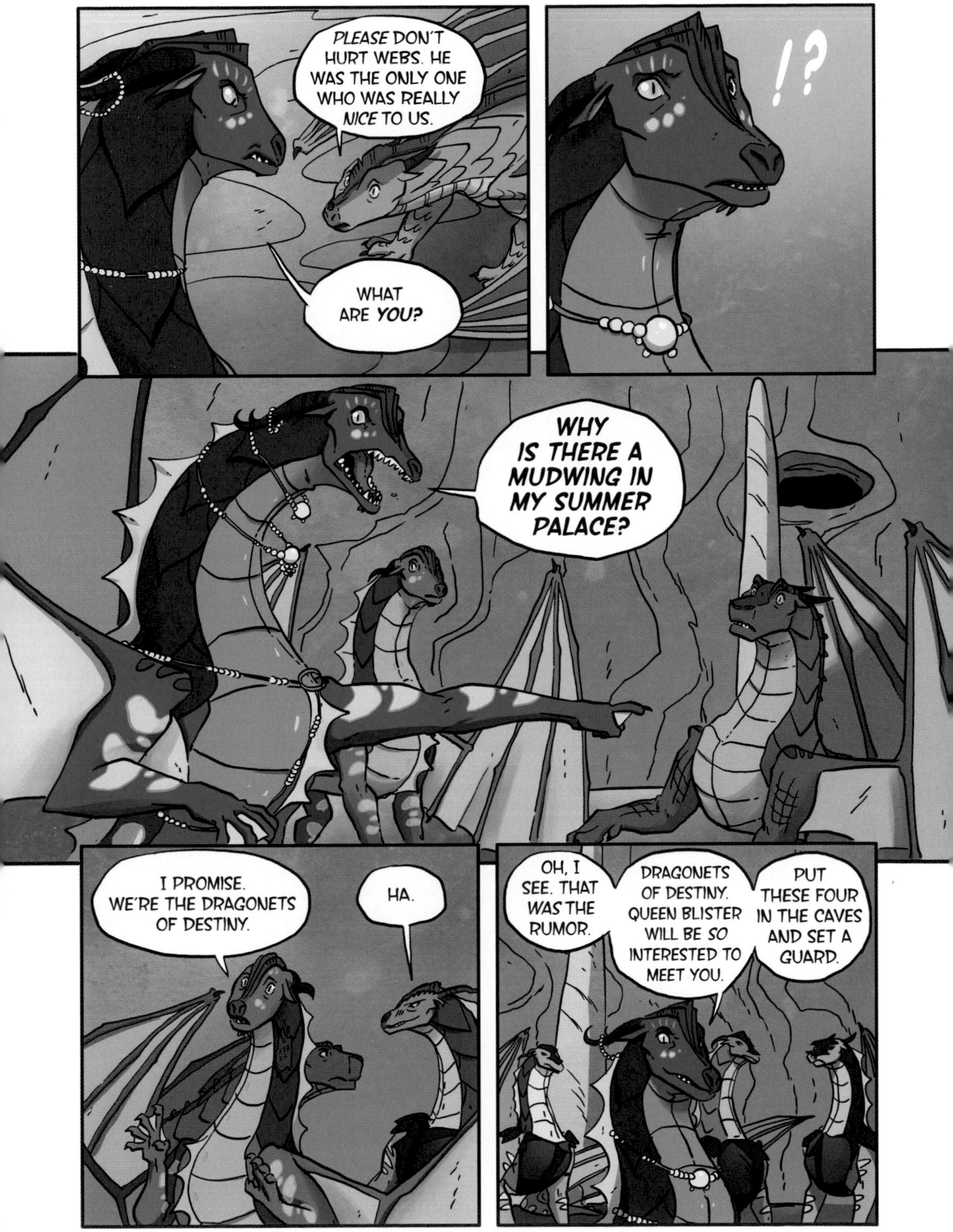
PLEASE DON'T HURT WEBS. HE WAS THE ONLY ONE WHO WAS REALLY NICE TO US.
WHAT ARE YOU?
!?
WHY IS THERE A MUDWING IN MY SUMMER PALACE?
I PROMISE. WE'RE THE DRAGONETS OF DESTINY.
HA.
OH, I SEE. THAT WAS THE RUMOR.
DRAGONETS OF DESTINY. QUEEN BLISTER WILL BE SO INTERESTED TO MEET YOU.
PUT THESE FOUR IN THE CAVES AND SET A GUARD.

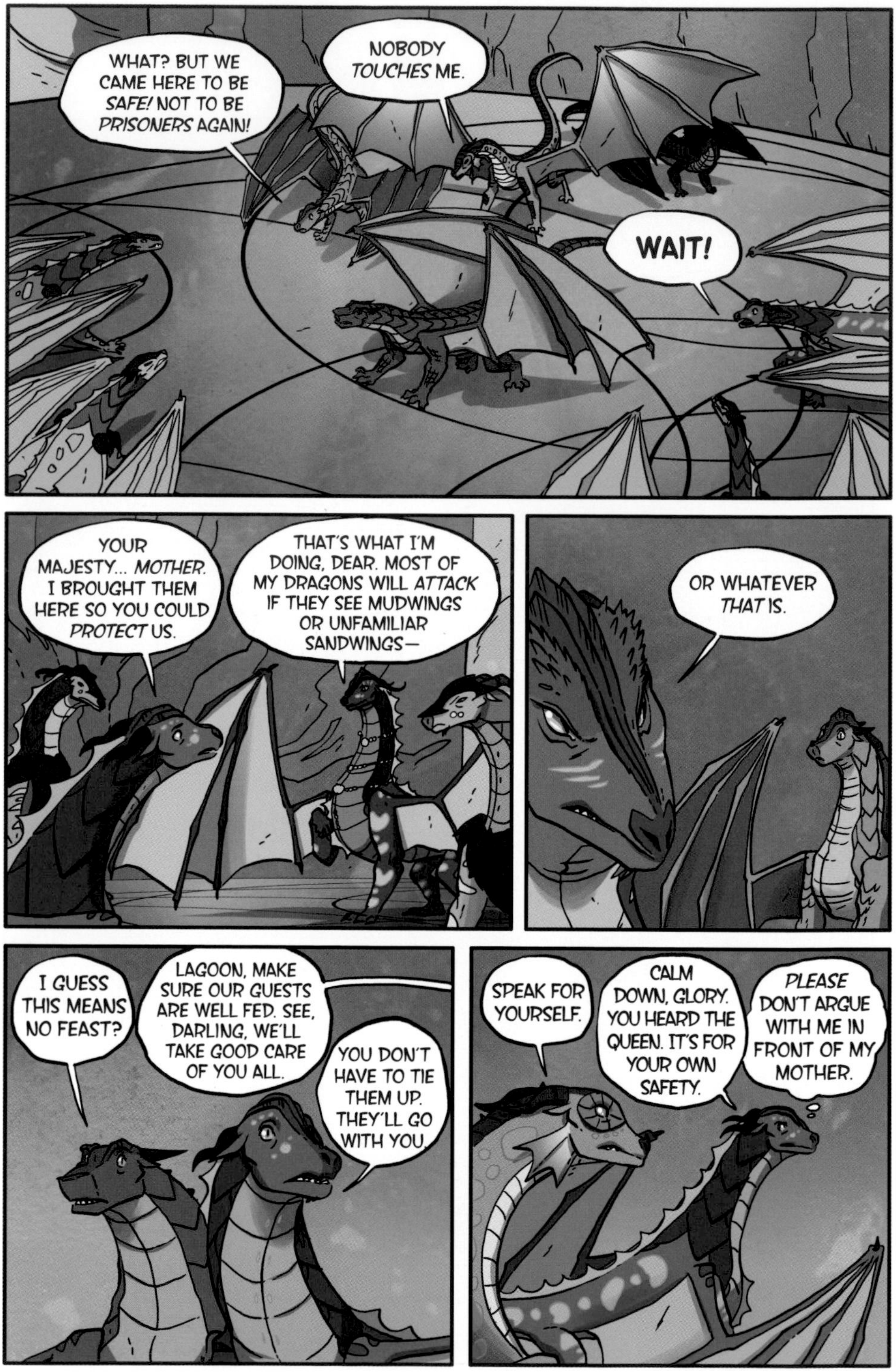
WHAT? BUT WE CAME HERE TO BE SAFE! NOT TO BE PRISONERS AGAIN!
NOBODY TOUCHES ME.
WAIT!
YOUR MAJESTY... MOTHER. I BROUGHT THEM HERE SO YOU COULD PROTECT US.
THAT'S WHAT I'M DOING, DEAR. MOST OF MY DRAGONS WILL ATTACK IF THEY SEE MUDWINGS OR UNFAMILIAR SANDWINGS—
OR WHATEVER THAT IS.
I GUESS THIS MEANS NO FEAST?
LAGOON, MAKE SURE OUR GUESTS ARE WELL FED. SEE, DARLING, WE'LL TAKE GOOD CARE OF YOU ALL.
YOU DON'T HAVE TO TIE THEM UP. THEY'LL GO WITH YOU.
SPEAK FOR YOURSELF.
CALM DOWN, GLORY. YOU HEARD THE QUEEN. IT'S FOR YOUR OWN SAFETY.
PLEASE DON'T ARGUE WITH ME IN FRONT OF MY MOTHER.

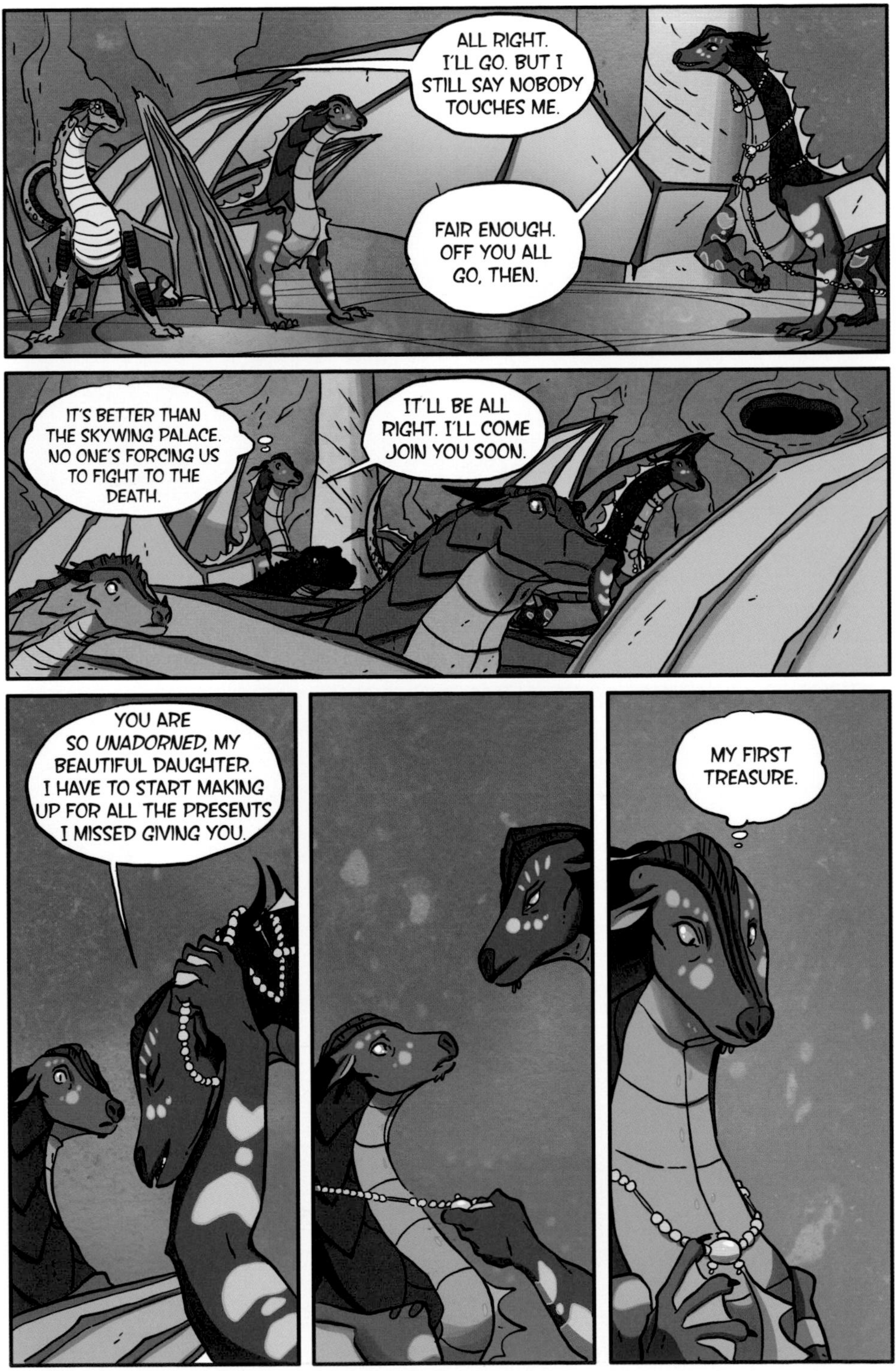
ALL RIGHT. I'LL GO. BUT I STILL SAY NOBODY TOUCHES ME.
FAIR ENOUGH. OFF YOU ALL GO, THEN.
IT'S BETTER THAN THE SKYWING PALACE. NO ONE'S FORCING US TO FIGHT TO THE DEATH.
IT'LL BE ALL RIGHT. I'LL COME JOIN YOU SOON.
YOU ARE SO *UNADORNED*, MY BEAUTIFUL DAUGHTER. I HAVE TO START MAKING UP FOR ALL THE PRESENTS I MISSED GIVING YOU.
MY FIRST TREASURE.

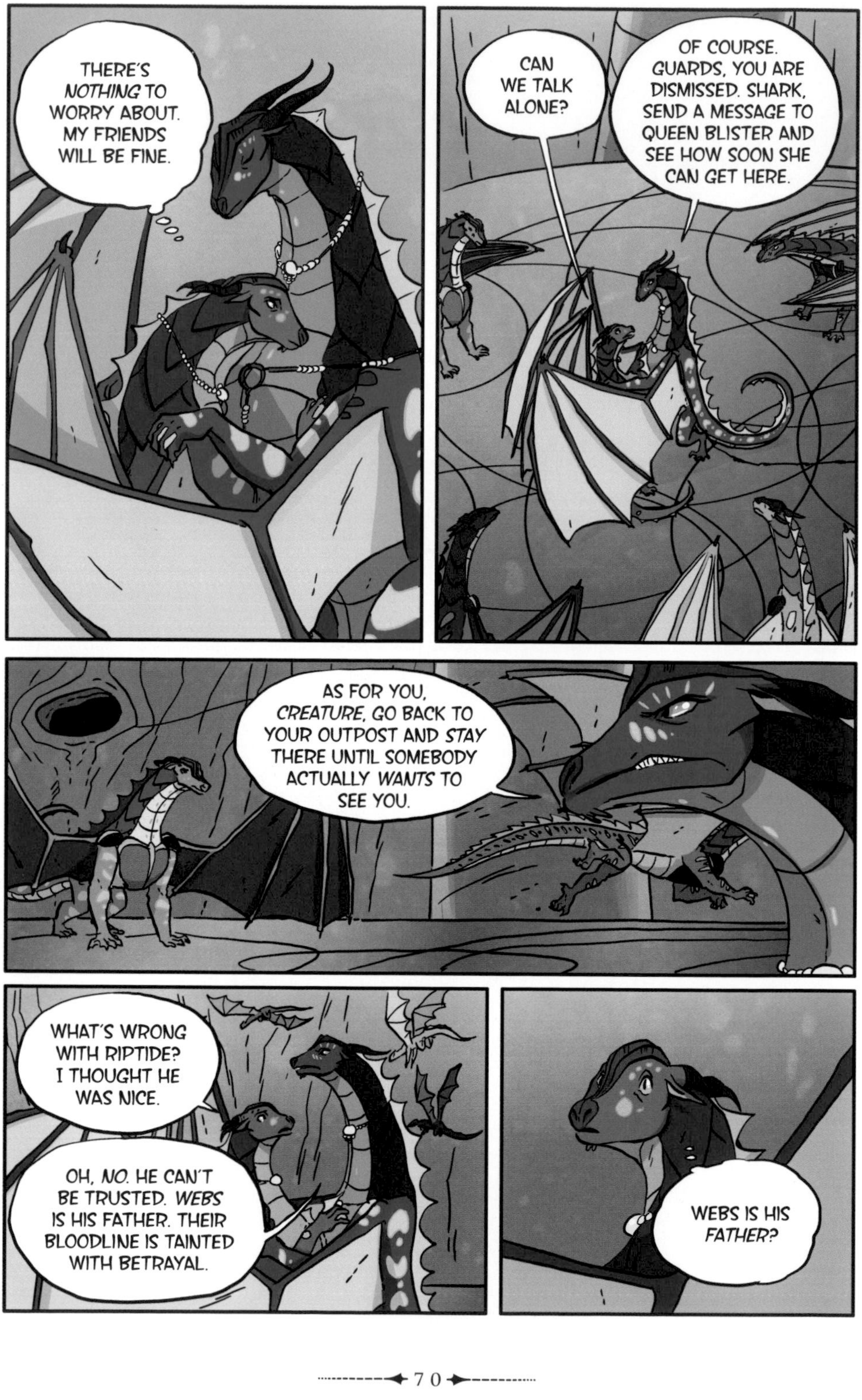
THERE'S *NOTHING* TO WORRY ABOUT. MY FRIENDS WILL BE FINE.
CAN WE TALK ALONE?
OF COURSE. GUARDS, YOU ARE DISMISSED. SHARK, SEND A MESSAGE TO QUEEN BLISTER AND SEE HOW SOON SHE CAN GET HERE.
AS FOR YOU, *CREATURE*, GO BACK TO YOUR OUTPOST AND *STAY* THERE UNTIL SOMEBODY ACTUALLY *WANTS* TO SEE YOU.
WHAT'S WRONG WITH RIPTIDE? I THOUGHT HE WAS NICE.
OH, *NO*. HE CAN'T BE TRUSTED. *WEBS* IS HIS FATHER. THEIR BLOODLINE IS TAINTED WITH BETRAYAL.
WEBS IS HIS *FATHER*?

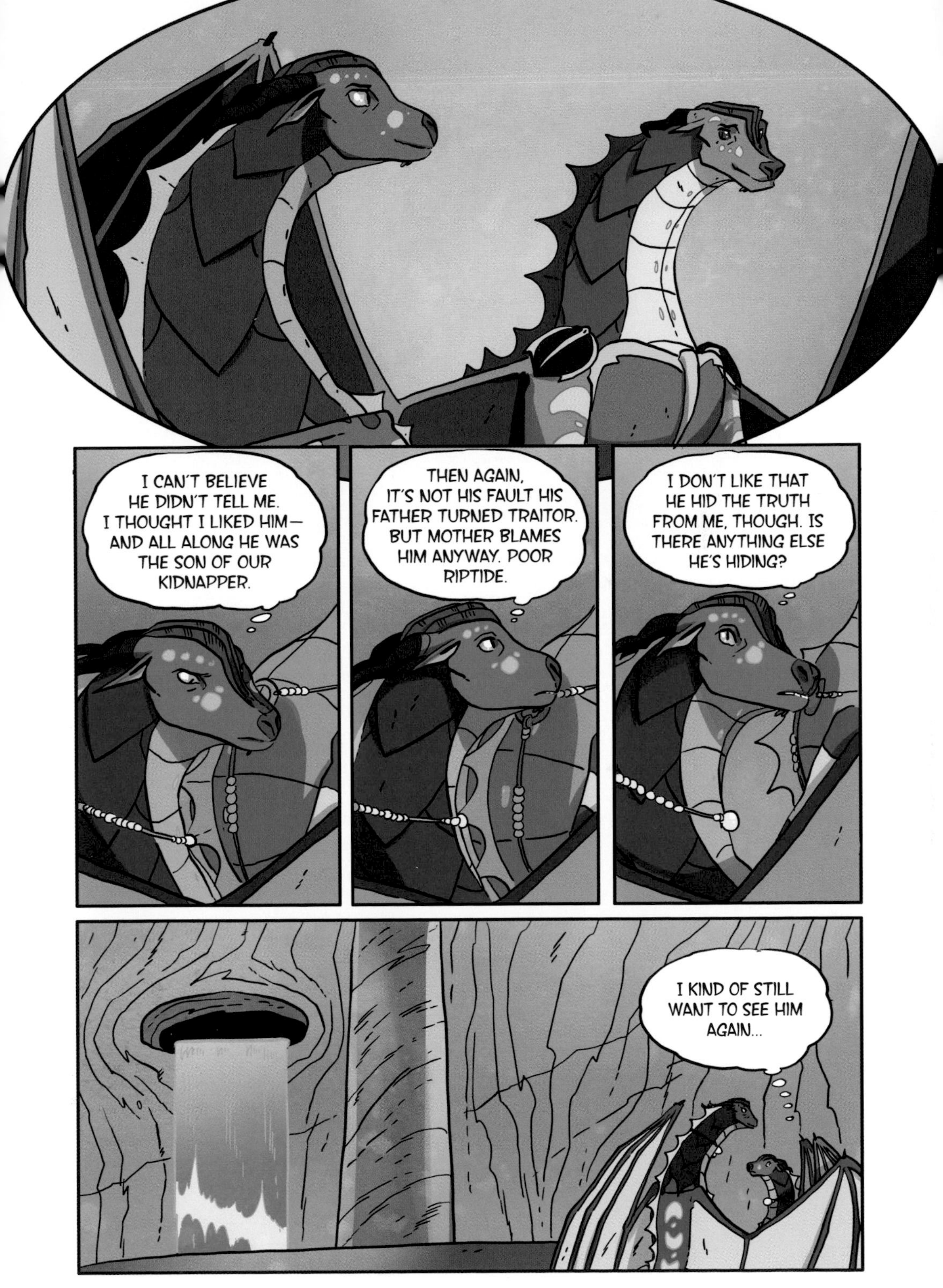
I CAN'T BELIEVE HE DIDN'T TELL ME. I THOUGHT I LIKED HIM—AND ALL ALONG HE WAS THE SON OF OUR KIDNAPPER.
THEN AGAIN, IT'S NOT HIS FAULT HIS FATHER TURNED TRAITOR. BUT MOTHER BLAMES HIM ANYWAY. POOR RIPTIDE.
I DON'T LIKE THAT HE HID THE TRUTH FROM ME, THOUGH. IS THERE ANYTHING ELSE HE'S HIDING?
I KIND OF STILL WANT TO SEE HIM AGAIN...

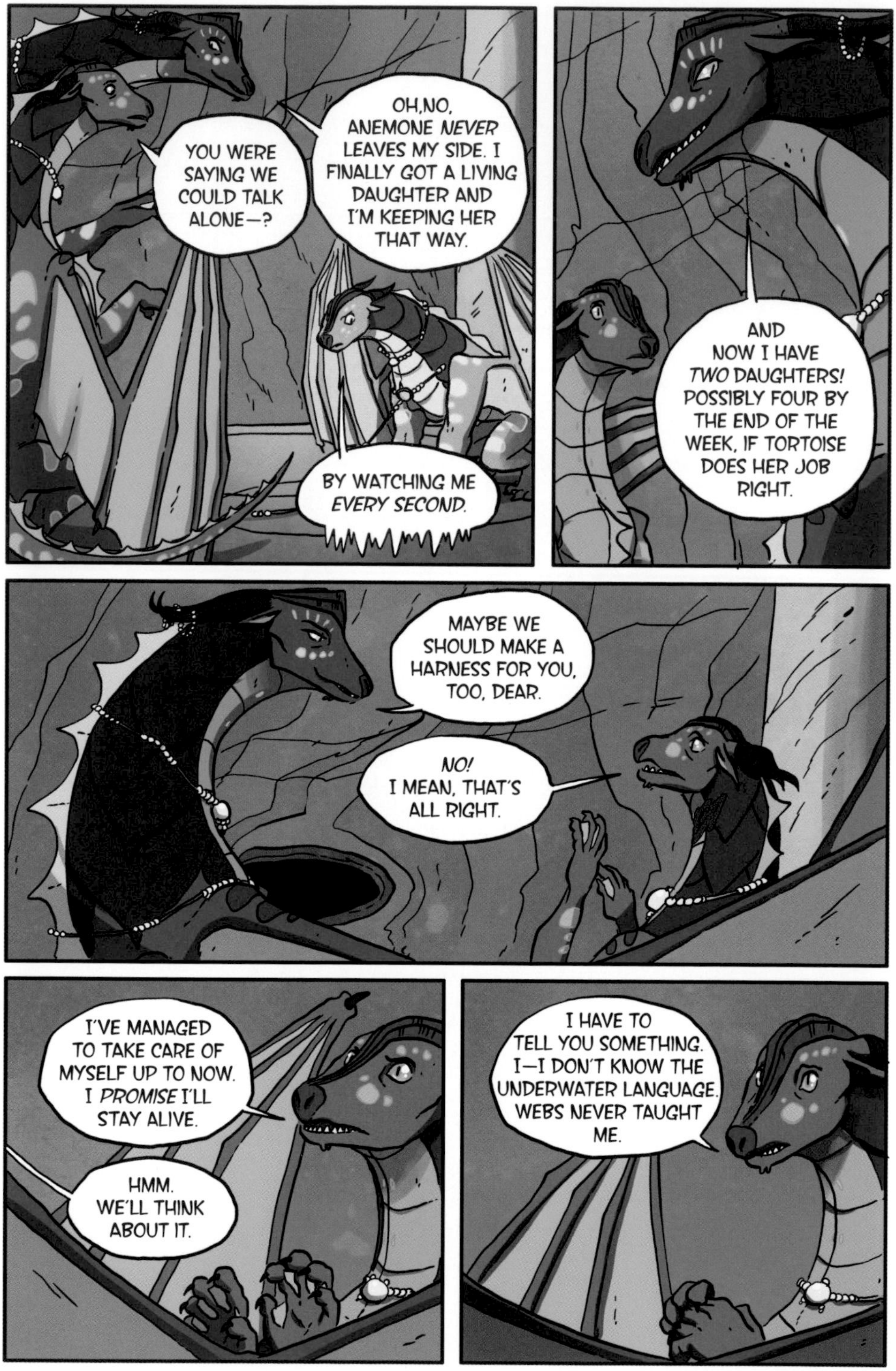
YOU WERE SAYING WE COULD TALK ALONE—?
OH,NO, ANEMONE *NEVER* LEAVES MY SIDE. I FINALLY GOT A LIVING DAUGHTER AND I'M KEEPING HER THAT WAY.
BY WATCHING ME *EVERY SECOND.*
AND NOW I HAVE *TWO* DAUGHTERS! POSSIBLY FOUR BY THE END OF THE WEEK, IF TORTOISE DOES HER JOB RIGHT.
MAYBE WE SHOULD MAKE A HARNESS FOR YOU, TOO, DEAR.
NO! I MEAN, THAT'S ALL RIGHT.
I'VE MANAGED TO TAKE CARE OF MYSELF UP TO NOW. I *PROMISE* I'LL STAY ALIVE.
HMM. WE'LL THINK ABOUT IT.
I HAVE TO TELL YOU SOMETHING. I—I DON'T KNOW THE UNDERWATER LANGUAGE. WEBS NEVER TAUGHT ME.

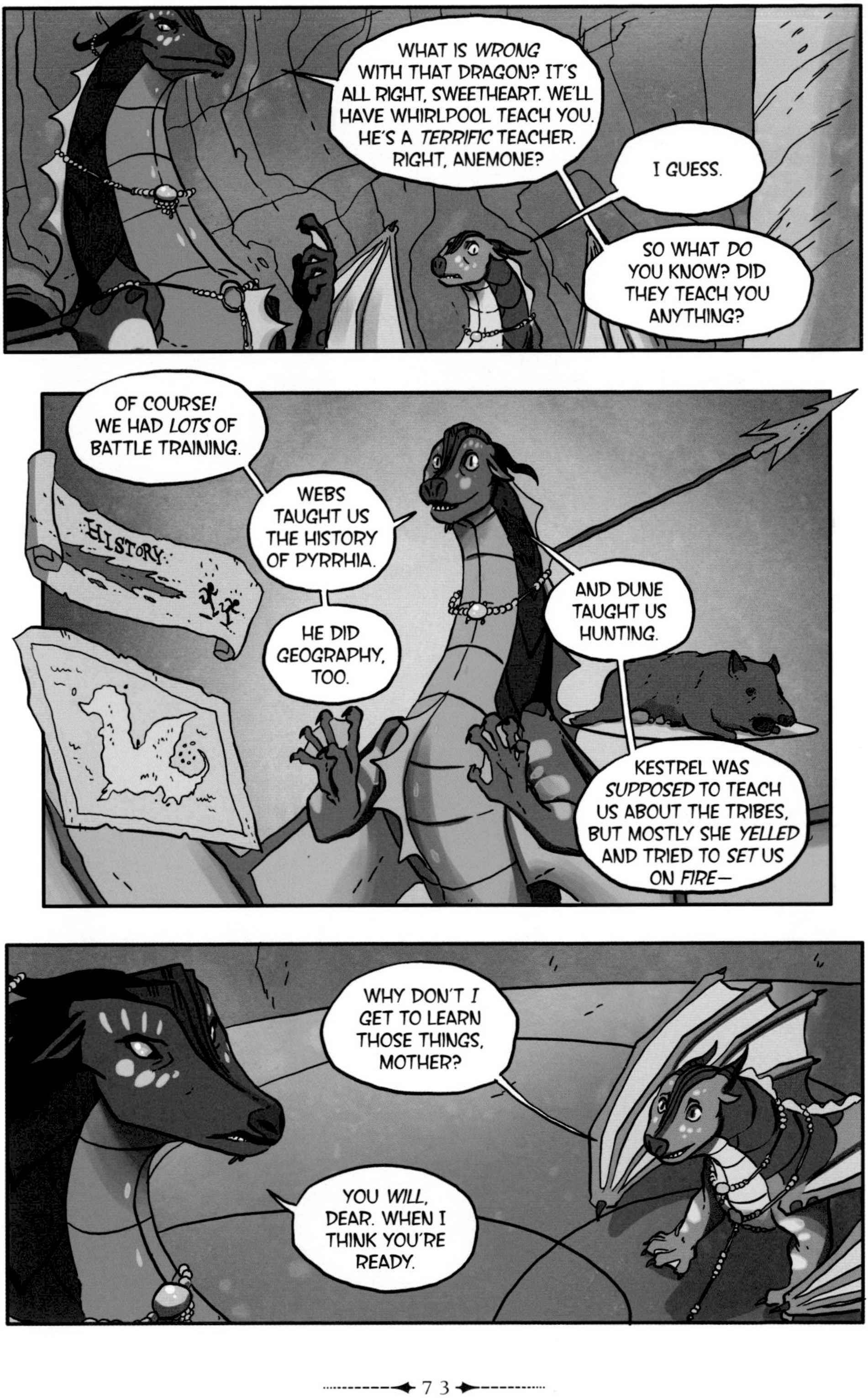
WHAT IS *WRONG* WITH THAT DRAGON? IT'S ALL RIGHT, SWEETHEART. WE'LL HAVE WHIRLPOOL TEACH YOU. HE'S A *TERRIFIC* TEACHER. RIGHT, ANEMONE?
I GUESS.
SO WHAT *DO* YOU KNOW? DID THEY TEACH YOU ANYTHING?
OF COURSE! WE HAD *LOTS* OF BATTLE TRAINING.
WEBS TAUGHT US THE HISTORY OF PYRRHIA.
HE DID GEOGRAPHY, TOO.
AND DUNE TAUGHT US HUNTING.
KESTREL WAS *SUPPOSED* TO TEACH US ABOUT THE TRIBES, BUT MOSTLY SHE *YELLED* AND TRIED TO *SET* US ON *FIRE*—
HISTORY
WHY DON'T *I* GET TO LEARN THOSE THINGS, MOTHER?
YOU *WILL*, DEAR. WHEN I THINK YOU'RE READY.

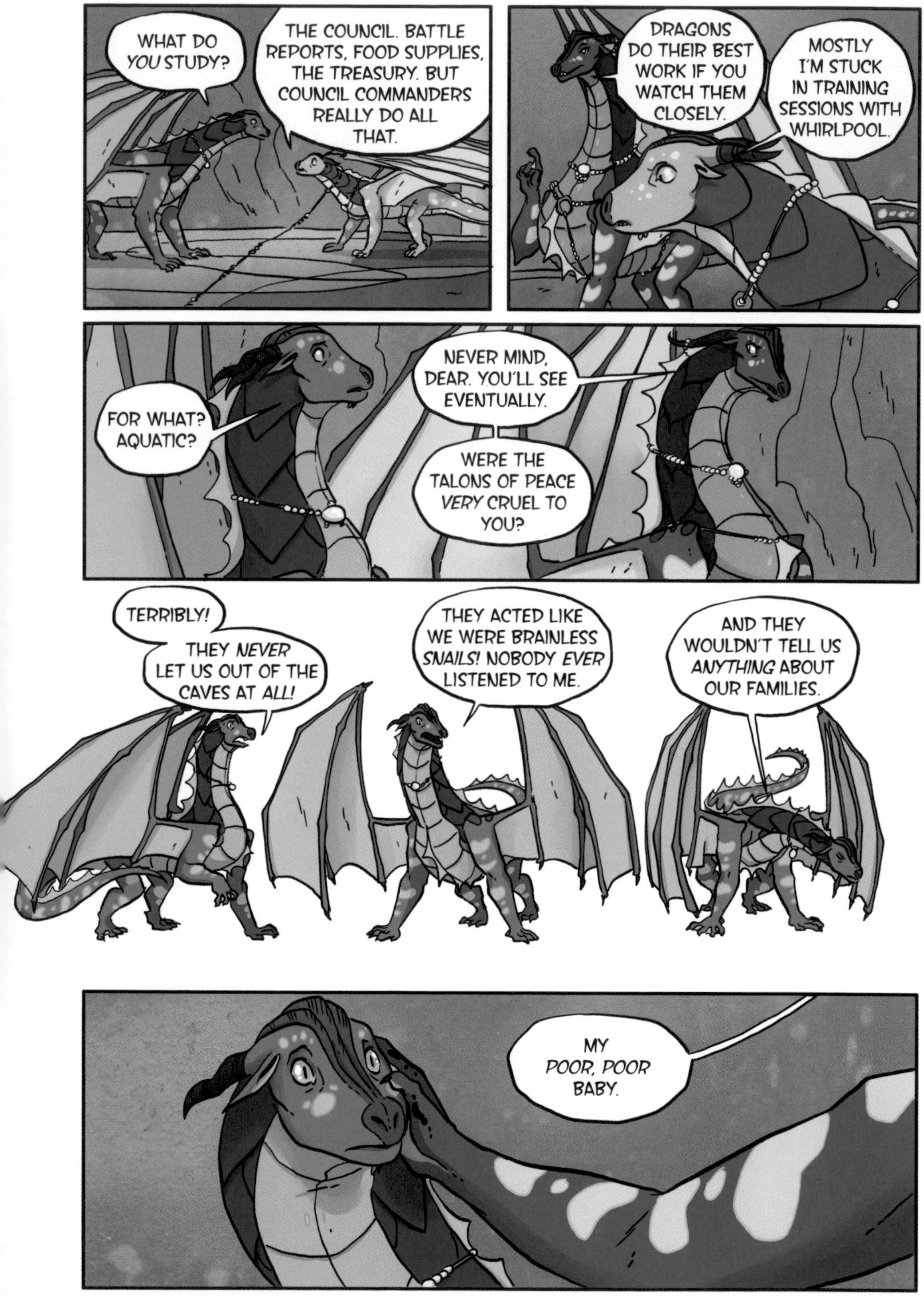
WHAT DO *YOU* STUDY?
THE COUNCIL. BATTLE REPORTS, FOOD SUPPLIES, THE TREASURY. BUT COUNCIL COMMANDERS REALLY DO ALL THAT.
DRAGONS DO THEIR BEST WORK IF YOU WATCH THEM CLOSELY.
MOSTLY I'M STUCK IN TRAINING SESSIONS WITH WHIRLPOOL.
FOR WHAT? AQUATIC?
NEVER MIND, DEAR. YOU'LL SEE EVENTUALLY.
WERE THE TALONS OF PEACE *VERY* CRUEL TO YOU?
TERRIBLY!
THEY *NEVER* LET US OUT OF THE CAVES AT *ALL*!
THEY ACTED LIKE WE WERE BRAINLESS *SNAILS!* NOBODY *EVER* LISTENED TO ME.
AND THEY WOULDN'T TELL US *ANYTHING* ABOUT OUR FAMILIES.
MY *POOR, POOR* BABY.

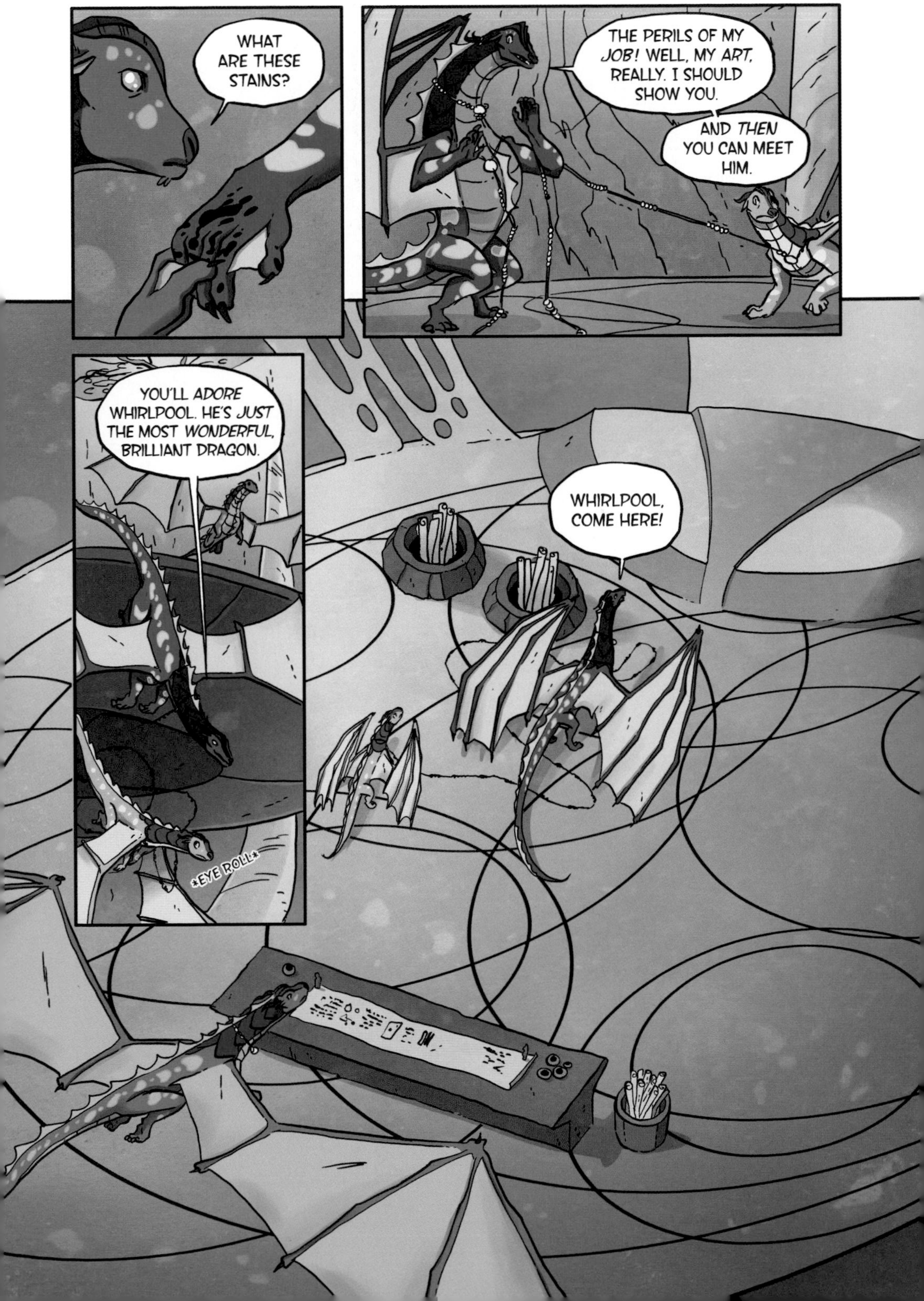
WHAT ARE THESE STAINS?
THE PERILS OF MY *JOB*! WELL, MY *ART*, REALLY. I SHOULD SHOW YOU.
AND *THEN* YOU CAN MEET HIM.
YOU'LL *ADORE* WHIRLPOOL. HE'S *JUST* THE MOST *WONDERFUL*, BRILLIANT DRAGON.
EYE ROLL
WHIRLPOOL, COME HERE!

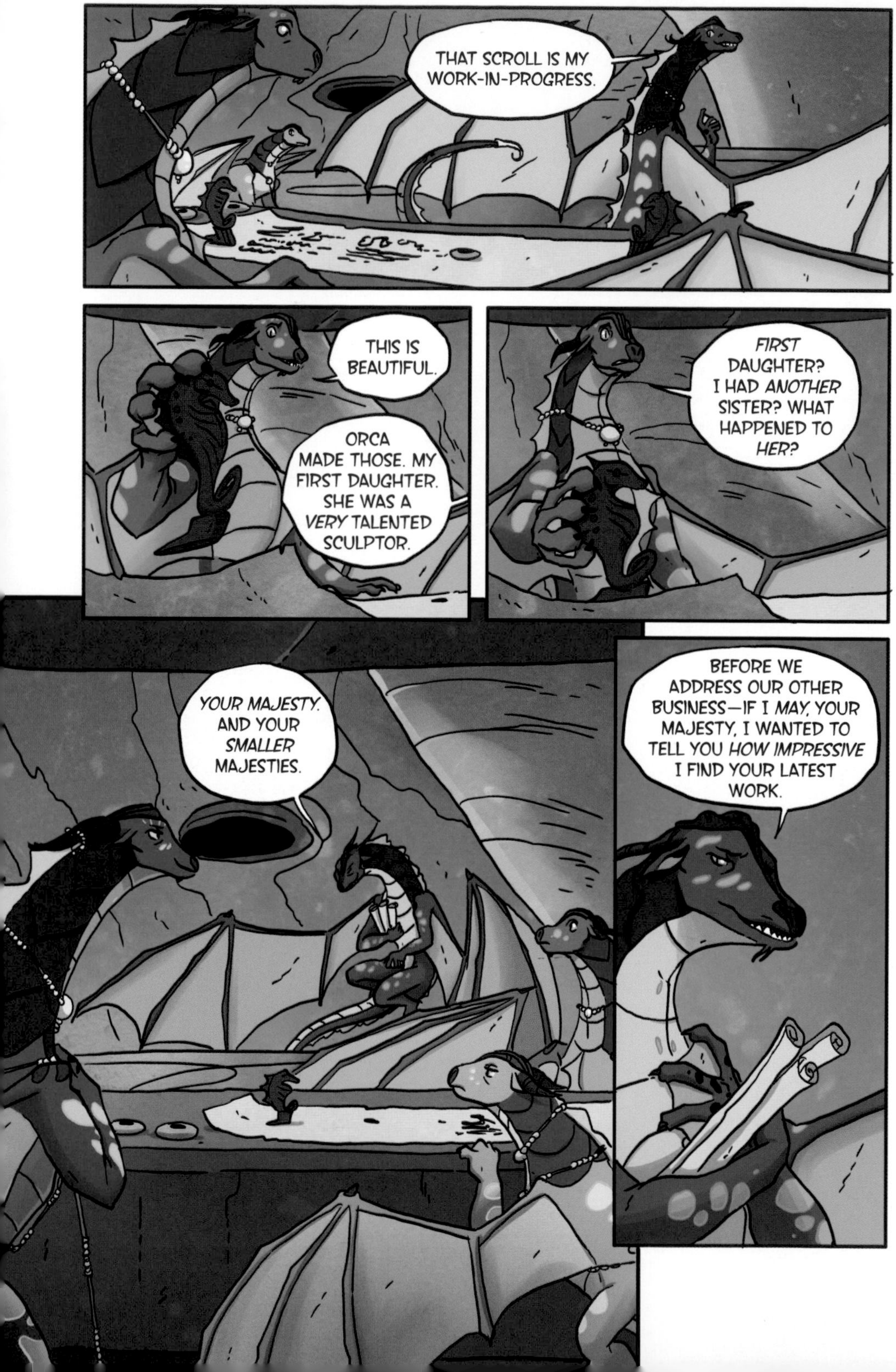
THAT SCROLL IS MY WORK-IN-PROGRESS.
THIS IS BEAUTIFUL.
ORCA MADE THOSE. MY FIRST DAUGHTER. SHE WAS A *VERY* TALENTED SCULPTOR.
FIRST DAUGHTER? I HAD *ANOTHER* SISTER? WHAT HAPPENED TO *HER*?
YOUR MAJESTY. AND YOUR *SMALLER* MAJESTIES.
BEFORE WE ADDRESS OUR OTHER BUSINESS—IF I *MAY*, YOUR MAJESTY, I WANTED TO TELL YOU *HOW IMPRESSIVE* I FIND YOUR LATEST WORK.

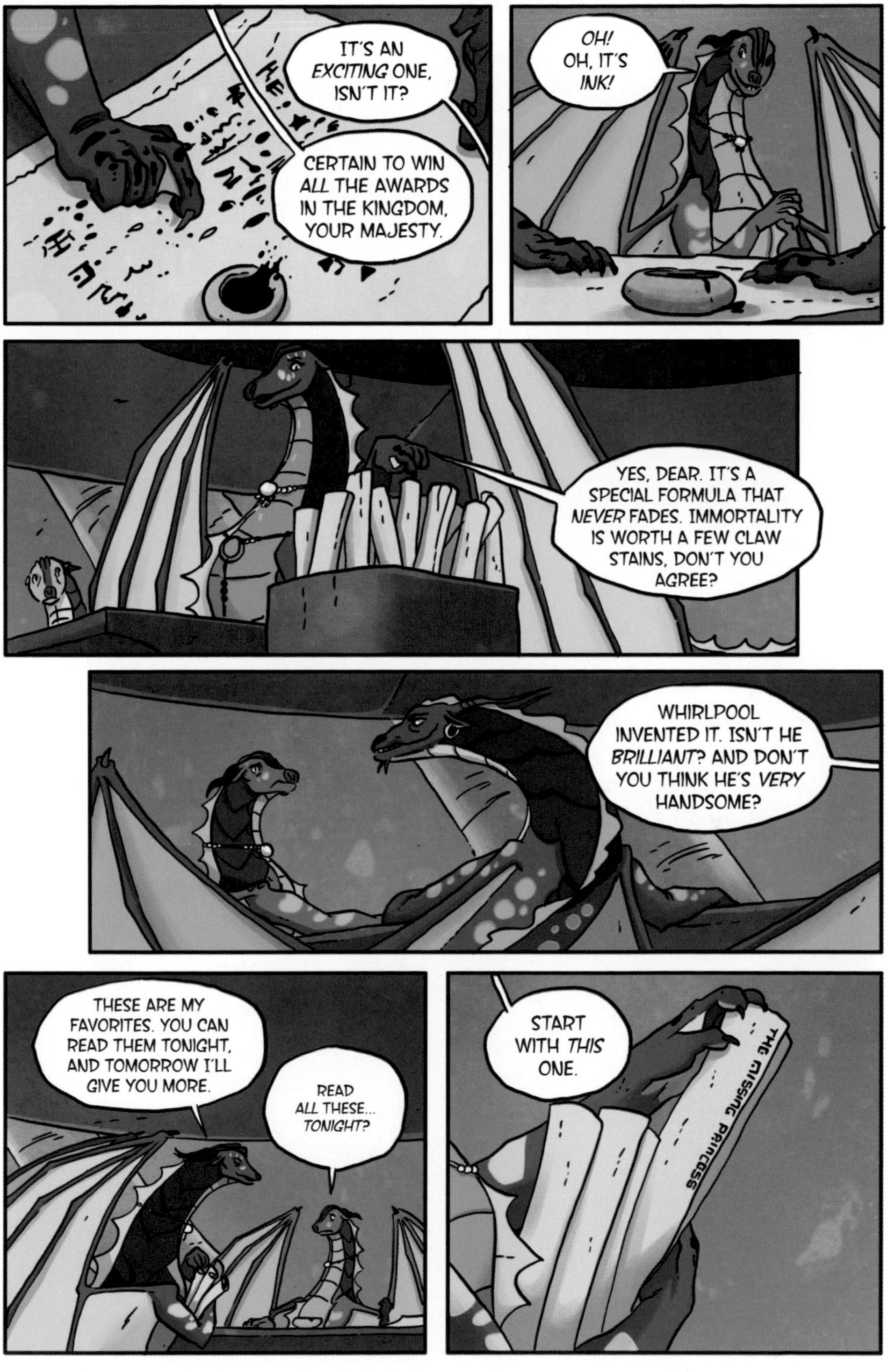
IT'S AN *EXCITING* ONE, ISN'T IT?
CERTAIN TO WIN *ALL* THE AWARDS IN THE KINGDOM, YOUR MAJESTY.
OH! OH, IT'S *INK!*
YES, DEAR. IT'S A SPECIAL FORMULA THAT *NEVER* FADES. IMMORTALITY IS WORTH A FEW CLAW STAINS, DON'T YOU AGREE?
WHIRLPOOL INVENTED IT. ISN'T HE *BRILLIANT*? AND DON'T YOU THINK HE'S *VERY* HANDSOME?
THESE ARE MY FAVORITES. YOU CAN READ THEM TONIGHT, AND TOMORROW I'LL GIVE YOU MORE.
READ ALL THESE... *TONIGHT?*
START WITH *THIS* ONE.
THE MISSING PRINCESS

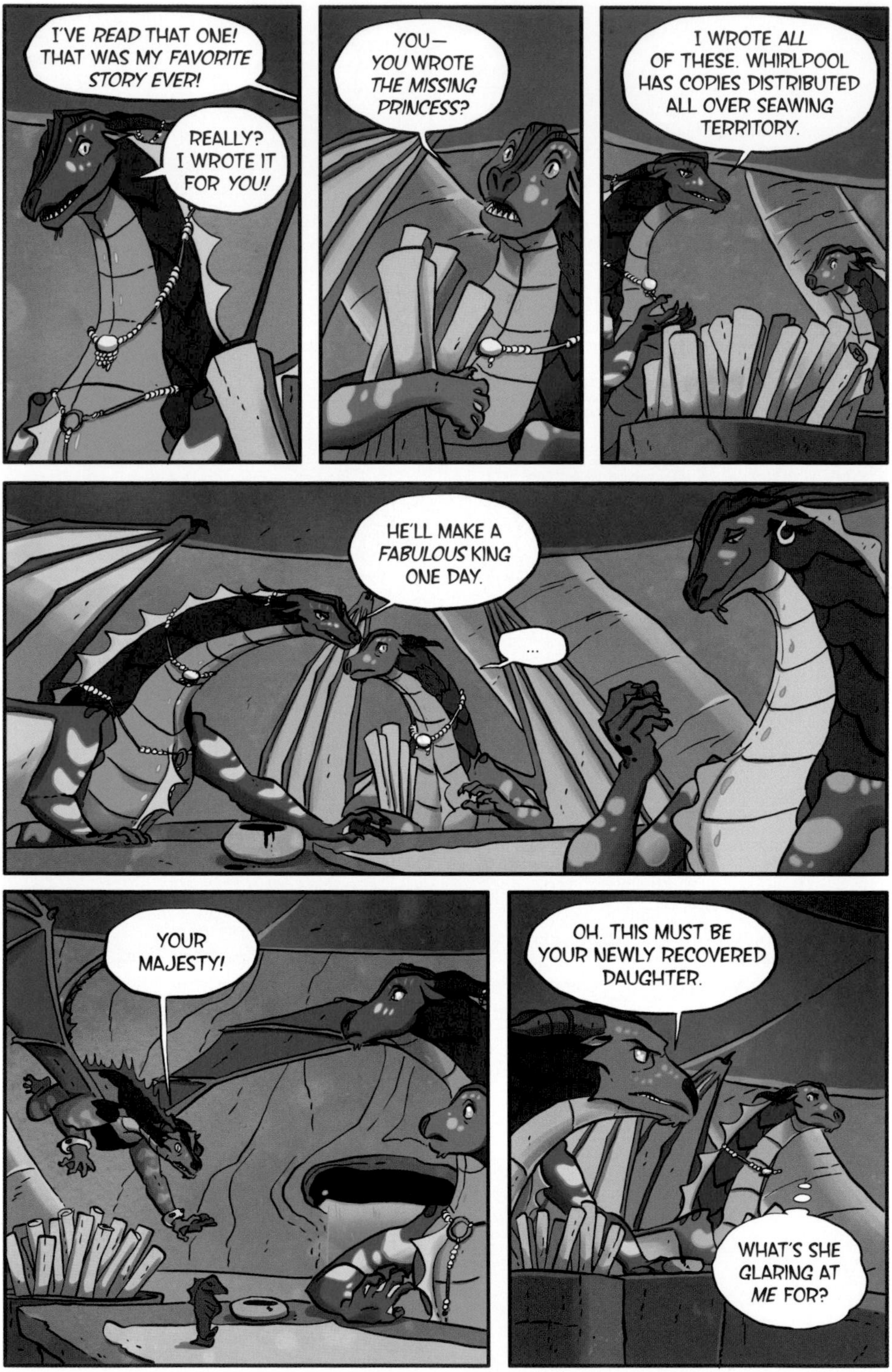

I'VE *READ* THAT ONE! THAT WAS MY *FAVORITE* STORY *EVER*!
REALLY? I WROTE IT FOR *YOU*!
YOU— *YOU* WROTE *THE MISSING PRINCESS*?
I WROTE *ALL* OF THESE. WHIRLPOOL HAS COPIES DISTRIBUTED ALL OVER SEAWING TERRITORY.
HE'LL MAKE A *FABULOUS* KING ONE DAY.
...
YOUR MAJESTY!
OH. THIS MUST BE YOUR NEWLY RECOVERED DAUGHTER.
WHAT'S SHE GLARING AT *ME* FOR?

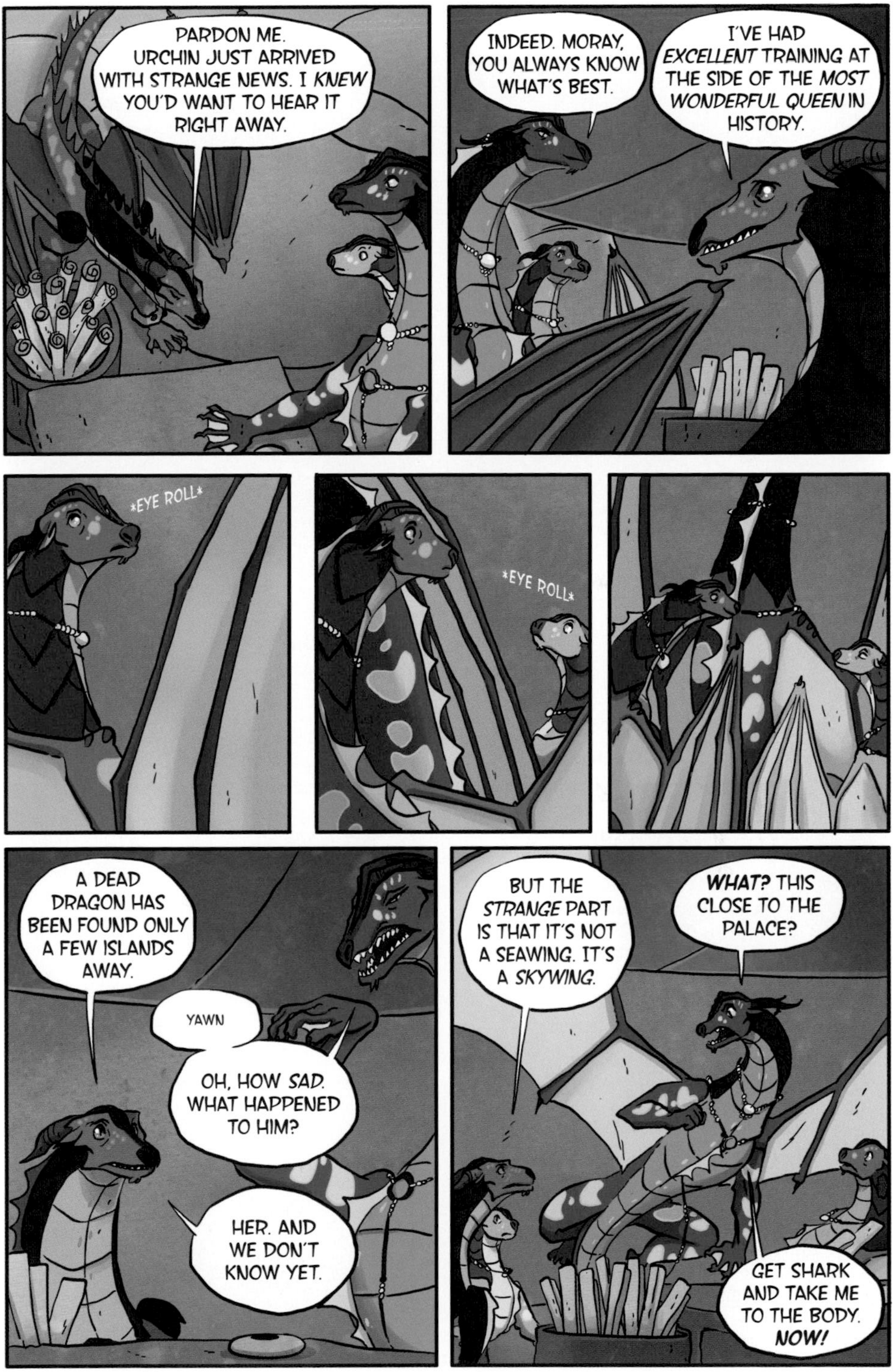
PARDON ME. URCHIN JUST ARRIVED WITH STRANGE NEWS. I *KNEW* YOU'D WANT TO HEAR IT RIGHT AWAY.
INDEED. MORAY, YOU ALWAYS KNOW WHAT'S BEST.
I'VE HAD *EXCELLENT* TRAINING AT THE SIDE OF THE *MOST WONDERFUL QUEEN* IN HISTORY.
EYE ROLL
EYE ROLL
A DEAD DRAGON HAS BEEN FOUND ONLY A FEW ISLANDS AWAY.
YAWN
OH, HOW *SAD*. WHAT HAPPENED TO HIM?
HER. AND WE DON'T KNOW YET.
BUT THE *STRANGE* PART IS THAT IT'S NOT A SEAWING. IT'S A *SKYWING*.
WHAT? THIS CLOSE TO THE PALACE?
GET SHARK AND TAKE ME TO THE BODY. ***NOW!***

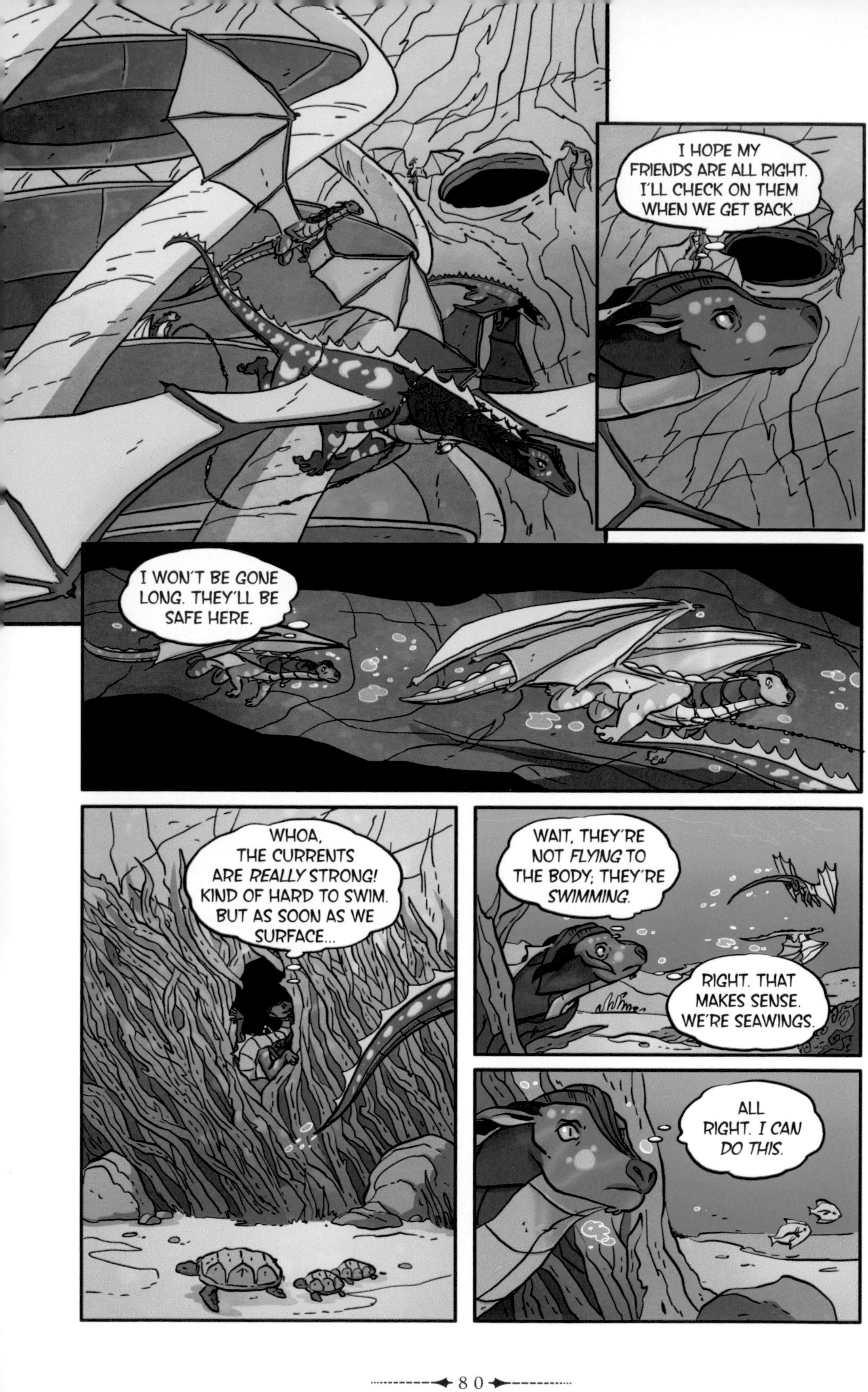
I HOPE MY FRIENDS ARE ALL RIGHT. I'LL CHECK ON THEM WHEN WE GET BACK.
I WON'T BE GONE LONG. THEY'LL BE SAFE HERE.
WHOA, THE CURRENTS ARE *REALLY* STRONG! KIND OF HARD TO SWIM. BUT AS SOON AS WE SURFACE...
WAIT, THEY'RE NOT *FLYING* TO THE BODY; THEY'RE *SWIMMING*.
RIGHT. THAT MAKES SENSE. WE'RE SEAWINGS.
ALL RIGHT. *I CAN DO THIS.*

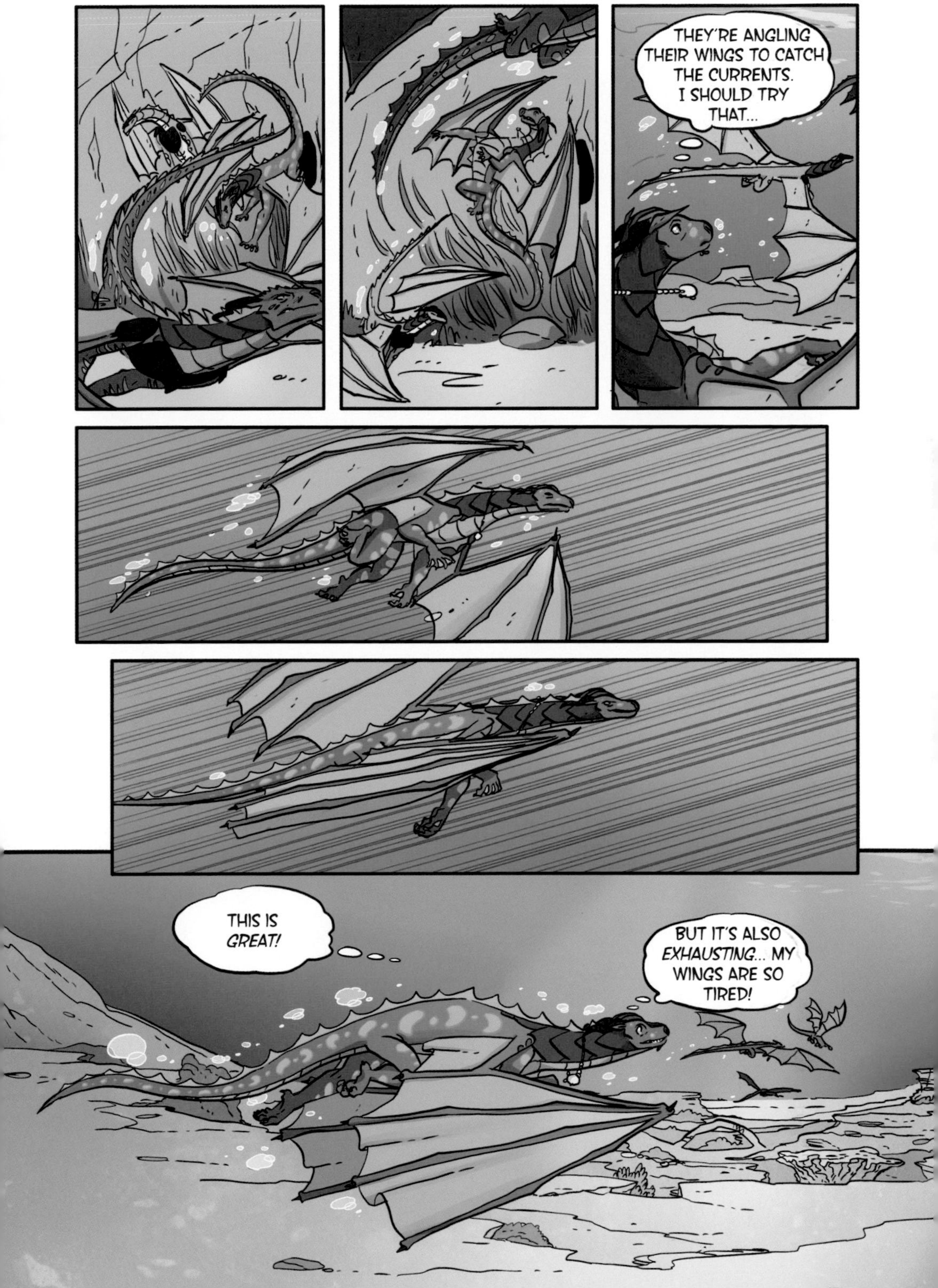
THEY'RE ANGLING THEIR WINGS TO CATCH THE CURRENTS. I SHOULD TRY THAT...
THIS IS *GREAT!*
BUT IT'S ALSO *EXHAUSTING*... MY WINGS ARE SO TIRED!

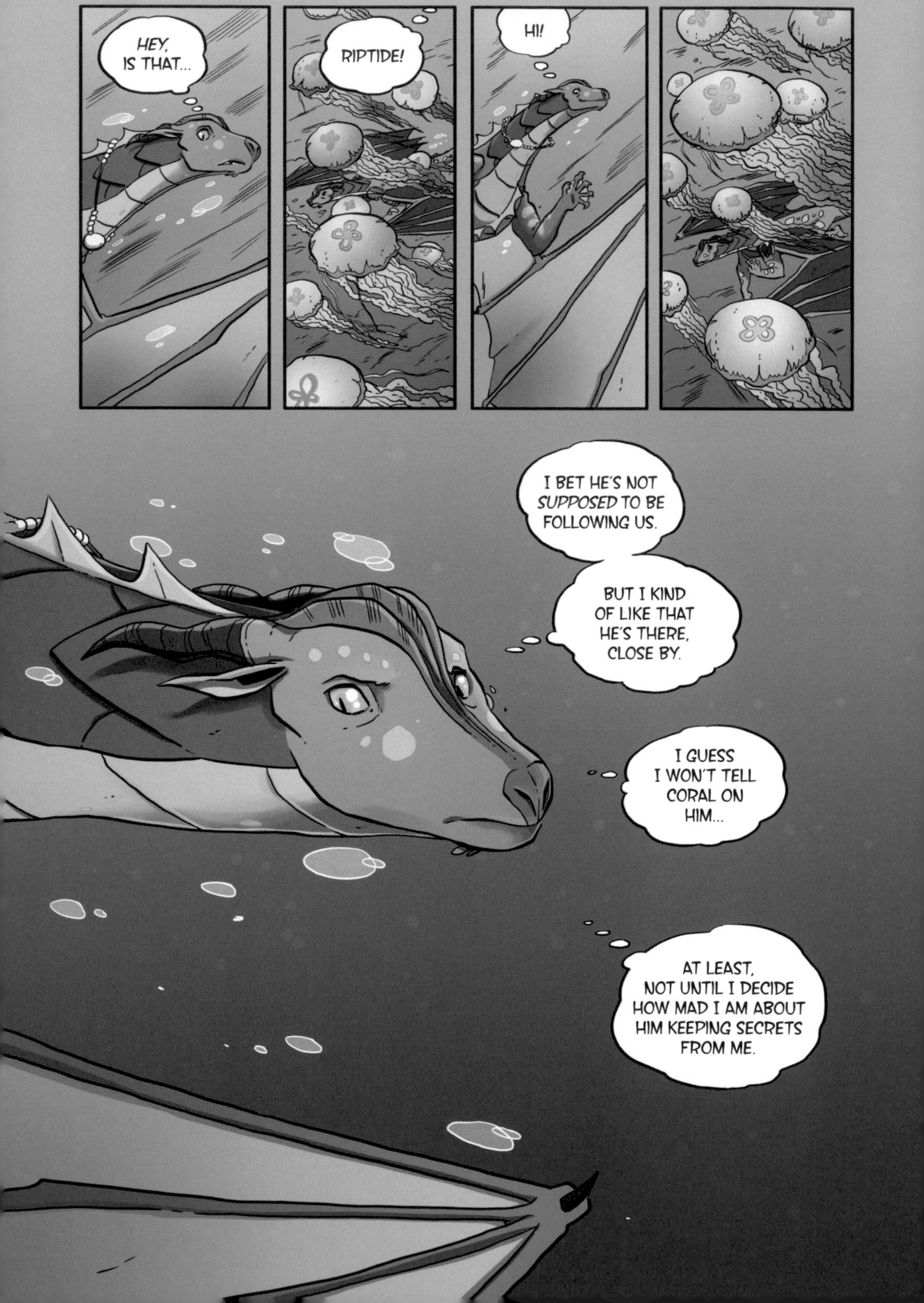
HEY, IS THAT...
RIPTIDE!
HI!
I BET HE'S NOT *SUPPOSED* TO BE FOLLOWING US.
BUT I KIND OF LIKE THAT HE'S THERE, CLOSE BY.
I GUESS I WON'T TELL CORAL ON HIM...
AT LEAST, NOT UNTIL I DECIDE HOW MAD I AM ABOUT HIM KEEPING SECRETS FROM ME.

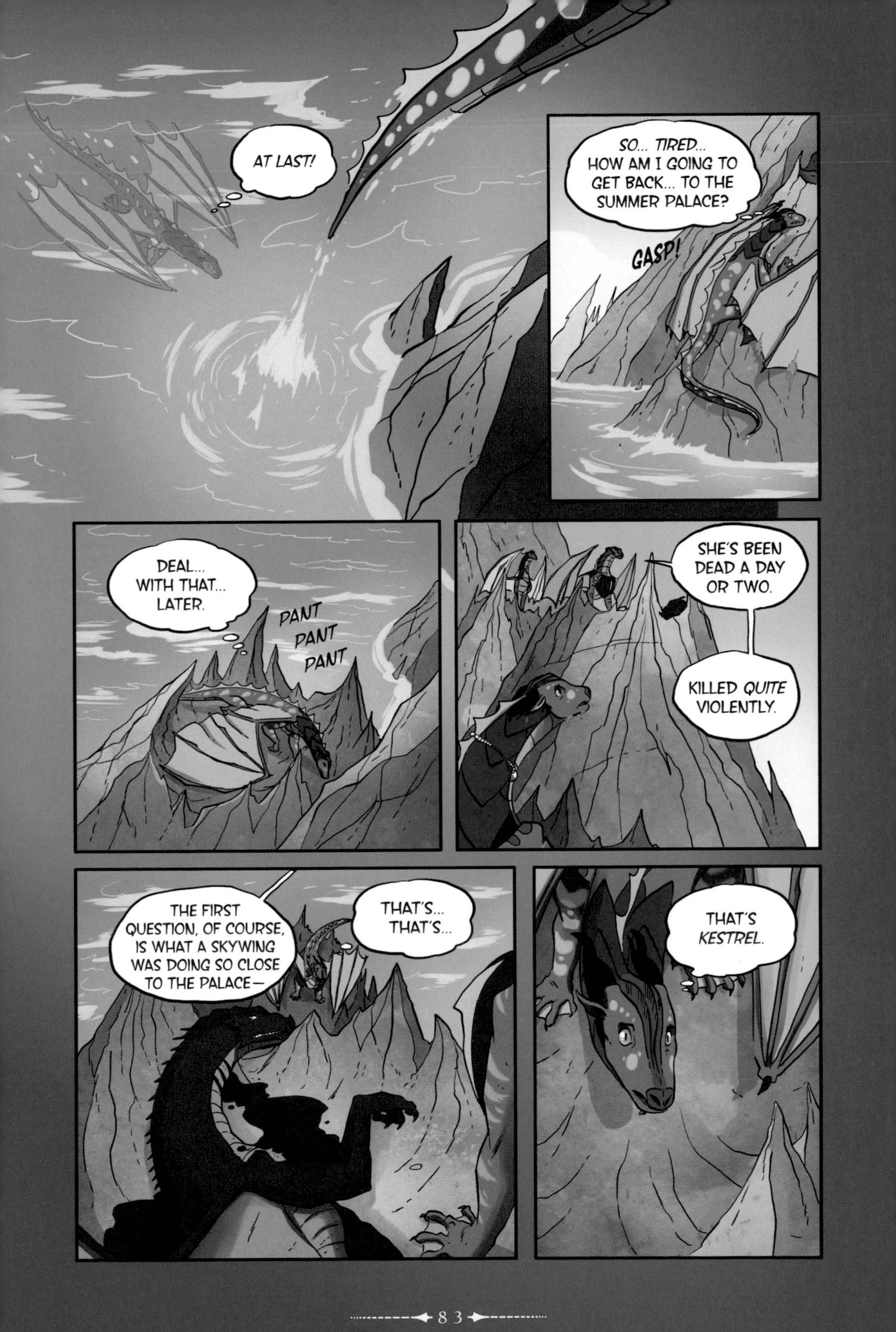
AT LAST!
SO... TIRED... HOW AM I GOING TO GET BACK... TO THE SUMMER PALACE?
GASP!
DEAL... WITH THAT... LATER.
PANT PANT PANT
SHE'S BEEN DEAD A DAY OR TWO.
KILLED *QUITE* VIOLENTLY.
THE FIRST QUESTION, OF COURSE, IS WHAT A SKYWING WAS DOING SO CLOSE TO THE PALACE—
THAT'S... THAT'S...
THAT'S *KESTREL*.

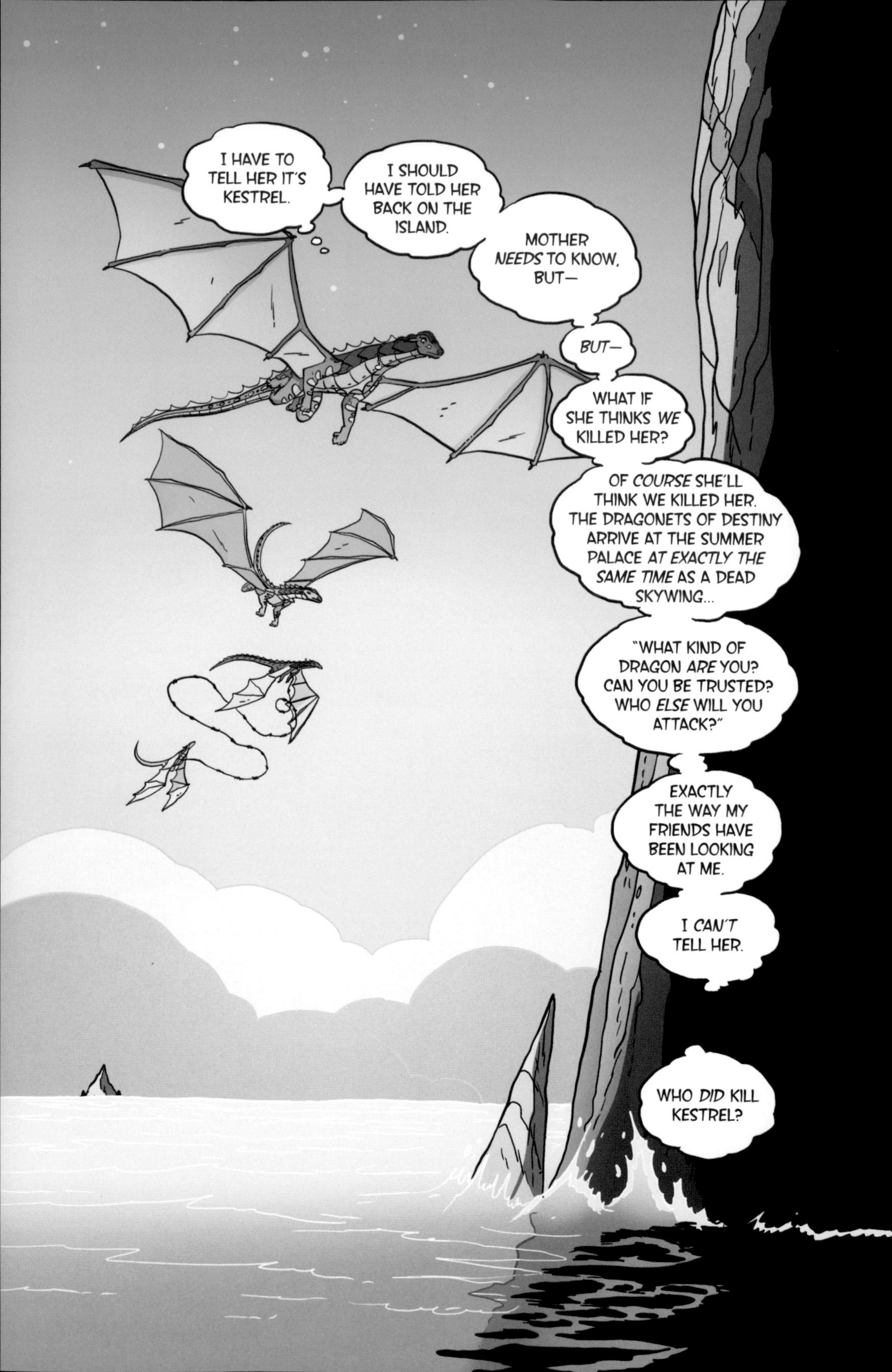
I HAVE TO TELL HER IT'S KESTREL.
I SHOULD HAVE TOLD HER BACK ON THE ISLAND.
MOTHER *NEEDS* TO KNOW, BUT—
BUT—
WHAT IF SHE THINKS *WE* KILLED HER?
OF *COURSE* SHE'LL THINK WE KILLED HER. THE DRAGONETS OF DESTINY ARRIVE AT THE SUMMER PALACE *AT EXACTLY THE SAME TIME* AS A DEAD SKYWING...
"WHAT KIND OF DRAGON *ARE* YOU? CAN YOU BE TRUSTED? WHO *ELSE* WILL YOU ATTACK?"
EXACTLY THE WAY MY FRIENDS HAVE BEEN LOOKING AT ME.
I *CAN'T* TELL HER.
WHO *DID* KILL KESTREL?

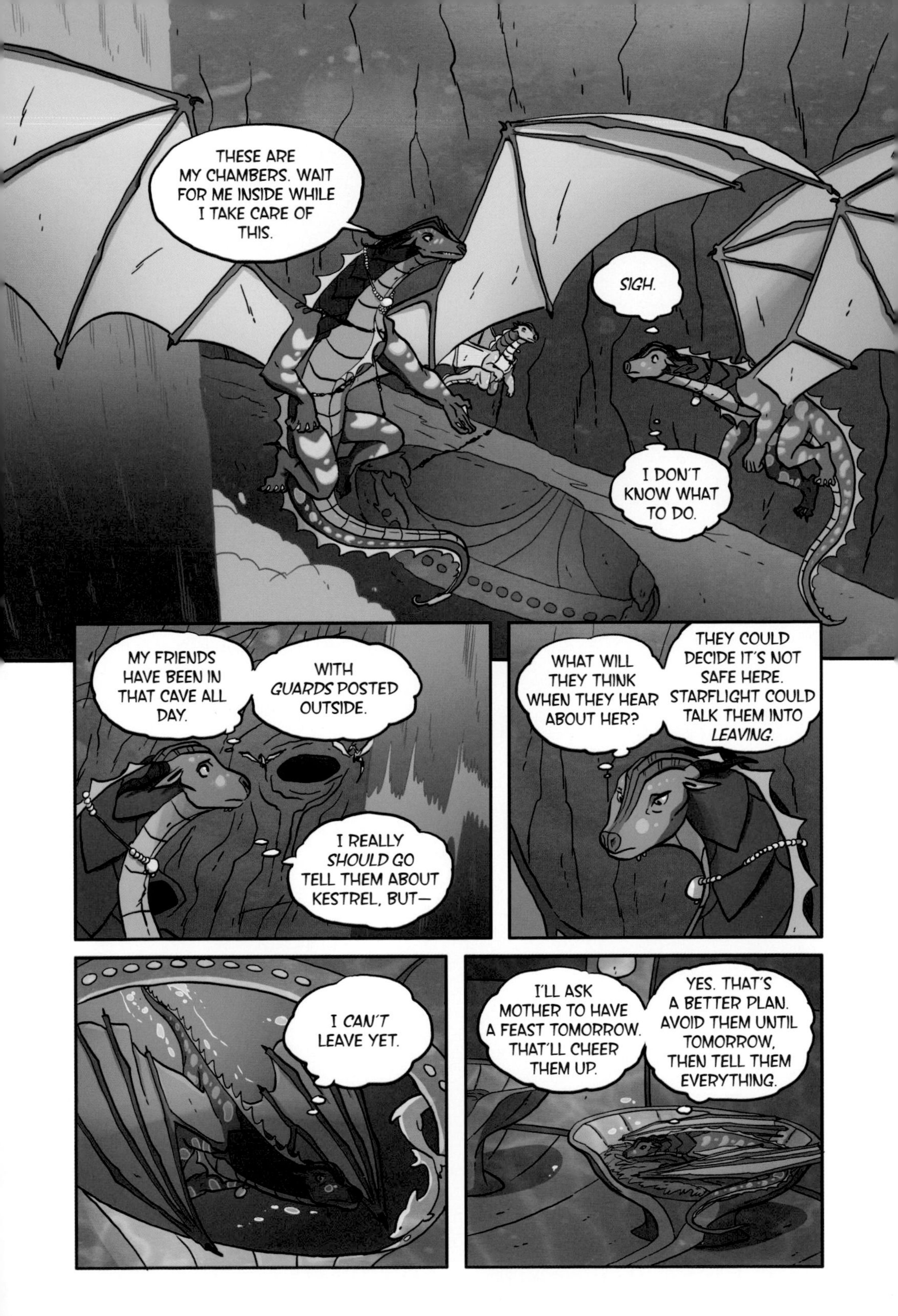
THESE ARE MY CHAMBERS. WAIT FOR ME INSIDE WHILE I TAKE CARE OF THIS.
SIGH.
I DON'T KNOW WHAT TO DO.
MY FRIENDS HAVE BEEN IN THAT CAVE ALL DAY.
WITH *GUARDS* POSTED OUTSIDE.
I REALLY *SHOULD* GO TELL THEM ABOUT KESTREL, BUT—
WHAT WILL THEY THINK WHEN THEY HEAR ABOUT HER?
THEY COULD DECIDE IT'S NOT SAFE HERE. STARFLIGHT COULD TALK THEM INTO *LEAVING*.
I *CAN'T* LEAVE YET.
I'LL ASK MOTHER TO HAVE A FEAST TOMORROW. THAT'LL CHEER THEM UP.
YES. THAT'S A BETTER PLAN. AVOID THEM UNTIL TOMORROW, THEN TELL THEM EVERYTHING.

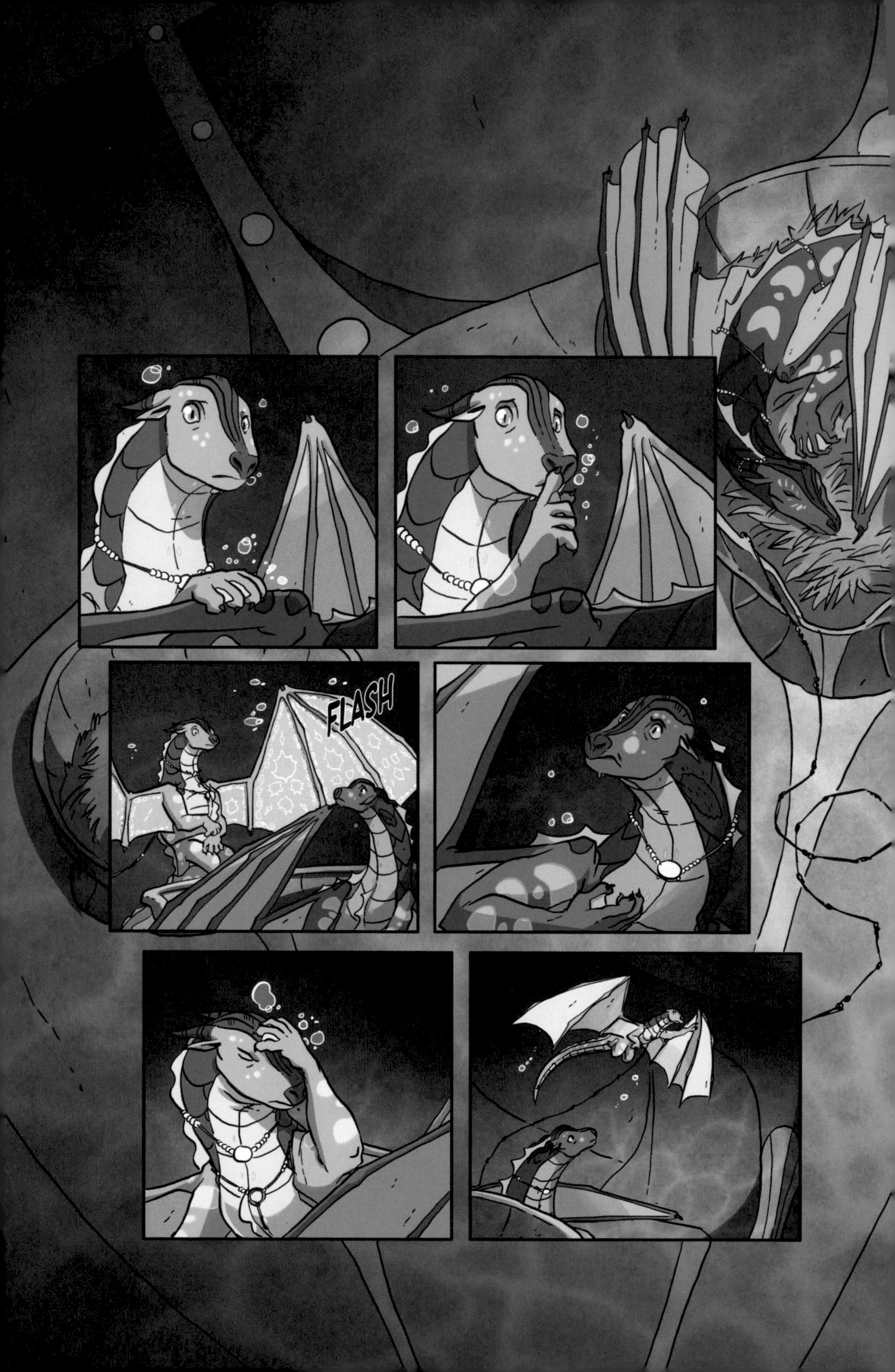
FLASH

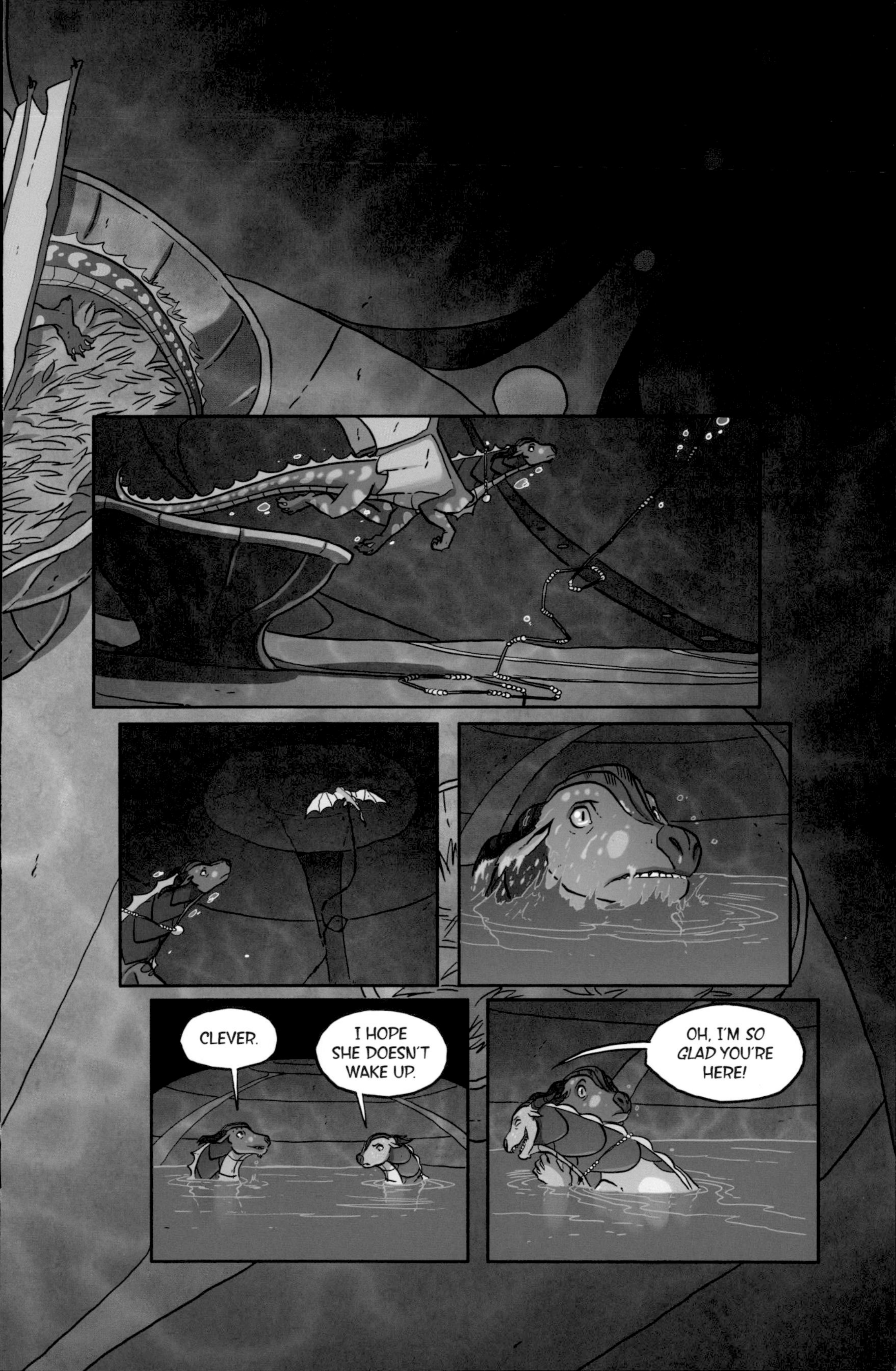
CLEVER.
I HOPE SHE DOESN'T WAKE UP.
OH, I'M *SO GLAD* YOU'RE HERE!

REALLY?

BUT AREN'T WE RIVALS? DON'T I THREATEN HER CHANCE AT THE THRONE?

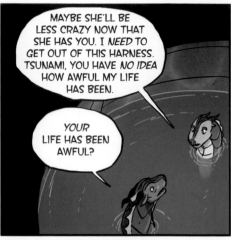

MAYBE SHE'LL BE LESS CRAZY NOW THAT SHE HAS YOU. I *NEED* TO GET OUT OF THIS HARNESS. TSUNAMI, YOU HAVE *NO IDEA* HOW AWFUL MY LIFE HAS BEEN.

YOUR LIFE HAS BEEN AWFUL?

TRY BEING RAISED WITH *NO OCEAN* BY DRAGONS WHO *HATE* YOU AND TREAT YOU LIKE A *TADPOLE.*

I *AM* TREATED LIKE A TADPOLE!

YOU'RE ONLY, WHAT, ONE YEAR OLD? I'M SURE THAT'LL CHANGE.

WELL, *MOSTLY* SURE.

HALFWAY SURE.

AT LEAST *YOU* HAVE FRIENDS!

WELL, I WAS SORT OF STUCK WITH THOSE FOUR. AND THEY'RE ALWAYS *ARGUING* WITH ME OR GETTING *MAD* ABOUT SOMETHING.

THEY SEEM GREAT. I ALWAYS WANTED BROTHERS AND SISTERS.

DON'T YOU HAVE BROTHERS?

LOTS. BUT MOTHER THINKS THEY PLAY TOO ROUGH.

I'M NOT ALLOWED TO PLAY WITH *ANYONE.*

MOTHER'S *OBSESSED* WITH FINDING OUT WHO'S KILLING HER DAUGHTERS. SHE SUSPECTS ALMOST EVERYONE.

EXCEPT MORAY, WHO'S PERFECT AND *BORING.*

I GUESS MY FRIENDS ARE ALL RIGHT WHEN THEY'RE NOT COMPLAINING.

THEY COMPLAIN A *LOT,* THOUGH.

I COMPLAINED ONCE. MOTHER NEARLY GOT ME A MUZZLE TO MATCH THE HARNESS.

AT LEAST SOMEBODY LOVES YOU.

SHE LOVES YOU, TOO.

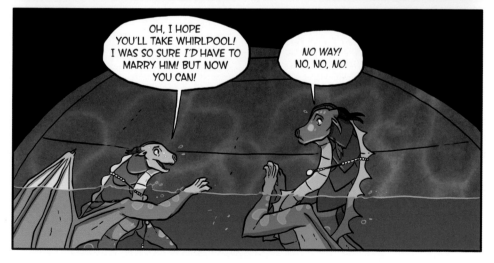

OH, I HOPE YOU'LL TAKE WHIRLPOOL! I WAS SO SURE *I'D* HAVE TO MARRY HIM! BUT NOW YOU CAN!

NO WAY! NO, NO, *NO.*

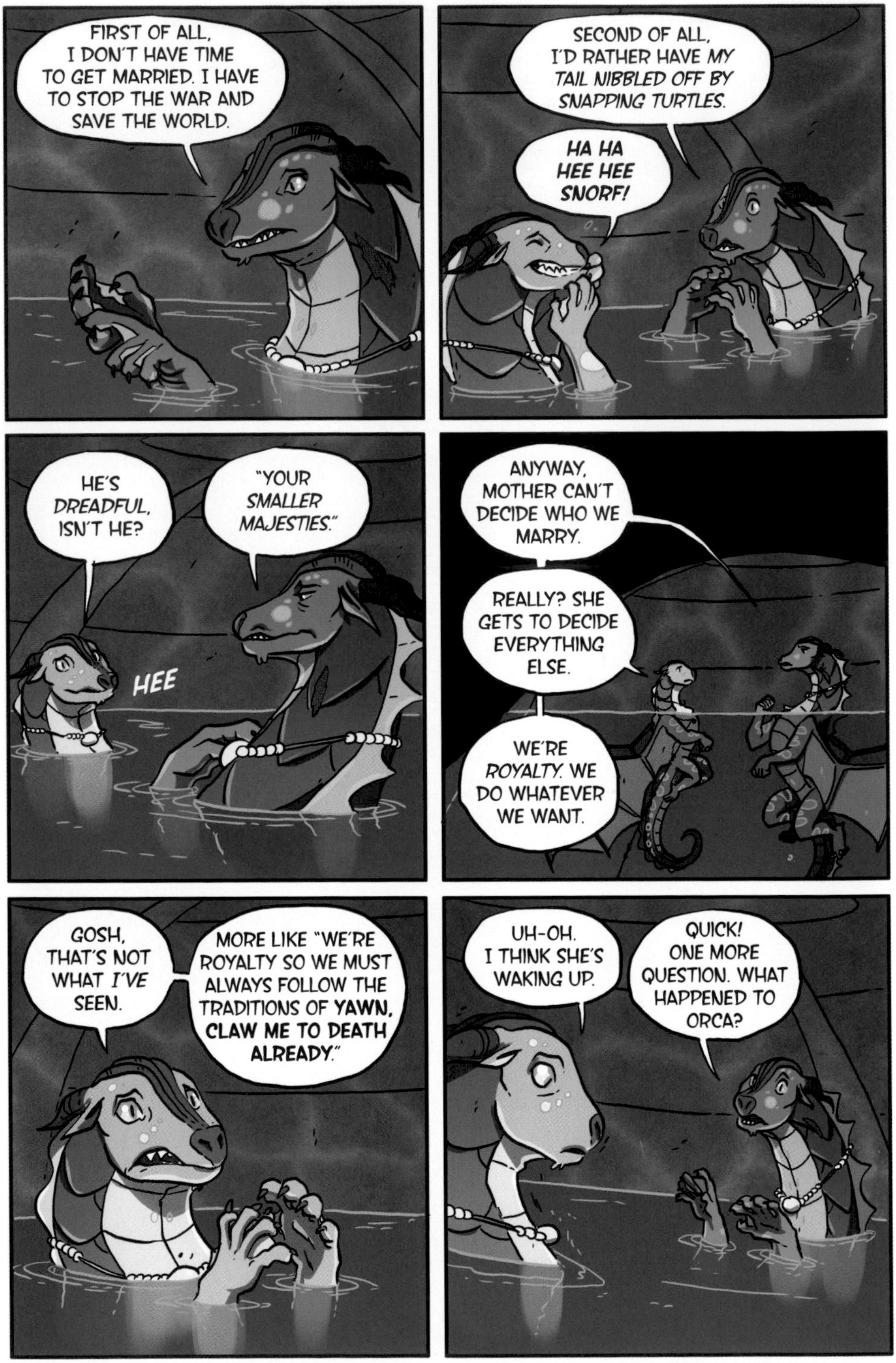
FIRST OF ALL, I DON'T HAVE TIME TO GET MARRIED. I HAVE TO STOP THE WAR AND SAVE THE WORLD.
SECOND OF ALL, I'D RATHER HAVE *MY TAIL NIBBLED OFF BY SNAPPING TURTLES.*
HA HA HEE HEE SNORF!
HE'S *DREADFUL,* ISN'T HE?
"YOUR *SMALLER MAJESTIES.*"
HEE
ANYWAY, MOTHER CAN'T DECIDE WHO WE MARRY.
REALLY? SHE GETS TO DECIDE EVERYTHING ELSE.
WE'RE *ROYALTY.* WE DO WHATEVER WE WANT.
GOSH, THAT'S NOT WHAT *I'VE* SEEN.
MORE LIKE "WE'RE ROYALTY SO WE MUST ALWAYS FOLLOW THE TRADITIONS OF **YAWN, CLAW ME TO DEATH ALREADY.**"
UH-OH. I THINK SHE'S WAKING UP.
QUICK! ONE MORE QUESTION. WHAT HAPPENED TO ORCA?

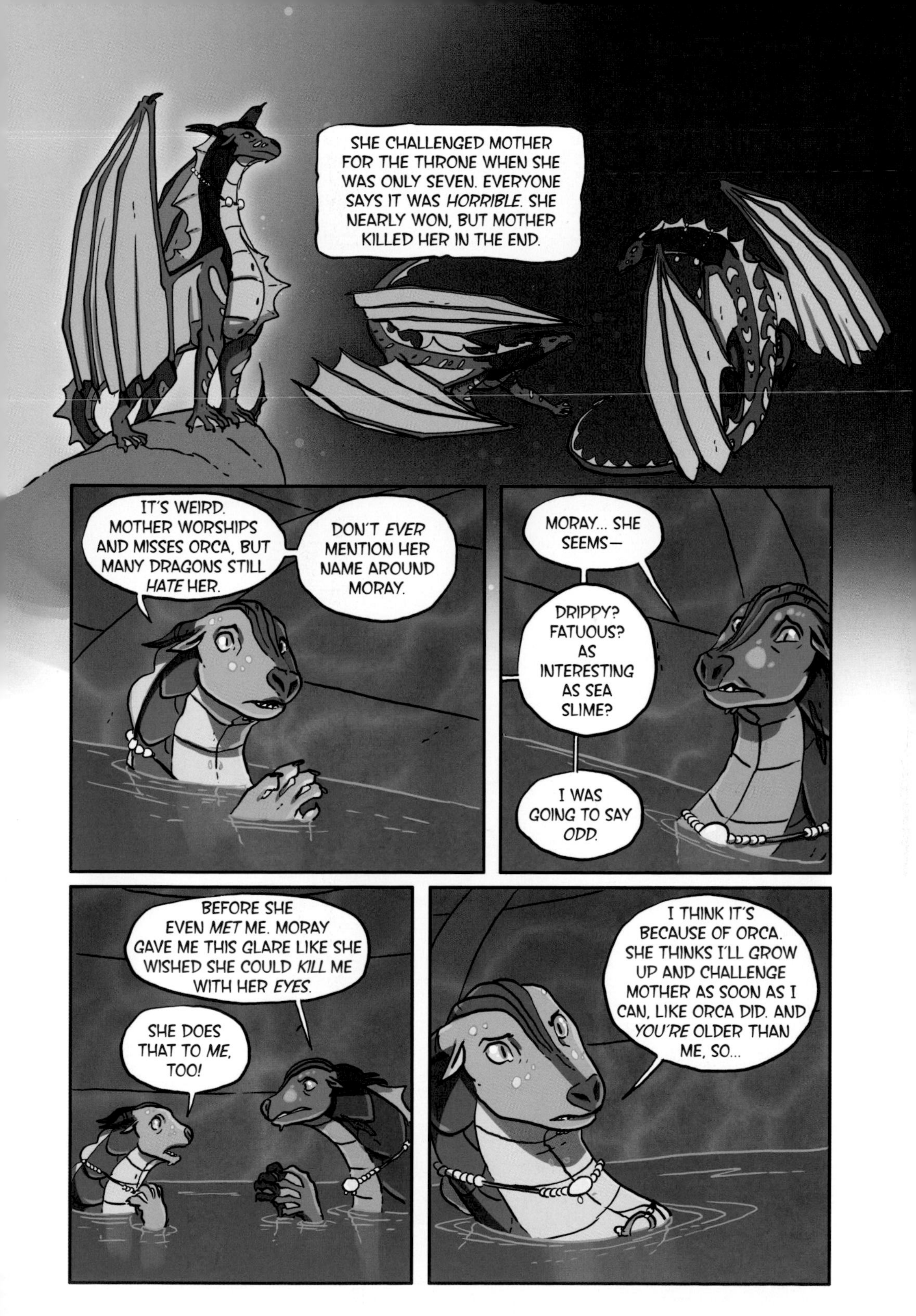
SHE CHALLENGED MOTHER FOR THE THRONE WHEN SHE WAS ONLY SEVEN. EVERYONE SAYS IT WAS *HORRIBLE*. SHE NEARLY WON, BUT MOTHER KILLED HER IN THE END.
IT'S WEIRD. MOTHER WORSHIPS AND MISSES ORCA, BUT MANY DRAGONS STILL *HATE* HER.
DON'T *EVER* MENTION HER NAME AROUND MORAY.
MORAY... SHE SEEMS—
DRIPPY? FATUOUS? AS INTERESTING AS SEA SLIME?
I WAS GOING TO SAY *ODD*.
BEFORE SHE EVEN *MET* ME, MORAY GAVE ME THIS GLARE LIKE SHE WISHED SHE COULD *KILL* ME WITH HER *EYES*.
SHE DOES THAT TO *ME*, TOO!
I THINK IT'S BECAUSE OF ORCA. SHE THINKS I'LL GROW UP AND CHALLENGE MOTHER AS SOON AS I CAN, LIKE ORCA DID. AND *YOU'RE* OLDER THAN ME, SO...

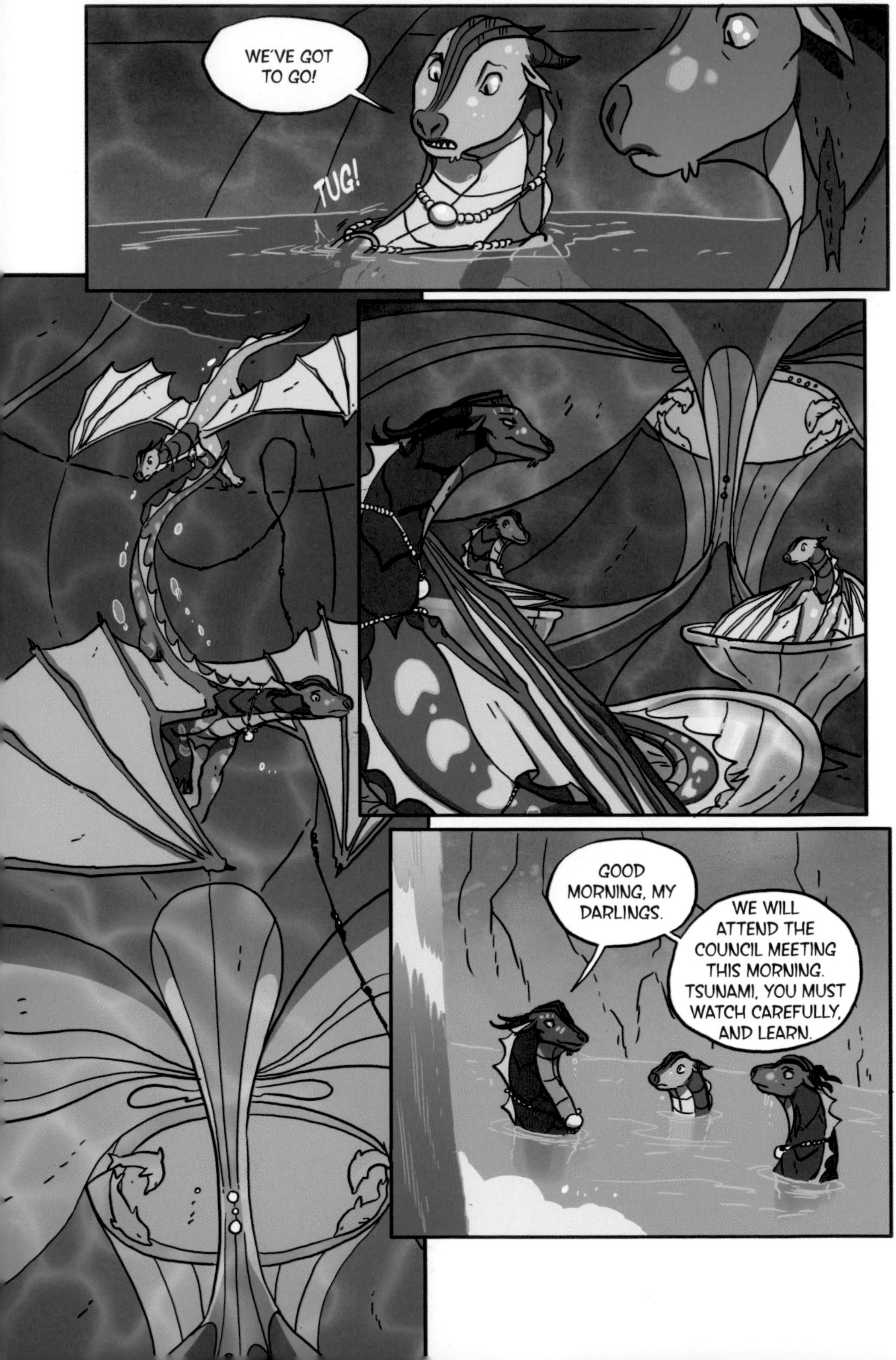
WE'VE GOT TO GO!
TUG!
GOOD MORNING, MY DARLINGS.
WE WILL ATTEND THE COUNCIL MEETING THIS MORNING. TSUNAMI, YOU MUST WATCH CAREFULLY, AND LEARN.

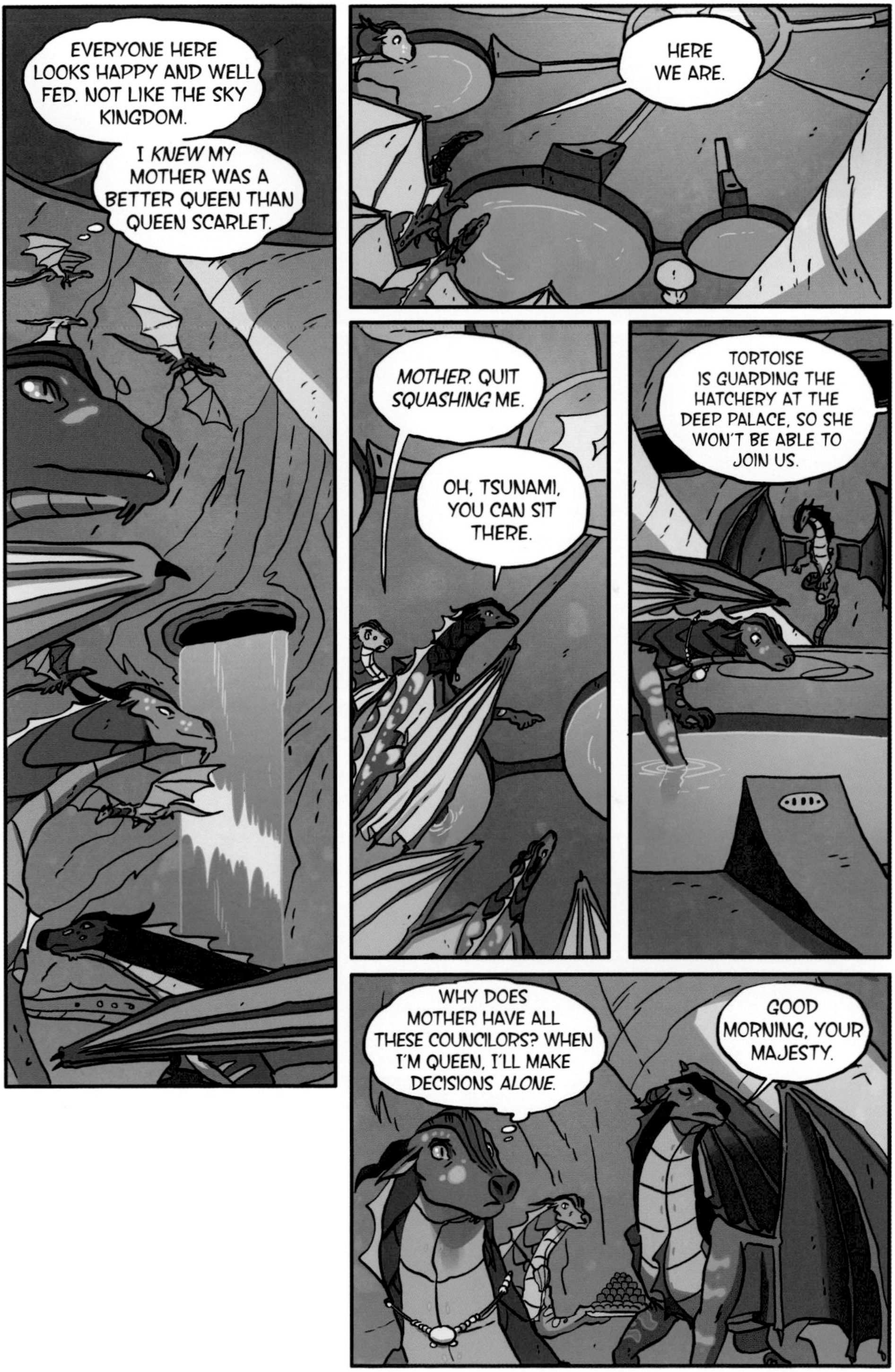
EVERYONE HERE LOOKS HAPPY AND WELL FED. NOT LIKE THE SKY KINGDOM.
I *KNEW* MY MOTHER WAS A BETTER QUEEN THAN QUEEN SCARLET.
HERE WE ARE.
MOTHER. QUIT *SQUASHING* ME.
OH, TSUNAMI, YOU CAN SIT THERE.
TORTOISE IS GUARDING THE HATCHERY AT THE DEEP PALACE, SO SHE WON'T BE ABLE TO JOIN US.
WHY DOES MOTHER HAVE ALL THESE COUNCILORS? WHEN I'M QUEEN, I'LL MAKE DECISIONS *ALONE.*
GOOD MORNING, YOUR MAJESTY.

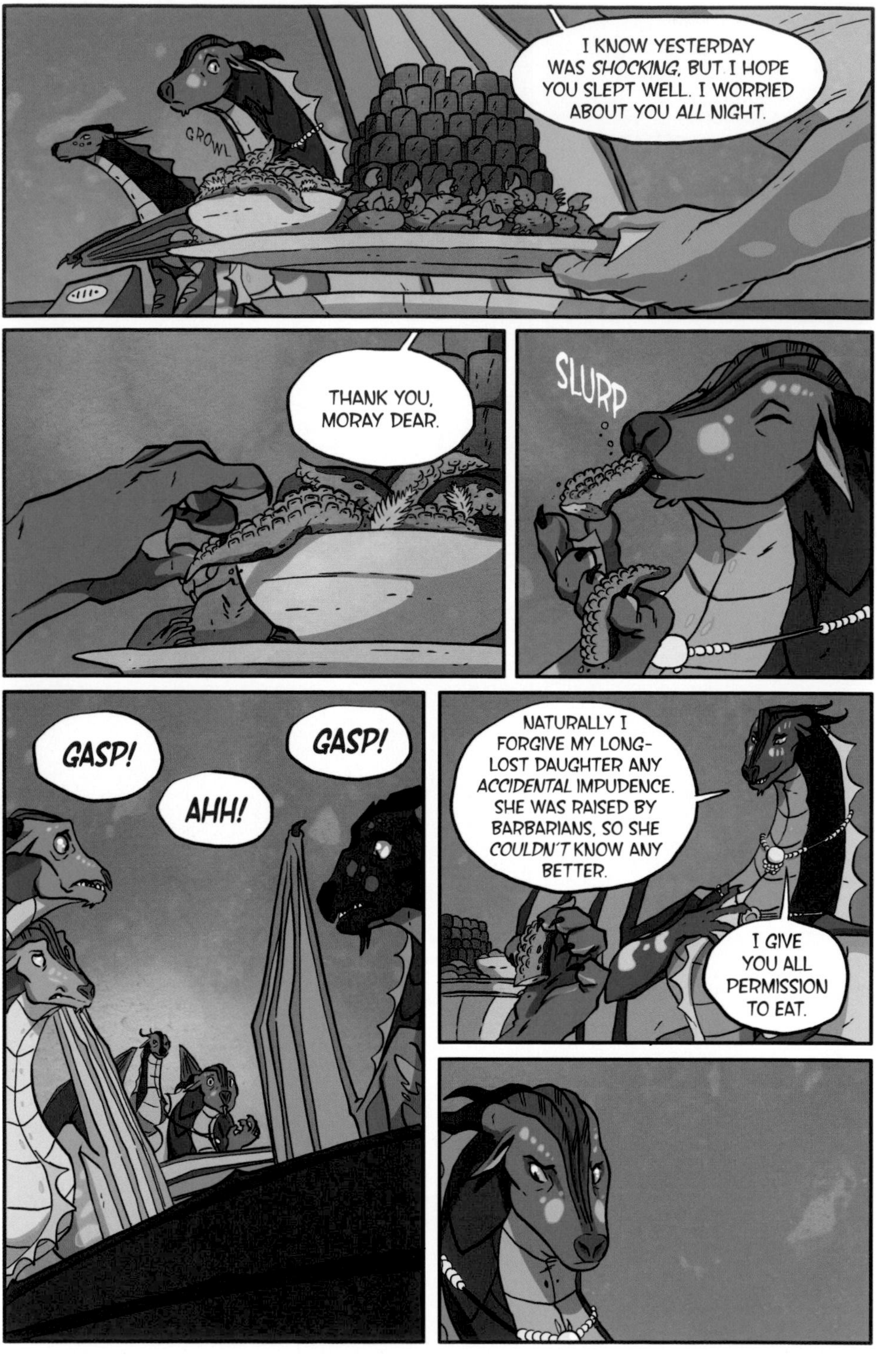
I KNOW YESTERDAY WAS *SHOCKING*, BUT I HOPE YOU SLEPT WELL. I WORRIED ABOUT YOU *ALL* NIGHT.
GROWL
THANK YOU, MORAY DEAR.
SLURP
GASP!
AHH!
GASP!
NATURALLY I FORGIVE MY LONG-LOST DAUGHTER ANY *ACCIDENTAL* IMPUDENCE. SHE WAS RAISED BY BARBARIANS, SO SHE *COULDN'T* KNOW ANY BETTER.
I GIVE YOU ALL PERMISSION TO EAT.

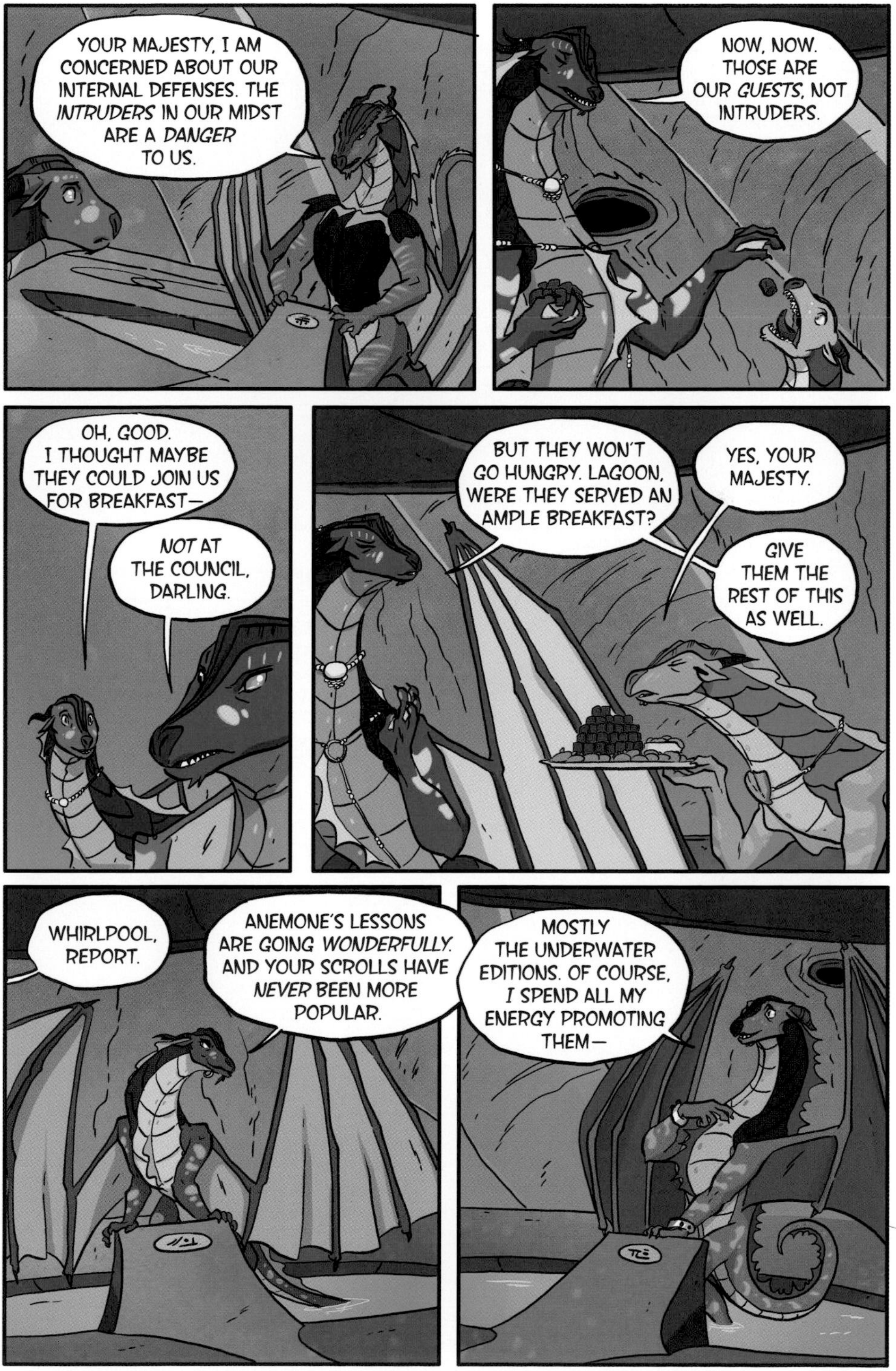
YOUR MAJESTY, I AM CONCERNED ABOUT OUR INTERNAL DEFENSES. THE *INTRUDERS* IN OUR MIDST ARE A *DANGER* TO US.
NOW, NOW. THOSE ARE OUR *GUESTS*, NOT INTRUDERS.
OH, GOOD. I THOUGHT MAYBE THEY COULD JOIN US FOR BREAKFAST—
NOT AT THE COUNCIL, DARLING.
BUT THEY WON'T GO HUNGRY. LAGOON, WERE THEY SERVED AN AMPLE BREAKFAST?
YES, YOUR MAJESTY.
GIVE THEM THE REST OF THIS AS WELL.
WHIRLPOOL, REPORT.
ANEMONE'S LESSONS ARE GOING *WONDERFULLY*. AND YOUR SCROLLS HAVE *NEVER* BEEN MORE POPULAR.
MOSTLY THE UNDERWATER EDITIONS. OF COURSE, *I* SPEND ALL MY ENERGY PROMOTING THEM—

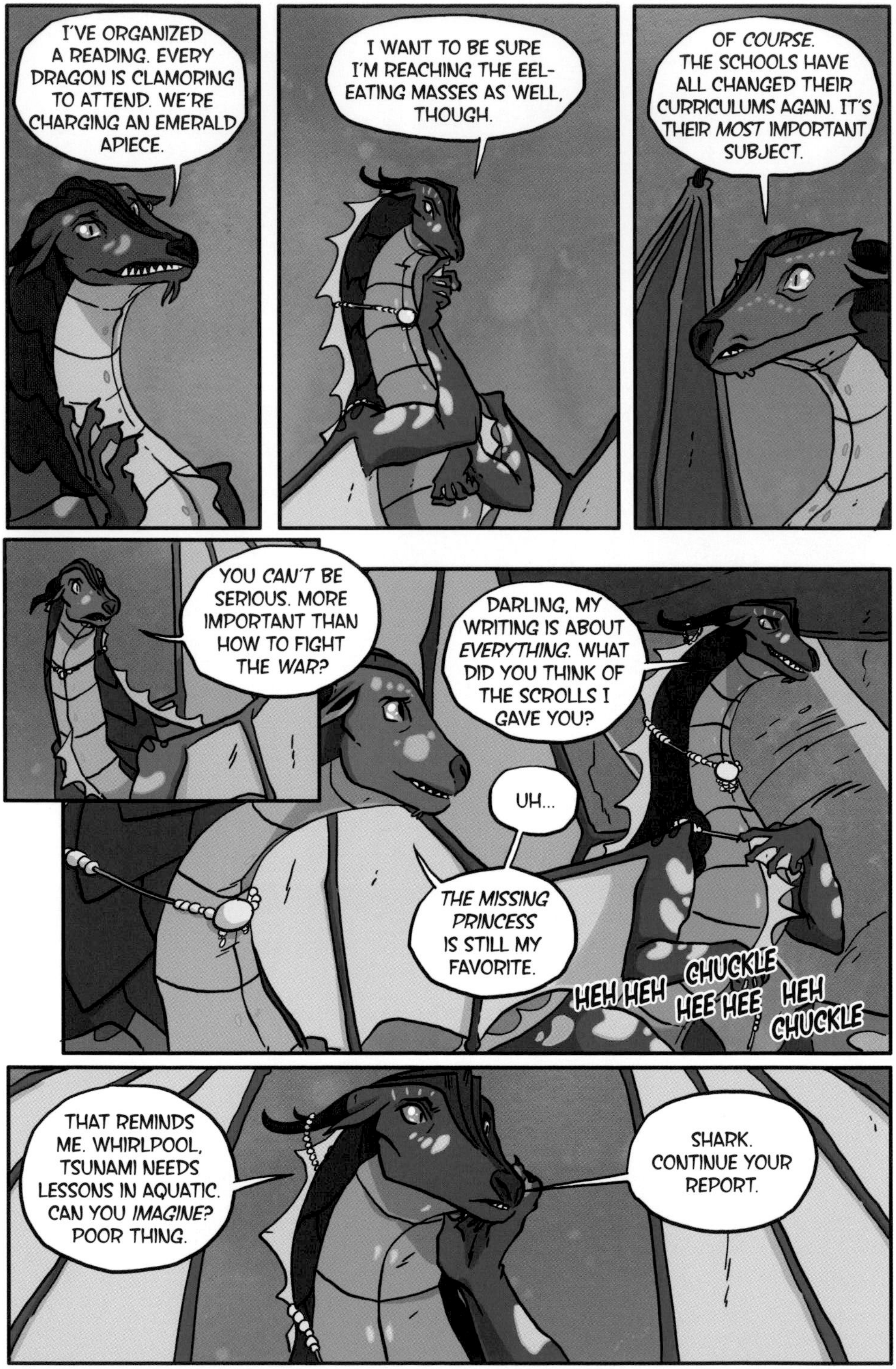
I'VE ORGANIZED A READING. EVERY DRAGON IS CLAMORING TO ATTEND. WE'RE CHARGING AN EMERALD APIECE.
I WANT TO BE SURE I'M REACHING THE EEL-EATING MASSES AS WELL, THOUGH.
OF *COURSE*. THE SCHOOLS HAVE ALL CHANGED THEIR CURRICULUMS AGAIN. IT'S THEIR *MOST* IMPORTANT SUBJECT.
YOU *CAN'T* BE SERIOUS. MORE IMPORTANT THAN HOW TO FIGHT THE *WAR*?
DARLING, MY WRITING IS ABOUT *EVERYTHING*. WHAT DID YOU THINK OF THE SCROLLS I GAVE YOU?
UH...
THE MISSING PRINCESS IS STILL MY FAVORITE.
HEH HEH
CHUCKLE
HEE HEE
HEH
CHUCKLE
THAT REMINDS ME. WHIRLPOOL, TSUNAMI NEEDS LESSONS IN AQUATIC. CAN YOU *IMAGINE*? POOR THING.
SHARK. CONTINUE YOUR REPORT.

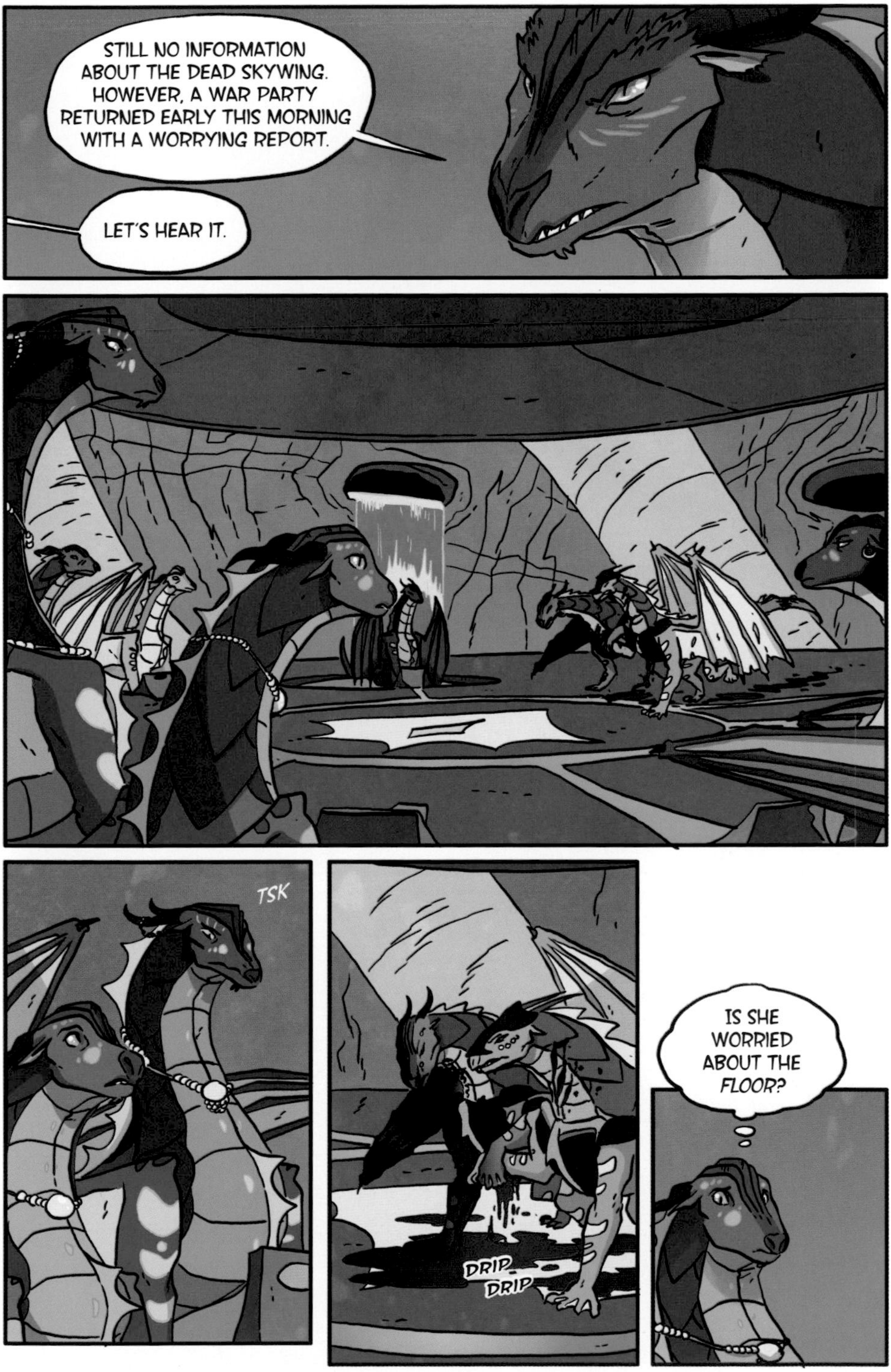
STILL NO INFORMATION ABOUT THE DEAD SKYWING. HOWEVER, A WAR PARTY RETURNED EARLY THIS MORNING WITH A WORRYING REPORT.
LET'S HEAR IT.
TSK
DRIP DRIP
IS SHE WORRIED ABOUT THE *FLOOR?*

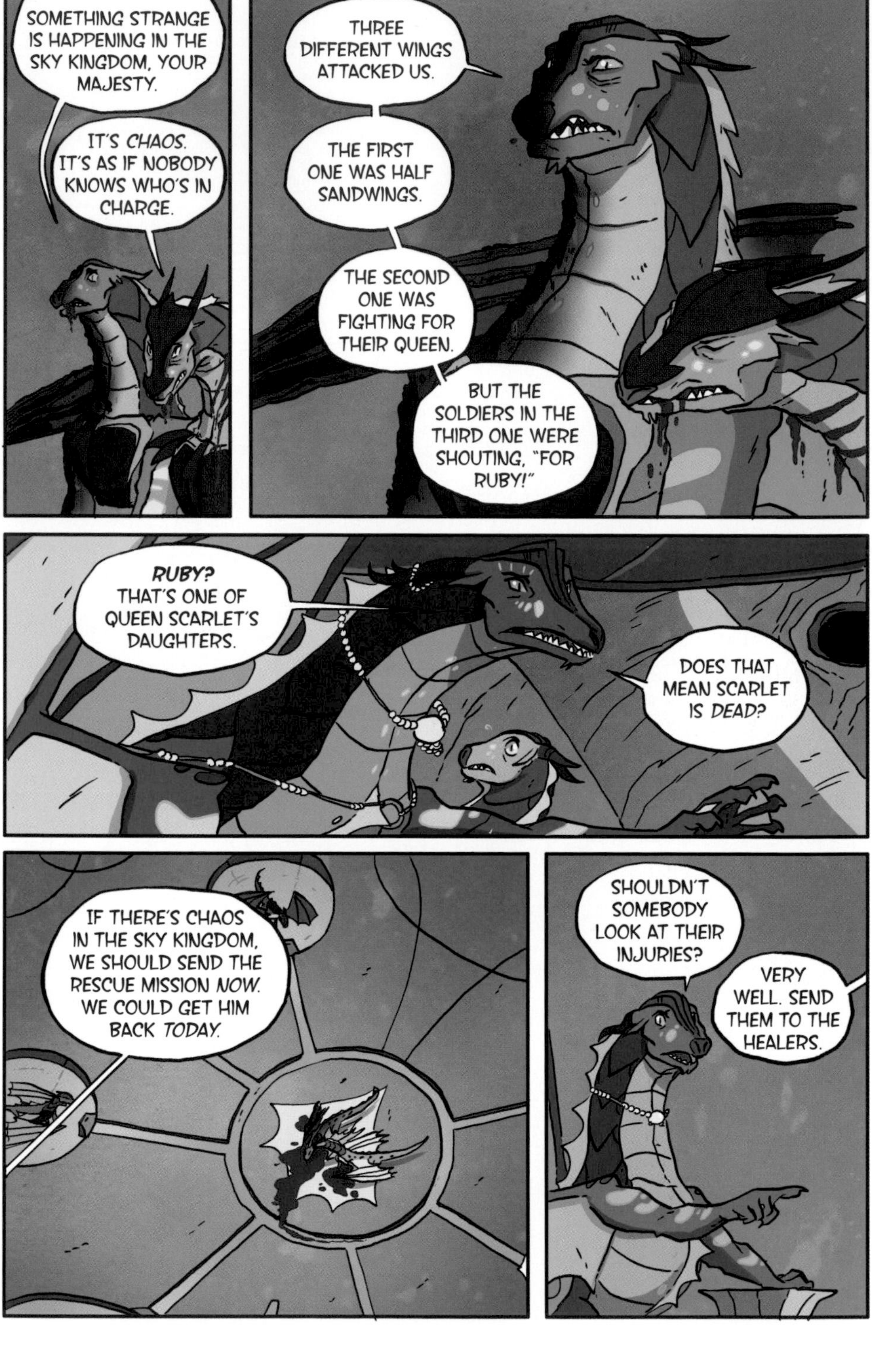
SOMETHING STRANGE IS HAPPENING IN THE SKY KINGDOM, YOUR MAJESTY.
IT'S *CHAOS*. IT'S AS IF NOBODY KNOWS WHO'S IN CHARGE.
THREE DIFFERENT WINGS ATTACKED US.
THE FIRST ONE WAS HALF SANDWINGS.
THE SECOND ONE WAS FIGHTING FOR THEIR QUEEN.
BUT THE SOLDIERS IN THE THIRD ONE WERE SHOUTING, "FOR RUBY!"
RUBY? THAT'S ONE OF QUEEN SCARLET'S DAUGHTERS.
DOES THAT MEAN SCARLET IS *DEAD?*
IF THERE'S CHAOS IN THE SKY KINGDOM, WE SHOULD SEND THE RESCUE MISSION *NOW*. WE COULD GET HIM BACK *TODAY*.
SHOULDN'T SOMEBODY LOOK AT THEIR INJURIES?
VERY WELL. SEND THEM TO THE HEALERS.

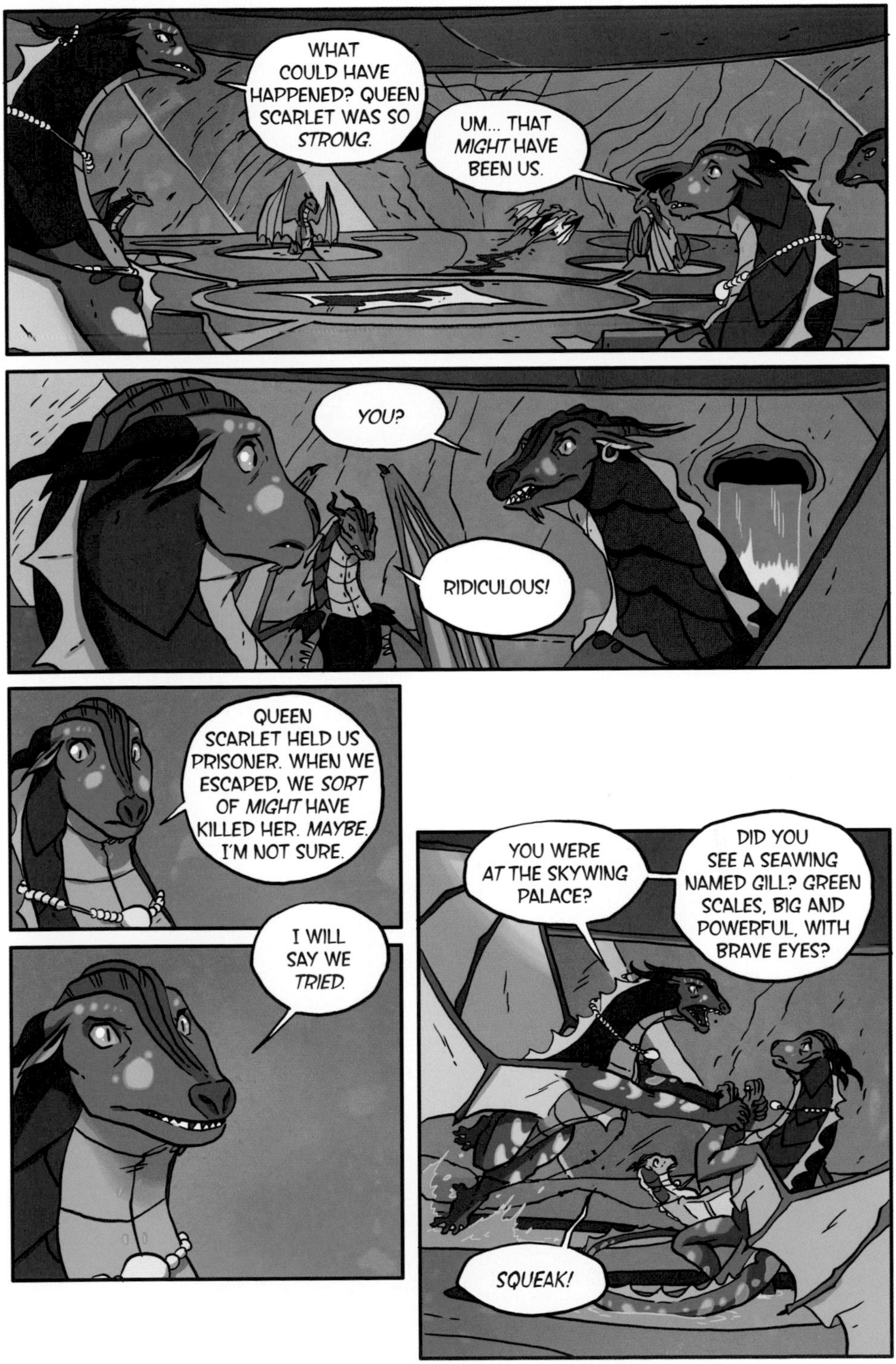
WHAT COULD HAVE HAPPENED? QUEEN SCARLET WAS SO *STRONG*.
UM... THAT *MIGHT* HAVE BEEN US.
YOU?
RIDICULOUS!
QUEEN SCARLET HELD US PRISONER. WHEN WE ESCAPED, WE *SORT* OF *MIGHT* HAVE KILLED HER. *MAYBE*. I'M NOT SURE.
I WILL SAY WE *TRIED*.
YOU WERE AT THE SKYWING PALACE?
DID YOU SEE A SEAWING NAMED GILL? GREEN SCALES, BIG AND POWERFUL, WITH BRAVE EYES?
SQUEAK!

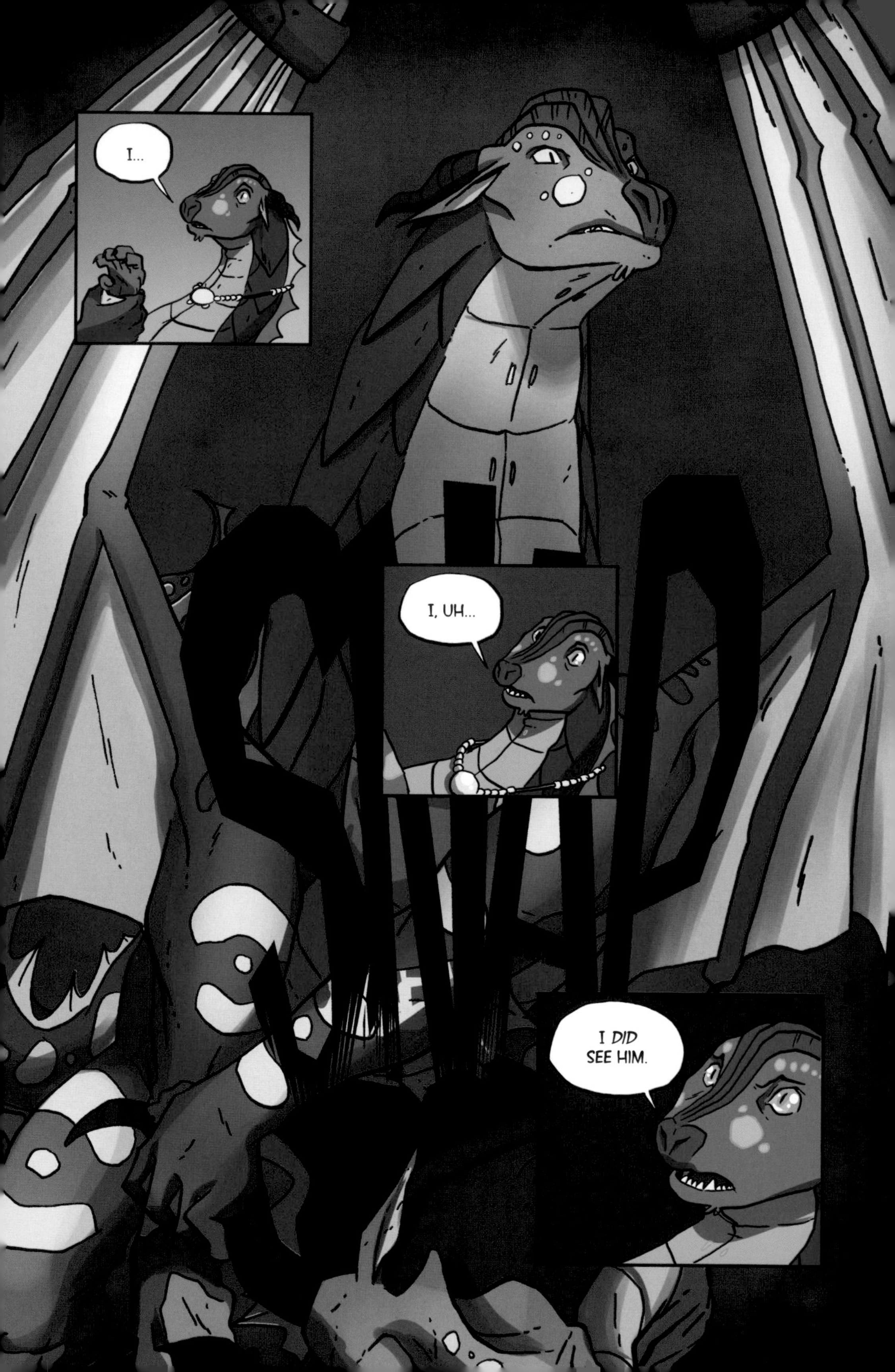
I...
I, UH...
I DID SEE HIM.

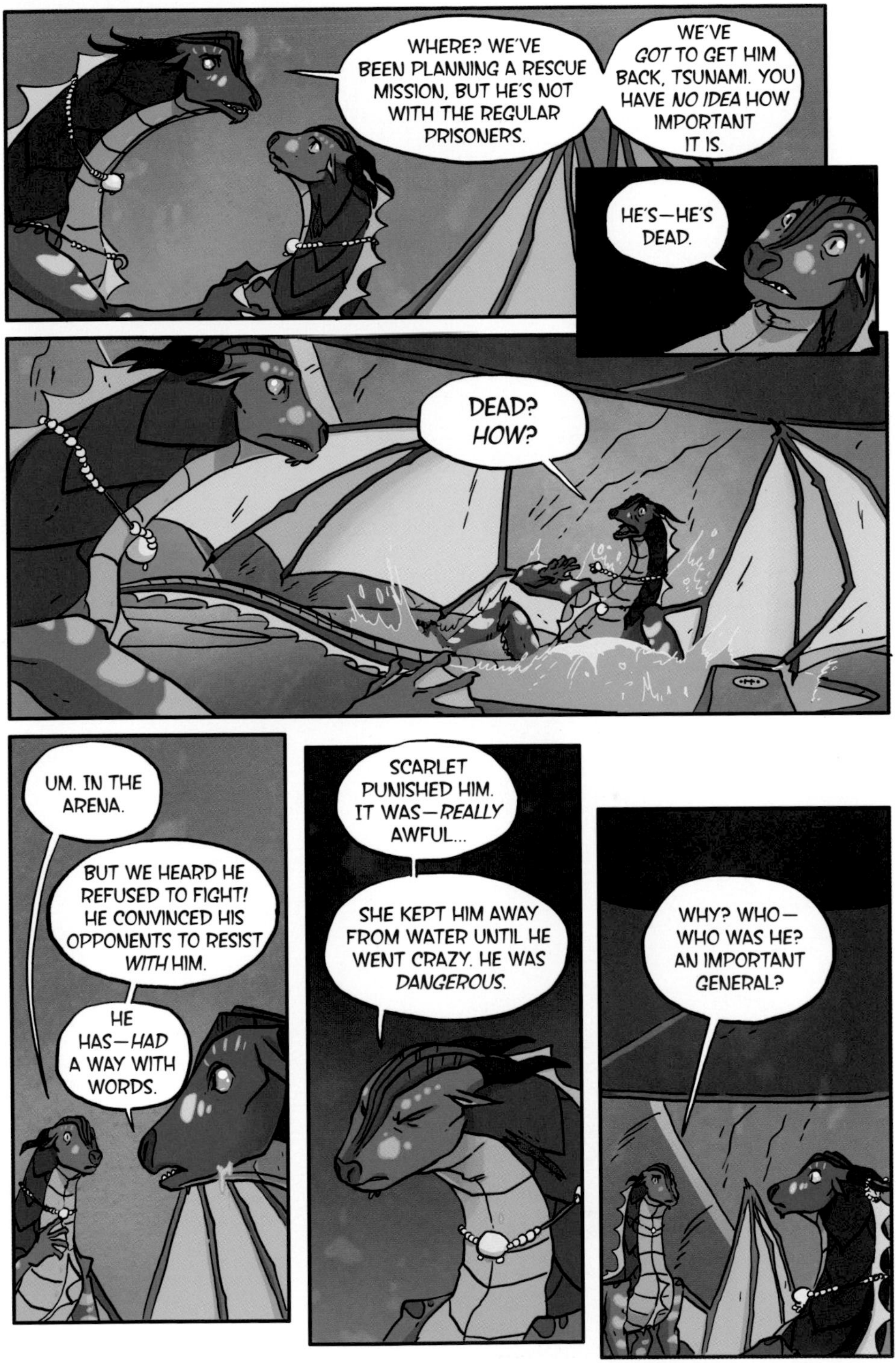
WHERE? WE'VE BEEN PLANNING A RESCUE MISSION, BUT HE'S NOT WITH THE REGULAR PRISONERS.
WE'VE *GOT* TO GET HIM BACK, TSUNAMI. YOU HAVE *NO IDEA* HOW IMPORTANT IT IS.
HE'S—HE'S DEAD.
DEAD? *HOW?*
UM. IN THE ARENA.
BUT WE HEARD HE REFUSED TO FIGHT! HE CONVINCED HIS OPPONENTS TO RESIST *WITH* HIM.
HE HAS—*HAD* A WAY WITH WORDS.
SCARLET PUNISHED HIM. IT WAS—*REALLY* AWFUL...
SHE KEPT HIM AWAY FROM WATER UNTIL HE WENT CRAZY. HE WAS *DANGEROUS*.
WHY? WHO—WHO WAS HE? AN IMPORTANT GENERAL?

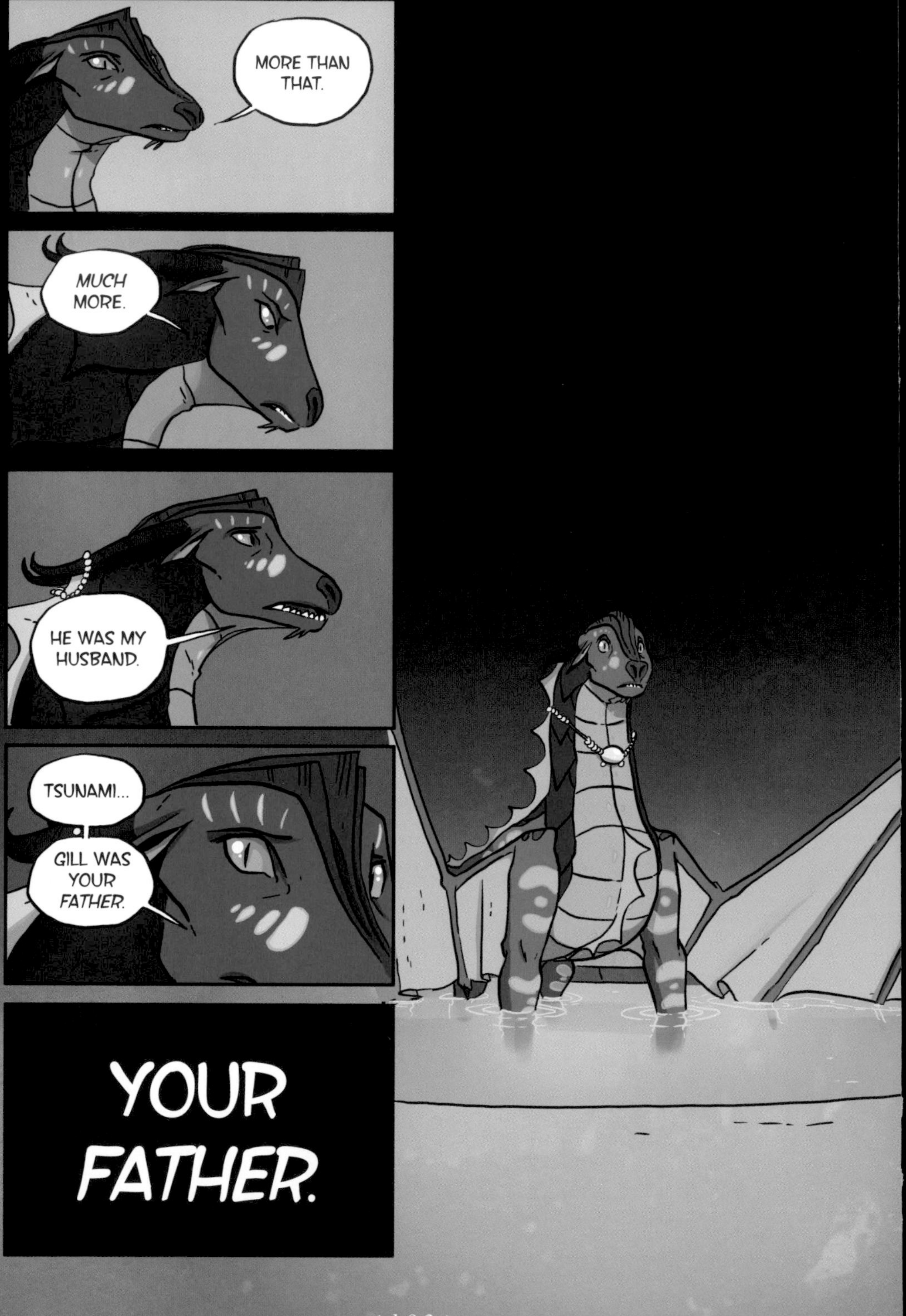
MORE THAN THAT.
MUCH MORE.
HE WAS MY HUSBAND.
TSUNAMI...
GILL WAS YOUR FATHER.
YOUR FATHER.

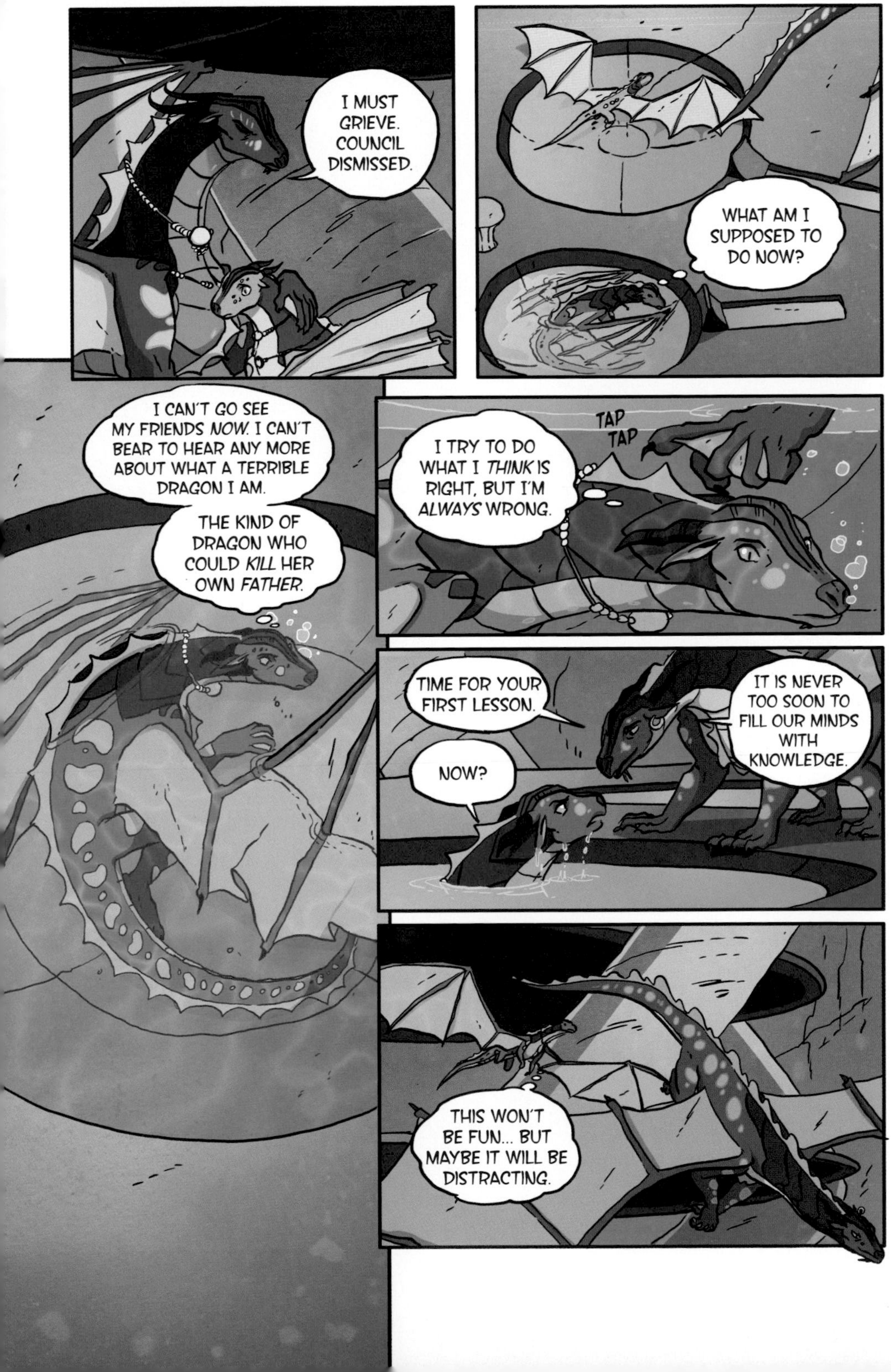
I MUST GRIEVE. COUNCIL DISMISSED.
WHAT AM I SUPPOSED TO DO NOW?
I CAN'T GO SEE MY FRIENDS *NOW*. I CAN'T BEAR TO HEAR ANY MORE ABOUT WHAT A TERRIBLE DRAGON I AM.
THE KIND OF DRAGON WHO COULD *KILL* HER OWN *FATHER*.
TAP TAP
I TRY TO DO WHAT I *THINK* IS RIGHT, BUT I'M *ALWAYS* WRONG.
TIME FOR YOUR FIRST LESSON.
IT IS NEVER TOO SOON TO FILL OUR MINDS WITH KNOWLEDGE.
NOW?
THIS WON'T BE FUN... BUT MAYBE IT WILL BE DISTRACTING.

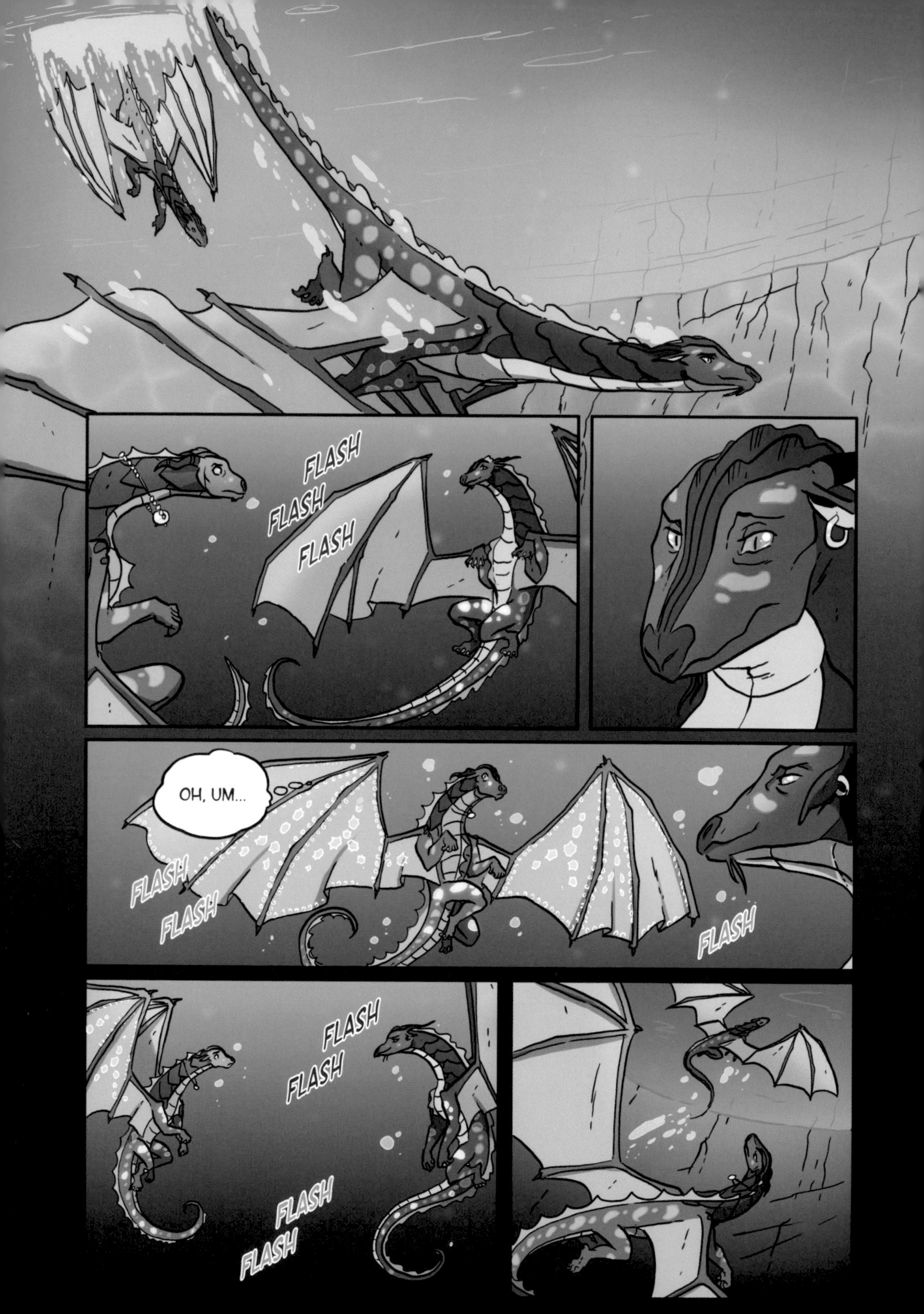
FLASH
FLASH
FLASH
OH, UM...
FLASH
FLASH
FLASH
FLASH
FLASH
FLASH
FLASH

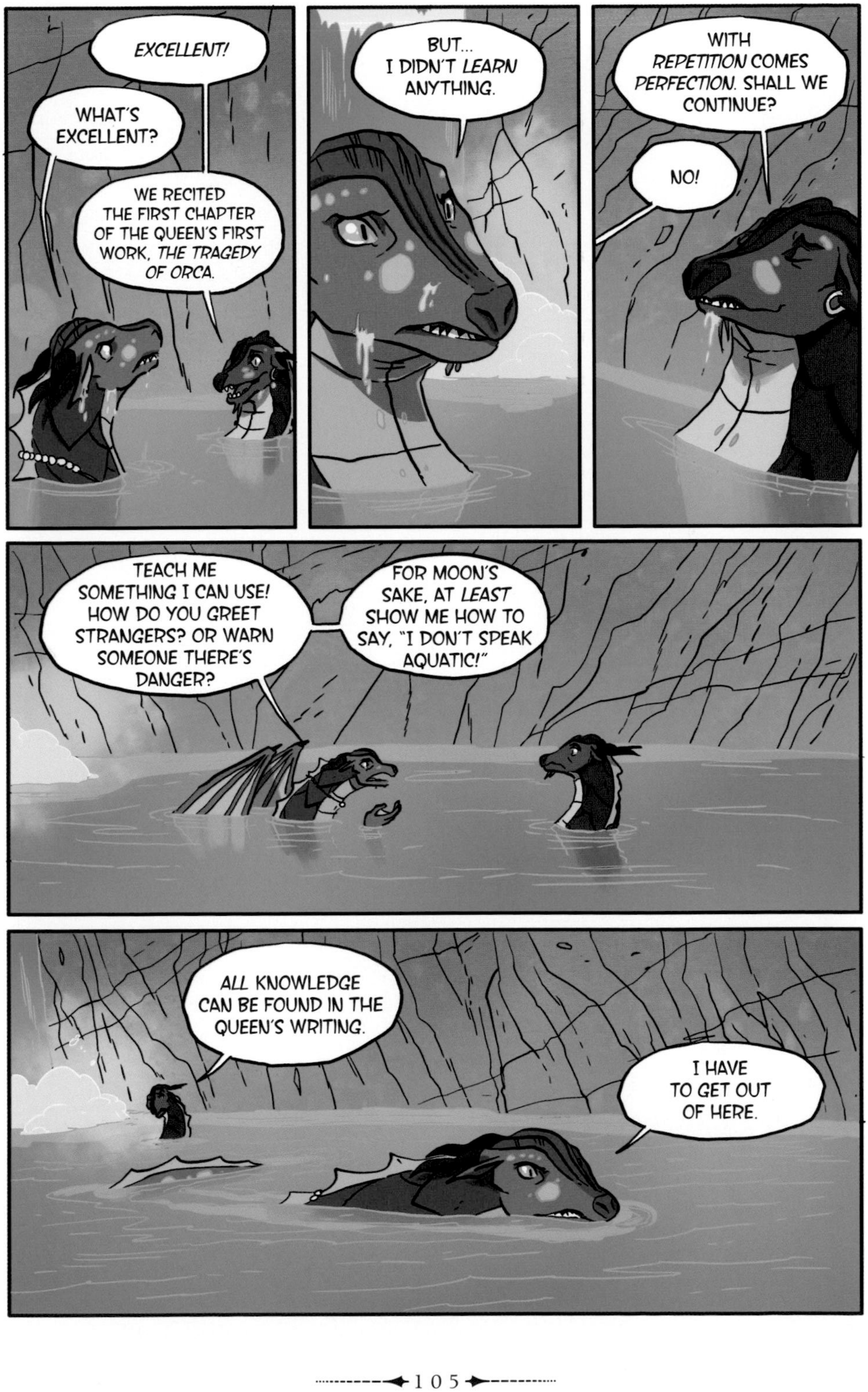
EXCELLENT!
WHAT'S EXCELLENT?
WE RECITED THE FIRST CHAPTER OF THE QUEEN'S FIRST WORK, *THE TRAGEDY OF ORCA*.
BUT... I DIDN'T *LEARN* ANYTHING.
WITH *REPETITION* COMES *PERFECTION*. SHALL WE CONTINUE?
NO!
TEACH ME SOMETHING I CAN USE! HOW DO YOU GREET STRANGERS? OR WARN SOMEONE THERE'S DANGER?
FOR MOON'S SAKE, AT *LEAST* SHOW ME HOW TO SAY, "I DON'T SPEAK AQUATIC!"
ALL KNOWLEDGE CAN BE FOUND IN THE QUEEN'S WRITING.
I HAVE TO GET OUT OF HERE.

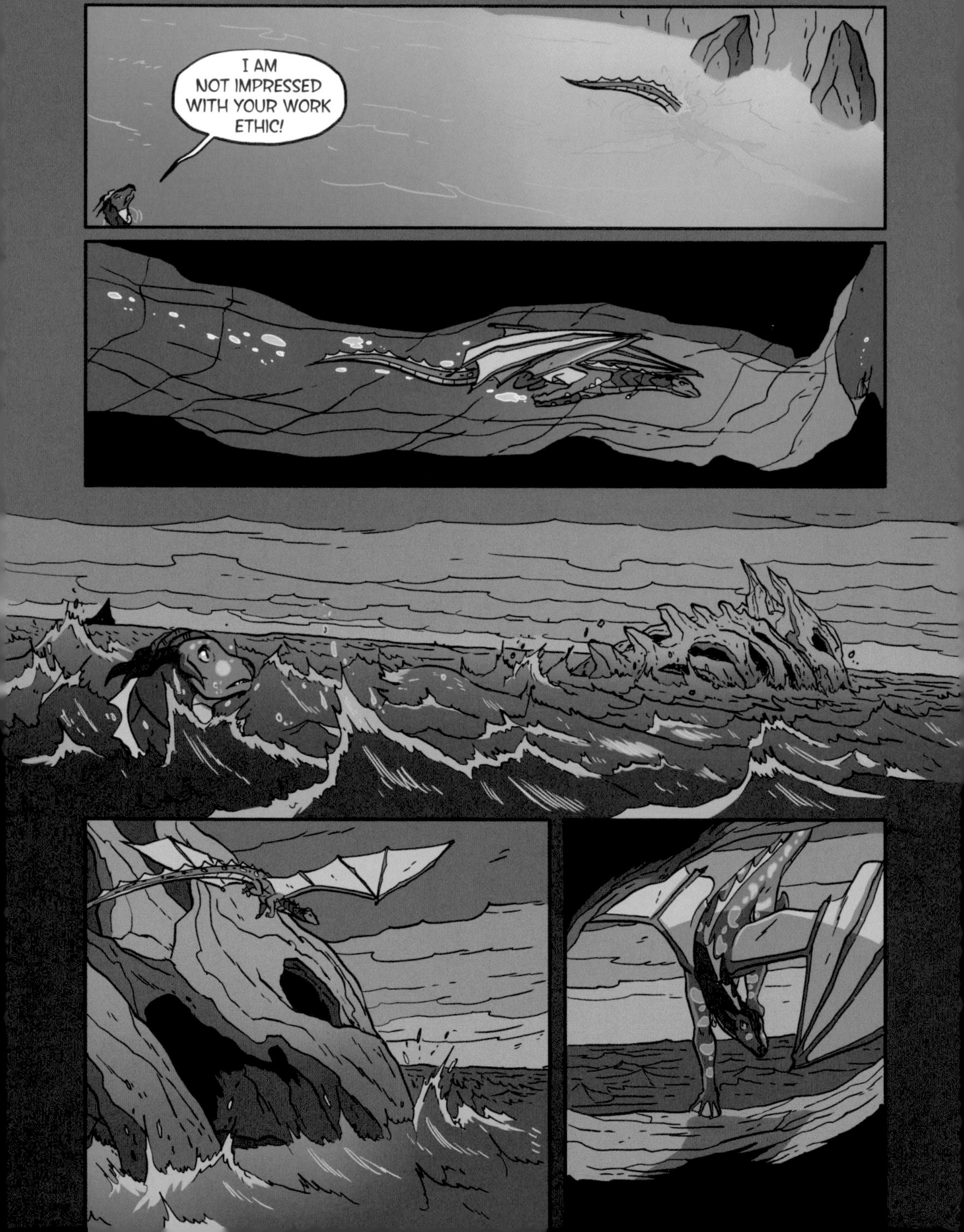
I AM NOT IMPRESSED WITH YOUR WORK ETHIC!

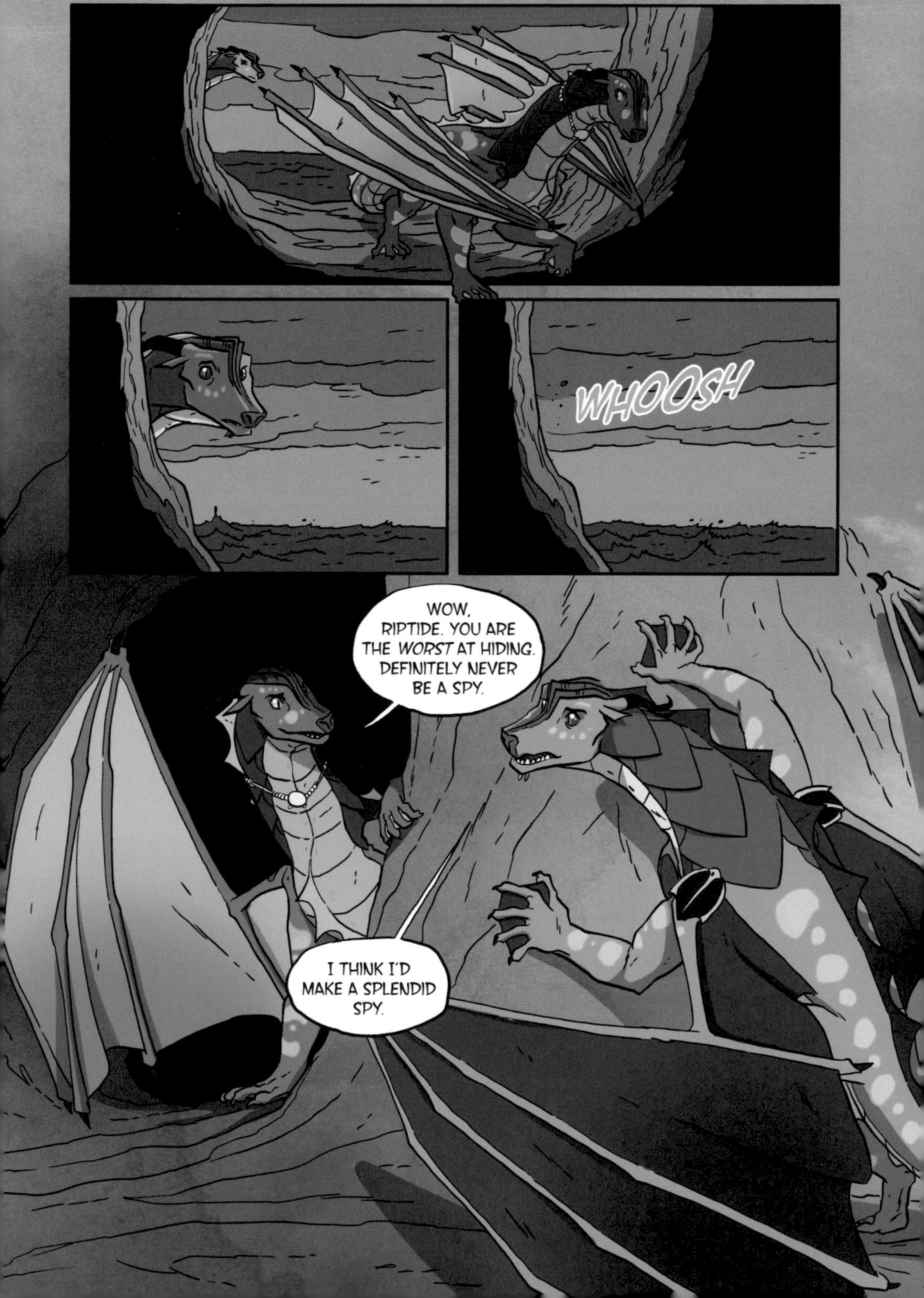

WHOOSH
WOW, RIPTIDE. YOU ARE THE *WORST* AT HIDING. DEFINITELY NEVER BE A SPY.
I THINK I'D MAKE A SPLENDID SPY.

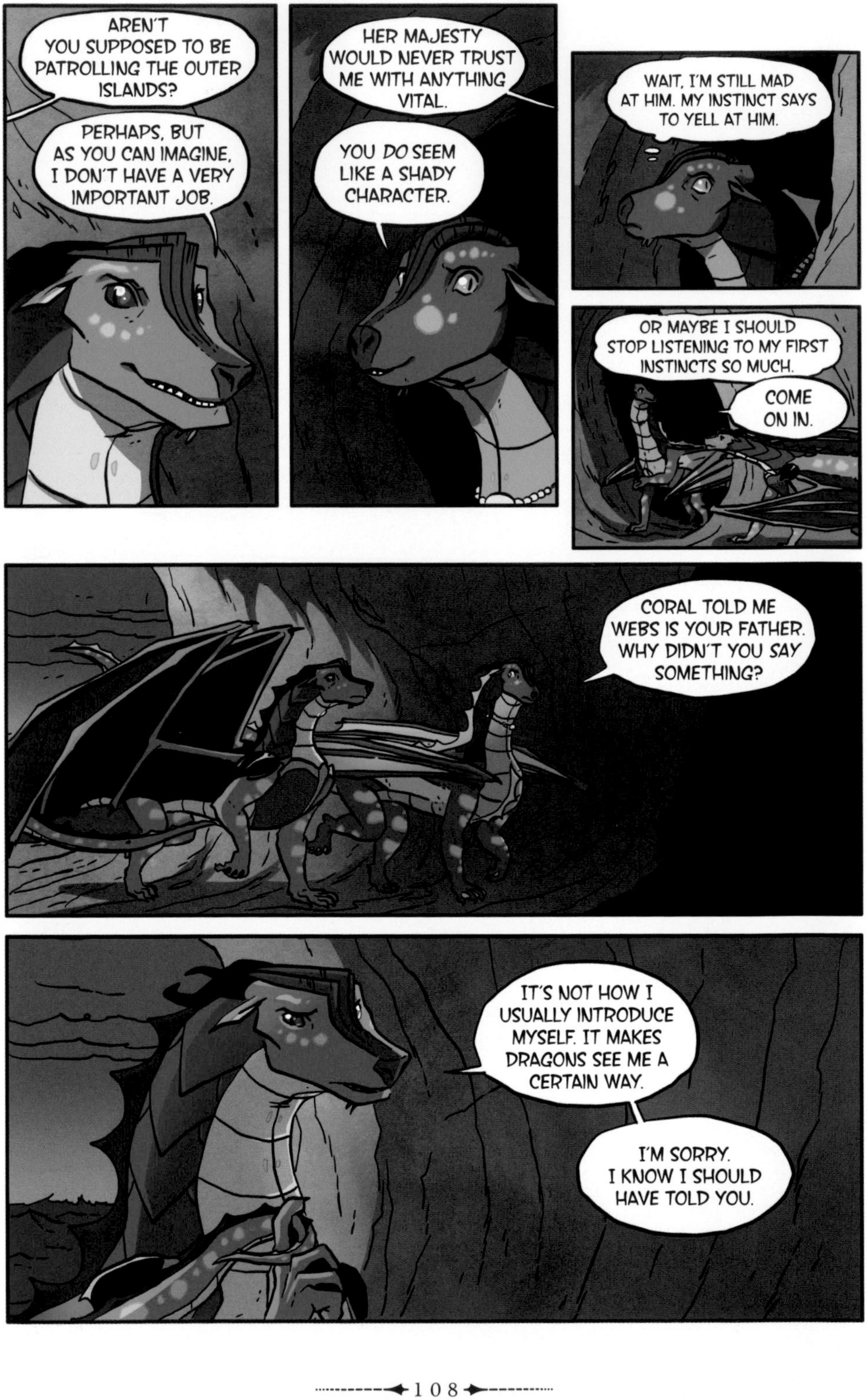
AREN'T YOU SUPPOSED TO BE PATROLLING THE OUTER ISLANDS?
PERHAPS, BUT AS YOU CAN IMAGINE, I DON'T HAVE A VERY IMPORTANT JOB.
HER MAJESTY WOULD NEVER TRUST ME WITH ANYTHING VITAL.
YOU *DO* SEEM LIKE A SHADY CHARACTER.
WAIT, I'M STILL MAD AT HIM. MY INSTINCT SAYS TO YELL AT HIM.
OR MAYBE I SHOULD STOP LISTENING TO MY FIRST INSTINCTS SO MUCH.
COME ON IN.
CORAL TOLD ME WEBS IS YOUR FATHER. WHY DIDN'T YOU *SAY* SOMETHING?
IT'S NOT HOW I USUALLY INTRODUCE MYSELF. IT MAKES DRAGONS SEE ME A CERTAIN WAY.
I'M SORRY. I KNOW I SHOULD HAVE TOLD YOU.

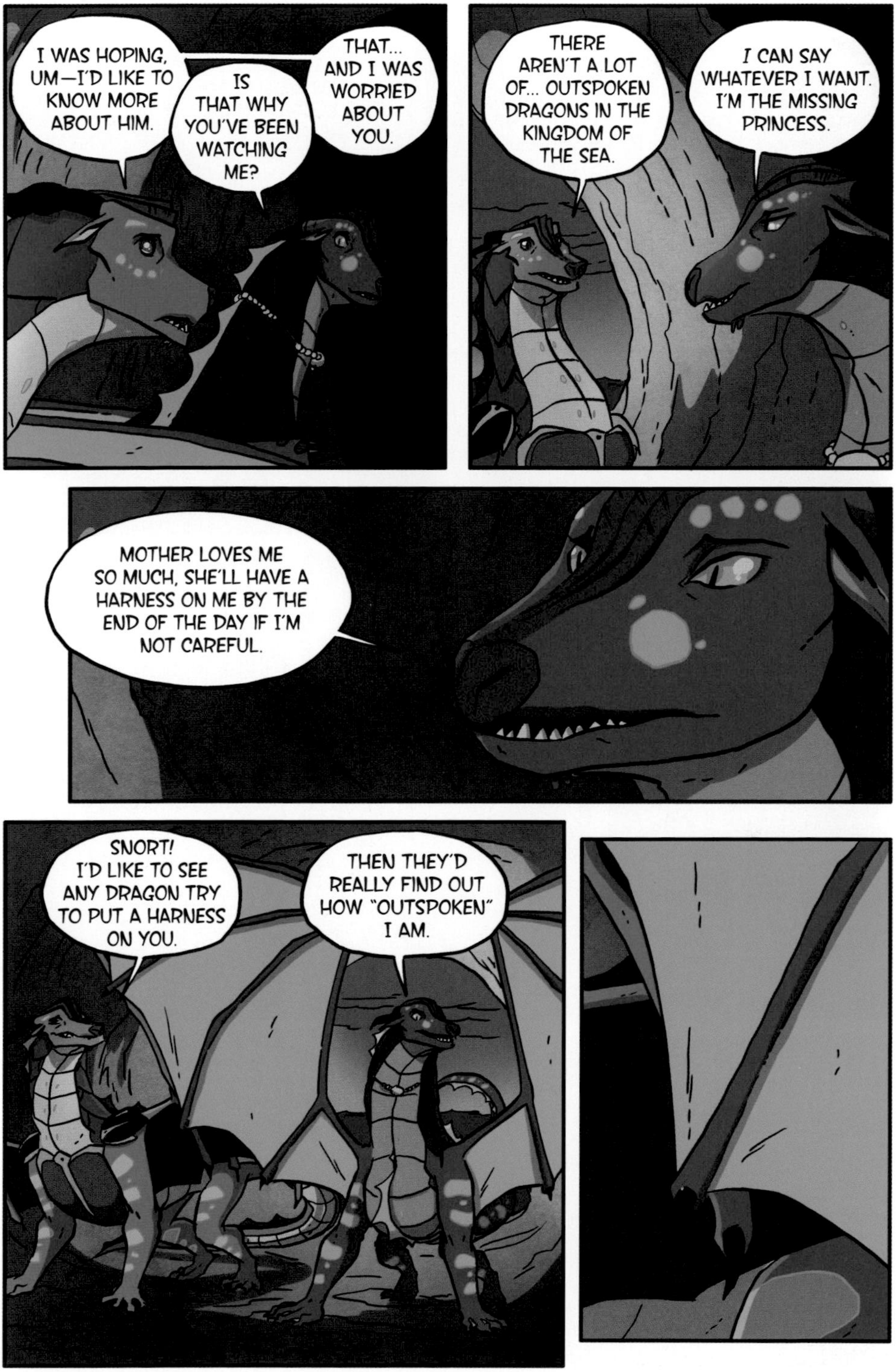

I WAS HOPING, UM—I'D LIKE TO KNOW MORE ABOUT HIM.
IS THAT WHY YOU'VE BEEN WATCHING ME?
THAT... AND I WAS WORRIED ABOUT YOU.
THERE AREN'T A LOT OF... OUTSPOKEN DRAGONS IN THE KINGDOM OF THE SEA.
I CAN SAY WHATEVER I WANT. I'M THE MISSING PRINCESS.
MOTHER LOVES ME SO MUCH, SHE'LL HAVE A HARNESS ON ME BY THE END OF THE DAY IF I'M NOT CAREFUL.
SNORT! I'D LIKE TO SEE ANY DRAGON TRY TO PUT A HARNESS ON YOU.
THEN THEY'D REALLY FIND OUT HOW "OUTSPOKEN" I AM.

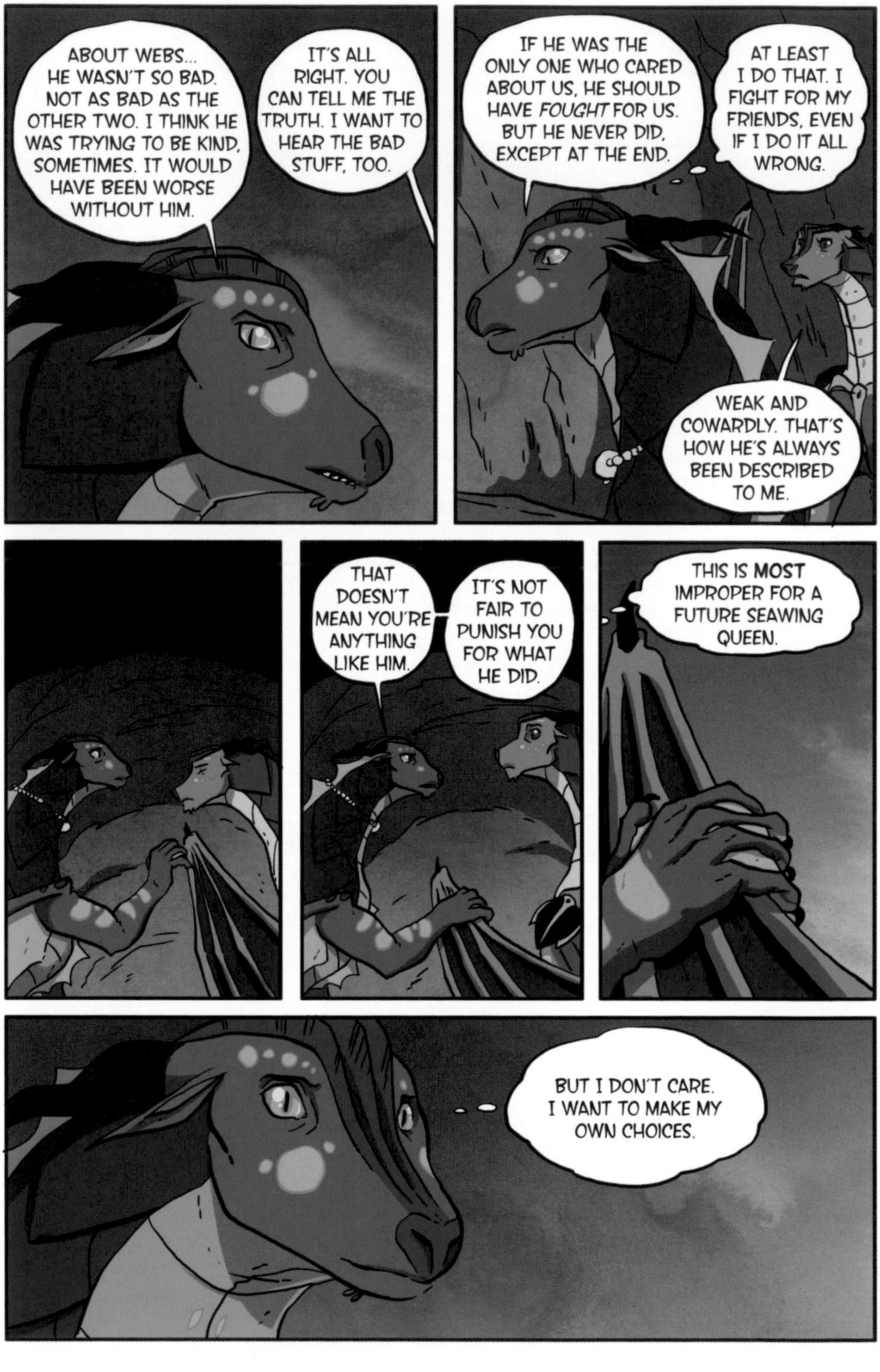
ABOUT WEBS... HE WASN'T SO BAD. NOT AS BAD AS THE OTHER TWO. I THINK HE WAS TRYING TO BE KIND, SOMETIMES. IT WOULD HAVE BEEN WORSE WITHOUT HIM.
IT'S ALL RIGHT. YOU CAN TELL ME THE TRUTH. I WANT TO HEAR THE BAD STUFF, TOO.
IF HE WAS THE ONLY ONE WHO CARED ABOUT US, HE SHOULD HAVE *FOUGHT* FOR US. BUT HE NEVER DID, EXCEPT AT THE END.
AT LEAST I DO THAT. I FIGHT FOR MY FRIENDS, EVEN IF I DO IT ALL WRONG.
WEAK AND COWARDLY. THAT'S HOW HE'S ALWAYS BEEN DESCRIBED TO ME.
THAT DOESN'T MEAN YOU'RE ANYTHING LIKE HIM.
IT'S NOT FAIR TO PUNISH YOU FOR WHAT HE DID.
THIS IS **MOST** IMPROPER FOR A FUTURE SEAWING QUEEN.
BUT I DON'T CARE. I WANT TO MAKE MY OWN CHOICES.

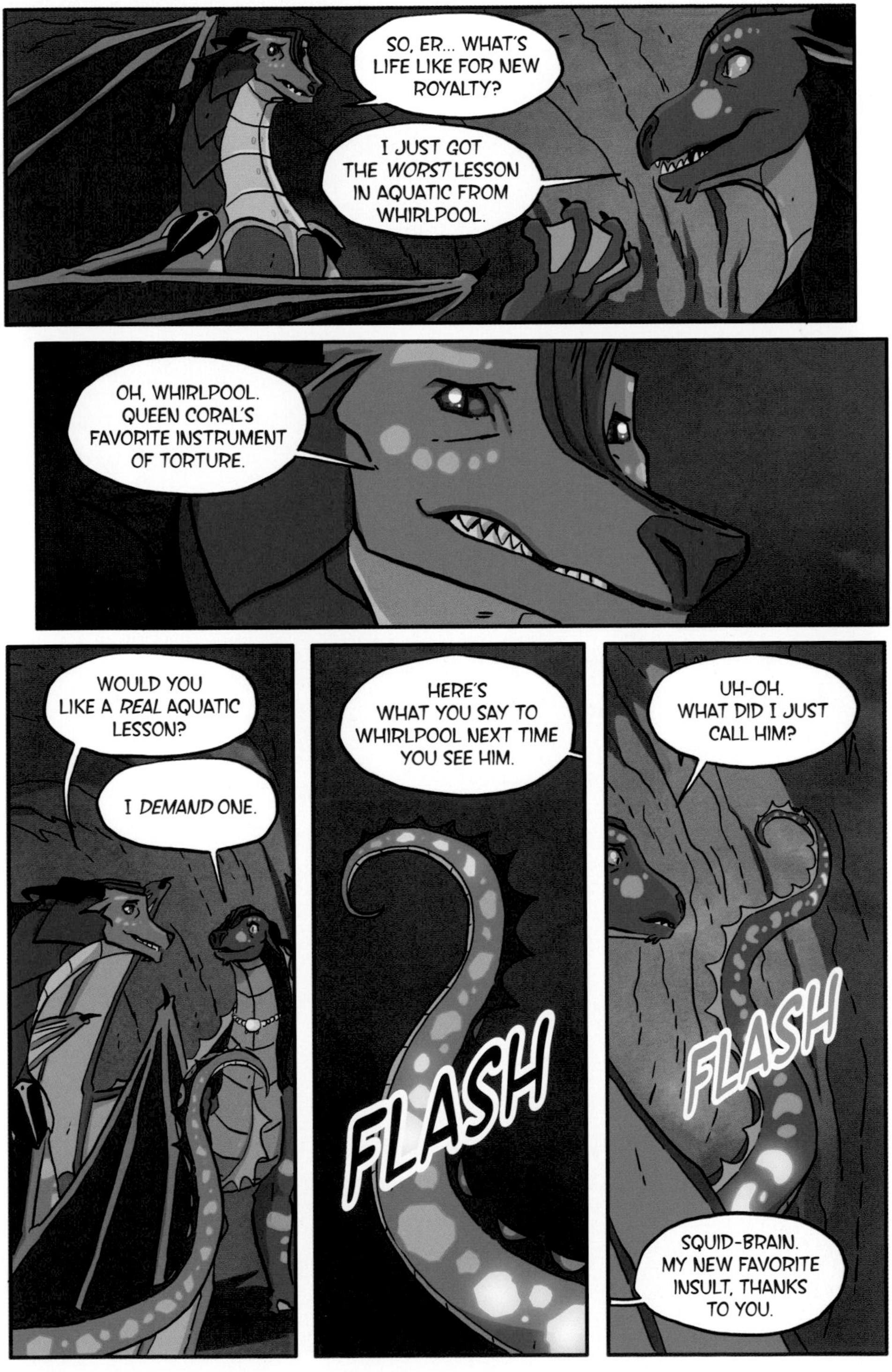
SO, ER... WHAT'S LIFE LIKE FOR NEW ROYALTY?
I JUST GOT THE *WORST* LESSON IN AQUATIC FROM WHIRLPOOL.
OH, WHIRLPOOL. QUEEN CORAL'S FAVORITE INSTRUMENT OF TORTURE.
WOULD YOU LIKE A *REAL* AQUATIC LESSON?
I *DEMAND* ONE.
HERE'S WHAT YOU SAY TO WHIRLPOOL NEXT TIME YOU SEE HIM.
FLASH
UH-OH. WHAT DID I JUST CALL HIM?
FLASH
SQUID-BRAIN. MY NEW FAVORITE INSULT, THANKS TO YOU.

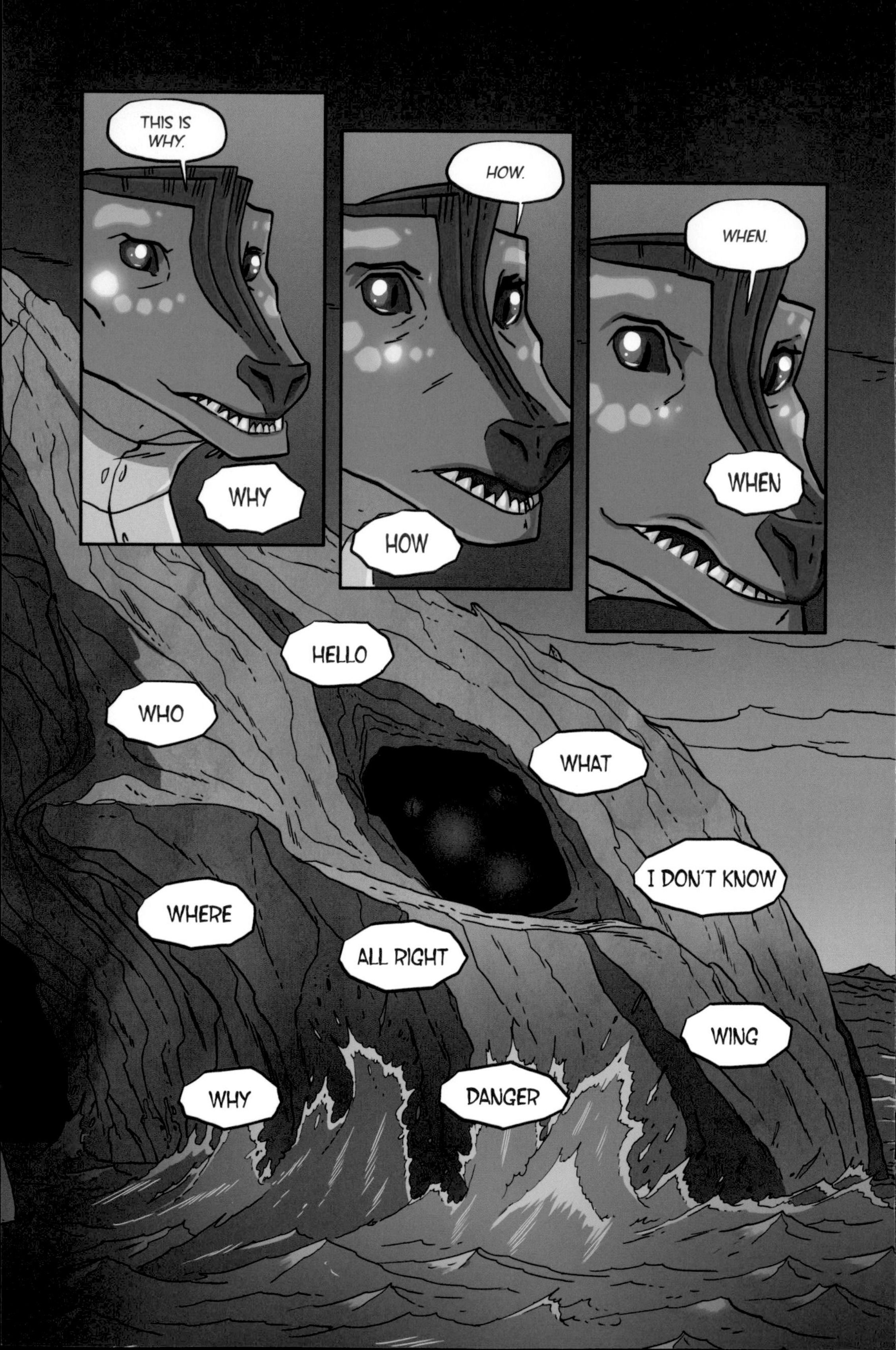
THIS IS WHY.
WHY
HOW.
HOW
WHEN.
WHEN
HELLO
WHO
WHAT
I DON'T KNOW
WHERE
ALL RIGHT
WING
WHY
DANGER

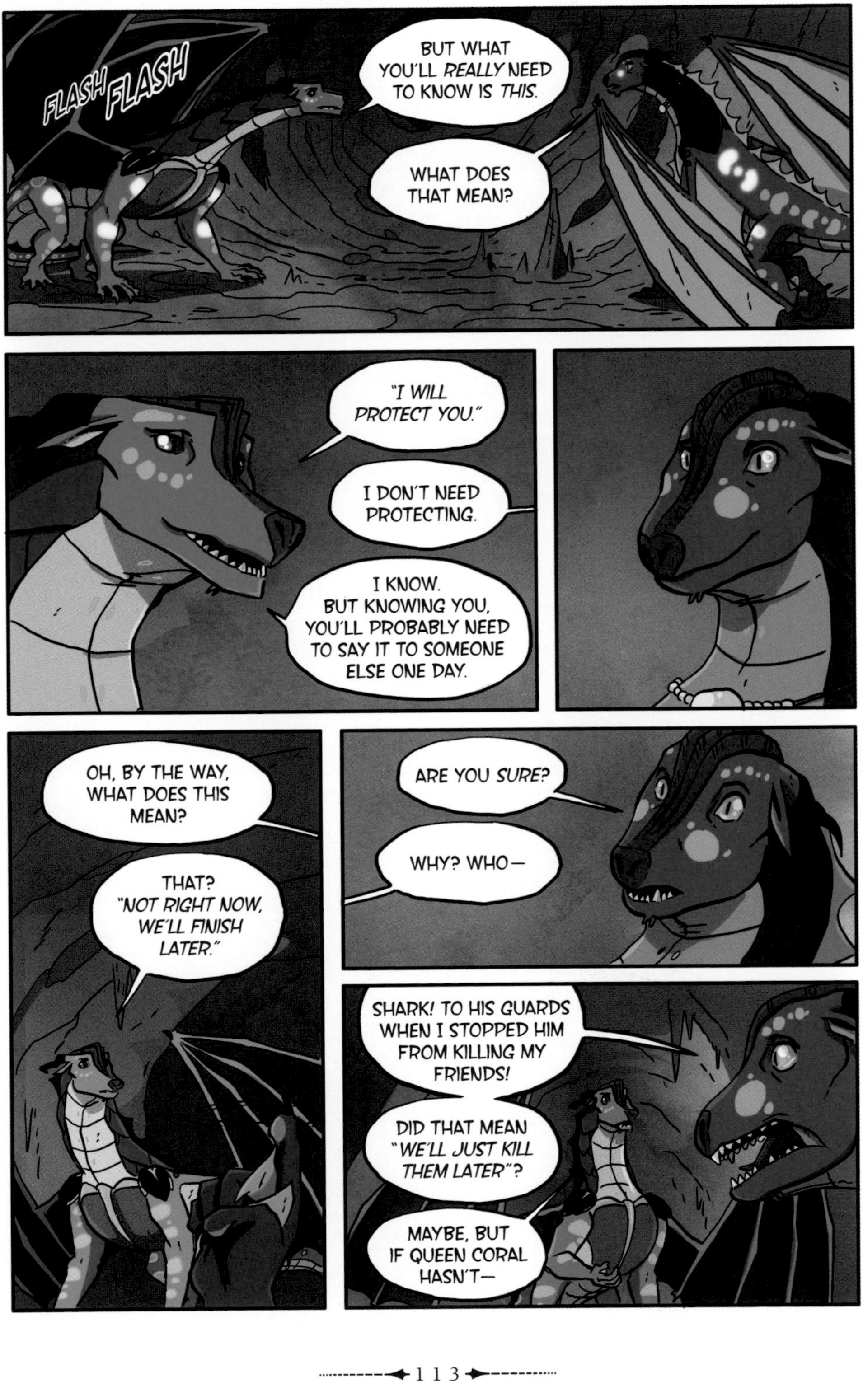
FLASH FLASH
BUT WHAT YOU'LL *REALLY* NEED TO KNOW IS *THIS*.
WHAT DOES THAT MEAN?
"I WILL PROTECT YOU."
I DON'T NEED PROTECTING.
I KNOW. BUT KNOWING YOU, YOU'LL PROBABLY NEED TO SAY IT TO SOMEONE ELSE ONE DAY.
OH, BY THE WAY, WHAT DOES THIS MEAN?
THAT? *"NOT RIGHT NOW, WE'LL FINISH LATER."*
ARE YOU *SURE*?
WHY? WHO—
SHARK! TO HIS GUARDS WHEN I STOPPED HIM FROM KILLING MY FRIENDS!
DID THAT MEAN *"WE'LL JUST KILL THEM LATER"*?
MAYBE, BUT IF QUEEN CORAL HASN'T—

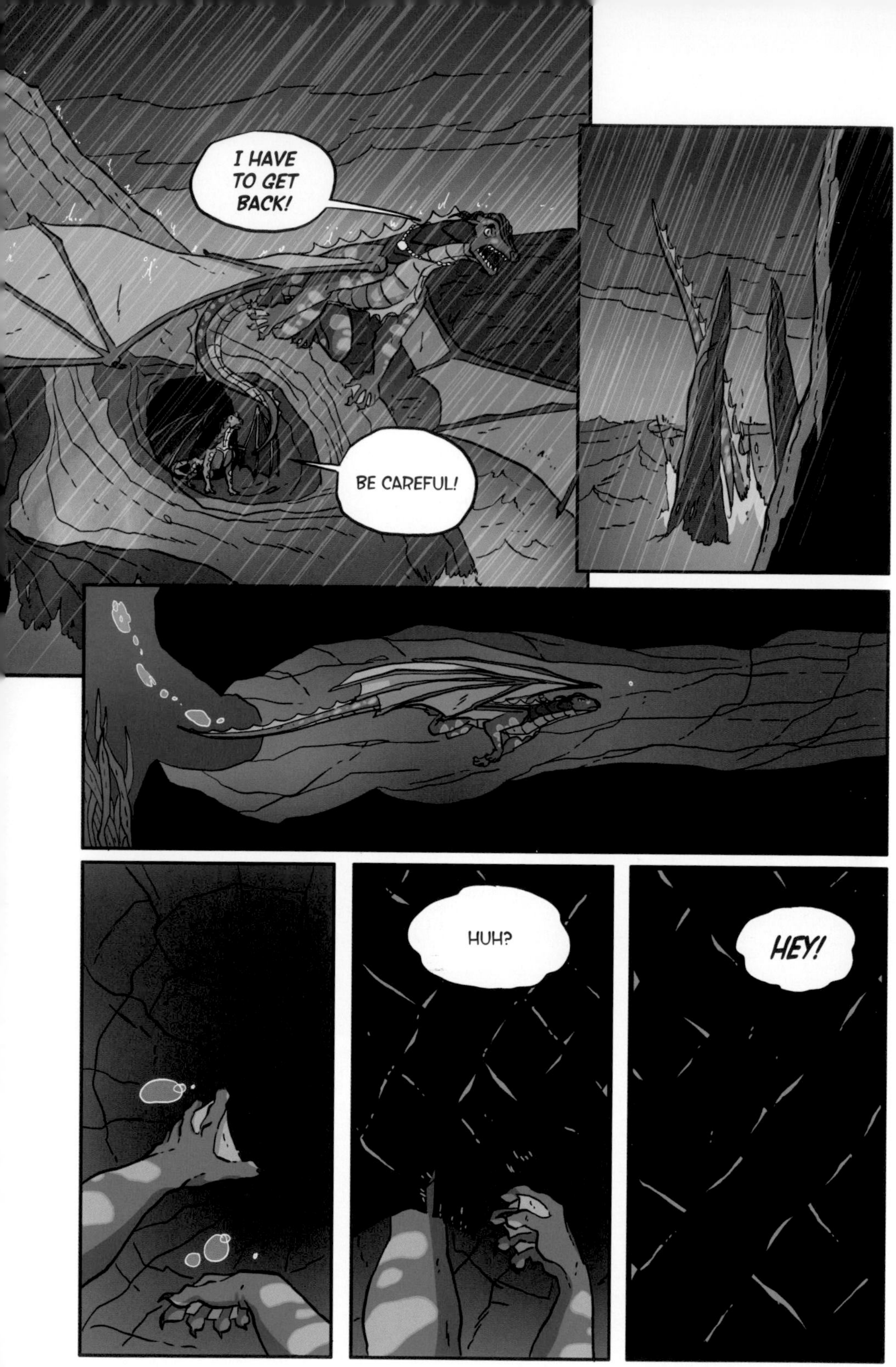
I HAVE TO GET BACK!
BE CAREFUL!
HUH?
HEY!

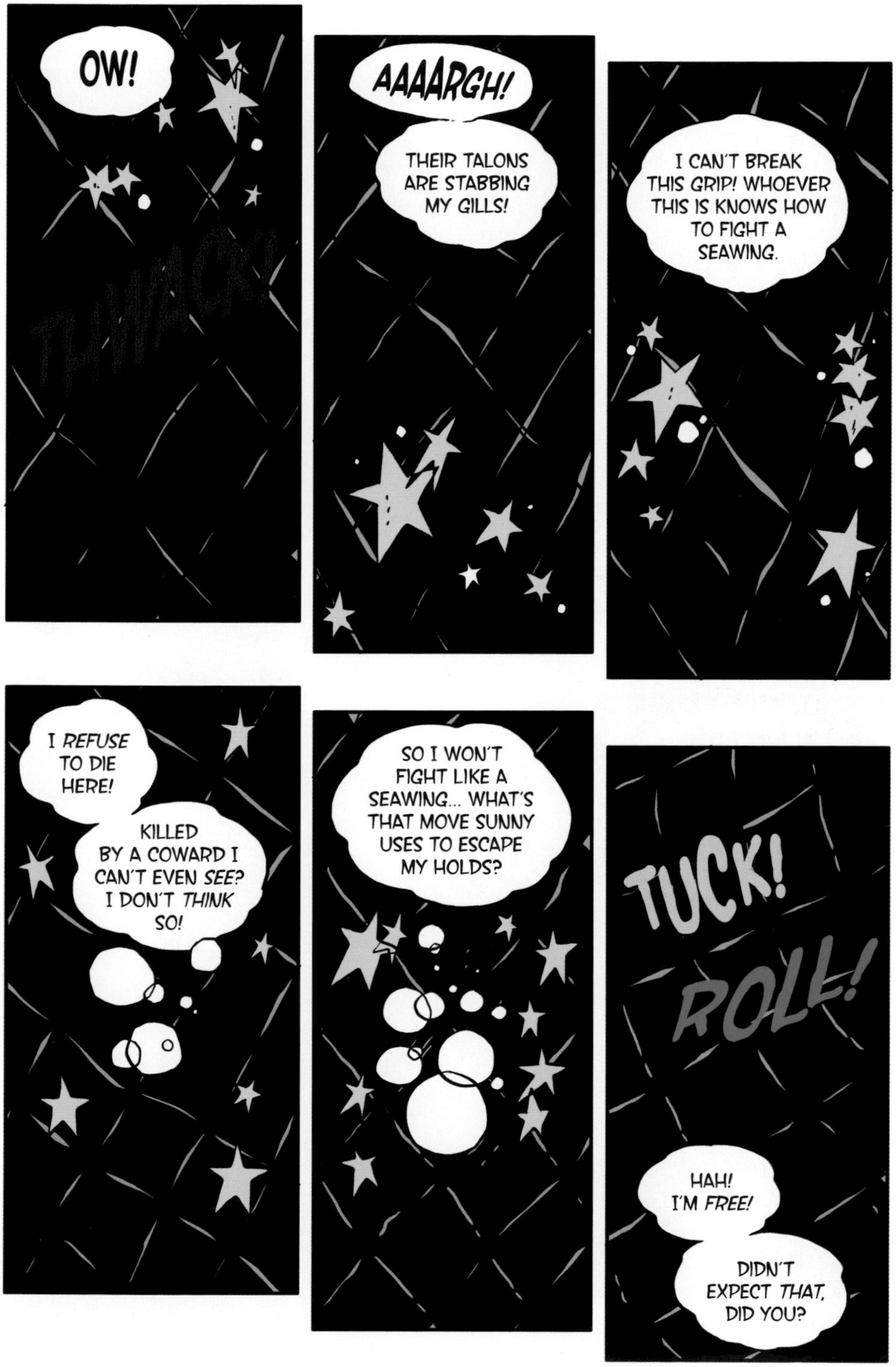
OW!
THWACK!
AAAARGH!
THEIR TALONS ARE STABBING MY GILLS!
I CAN'T BREAK THIS GRIP! WHOEVER THIS IS KNOWS HOW TO FIGHT A SEAWING.
I *REFUSE* TO DIE HERE!
KILLED BY A COWARD I CAN'T EVEN *SEE*? I DON'T *THINK* SO!
SO I WON'T FIGHT LIKE A SEAWING... WHAT'S THAT MOVE SUNNY USES TO ESCAPE MY HOLDS?
TUCK!
ROLL!
HAH! I'M *FREE!*
DIDN'T EXPECT *THAT*, DID YOU?

WHY WON'T THIS THING COME OFF?
TUG! TUG!
I THINK I HEAR THEM...
KICK!
CLLAANG!
OW!! ARE THEY WEARING METAL?
OOOWW!
THAT THING GLORY DOES, CHANGING COLORS TO DISTRACT PEOPLE... WHAT IF I LIGHT ALL MY SCALES UP AS BRIGHT AS THEY'LL GO?
HA! GOT YOU NOW...

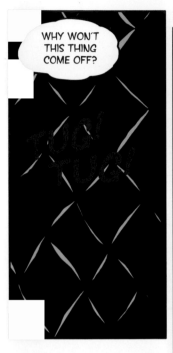

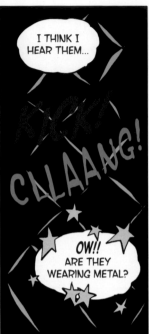

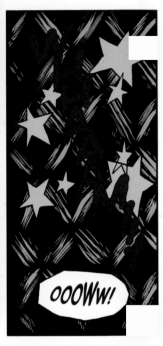

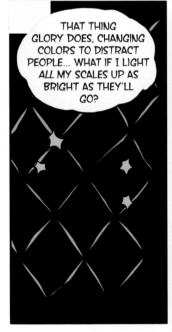

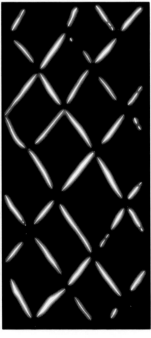

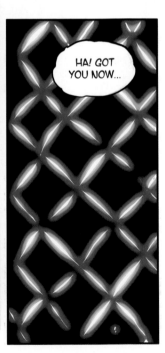

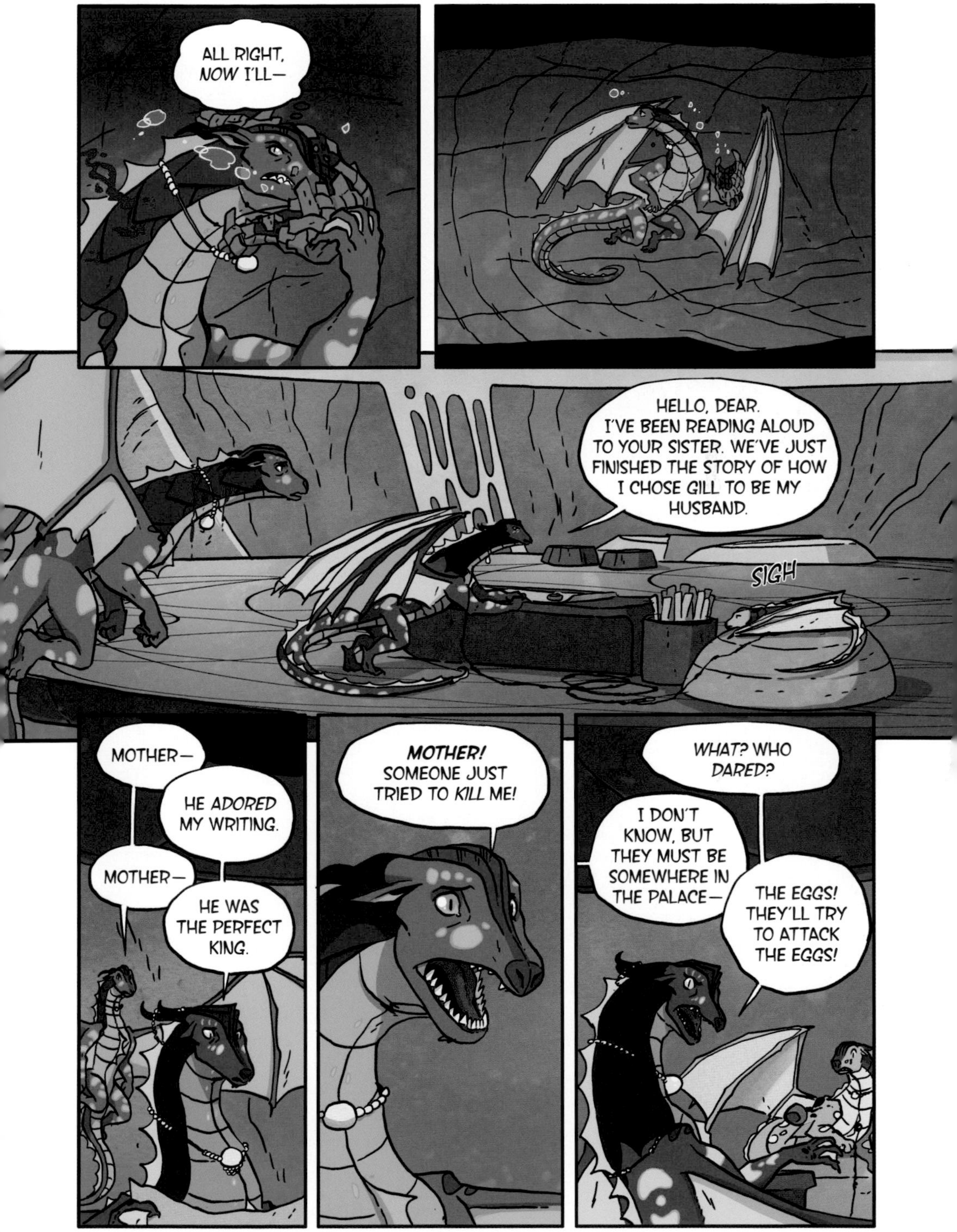
ALL RIGHT, NOW I'LL—
HELLO, DEAR. I'VE BEEN READING ALOUD TO YOUR SISTER. WE'VE JUST FINISHED THE STORY OF HOW I CHOSE GILL TO BE MY HUSBAND.
SIGH
MOTHER—
HE *ADORED* MY WRITING.
MOTHER—
HE WAS THE PERFECT KING.
MOTHER! SOMEONE JUST TRIED TO *KILL* ME!
WHAT? WHO *DARED?*
I DON'T KNOW, BUT THEY MUST BE SOMEWHERE IN THE PALACE—
THE EGGS! THEY'LL TRY TO ATTACK THE EGGS!

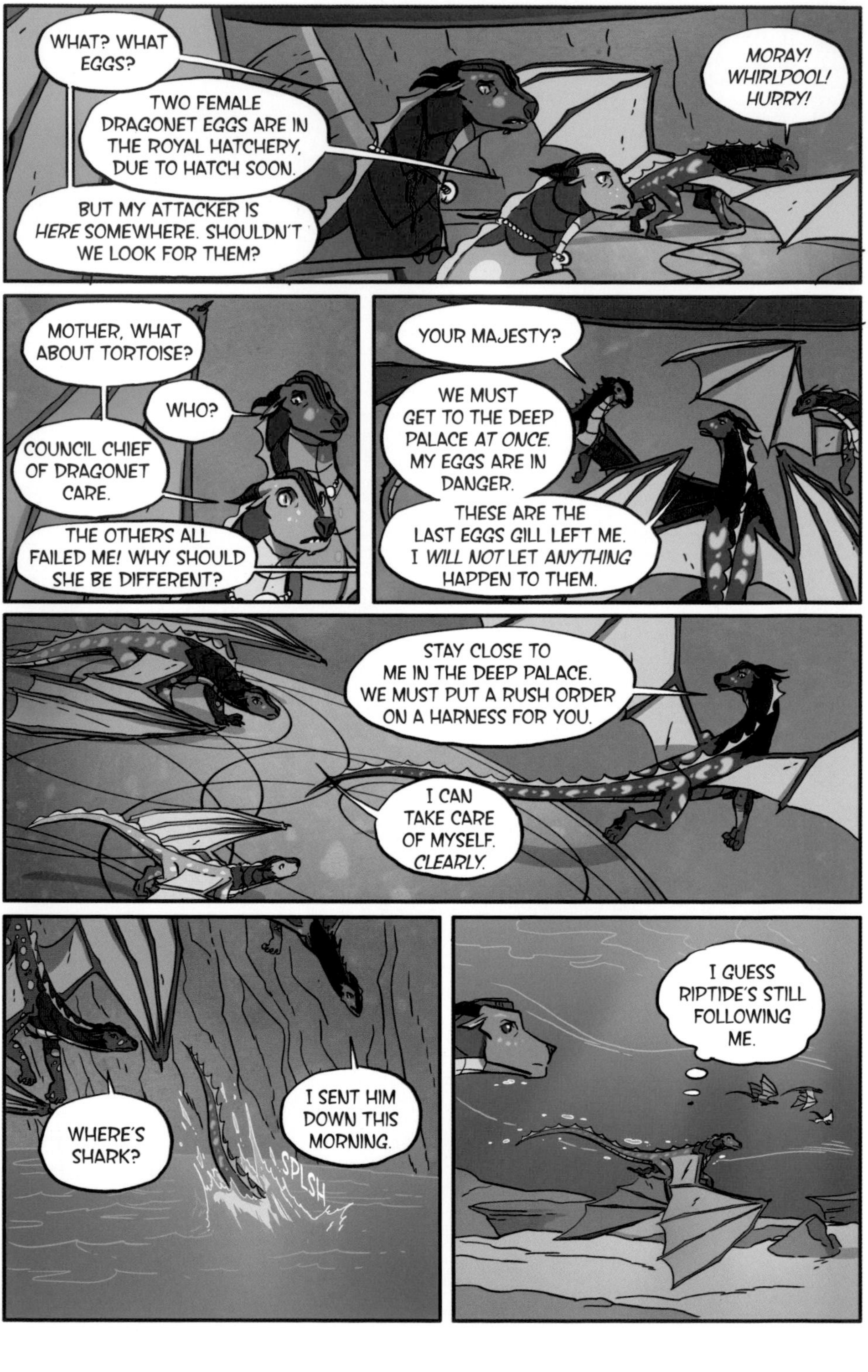
WHAT? WHAT EGGS?
TWO FEMALE DRAGONET EGGS ARE IN THE ROYAL HATCHERY, DUE TO HATCH SOON.
BUT MY ATTACKER IS *HERE* SOMEWHERE. SHOULDN'T WE LOOK FOR THEM?
MORAY! WHIRLPOOL! HURRY!
MOTHER, WHAT ABOUT TORTOISE?
WHO?
COUNCIL CHIEF OF DRAGONET CARE.
THE OTHERS ALL FAILED ME! WHY SHOULD SHE BE DIFFERENT?
YOUR MAJESTY?
WE MUST GET TO THE DEEP PALACE *AT ONCE.* MY EGGS ARE IN DANGER.
THESE ARE THE LAST EGGS GILL LEFT ME. I *WILL NOT* LET *ANYTHING* HAPPEN TO THEM.
STAY CLOSE TO ME IN THE DEEP PALACE. WE MUST PUT A RUSH ORDER ON A HARNESS FOR YOU.
I CAN TAKE CARE OF MYSELF. *CLEARLY.*
WHERE'S SHARK?
I SENT HIM DOWN THIS MORNING.
SPLSH
I GUESS RIPTIDE'S STILL FOLLOWING ME.

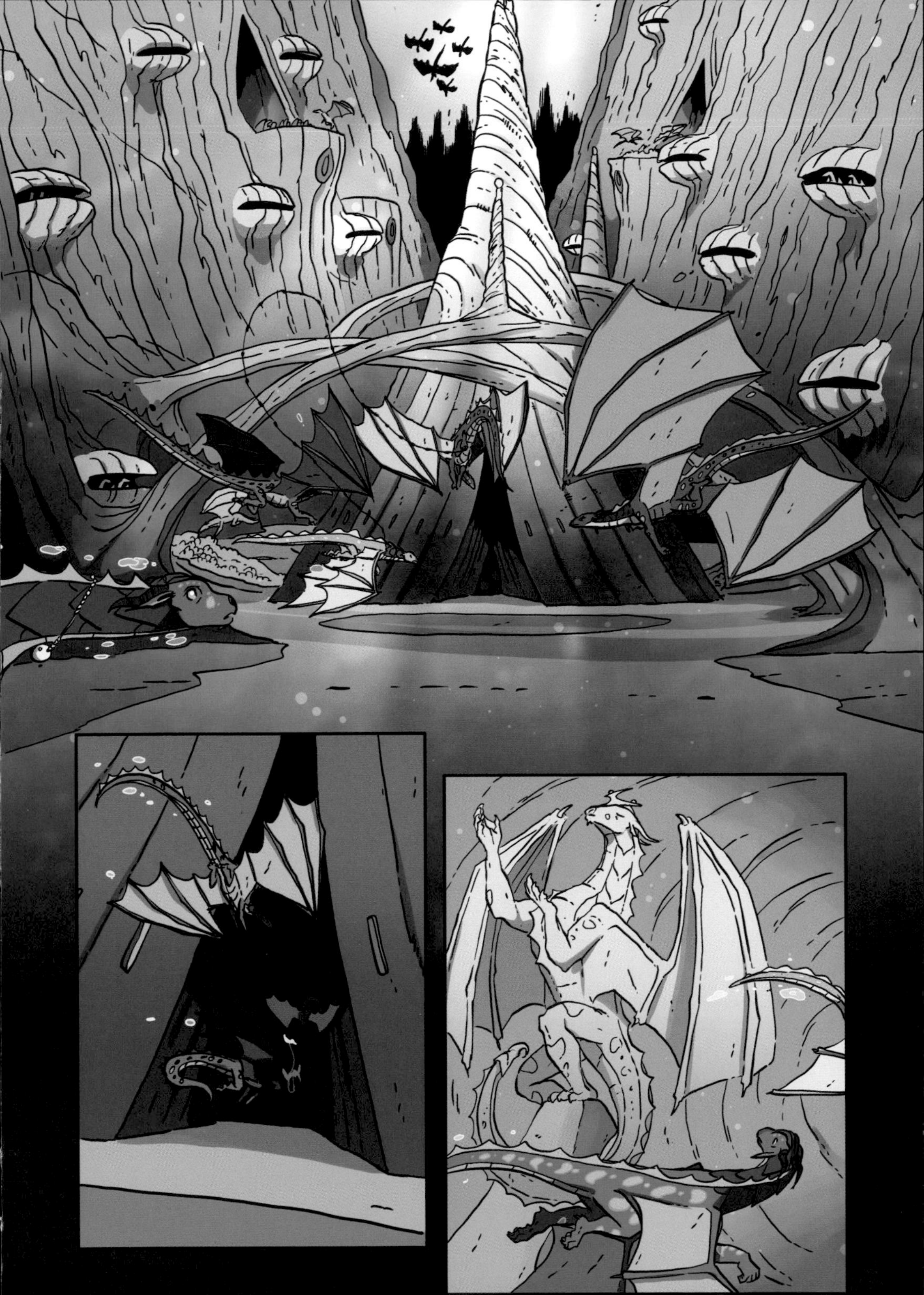

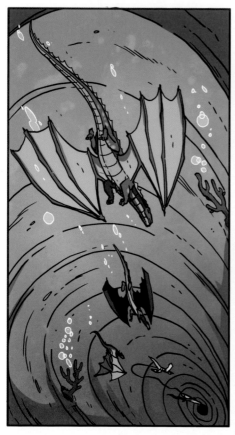

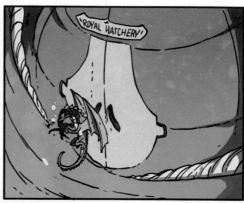

"ROYAL HATCHERY"

ROOOAARRRRR!

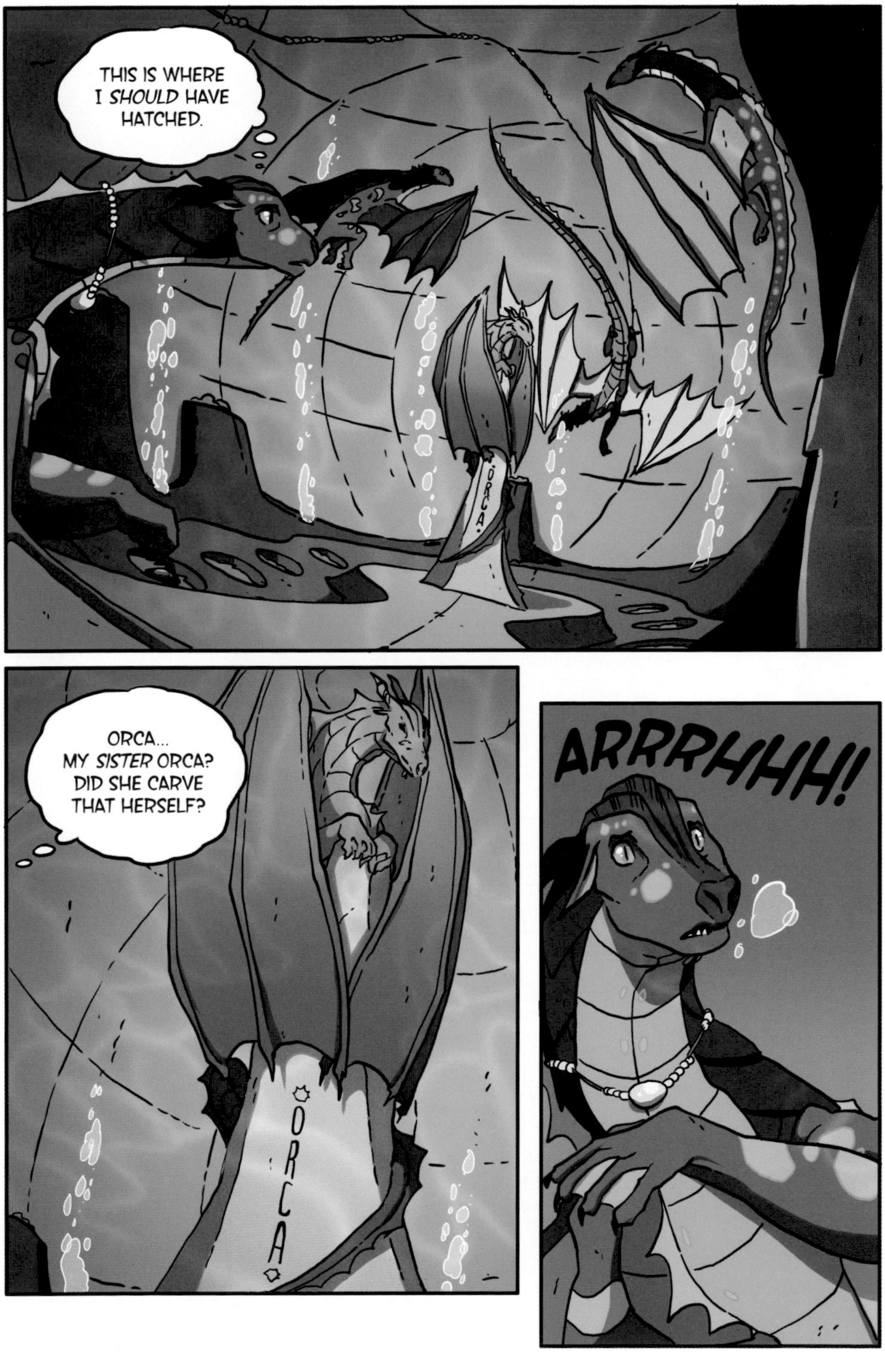
THIS IS WHERE I *SHOULD* HAVE HATCHED.
ORCA
ORCA... MY *SISTER* ORCA? DID SHE CARVE THAT HERSELF?
ORCA
ARRRHHH!

AHHHHH!

WHO COULD DO THAT TO A BABY DRAGON?

TO MY SISTER.

I UNDERSTAND WHY CORAL IS SO PROTECTIVE NOW.

NOTHING WILL *EVER*, *EVER* HURT ANEMONE, NOT WHILE *I'M* AROUND.

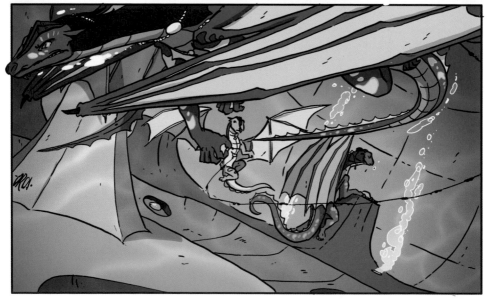

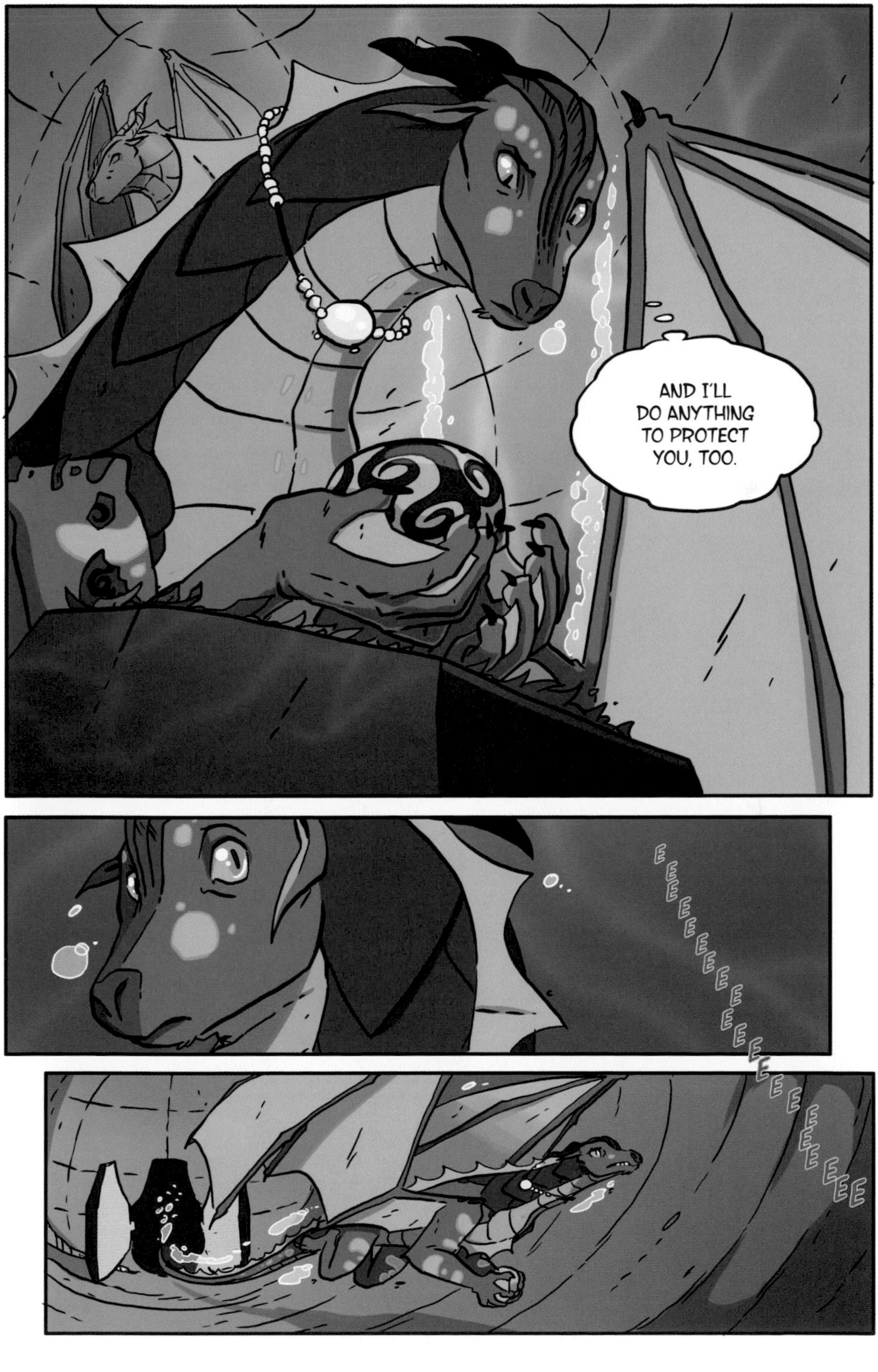
AND I'LL DO ANYTHING TO PROTECT YOU, TOO.
EEEEEEEEEEEEEEEEEEEEE

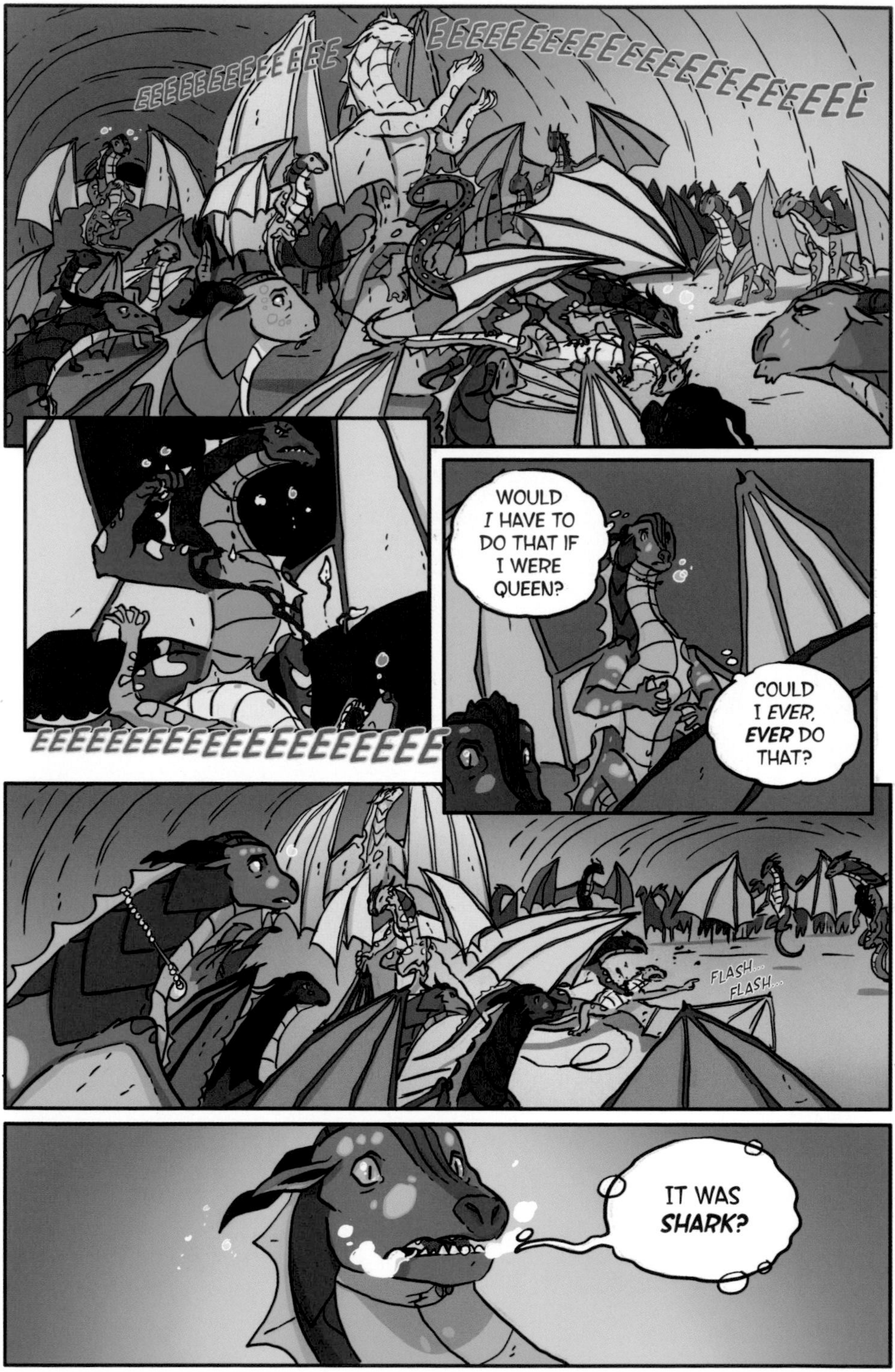
EEEEEEEEEEEEE
EEEEEEEEEEEEEEEEEEEEEEEEEE
EEEEEEEEEEEEEEEEEEEEEEEE
WOULD I HAVE TO DO THAT IF I WERE QUEEN?
COULD I *EVER*, ***EVER*** DO THAT?
FLASH... FLASH...
IT WAS **SHARK?**

I WILL PROTECT.

HOW?

I WILL PROTECT.

BUT I HOPE YOU DON'T DO *THAT* TO *ME*...

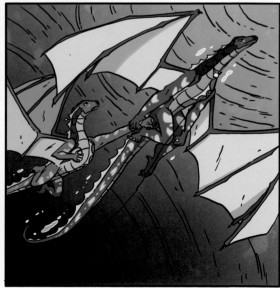

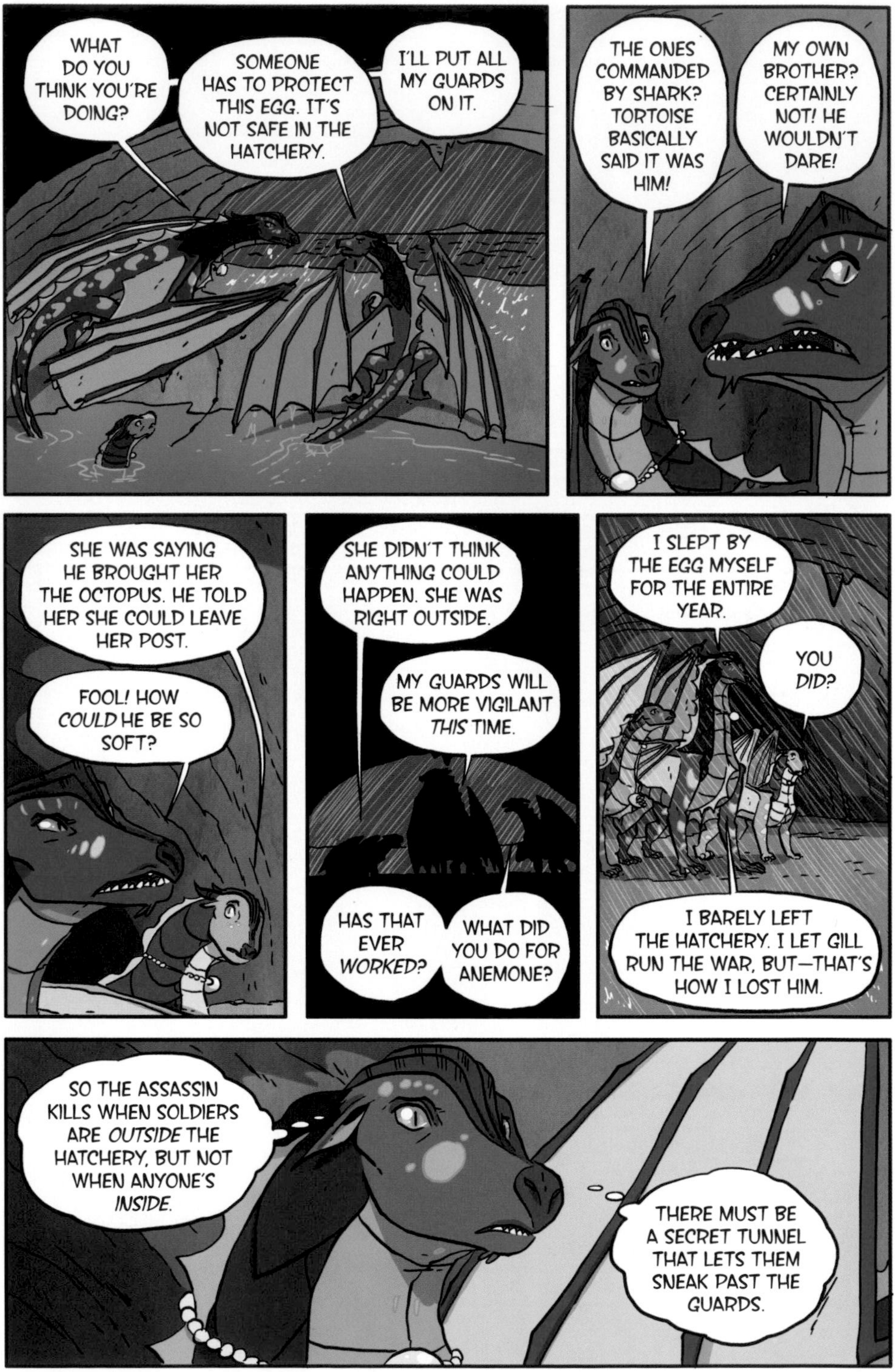
WHAT DO YOU THINK YOU'RE DOING?
SOMEONE HAS TO PROTECT THIS EGG. IT'S NOT SAFE IN THE HATCHERY.
I'LL PUT ALL MY GUARDS ON IT.
THE ONES COMMANDED BY SHARK? TORTOISE BASICALLY SAID IT WAS HIM!
MY OWN BROTHER? CERTAINLY NOT! HE WOULDN'T DARE!
SHE WAS SAYING HE BROUGHT HER THE OCTOPUS. HE TOLD HER SHE COULD LEAVE HER POST.
FOOL! HOW *COULD* HE BE SO SOFT?
SHE DIDN'T THINK ANYTHING COULD HAPPEN. SHE WAS RIGHT OUTSIDE.
MY GUARDS WILL BE MORE VIGILANT *THIS* TIME.
HAS THAT EVER *WORKED*?
WHAT DID YOU DO FOR ANEMONE?
I SLEPT BY THE EGG MYSELF FOR THE ENTIRE YEAR.
YOU *DID*?
I BARELY LEFT THE HATCHERY. I LET GILL RUN THE WAR, BUT—THAT'S HOW I LOST HIM.
SO THE ASSASSIN KILLS WHEN SOLDIERS ARE *OUTSIDE* THE HATCHERY, BUT NOT WHEN ANYONE'S *INSIDE*.
THERE MUST BE A SECRET TUNNEL THAT LETS THEM SNEAK PAST THE GUARDS.

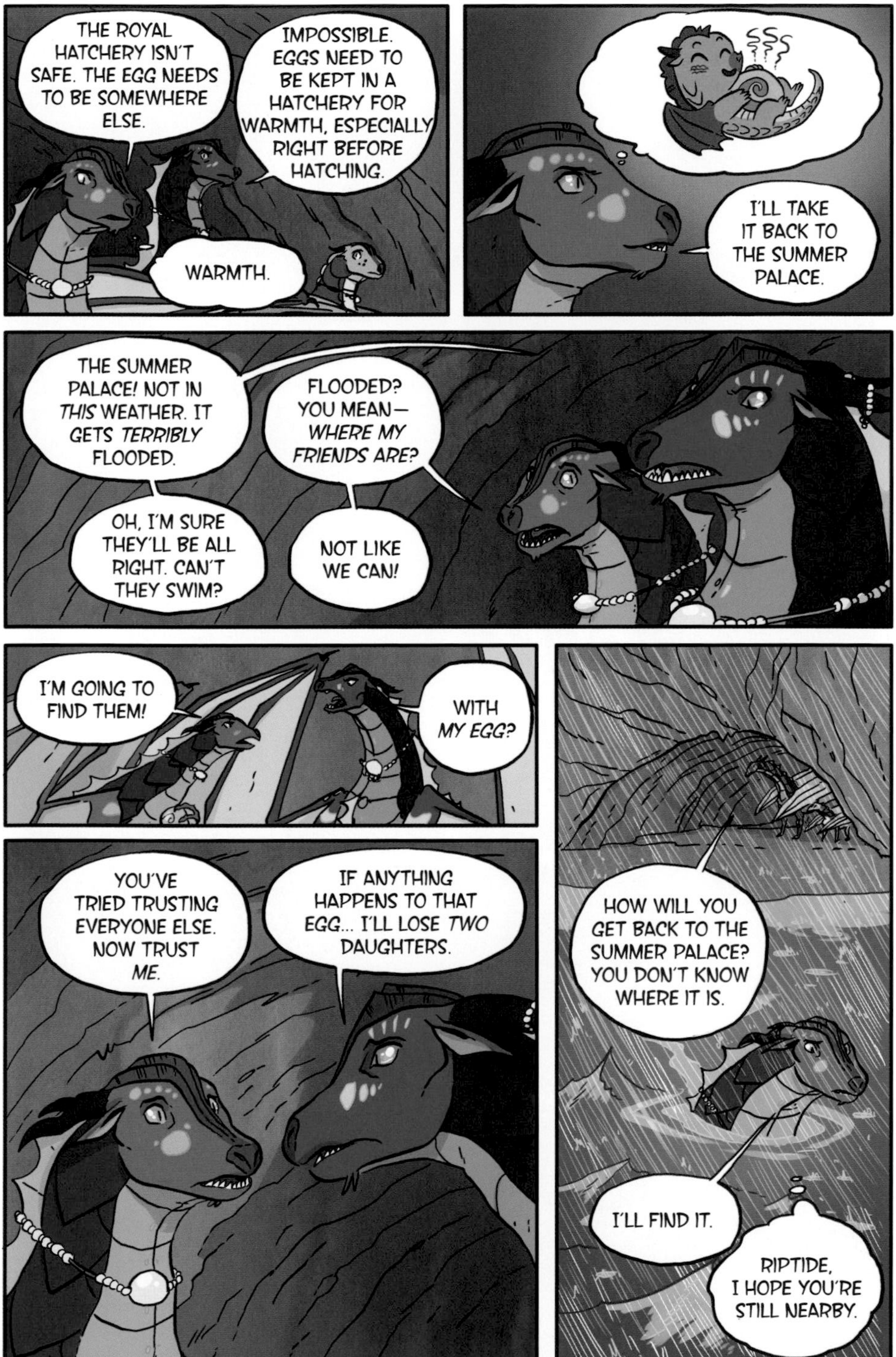
THE ROYAL HATCHERY ISN'T SAFE. THE EGG NEEDS TO BE SOMEWHERE ELSE.
IMPOSSIBLE. EGGS NEED TO BE KEPT IN A HATCHERY FOR WARMTH, ESPECIALLY RIGHT BEFORE HATCHING.
WARMTH.
I'LL TAKE IT BACK TO THE SUMMER PALACE.
THE SUMMER PALACE! NOT IN *THIS* WEATHER. IT GETS *TERRIBLY* FLOODED.
FLOODED? YOU MEAN— *WHERE MY FRIENDS ARE?*
OH, I'M SURE THEY'LL BE ALL RIGHT. CAN'T THEY SWIM?
NOT LIKE WE CAN!
I'M GOING TO FIND THEM!
WITH *MY EGG?*
YOU'VE TRIED TRUSTING EVERYONE ELSE. NOW TRUST *ME*.
IF ANYTHING HAPPENS TO THAT EGG... I'LL LOSE *TWO* DAUGHTERS.
HOW WILL YOU GET BACK TO THE SUMMER PALACE? YOU DON'T KNOW WHERE IT IS.
I'LL FIND IT.
RIPTIDE, I HOPE YOU'RE STILL NEARBY.

HE'LL NEVER FIND ME LIKE *THIS.*

LUCKILY, I KNOW A TRICK OR TWO NOW.

FLASH!

RIPTIDE!

FLASH

I HOPE HE MEANT *FOLLOW ME* AND NOT *WATCH OUT FOR THAT MONSTER WHO EATS DRAGON EGGS.*

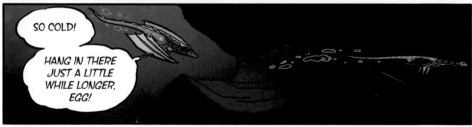

SO COLD!

HANG IN THERE JUST A LITTLE WHILE LONGER, EGG!

I GUESS I'LL GO BACK—

NO! COME WITH ME! PLEASE?

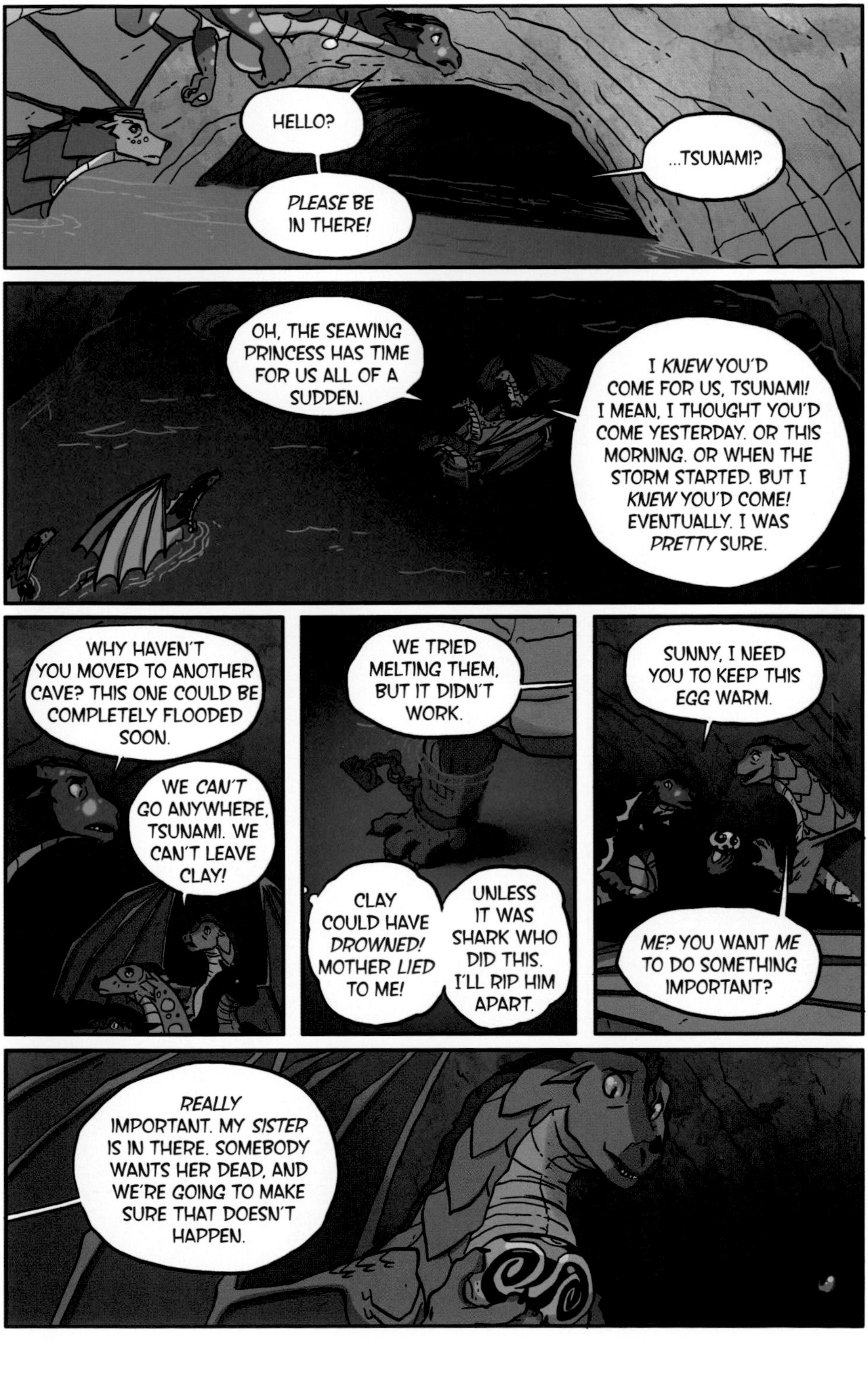
HELLO?
PLEASE BE IN THERE!
...TSUNAMI?
OH, THE SEAWING PRINCESS HAS TIME FOR US ALL OF A SUDDEN.
I KNEW YOU'D COME FOR US, TSUNAMI! I MEAN, I THOUGHT YOU'D COME YESTERDAY. OR THIS MORNING. OR WHEN THE STORM STARTED. BUT I KNEW YOU'D COME! EVENTUALLY. I WAS PRETTY SURE.
WHY HAVEN'T YOU MOVED TO ANOTHER CAVE? THIS ONE COULD BE COMPLETELY FLOODED SOON.
WE CAN'T GO ANYWHERE, TSUNAMI. WE CAN'T LEAVE CLAY!
WE TRIED MELTING THEM, BUT IT DIDN'T WORK.
CLAY COULD HAVE DROWNED! MOTHER LIED TO ME!
UNLESS IT WAS SHARK WHO DID THIS. I'LL RIP HIM APART.
SUNNY, I NEED YOU TO KEEP THIS EGG WARM.
ME? YOU WANT ME TO DO SOMETHING IMPORTANT?
REALLY IMPORTANT. MY SISTER IS IN THERE. SOMEBODY WANTS HER DEAD, AND WE'RE GOING TO MAKE SURE THAT DOESN'T HAPPEN.

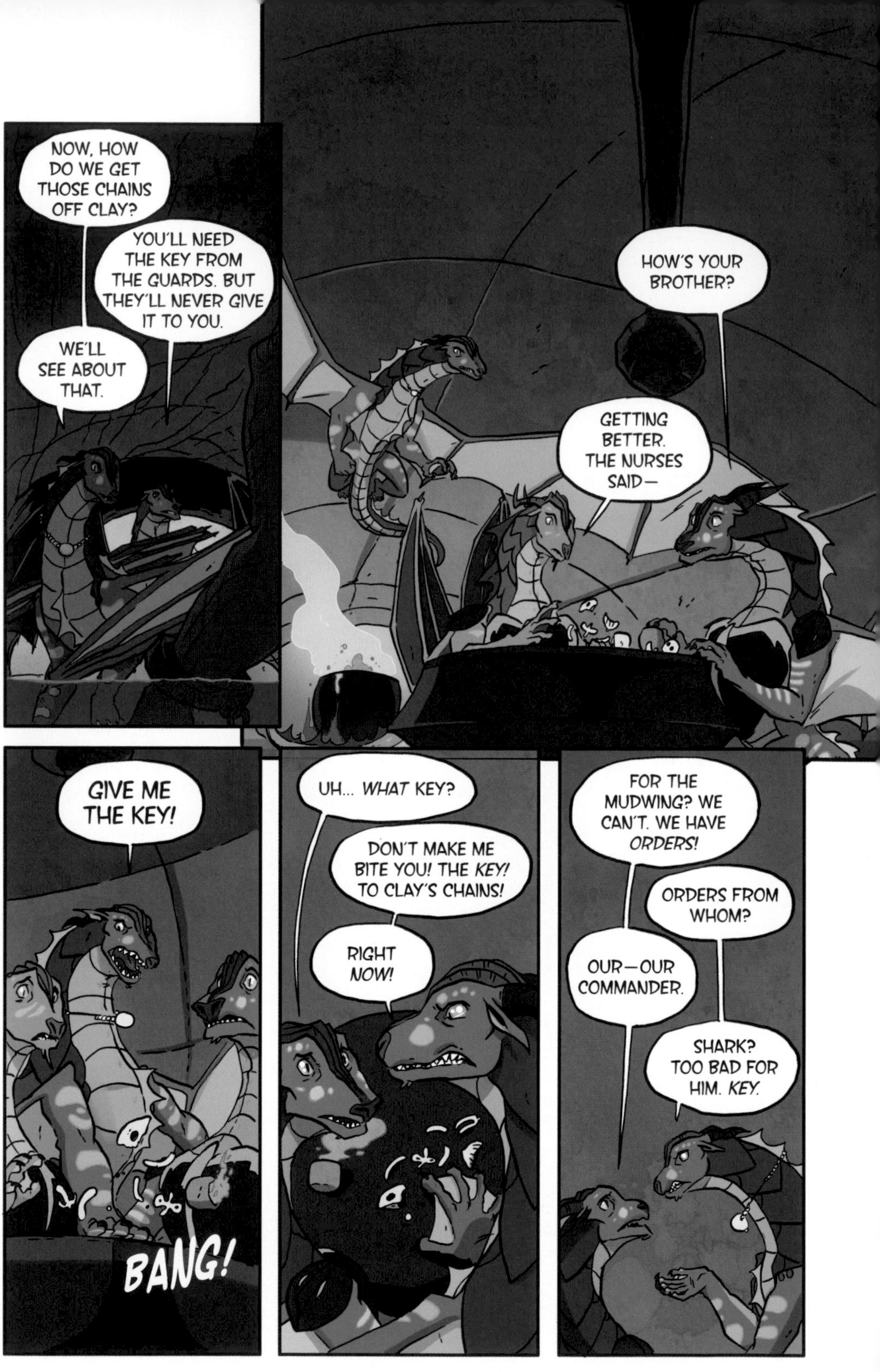
NOW, HOW DO WE GET THOSE CHAINS OFF CLAY?
YOU'LL NEED THE KEY FROM THE GUARDS. BUT THEY'LL NEVER GIVE IT TO YOU.
WE'LL SEE ABOUT THAT.
HOW'S YOUR BROTHER?
GETTING BETTER. THE NURSES SAID—
GIVE ME THE KEY!
BANG!
UH... *WHAT* KEY?
DON'T MAKE ME BITE YOU! THE *KEY!* TO CLAY'S CHAINS!
RIGHT *NOW!*
FOR THE MUDWING? WE CAN'T. WE HAVE *ORDERS!*
ORDERS FROM WHOM?
OUR—OUR COMMANDER.
SHARK? TOO BAD FOR HIM. *KEY.*

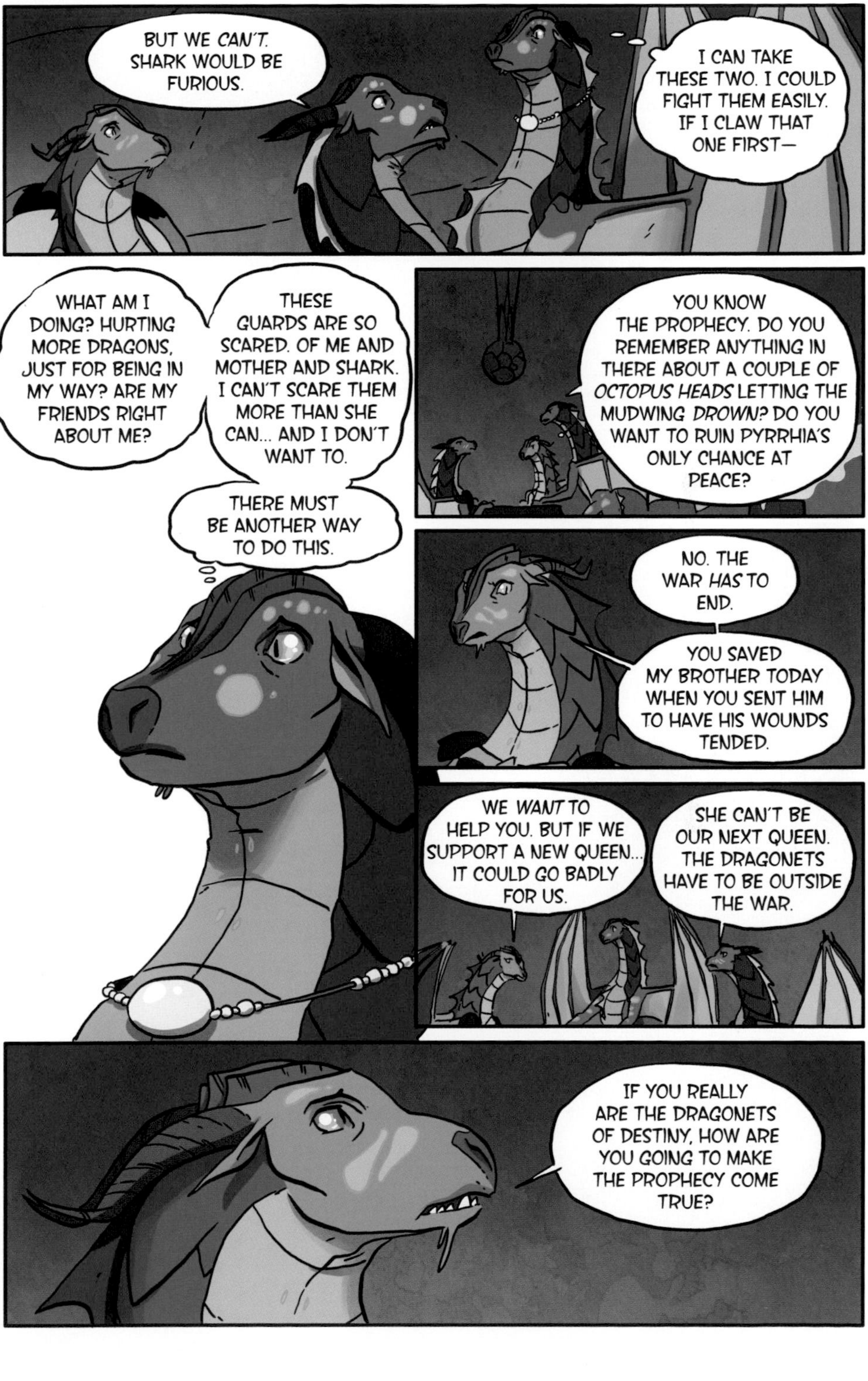
BUT WE *CAN'T.* SHARK WOULD BE FURIOUS.
I CAN TAKE THESE TWO. I COULD FIGHT THEM EASILY. IF I CLAW THAT ONE FIRST—
WHAT AM I DOING? HURTING MORE DRAGONS, JUST FOR BEING IN MY WAY? ARE MY FRIENDS RIGHT ABOUT ME?
THESE GUARDS ARE SO SCARED. OF ME AND MOTHER AND SHARK. I CAN'T SCARE THEM MORE THAN SHE CAN... AND I DON'T WANT TO.
THERE MUST BE ANOTHER WAY TO DO THIS.
YOU KNOW THE PROPHECY. DO YOU REMEMBER ANYTHING IN THERE ABOUT A COUPLE OF *OCTOPUS HEADS* LETTING THE MUDWING *DROWN?* DO YOU WANT TO RUIN PYRRHIA'S ONLY CHANCE AT PEACE?
NO. THE WAR *HAS* TO END.
YOU SAVED MY BROTHER TODAY WHEN YOU SENT HIM TO HAVE HIS WOUNDS TENDED.
WE *WANT* TO HELP YOU. BUT IF WE SUPPORT A NEW QUEEN... IT COULD GO BADLY FOR US.
SHE CAN'T BE OUR NEXT QUEEN. THE DRAGONETS HAVE TO BE OUTSIDE THE WAR.
IF YOU REALLY ARE THE DRAGONETS OF DESTINY, HOW ARE YOU GOING TO MAKE THE PROPHECY COME TRUE?

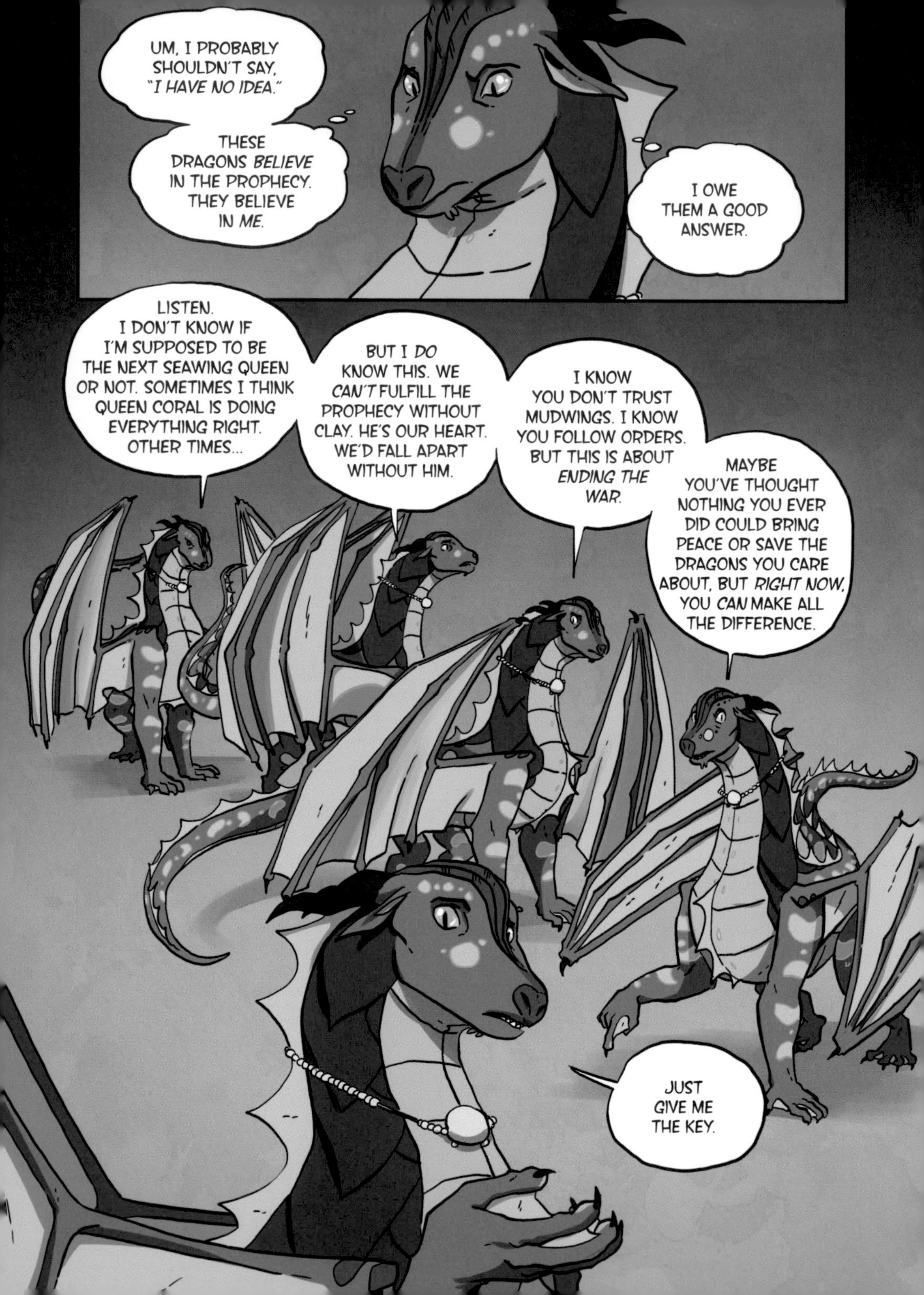
UM, I PROBABLY SHOULDN'T SAY, *"I HAVE NO IDEA."*
THESE DRAGONS *BELIEVE* IN THE PROPHECY. THEY BELIEVE IN *ME*.
I OWE THEM A GOOD ANSWER.
LISTEN. I DON'T KNOW IF I'M SUPPOSED TO BE THE NEXT SEAWING QUEEN OR NOT. SOMETIMES I THINK QUEEN CORAL IS DOING EVERYTHING RIGHT. OTHER TIMES...
BUT I *DO* KNOW THIS. WE *CAN'T* FULFILL THE PROPHECY WITHOUT CLAY. HE'S OUR HEART. WE'D FALL APART WITHOUT HIM.
I KNOW YOU DON'T TRUST MUDWINGS. I KNOW YOU FOLLOW ORDERS. BUT THIS IS ABOUT *ENDING THE WAR*.
MAYBE YOU'VE THOUGHT NOTHING YOU EVER DID COULD BRING PEACE OR SAVE THE DRAGONS YOU CARE ABOUT, BUT *RIGHT NOW*, YOU *CAN* MAKE ALL THE DIFFERENCE.
JUST GIVE ME THE KEY.

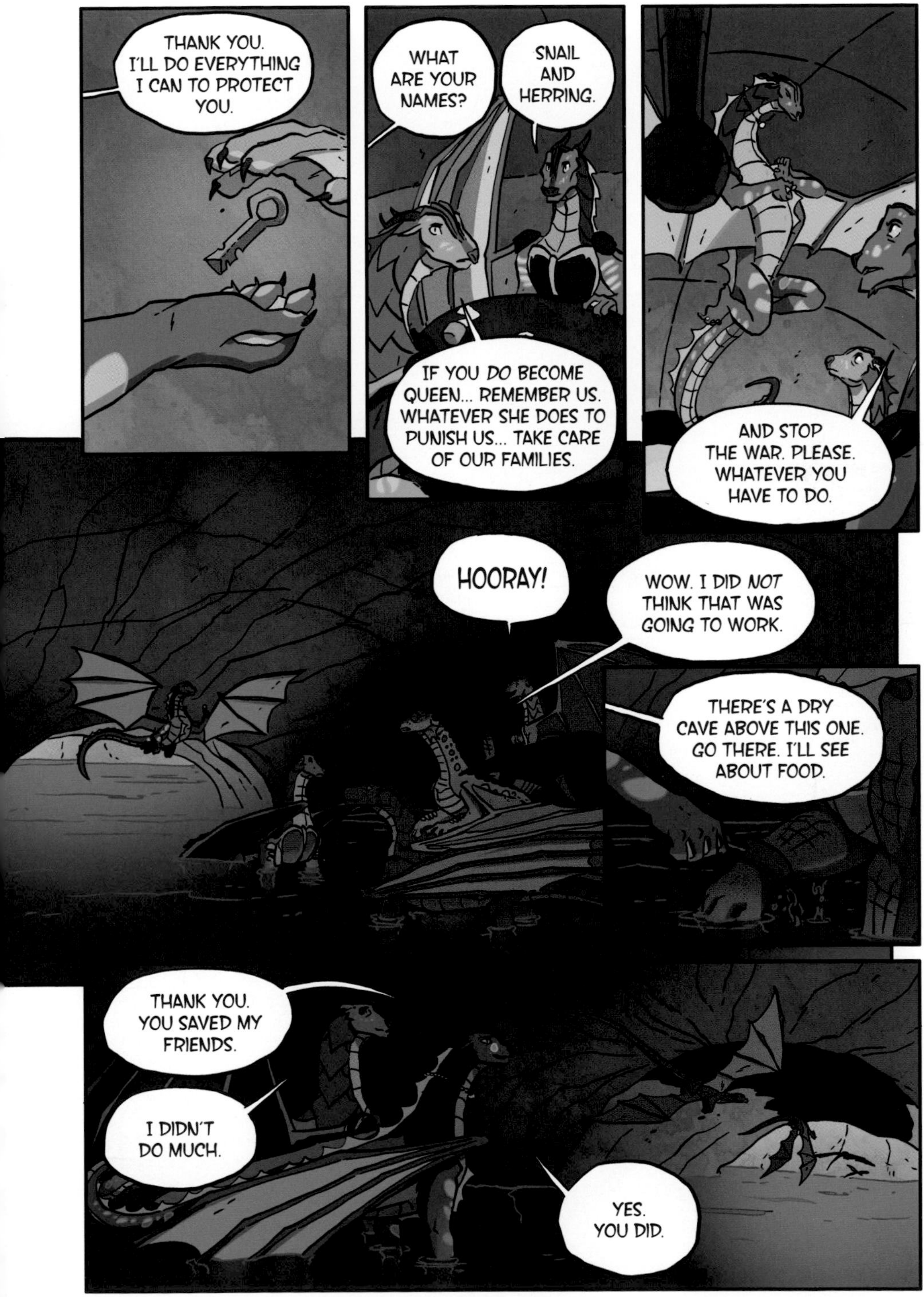
THANK YOU. I'LL DO EVERYTHING I CAN TO PROTECT YOU.
WHAT ARE YOUR NAMES?
SNAIL AND HERRING.
IF YOU *DO* BECOME QUEEN... REMEMBER US. WHATEVER SHE DOES TO PUNISH US... TAKE CARE OF OUR FAMILIES.
AND STOP THE WAR. PLEASE. WHATEVER YOU HAVE TO DO.
HOORAY!
WOW. I DID *NOT* THINK THAT WAS GOING TO WORK.
THERE'S A DRY CAVE ABOVE THIS ONE. GO THERE. I'LL SEE ABOUT FOOD.
THANK YOU. YOU SAVED MY FRIENDS.
I DIDN'T DO MUCH.
YES. YOU DID.

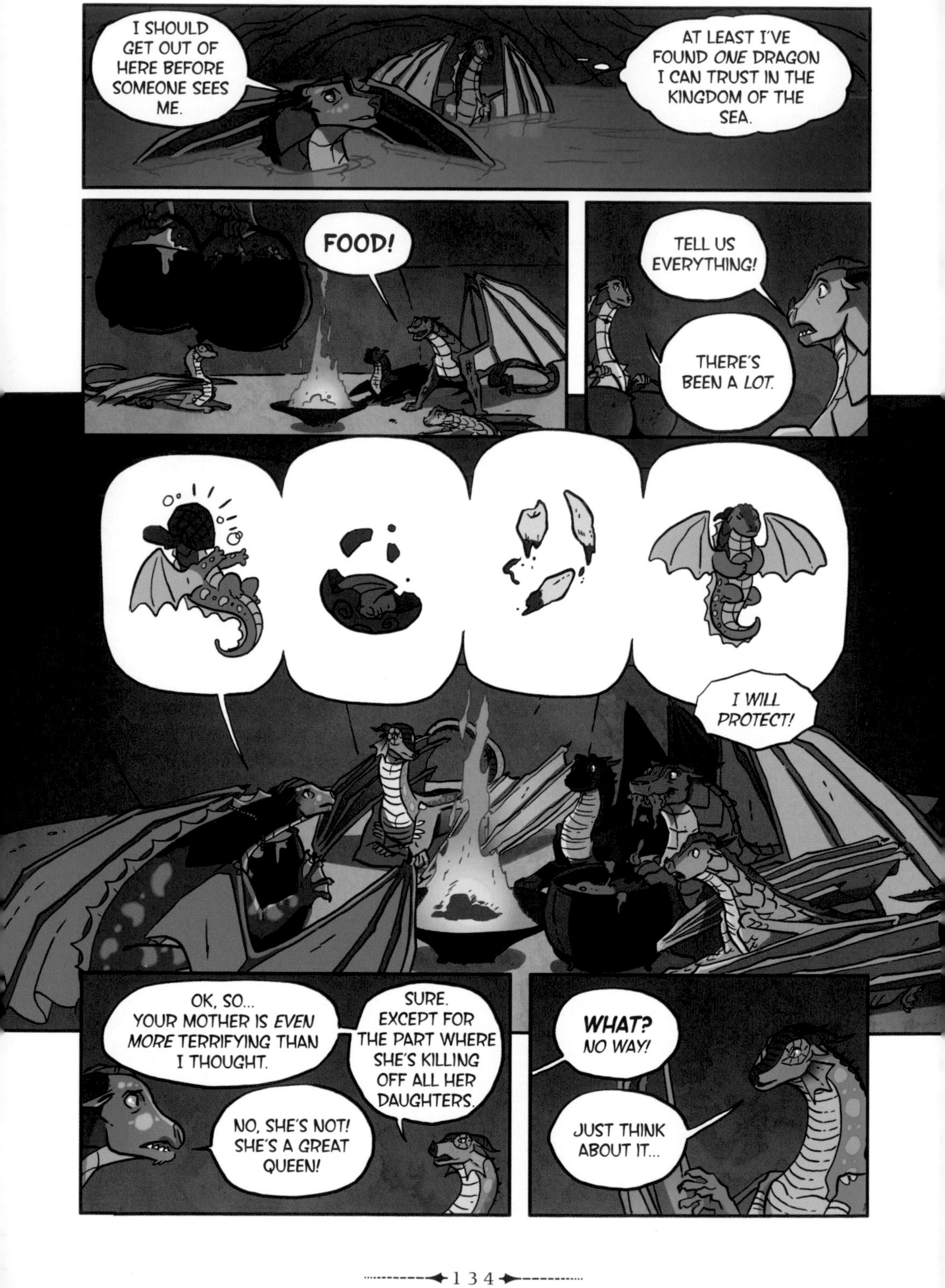
I SHOULD GET OUT OF HERE BEFORE SOMEONE SEES ME.
AT LEAST I'VE FOUND *ONE* DRAGON I CAN TRUST IN THE KINGDOM OF THE SEA.
FOOD!
TELL US EVERYTHING!
THERE'S BEEN A *LOT*.
I WILL PROTECT!
OK, SO... YOUR MOTHER IS *EVEN MORE* TERRIFYING THAN I THOUGHT.
NO, SHE'S NOT! SHE'S A GREAT QUEEN!
SURE. EXCEPT FOR THE PART WHERE SHE'S KILLING OFF ALL HER DAUGHTERS.
WHAT? NO WAY!
JUST THINK ABOUT IT...

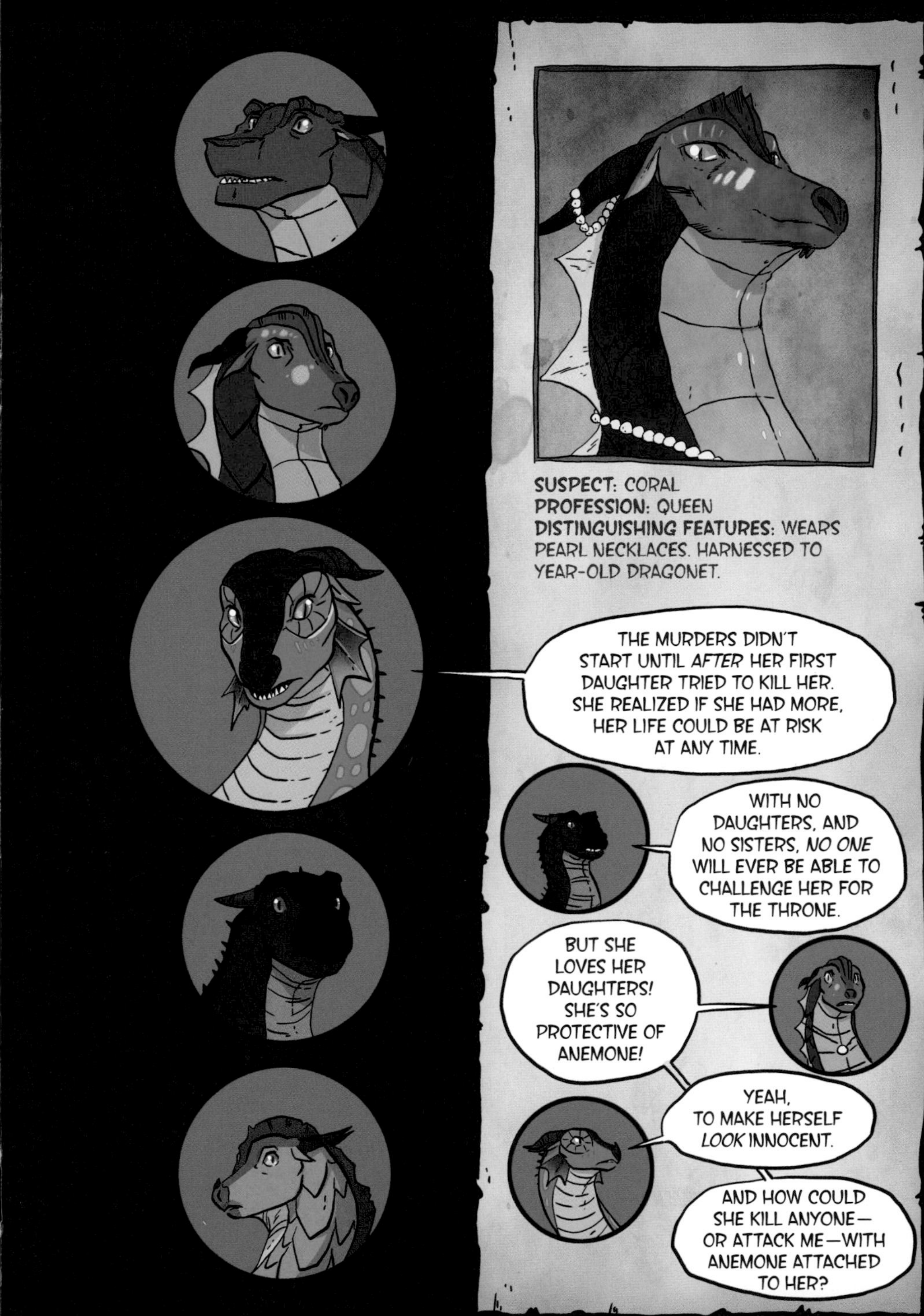
SUSPECT: CORAL
PROFESSION: QUEEN
DISTINGUISHING FEATURES: WEARS PEARL NECKLACES. HARNESSED TO YEAR-OLD DRAGONET.
THE MURDERS DIDN'T START UNTIL *AFTER* HER FIRST DAUGHTER TRIED TO KILL HER. SHE REALIZED IF SHE HAD MORE, HER LIFE COULD BE AT RISK AT ANY TIME.
WITH NO DAUGHTERS, AND NO SISTERS, *NO ONE* WILL EVER BE ABLE TO CHALLENGE HER FOR THE THRONE.
BUT SHE LOVES HER DAUGHTERS! SHE'S SO PROTECTIVE OF ANEMONE!
YEAH, TO MAKE HERSELF *LOOK* INNOCENT.
AND HOW COULD SHE KILL ANYONE— OR ATTACK ME—WITH ANEMONE ATTACHED TO HER?

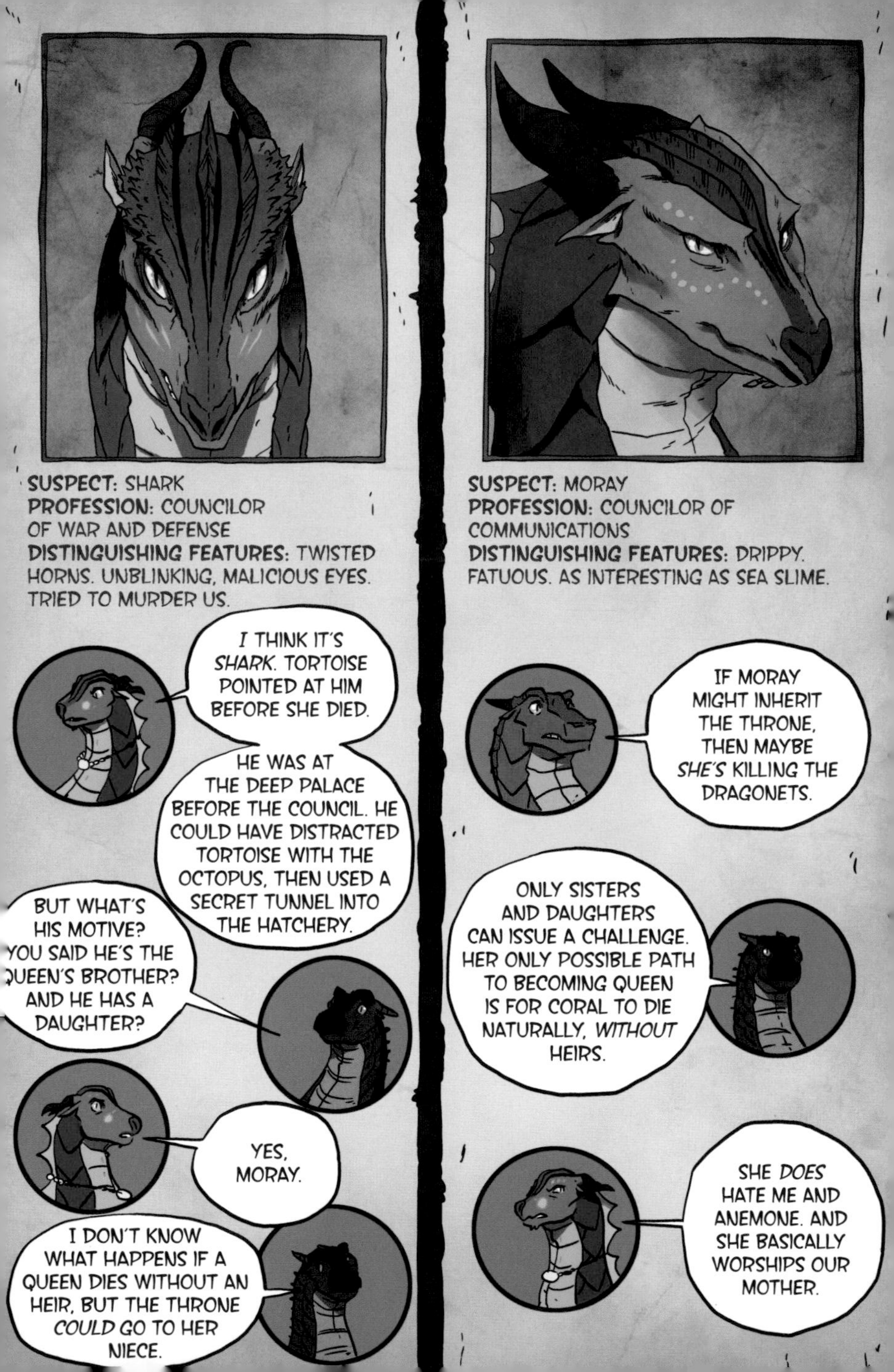
SUSPECT: SHARK
PROFESSION: COUNCILOR OF WAR AND DEFENSE
DISTINGUISHING FEATURES: TWISTED HORNS. UNBLINKING, MALICIOUS EYES. TRIED TO MURDER US.
I THINK IT'S SHARK. TORTOISE POINTED AT HIM BEFORE SHE DIED.
HE WAS AT THE DEEP PALACE BEFORE THE COUNCIL. HE COULD HAVE DISTRACTED TORTOISE WITH THE OCTOPUS, THEN USED A SECRET TUNNEL INTO THE HATCHERY.
BUT WHAT'S HIS MOTIVE? YOU SAID HE'S THE QUEEN'S BROTHER? AND HE HAS A DAUGHTER?
YES, MORAY.
I DON'T KNOW WHAT HAPPENS IF A QUEEN DIES WITHOUT AN HEIR, BUT THE THRONE COULD GO TO HER NIECE.
SUSPECT: MORAY
PROFESSION: COUNCILOR OF COMMUNICATIONS
DISTINGUISHING FEATURES: DRIPPY. FATUOUS. AS INTERESTING AS SEA SLIME.
IF MORAY MIGHT INHERIT THE THRONE, THEN MAYBE SHE'S KILLING THE DRAGONETS.
ONLY SISTERS AND DAUGHTERS CAN ISSUE A CHALLENGE. HER ONLY POSSIBLE PATH TO BECOMING QUEEN IS FOR CORAL TO DIE NATURALLY, WITHOUT HEIRS.
SHE DOES HATE ME AND ANEMONE. AND SHE BASICALLY WORSHIPS OUR MOTHER.

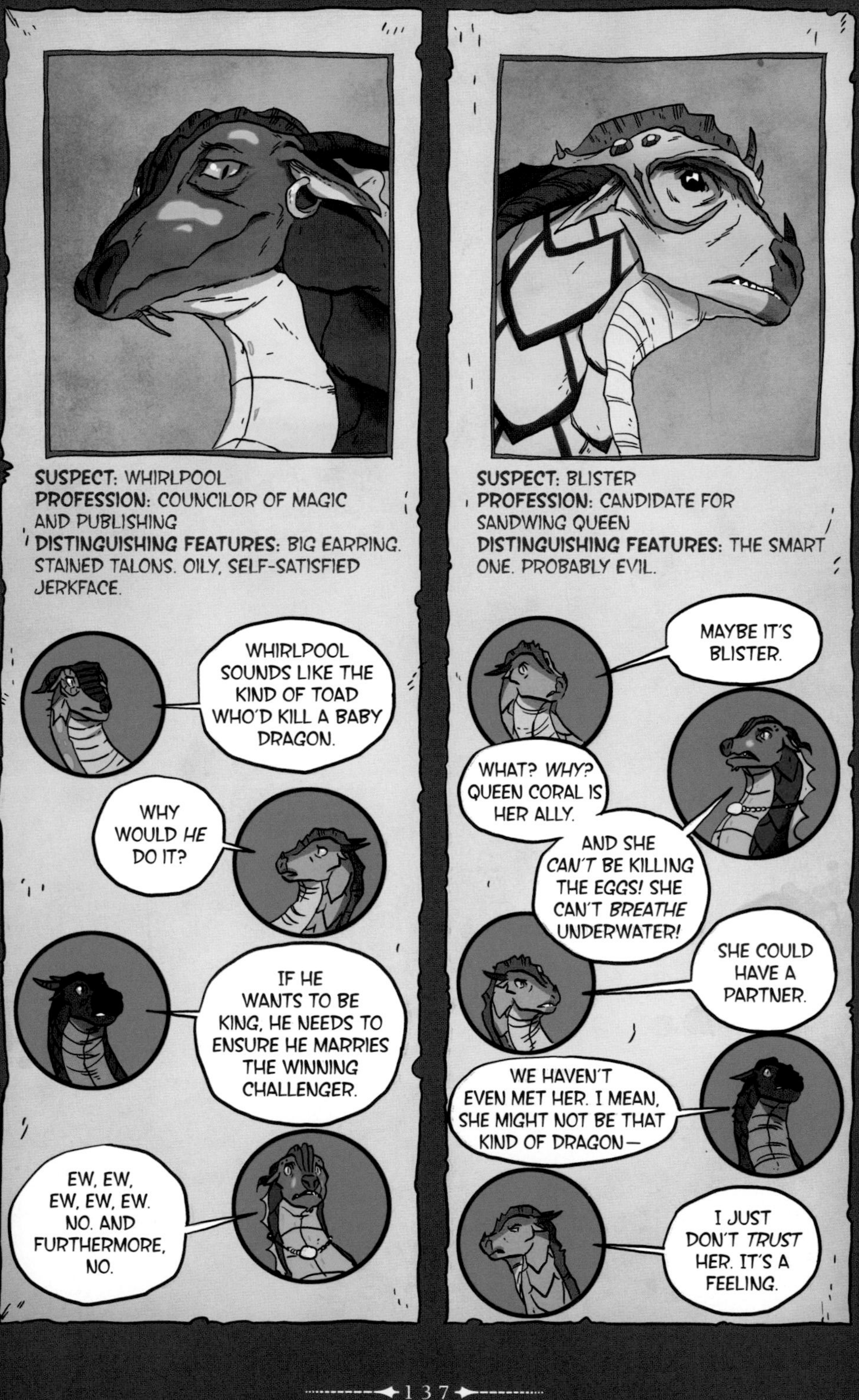

SUSPECT: WHIRLPOOL
PROFESSION: COUNCILOR OF MAGIC AND PUBLISHING
DISTINGUISHING FEATURES: BIG EARRING. STAINED TALONS. OILY, SELF-SATISFIED JERKFACE.
WHIRLPOOL SOUNDS LIKE THE KIND OF TOAD WHO'D KILL A BABY DRAGON.
WHY WOULD HE DO IT?
IF HE WANTS TO BE KING, HE NEEDS TO ENSURE HE MARRIES THE WINNING CHALLENGER.
EW, EW, EW, EW, EW. NO. AND FURTHERMORE, NO.
SUSPECT: BLISTER
PROFESSION: CANDIDATE FOR SANDWING QUEEN
DISTINGUISHING FEATURES: THE SMART ONE. PROBABLY EVIL.
MAYBE IT'S BLISTER.
WHAT? WHY? QUEEN CORAL IS HER ALLY.
AND SHE CAN'T BE KILLING THE EGGS! SHE CAN'T BREATHE UNDERWATER!
SHE COULD HAVE A PARTNER.
WE HAVEN'T EVEN MET HER. I MEAN, SHE MIGHT NOT BE THAT KIND OF DRAGON—
I JUST DON'T TRUST HER. IT'S A FEELING.

TSUNAMI, IT DOESN'T SOUND LIKE YOU'RE SAFE HERE. MAYBE WE SHOULD GO.

OR – *WE* COULD GO. *YOU* CAN STAY IF YOU REALLY WANT TO.

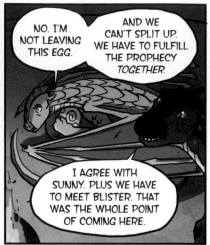

NO. I'M NOT LEAVING THIS EGG.

AND WE CAN'T SPLIT UP. WE HAVE TO FULFILL THE PROPHECY *TOGETHER.*

I AGREE WITH SUNNY. PLUS WE HAVE TO MEET BLISTER. THAT WAS THE WHOLE POINT OF COMING HERE.

THEN YOU SHOULD STAY WITH US TONIGHT. SO WE CAN KEEP EACH OTHER SAFE.

THANK THE *MOONS.*

...ALL RIGHT. THEN I CAN HELP PROTECT THE EGG, TOO.

YAY!

IT'S SO HARD FITTING IN WITH THE OTHER SEAWINGS.

I WISH MOTHER WAS MORE LIKE THE QUEEN FROM *THE MISSING PRINCESS.*

SHE WAS SO HAPPY TO SEE ME AT FIRST, BUT SOMETIMES SHE SCARES ME...

BUT *THIS...* THIS FEELS RIGHT.

SNOOORE

OH, I FORGOT TO TELL THEM... ABOUT KESTREL...

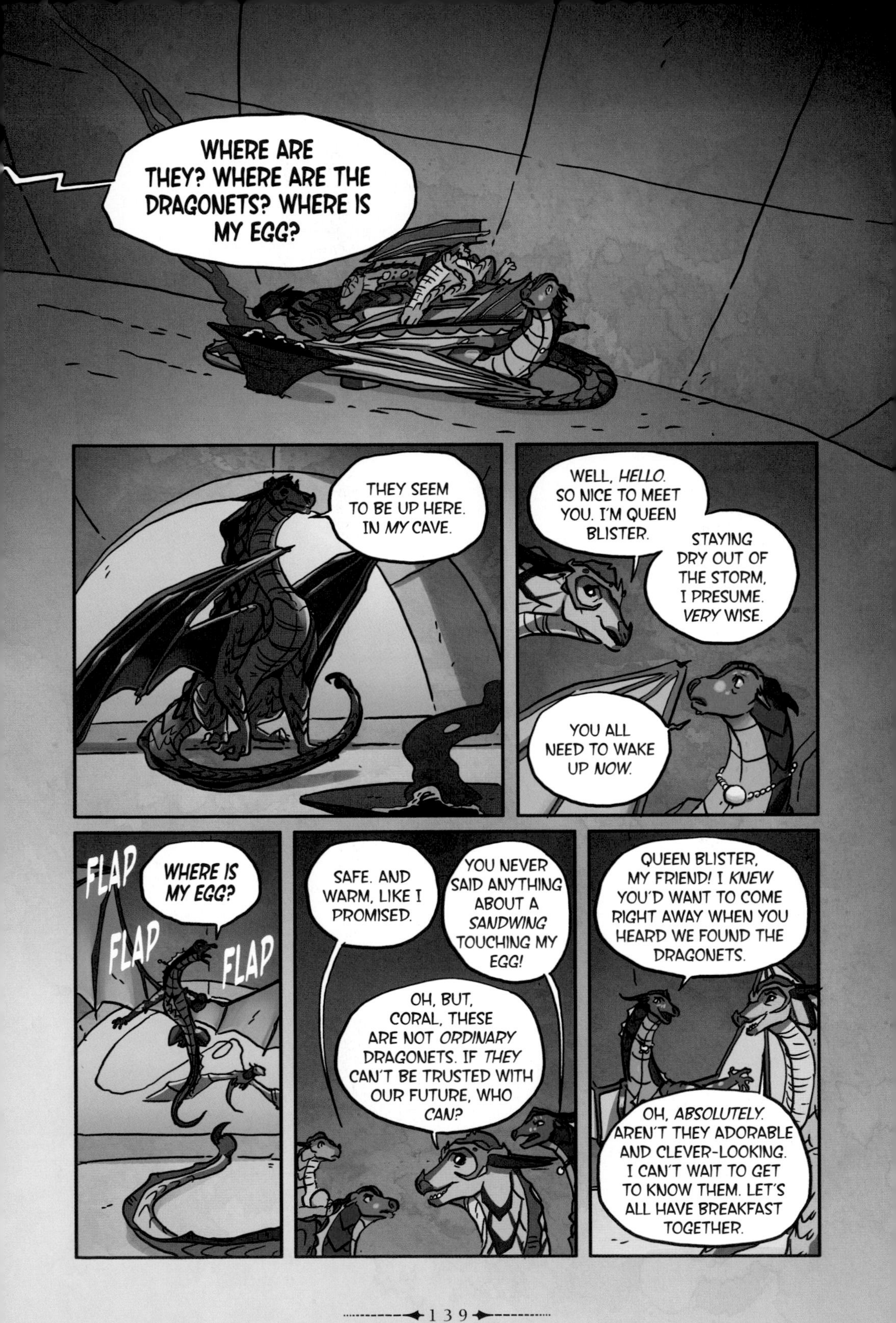
WHERE ARE THEY? WHERE ARE THE DRAGONETS? WHERE IS MY EGG?
THEY SEEM TO BE UP HERE. IN MY CAVE.
WELL, HELLO. SO NICE TO MEET YOU. I'M QUEEN BLISTER.
STAYING DRY OUT OF THE STORM, I PRESUME. VERY WISE.
YOU ALL NEED TO WAKE UP NOW.
FLAP
WHERE IS MY EGG?
FLAP
FLAP
SAFE. AND WARM, LIKE I PROMISED.
YOU NEVER SAID ANYTHING ABOUT A SANDWING TOUCHING MY EGG!
OH, BUT, CORAL, THESE ARE NOT ORDINARY DRAGONETS. IF THEY CAN'T BE TRUSTED WITH OUR FUTURE, WHO CAN?
QUEEN BLISTER, MY FRIEND! I KNEW YOU'D WANT TO COME RIGHT AWAY WHEN YOU HEARD WE FOUND THE DRAGONETS.
OH, ABSOLUTELY. AREN'T THEY ADORABLE AND CLEVER-LOOKING. I CAN'T WAIT TO GET TO KNOW THEM. LET'S ALL HAVE BREAKFAST TOGETHER.

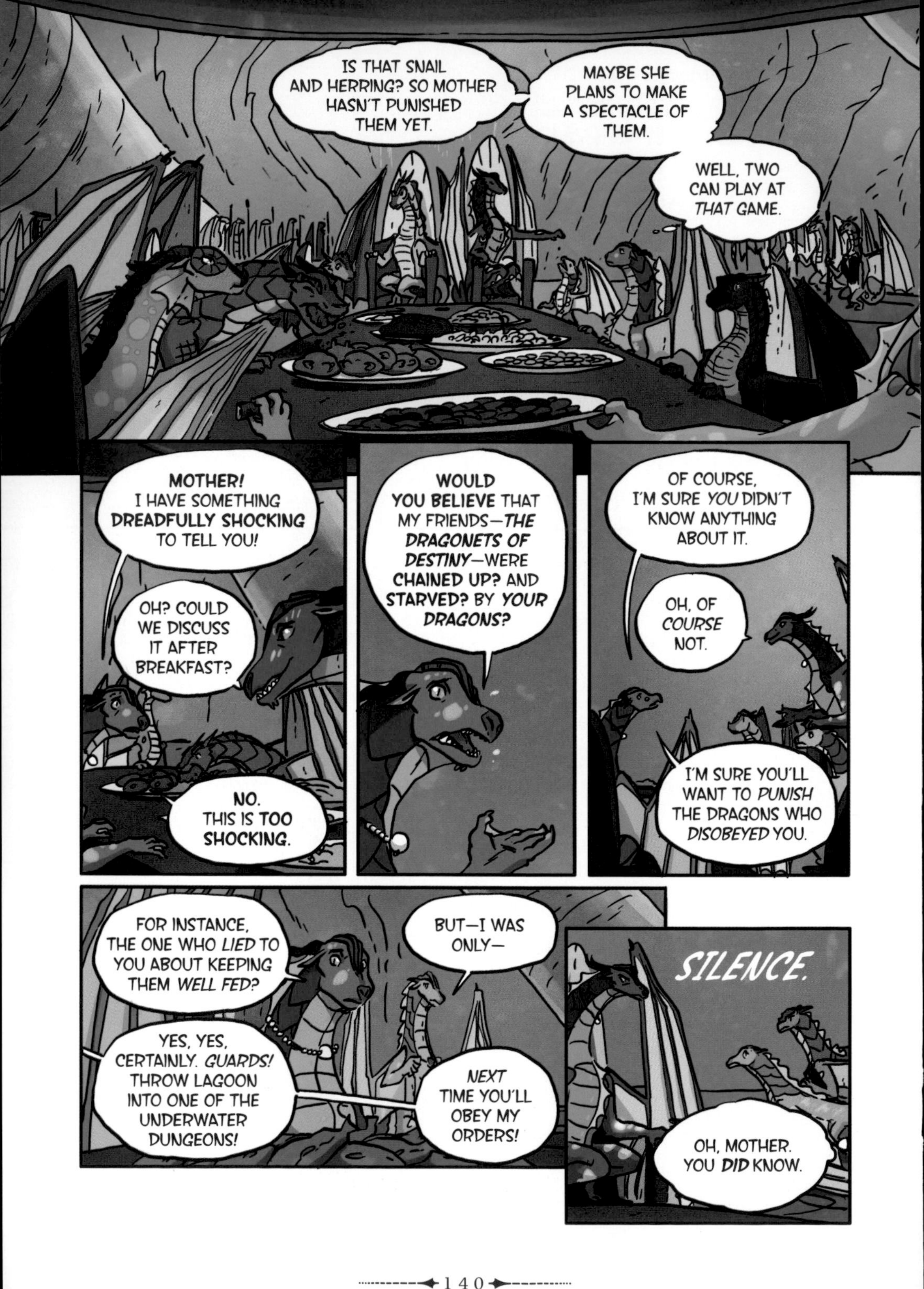
IS THAT SNAIL AND HERRING? SO MOTHER HASN'T PUNISHED THEM YET.
MAYBE SHE PLANS TO MAKE A SPECTACLE OF THEM.
WELL, TWO CAN PLAY AT *THAT* GAME.
MOTHER! I HAVE SOMETHING **DREADFULLY SHOCKING** TO TELL YOU!
OH? COULD WE DISCUSS IT AFTER BREAKFAST?
NO. THIS IS **TOO SHOCKING.**
WOULD YOU BELIEVE THAT MY FRIENDS—***THE DRAGONETS OF DESTINY***—WERE **CHAINED UP?** AND **STARVED?** BY ***YOUR DRAGONS?***
OF COURSE, I'M SURE *YOU* DIDN'T KNOW ANYTHING ABOUT IT.
OH, OF *COURSE* NOT.
I'M SURE YOU'LL WANT TO *PUNISH* THE DRAGONS WHO *DISOBEYED* YOU.
FOR INSTANCE, THE ONE WHO *LIED* TO YOU ABOUT KEEPING THEM *WELL FED?*
BUT—I WAS ONLY—
YES, YES, CERTAINLY. *GUARDS!* THROW LAGOON INTO ONE OF THE UNDERWATER DUNGEONS!
NEXT TIME YOU'LL OBEY MY ORDERS!
SILENCE.
OH, MOTHER. YOU **DID** KNOW.

AND **GUESS WHO** ORDERED YOUR GUARDS TO CHAIN UP CLAY? **COMMANDER SHARK!** IS THAT NOT **UTTERLY SHOCKING?**

IT IS.

IMAGINE THESE POOR GUARDS' DISTRESS, HAVING TO CHOOSE BETWEEN THEIR COMMANDER AND THEIR QUEEN! NATURALLY, THEY CHOSE *YOU.*

THAT'S WHY THEY GAVE ME THE KEY. THEY UNDERSTOOD THAT'S WHAT *YOU* WOULD HAVE WANTED.

IT SOUNDS LIKE THOSE GUARDS ARE PRACTICALLY HEROES.

AND SHARK—

TO THE DUNGEON WITH HIM AS WELL.

SHE'LL PROBABLY LET HIM OUT AS SOON AS SHE CAN. BUT AT LEAST WE'LL ALL BE SAFER FOR A DAY OR TWO.

SUCH EXCITEMENT. IF WE'RE QUITE FINISHED WITH OUR MORNING THEATRICS, LET'S CHAT ABOUT OUR BRAVE, CLEVER DRAGONETS OF DESTINY.

GLORY, I'D HEARD YOU WEREN'T A SKYWING, BUT THAT DOESN'T BOTHER *ME.* SKYWINGS ARE OVERRATED, IF YOU ASK ME.

YOU *HEARD?* HOW? *NOBODY* KNEW, NOT EVEN THE OTHER TALONS!

LET'S JUST SAY I HAVE FRIENDS. *NIGHTWING* FRIENDS.

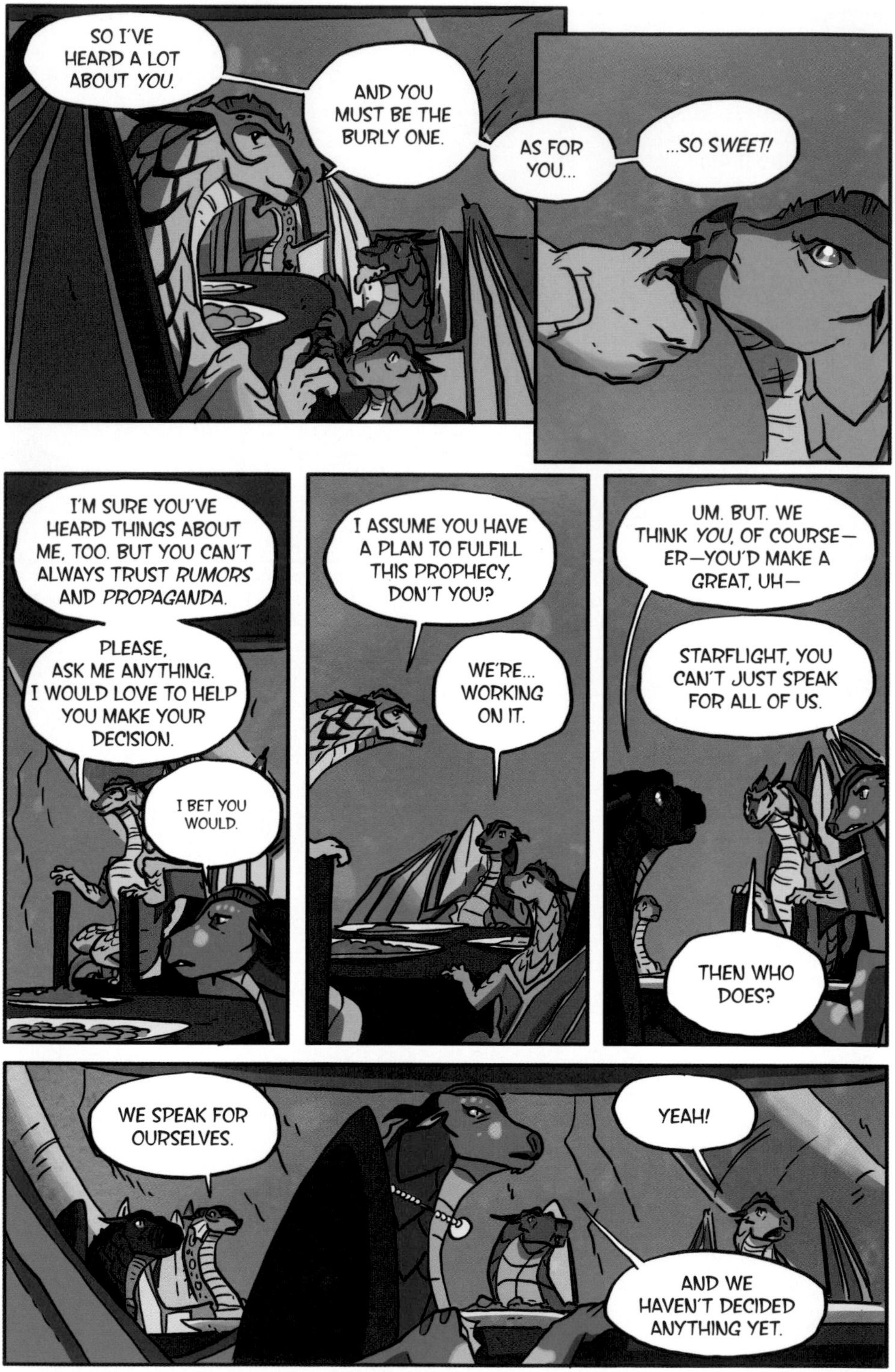
SO I'VE HEARD A LOT ABOUT *YOU.*
AND YOU MUST BE THE BURLY ONE.
AS FOR YOU...
...SO *SWEET!*
I'M SURE YOU'VE HEARD THINGS ABOUT ME, TOO. BUT YOU CAN'T ALWAYS TRUST *RUMORS* AND *PROPAGANDA.*
PLEASE, ASK ME ANYTHING. I WOULD LOVE TO HELP YOU MAKE YOUR DECISION.
I BET YOU WOULD.
I ASSUME YOU HAVE A PLAN TO FULFILL THIS PROPHECY, DON'T YOU?
WE'RE... WORKING ON IT.
UM. BUT. WE THINK *YOU,* OF COURSE— ER—YOU'D MAKE A GREAT, UH—
STARFLIGHT, YOU CAN'T JUST SPEAK FOR ALL OF US.
THEN WHO DOES?
WE SPEAK FOR OURSELVES.
YEAH!
AND WE HAVEN'T DECIDED ANYTHING YET.

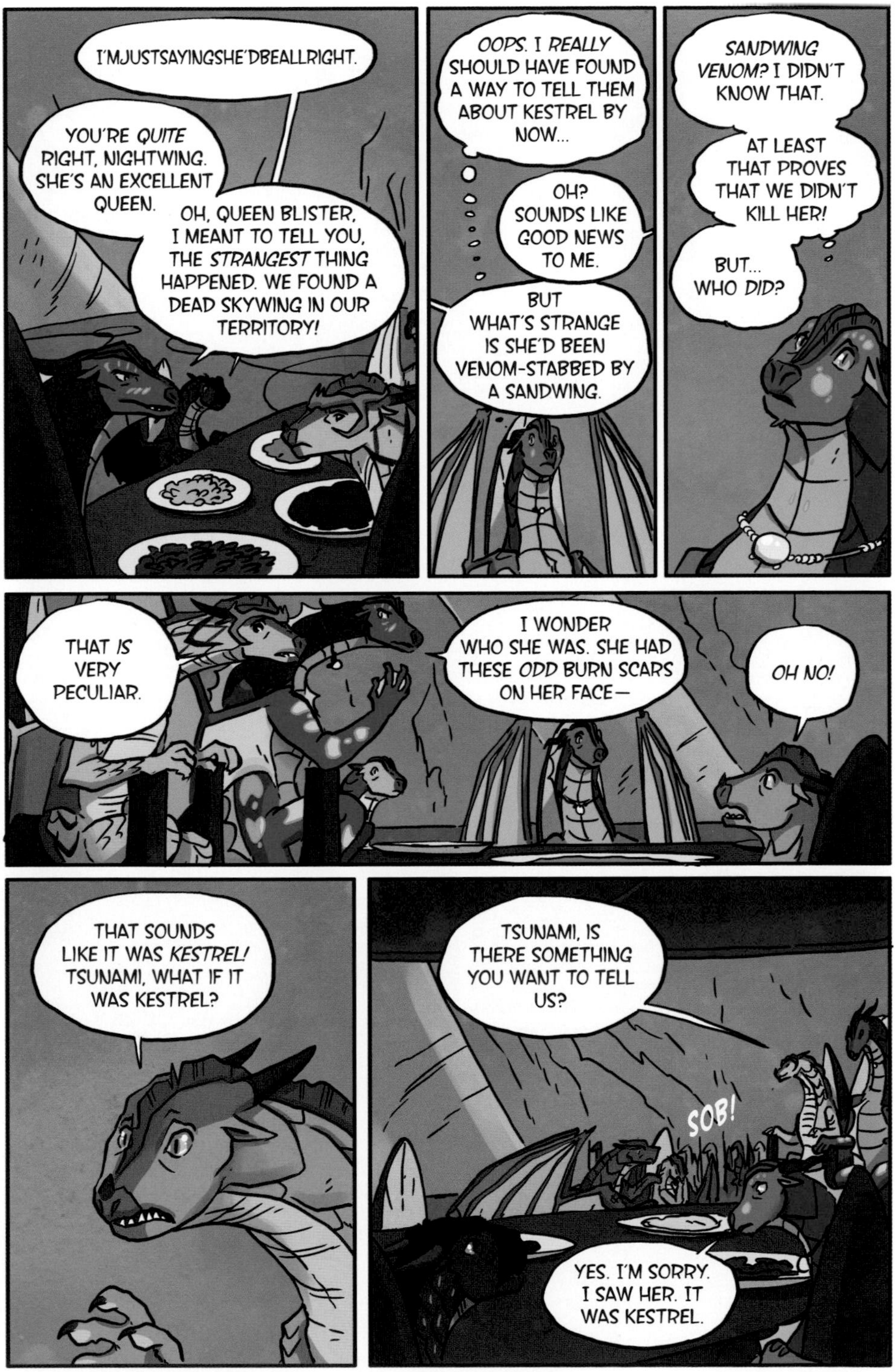
I'MJUSTSAYINGSHE'DBEALLRIGHT.
YOU'RE *QUITE* RIGHT, NIGHTWING. SHE'S AN EXCELLENT QUEEN.
OH, QUEEN BLISTER, I MEANT TO TELL YOU, THE *STRANGEST* THING HAPPENED. WE FOUND A DEAD SKYWING IN OUR TERRITORY!
OOPS. I *REALLY* SHOULD HAVE FOUND A WAY TO TELL THEM ABOUT KESTREL BY NOW...
OH? SOUNDS LIKE GOOD NEWS TO ME.
BUT WHAT'S STRANGE IS SHE'D BEEN VENOM-STABBED BY A SANDWING.
SANDWING VENOM? I DIDN'T KNOW THAT.
AT LEAST THAT PROVES THAT WE DIDN'T KILL HER!
BUT... WHO *DID?*
THAT *IS* VERY PECULIAR.
I WONDER WHO SHE WAS. SHE HAD THESE *ODD* BURN SCARS ON HER FACE—
OH NO!
THAT SOUNDS LIKE IT WAS *KESTREL!* TSUNAMI, WHAT IF IT WAS KESTREL?
TSUNAMI, IS THERE SOMETHING YOU WANT TO TELL US?
SOB!
YES. I'M SORRY. I SAW HER. IT WAS KESTREL.

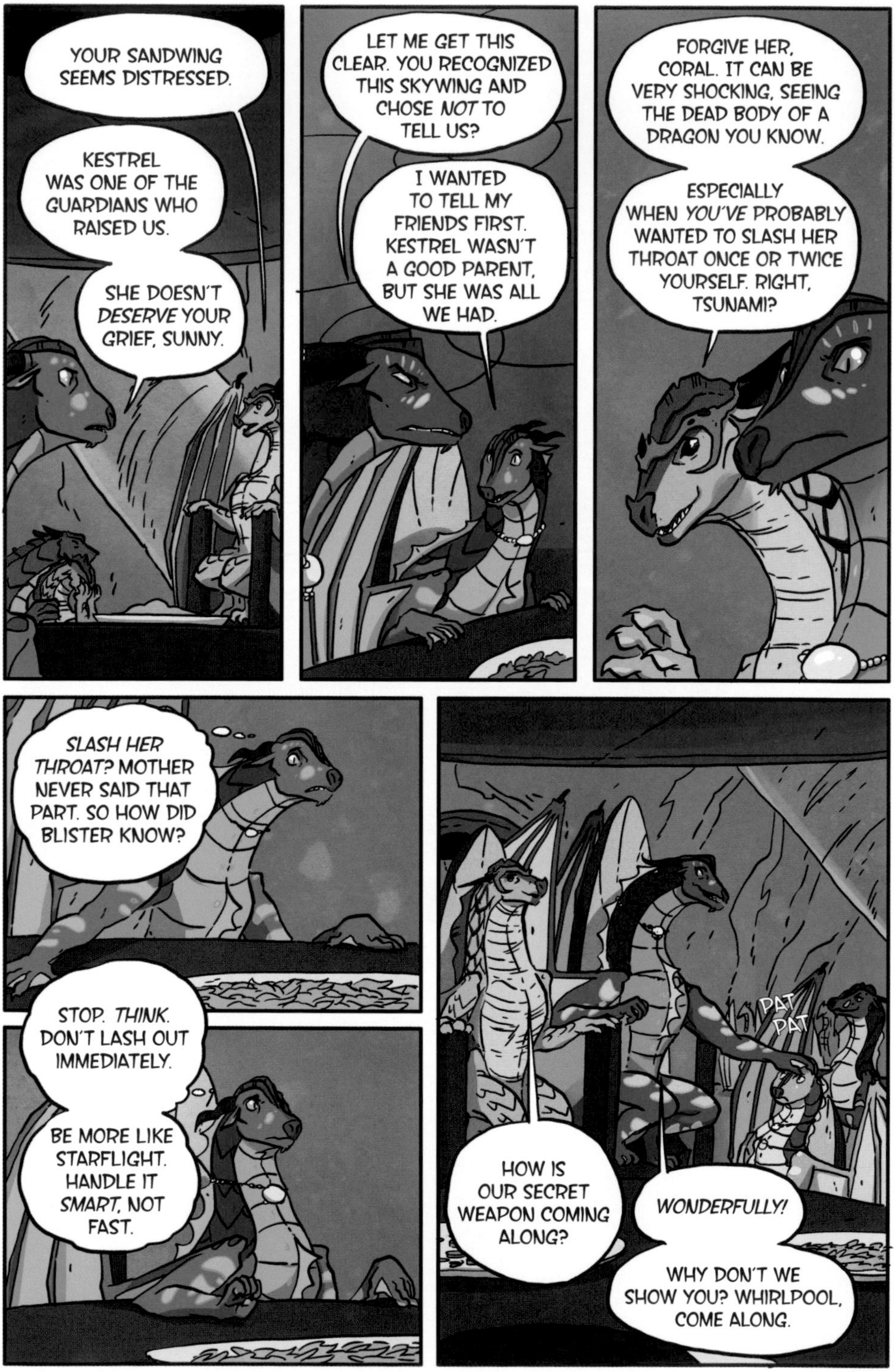
YOUR SANDWING SEEMS DISTRESSED.
KESTREL WAS ONE OF THE GUARDIANS WHO RAISED US.
SHE DOESN'T *DESERVE* YOUR GRIEF, SUNNY.
LET ME GET THIS CLEAR. YOU RECOGNIZED THIS SKYWING AND CHOSE *NOT* TO TELL US?
I WANTED TO TELL MY FRIENDS FIRST. KESTREL WASN'T A GOOD PARENT, BUT SHE WAS ALL WE HAD.
FORGIVE HER, CORAL. IT CAN BE VERY SHOCKING, SEEING THE DEAD BODY OF A DRAGON YOU KNOW.
ESPECIALLY WHEN *YOU'VE* PROBABLY WANTED TO SLASH HER THROAT ONCE OR TWICE YOURSELF. RIGHT, TSUNAMI?
SLASH HER THROAT? MOTHER NEVER SAID THAT PART. SO HOW DID BLISTER KNOW?
STOP. *THINK.* DON'T LASH OUT IMMEDIATELY.
BE MORE LIKE STARFLIGHT. HANDLE IT *SMART,* NOT FAST.
PAT PAT
HOW IS OUR SECRET WEAPON COMING ALONG?
WONDERFULLY!
WHY DON'T WE SHOW YOU? WHIRLPOOL, COME ALONG.

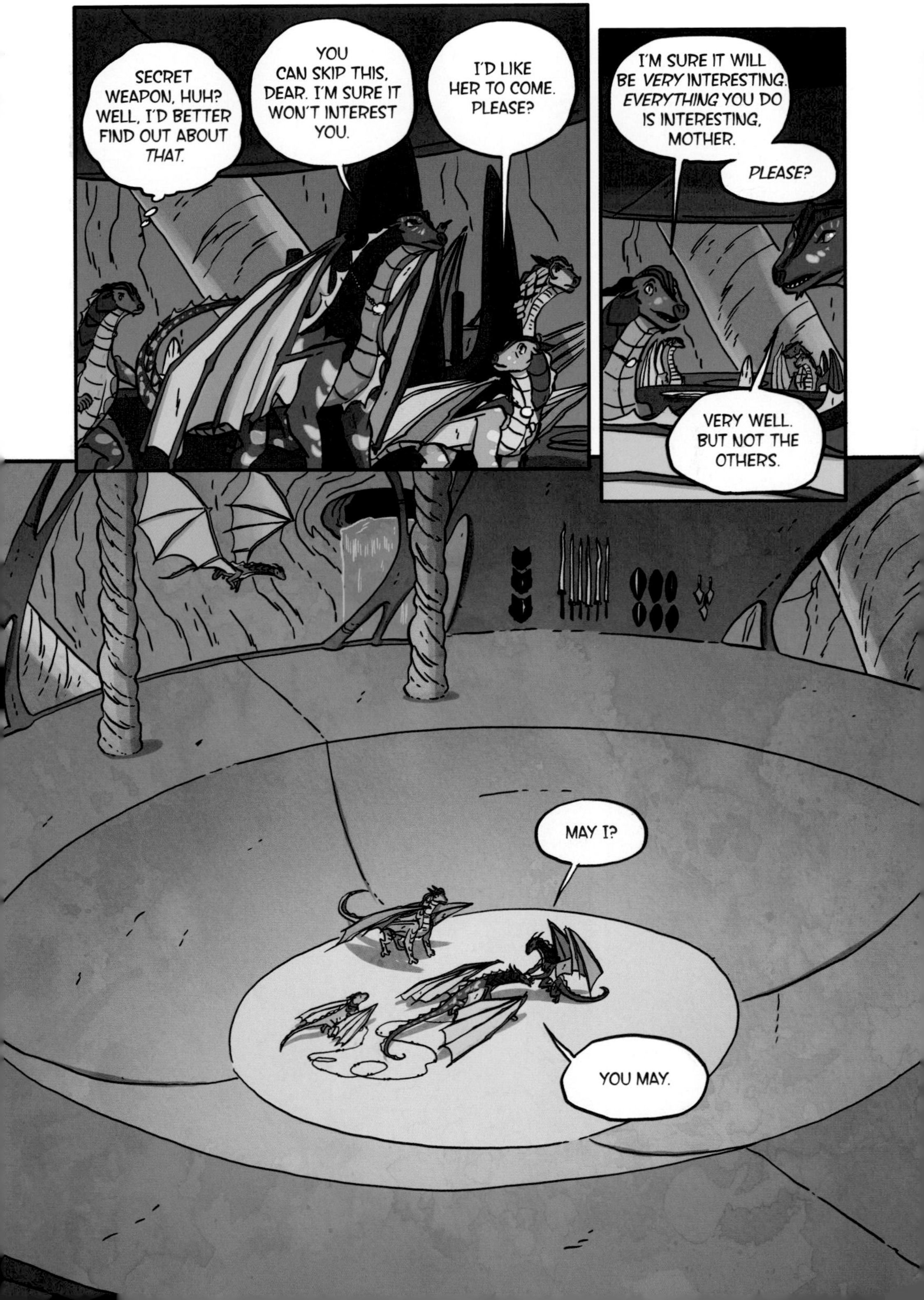
SECRET WEAPON, HUH? WELL, I'D BETTER FIND OUT ABOUT *THAT*.
YOU CAN SKIP THIS, DEAR. I'M SURE IT WON'T INTEREST YOU.
I'D LIKE HER TO COME. PLEASE?
I'M SURE IT WILL BE *VERY* INTERESTING. *EVERYTHING* YOU DO IS INTERESTING, MOTHER.
PLEASE?
VERY WELL. BUT NOT THE OTHERS.
MAY I?
YOU MAY.

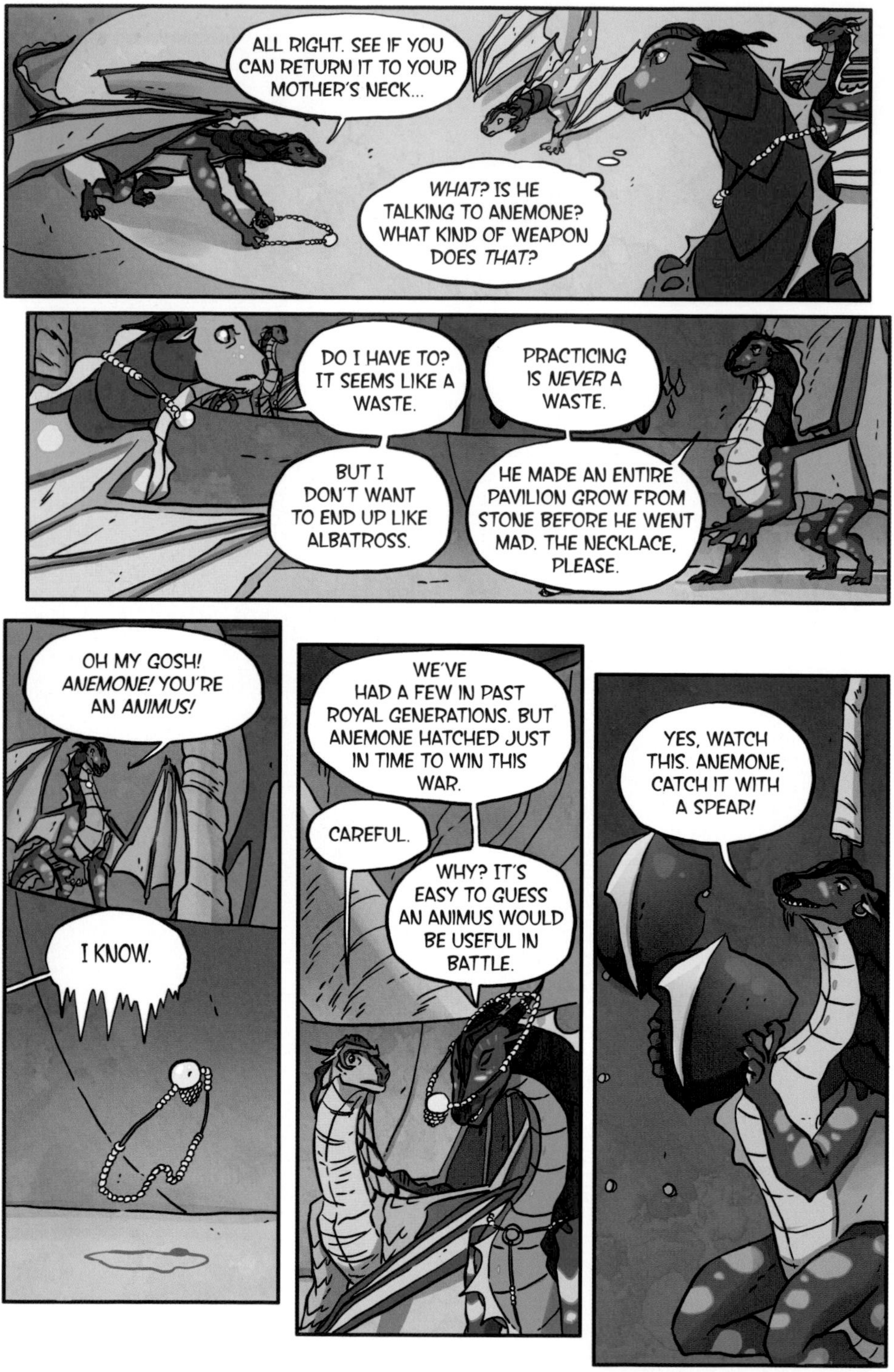
ALL RIGHT. SEE IF YOU CAN RETURN IT TO YOUR MOTHER'S NECK...
WHAT? IS HE TALKING TO ANEMONE? WHAT KIND OF WEAPON DOES *THAT?*
DO I HAVE TO? IT SEEMS LIKE A WASTE.
BUT I DON'T WANT TO END UP LIKE ALBATROSS.
PRACTICING IS *NEVER* A WASTE.
HE MADE AN ENTIRE PAVILION GROW FROM STONE BEFORE HE WENT MAD. THE NECKLACE, PLEASE.
OH MY *GOSH!* *ANEMONE!* YOU'RE AN *ANIMUS!*
I KNOW.
WE'VE HAD A FEW IN PAST ROYAL GENERATIONS. BUT ANEMONE HATCHED JUST IN TIME TO WIN THIS WAR.
CAREFUL.
WHY? IT'S EASY TO GUESS AN ANIMUS WOULD BE USEFUL IN BATTLE.
YES, WATCH THIS. ANEMONE, CATCH IT WITH A SPEAR!

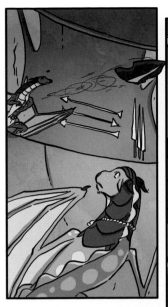

IMPRESSIVE. BUT NOT MUCH MORE THAN WHAT I SAW LAST TIME. WHAT ABOUT *BIGGER* OBJECTS? HOW MUCH LONGER MUST SHE TRAIN?

I'M SURE SHE'S NEARLY READY.

YEARS. LOTS OF YEARS.

CORAL—

LET'S TALK *PRIVATELY.*

TSUNAMI, ANEMONE, STAY HERE.

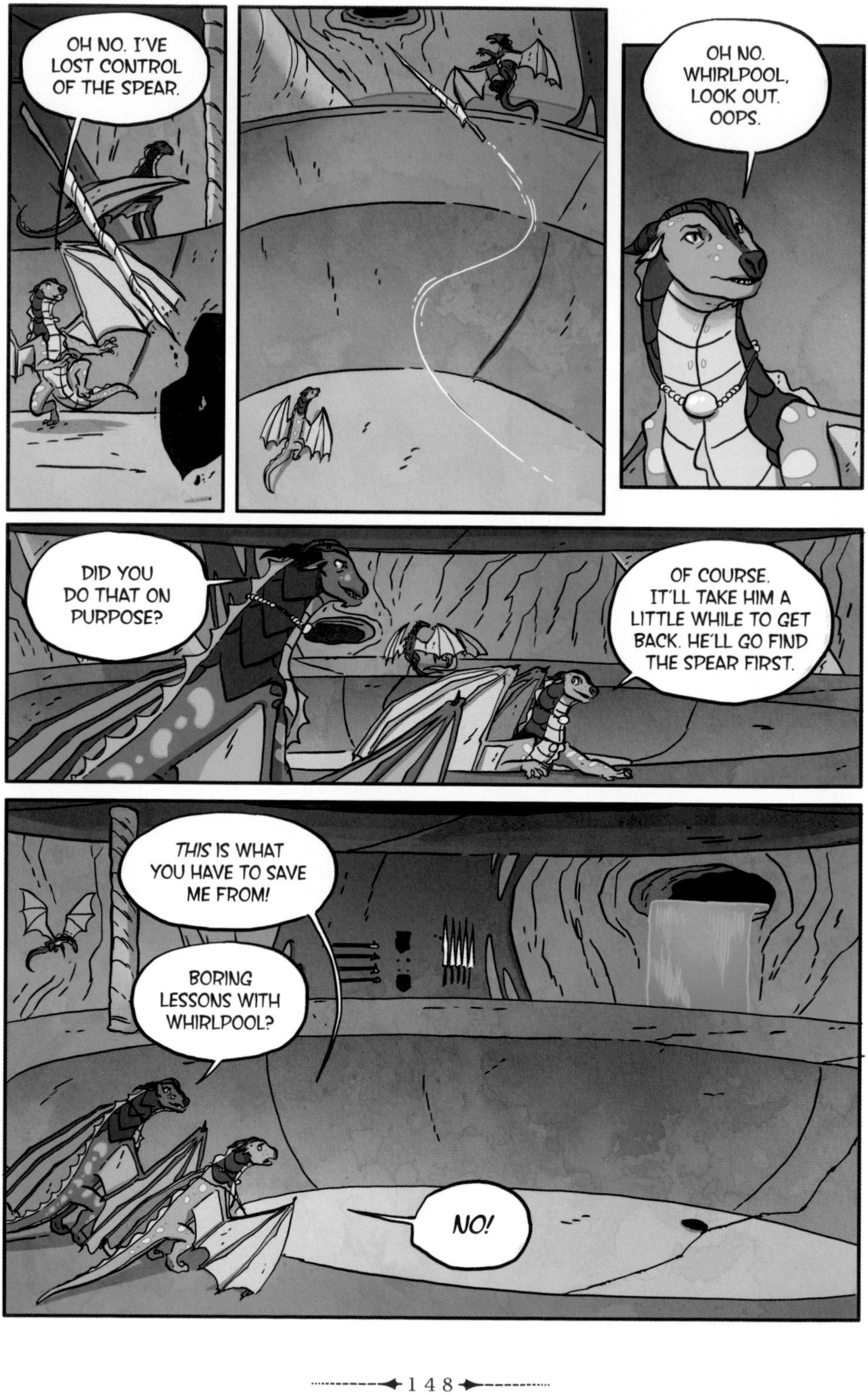
OH NO. I'VE LOST CONTROL OF THE SPEAR.
OH NO. WHIRLPOOL, LOOK OUT. OOPS.
DID YOU DO THAT ON PURPOSE?
OF COURSE. IT'LL TAKE HIM A LITTLE WHILE TO GET BACK. HE'LL GO FIND THE SPEAR FIRST.
THIS IS WHAT YOU HAVE TO SAVE ME FROM!
BORING LESSONS WITH WHIRLPOOL?
NO!

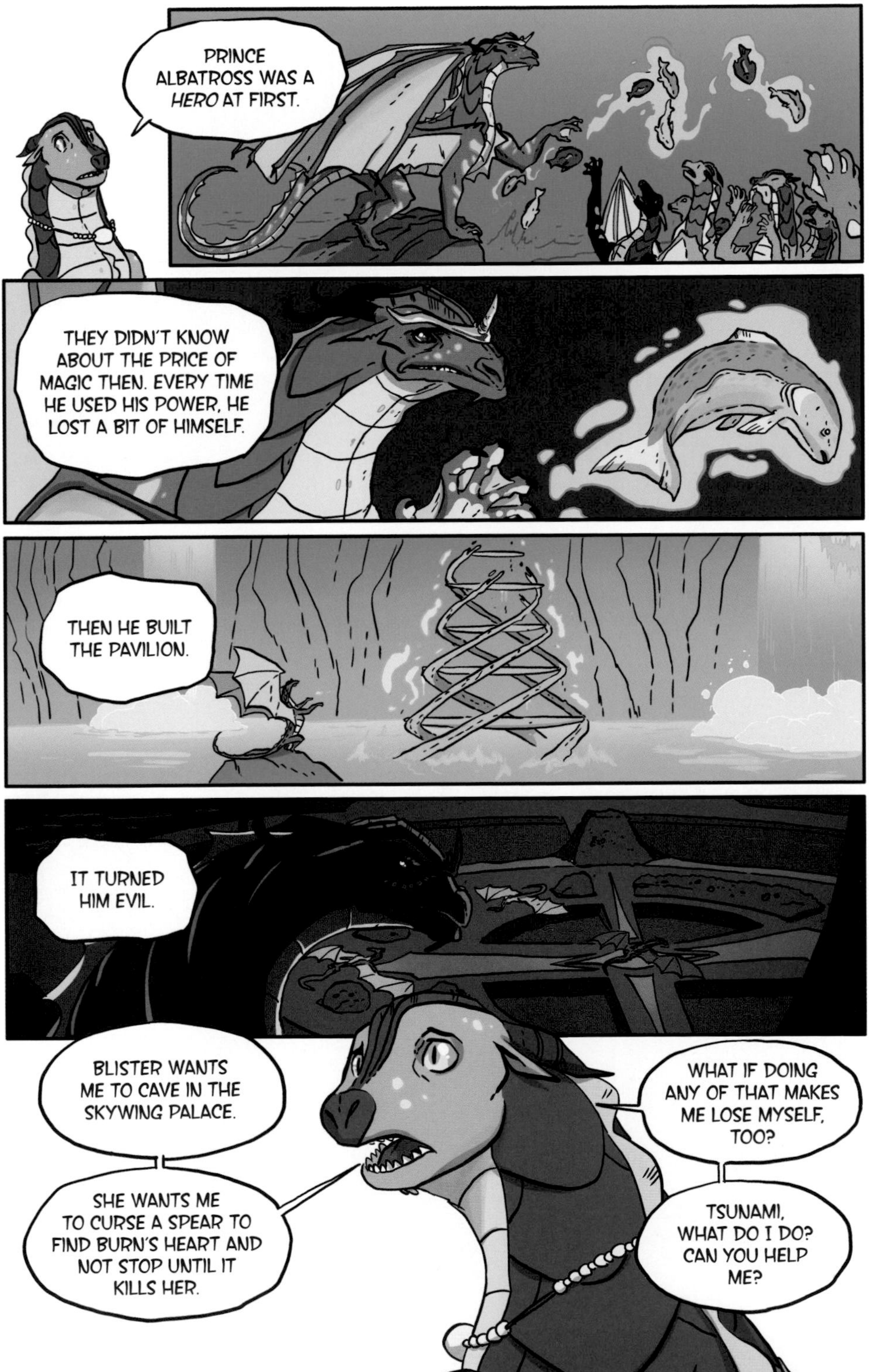
PRINCE ALBATROSS WAS A *HERO* AT FIRST.
THEY DIDN'T KNOW ABOUT THE PRICE OF MAGIC THEN. EVERY TIME HE USED HIS POWER, HE LOST A BIT OF HIMSELF.
THEN HE BUILT THE PAVILION.
IT TURNED HIM EVIL.
BLISTER WANTS ME TO CAVE IN THE SKYWING PALACE.
SHE WANTS ME TO CURSE A SPEAR TO FIND BURN'S HEART AND NOT STOP UNTIL IT KILLS HER.
WHAT IF DOING ANY OF THAT MAKES ME LOSE MYSELF, TOO?
TSUNAMI, WHAT DO I DO? CAN YOU HELP ME?

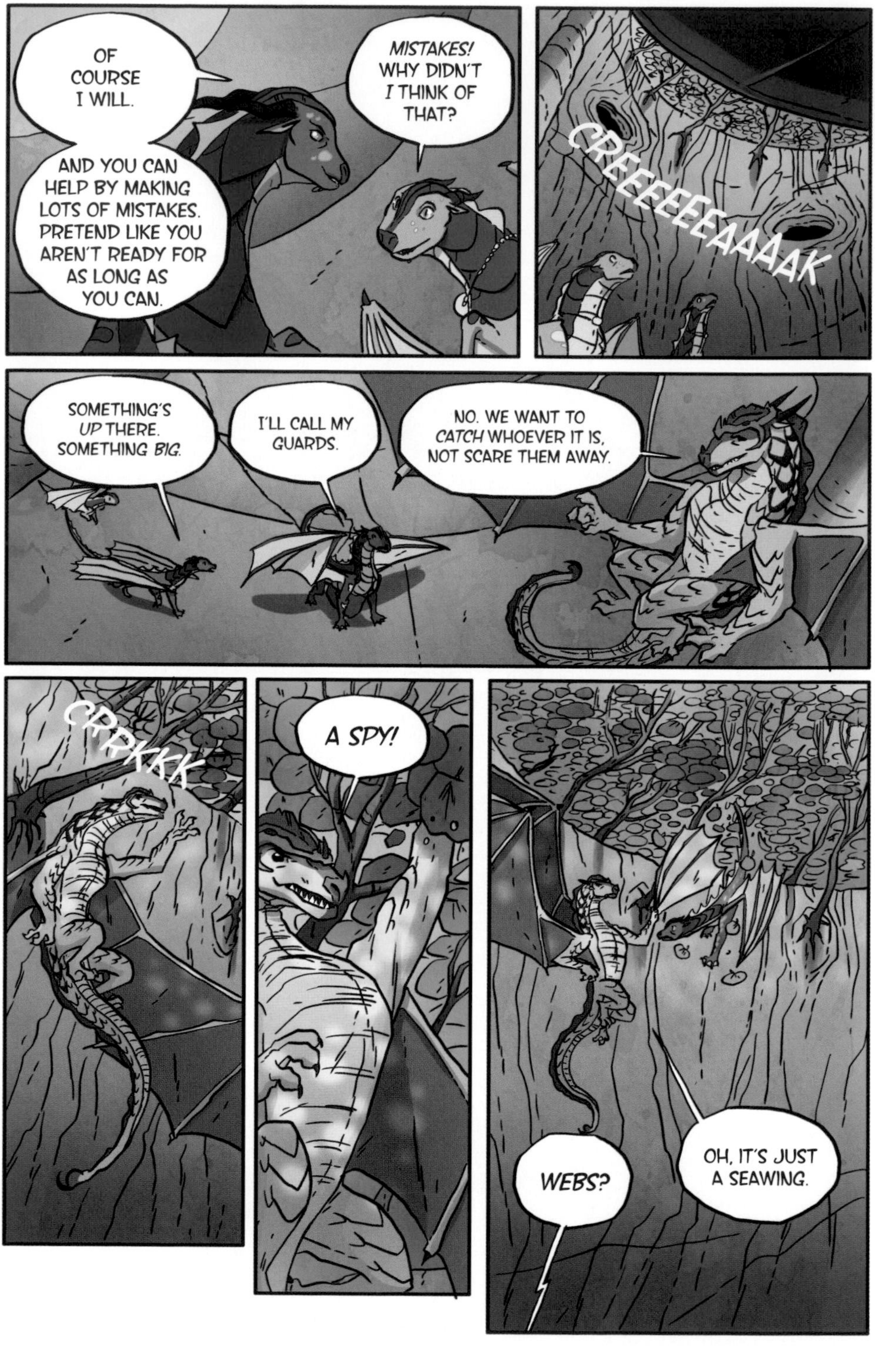

OF COURSE I WILL.
AND YOU CAN HELP BY MAKING LOTS OF MISTAKES. PRETEND LIKE YOU AREN'T READY FOR AS LONG AS YOU CAN.
MISTAKES! WHY DIDN'T I THINK OF THAT?
CREEEEEEAAAAK
SOMETHING'S UP THERE. SOMETHING BIG.
I'LL CALL MY GUARDS.
NO. WE WANT TO CATCH WHOEVER IT IS, NOT SCARE THEM AWAY.
CRRKKK
A SPY!
OH, IT'S JUST A SEAWING.
WEBS?

NOT *JUST* A SEAWING. THIS IS OUR TRIBE'S BIGGEST TRAITOR.

YOUR MAJESTY. PLEASE. I'VE COME TO BEG FOR MERCY.

MERCY? AFTER WHAT YOU DID?

MERCY *DENIED!*

CRACK!

MOTHER, DON'T... HE—HE MIGHT HAVE INFORMATION...

I...

WHY WOULD YOU SAVE HIS LIFE AFTER EVERYTHING HE *DID* TO YOU?

PERHAPS TSUNAMI MEANS THAT WE CAN NOW FIND OUT HOW HE SNUCK INTO THE ROYAL HATCHERY. *CLEVER* DRAGONET. SHE MUST GET HER BRAINS FROM YOU.

I SUPPOSE INTERROGATING HIM *WOULD* BE USEFUL.

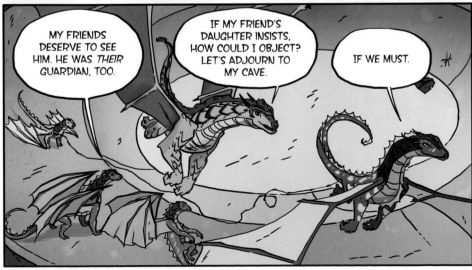

MY FRIENDS DESERVE TO SEE HIM. HE WAS *THEIR* GUARDIAN, TOO.

IF MY FRIEND'S DAUGHTER INSISTS, HOW COULD I OBJECT? LET'S ADJOURN TO MY CAVE.

IF WE MUST.

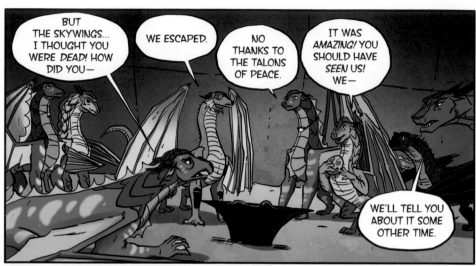

BUT THE SKYWINGS... I THOUGHT YOU WERE *DEAD!* HOW DID YOU—

WE ESCAPED.

NO THANKS TO THE TALONS OF PEACE.

IT WAS *AMAZING!* YOU SHOULD HAVE *SEEN* US! WE—

WE'LL TELL YOU ABOUT IT SOME OTHER TIME.

I WAS SURE YOU WERE TOO COWARDLY EVER TO RETURN.

I KNOW I'M NOT WORTHY, YOUR MAJESTY. BUT I—I HOPED...

WHY DID YOU STEAL ONE OF *MY* EGGS? IT COULD HAVE BEEN ANYONE'S!

THE EGG WAS SO BLUE. IT *HAD* TO BE THE ONE FROM THE PROPHECY.

I WOULD *NEVER* HAVE BETRAYED YOU FOR ANYTHING ELSE, BUT FOR PEACE...

HOW DID YOU GET INTO THE HATCHERY? I HAD GUARDS POSTED AT THAT DOOR EVERY MOMENT.

I DRUGGED THE GUARDS. I—I KNEW SOMEONE WHO HELPED ME. IT WASN'T THEIR FAULT.

WELL, I KILLED THEM ANYWAY.

AS FOR THE *SOMEONE* WHO HELPED YOU—YOUR WIFE, I ASSUME?

OF COURSE, THAT'S WHY SHE WAS REASSIGNED FROM THE KITCHENS TO THE FRONT LINES. TOO BAD THAT FIRST BATTLE WAS SUCH A BLOODBATH.

SOB!

NOW I KNOW THE DRAGONETS ARE SAFE, YOU CAN DO WHATEVER YOU LIKE TO ME.

I WILL. WE CAN *START* WITH YOU TELLING ME WHERE TO FIND THE TALONS OF PEACE.

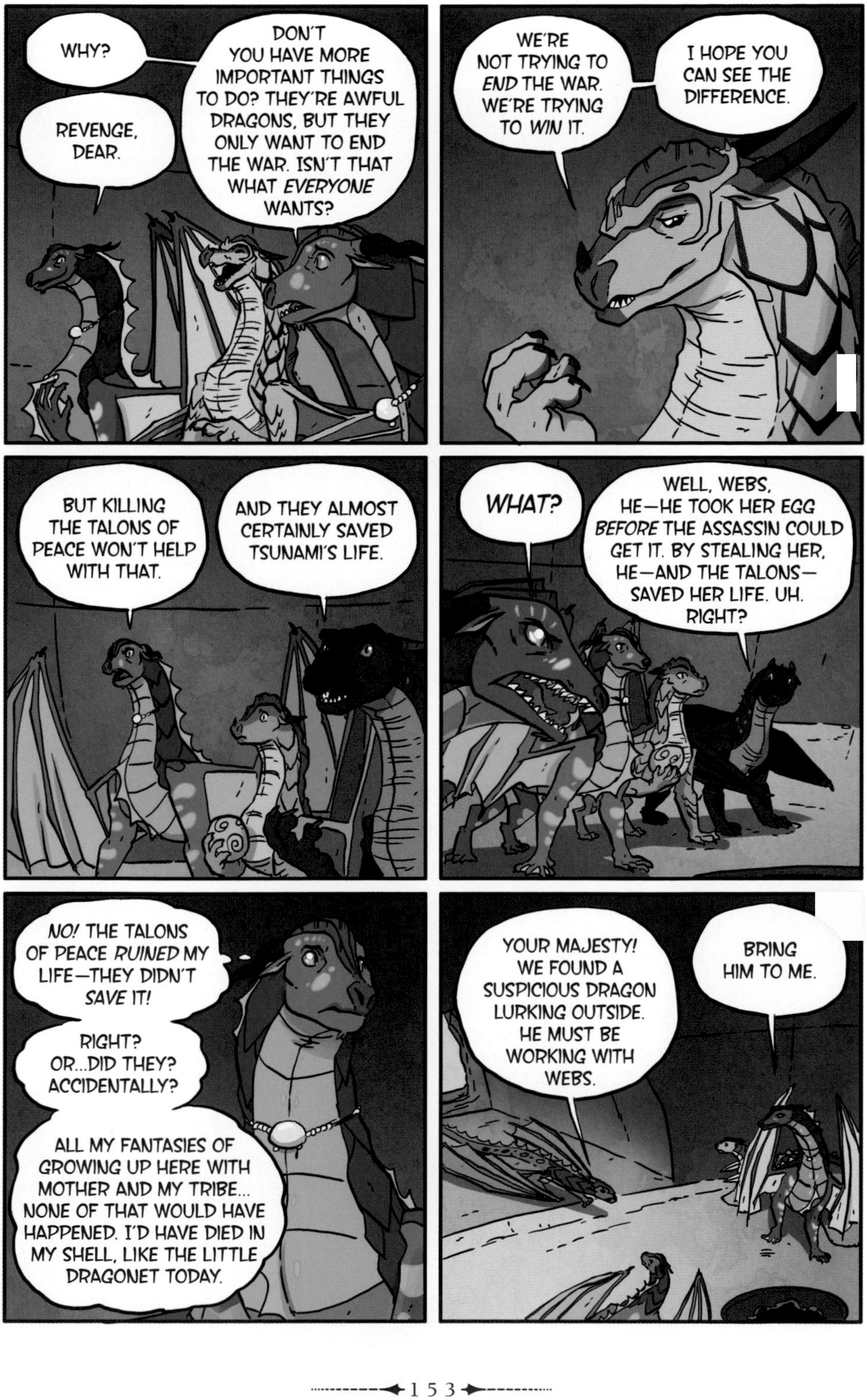
WHY?
REVENGE, DEAR.
DON'T YOU HAVE MORE IMPORTANT THINGS TO DO? THEY'RE AWFUL DRAGONS, BUT THEY ONLY WANT TO END THE WAR. ISN'T THAT WHAT *EVERYONE* WANTS?
WE'RE NOT TRYING TO *END* THE WAR. WE'RE TRYING TO *WIN* IT.
I HOPE YOU CAN SEE THE DIFFERENCE.
BUT KILLING THE TALONS OF PEACE WON'T HELP WITH THAT.
AND THEY ALMOST CERTAINLY SAVED TSUNAMI'S LIFE.
WHAT?
WELL, WEBS, HE—HE TOOK HER EGG *BEFORE* THE ASSASSIN COULD GET IT. BY STEALING HER, HE—AND THE TALONS—SAVED HER LIFE. UH. RIGHT?
NO! THE TALONS OF PEACE *RUINED* MY LIFE—THEY DIDN'T *SAVE* IT!
RIGHT? OR...DID THEY? ACCIDENTALLY?
ALL MY FANTASIES OF GROWING UP HERE WITH MOTHER AND MY TRIBE... NONE OF THAT WOULD HAVE HAPPENED. I'D HAVE DIED IN MY SHELL, LIKE THE LITTLE DRAGONET TODAY.
YOUR MAJESTY! WE FOUND A SUSPICIOUS DRAGON LURKING OUTSIDE. HE MUST BE WORKING WITH WEBS.
BRING HIM TO ME.

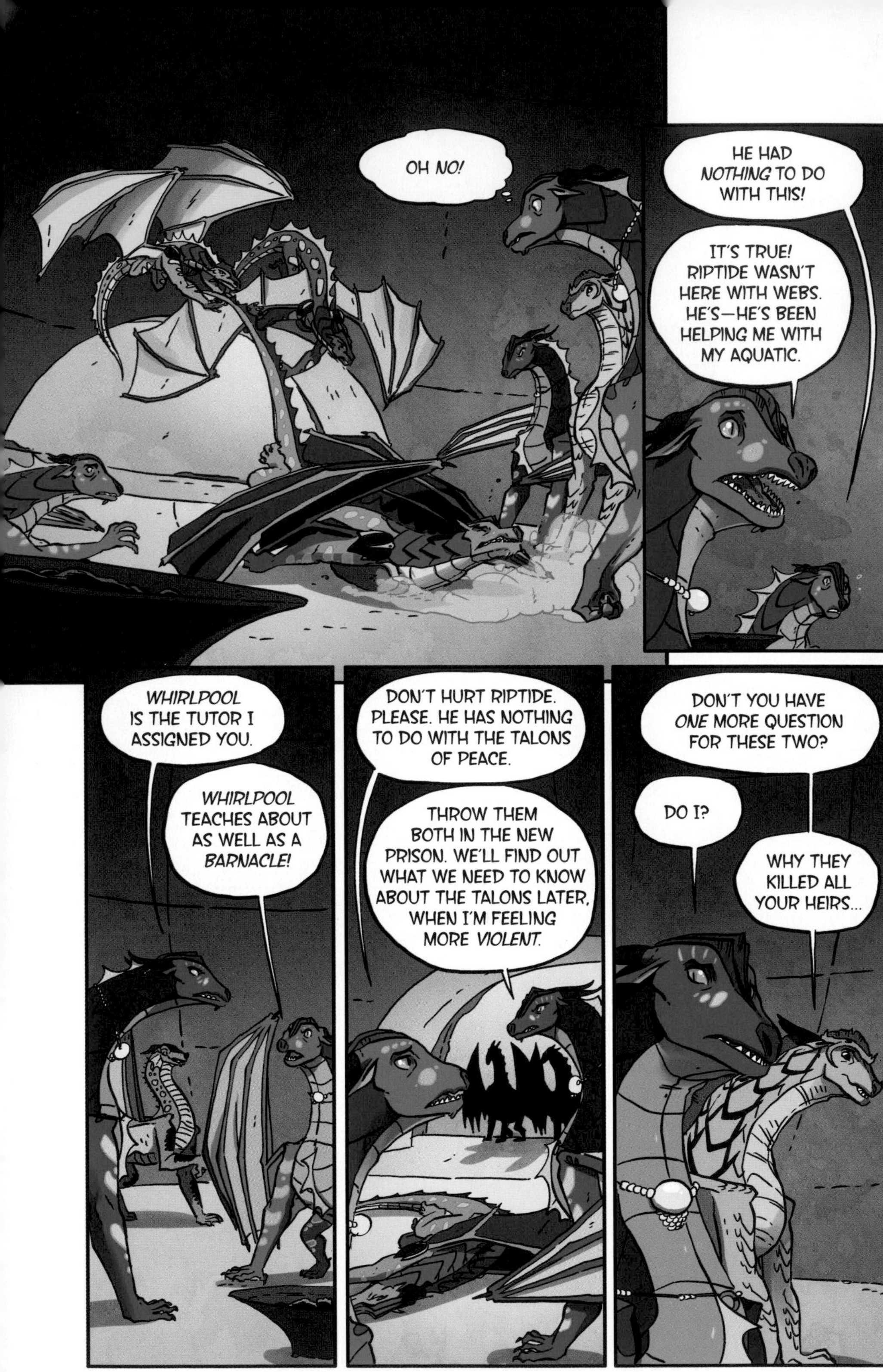
OH NO!
HE HAD NOTHING TO DO WITH THIS!
IT'S TRUE! RIPTIDE WASN'T HERE WITH WEBS. HE'S—HE'S BEEN HELPING ME WITH MY AQUATIC.
WHIRLPOOL IS THE TUTOR I ASSIGNED YOU.
WHIRLPOOL TEACHES ABOUT AS WELL AS A BARNACLE!
DON'T HURT RIPTIDE. PLEASE. HE HAS NOTHING TO DO WITH THE TALONS OF PEACE.
THROW THEM BOTH IN THE NEW PRISON. WE'LL FIND OUT WHAT WE NEED TO KNOW ABOUT THE TALONS LATER, WHEN I'M FEELING MORE VIOLENT.
DON'T YOU HAVE ONE MORE QUESTION FOR THESE TWO?
DO I?
WHY THEY KILLED ALL YOUR HEIRS...

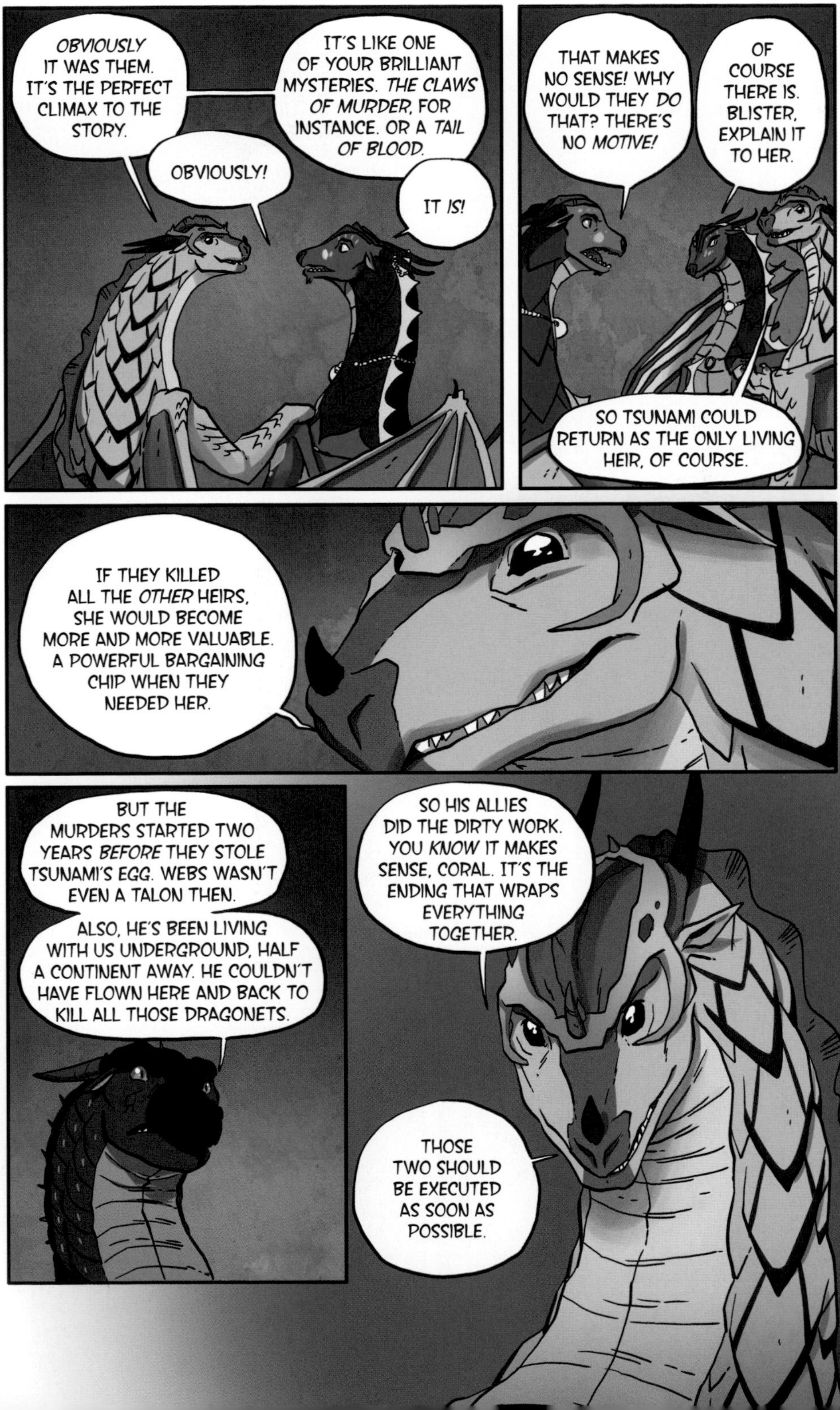

OBVIOUSLY IT WAS THEM. IT'S THE PERFECT CLIMAX TO THE STORY.
IT'S LIKE ONE OF YOUR BRILLIANT MYSTERIES. *THE CLAWS OF MURDER*, FOR INSTANCE. OR A *TAIL OF BLOOD*.
OBVIOUSLY!
IT *IS*!
THAT MAKES NO SENSE! WHY WOULD THEY *DO* THAT? THERE'S NO *MOTIVE*!
OF COURSE THERE IS. BLISTER, EXPLAIN IT TO HER.
SO TSUNAMI COULD RETURN AS THE ONLY LIVING HEIR, OF COURSE.
IF THEY KILLED ALL THE *OTHER* HEIRS, SHE WOULD BECOME MORE AND MORE VALUABLE. A POWERFUL BARGAINING CHIP WHEN THEY NEEDED HER.
BUT THE MURDERS STARTED TWO YEARS *BEFORE* THEY STOLE TSUNAMI'S EGG. WEBS WASN'T EVEN A TALON THEN.
ALSO, HE'S BEEN LIVING WITH US UNDERGROUND, HALF A CONTINENT AWAY. HE COULDN'T HAVE FLOWN HERE AND BACK TO KILL ALL THOSE DRAGONETS.
SO HIS ALLIES DID THE DIRTY WORK. YOU *KNOW* IT MAKES SENSE, CORAL. IT'S THE ENDING THAT WRAPS EVERYTHING TOGETHER.
THOSE TWO SHOULD BE EXECUTED AS SOON AS POSSIBLE.

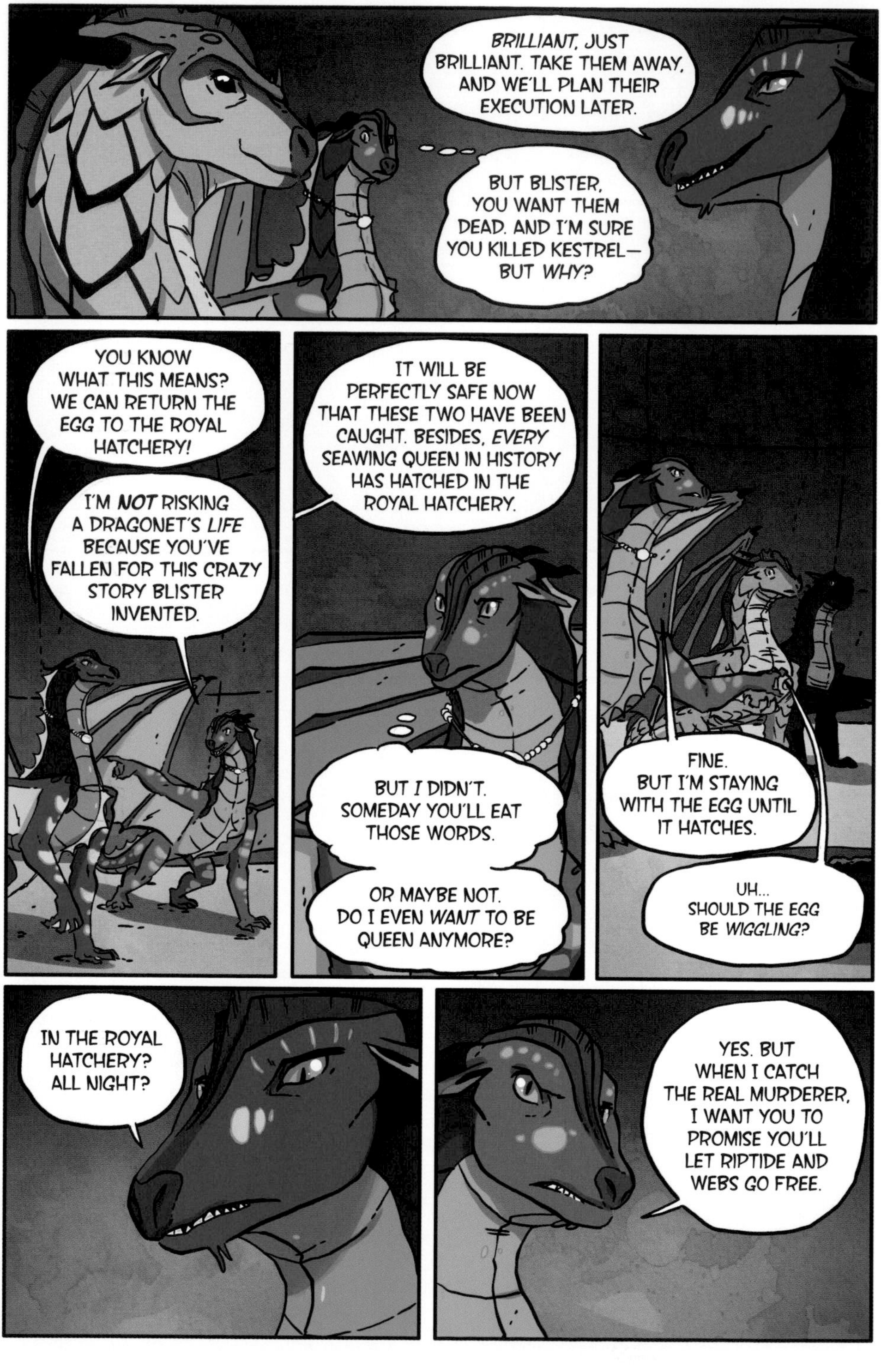
BRILLIANT, JUST BRILLIANT. TAKE THEM AWAY, AND WE'LL PLAN THEIR EXECUTION LATER.
BUT BLISTER, YOU WANT THEM DEAD. AND I'M SURE YOU KILLED KESTREL— BUT *WHY*?
YOU KNOW WHAT THIS MEANS? WE CAN RETURN THE EGG TO THE ROYAL HATCHERY!
I'M ***NOT*** RISKING A DRAGONET'S *LIFE* BECAUSE YOU'VE FALLEN FOR THIS CRAZY STORY BLISTER INVENTED.
IT WILL BE PERFECTLY SAFE NOW THAT THESE TWO HAVE BEEN CAUGHT. BESIDES, *EVERY* SEAWING QUEEN IN HISTORY HAS HATCHED IN THE ROYAL HATCHERY.
BUT *I* DIDN'T. SOMEDAY YOU'LL EAT THOSE WORDS.
OR MAYBE NOT. DO I EVEN *WANT* TO BE QUEEN ANYMORE?
FINE. BUT I'M STAYING WITH THE EGG UNTIL IT HATCHES.
UH... SHOULD THE EGG BE *WIGGLING*?
IN THE ROYAL HATCHERY? ALL NIGHT?
YES. BUT WHEN I CATCH THE REAL MURDERER, I WANT YOU TO PROMISE YOU'LL LET RIPTIDE AND WEBS GO FREE.

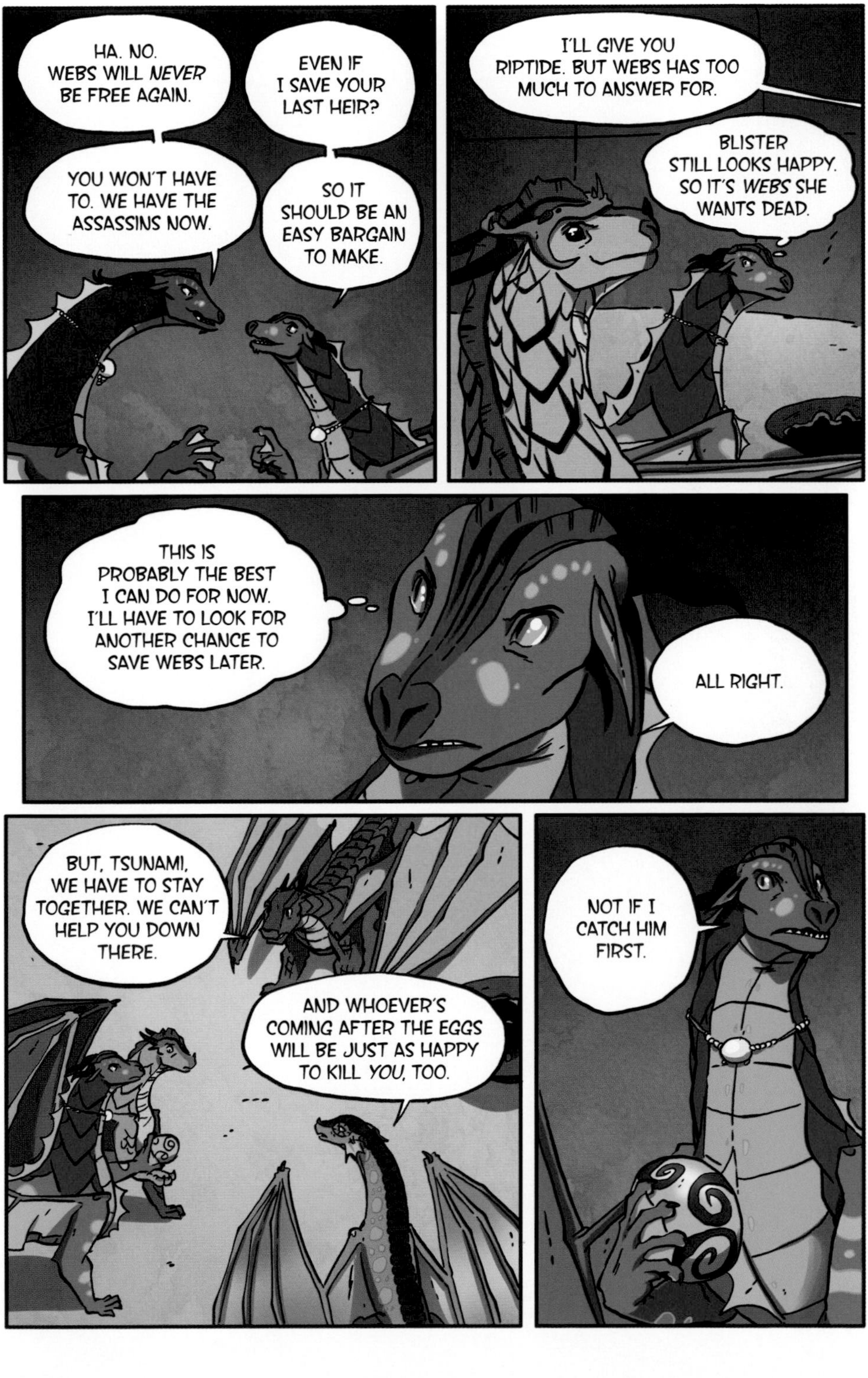
HA. NO. WEBS WILL *NEVER* BE FREE AGAIN.
EVEN IF I SAVE YOUR LAST HEIR?
YOU WON'T HAVE TO. WE HAVE THE ASSASSINS NOW.
SO IT SHOULD BE AN EASY BARGAIN TO MAKE.
I'LL GIVE YOU RIPTIDE. BUT WEBS HAS TOO MUCH TO ANSWER FOR.
BLISTER STILL LOOKS HAPPY. SO IT'S *WEBS* SHE WANTS DEAD.
THIS IS PROBABLY THE BEST I CAN DO FOR NOW. I'LL HAVE TO LOOK FOR ANOTHER CHANCE TO SAVE WEBS LATER.
ALL RIGHT.
BUT, TSUNAMI, WE HAVE TO STAY TOGETHER. WE CAN'T HELP YOU DOWN THERE.
AND WHOEVER'S COMING AFTER THE EGGS WILL BE JUST AS HAPPY TO KILL *YOU*, TOO.
NOT IF I CATCH HIM FIRST.

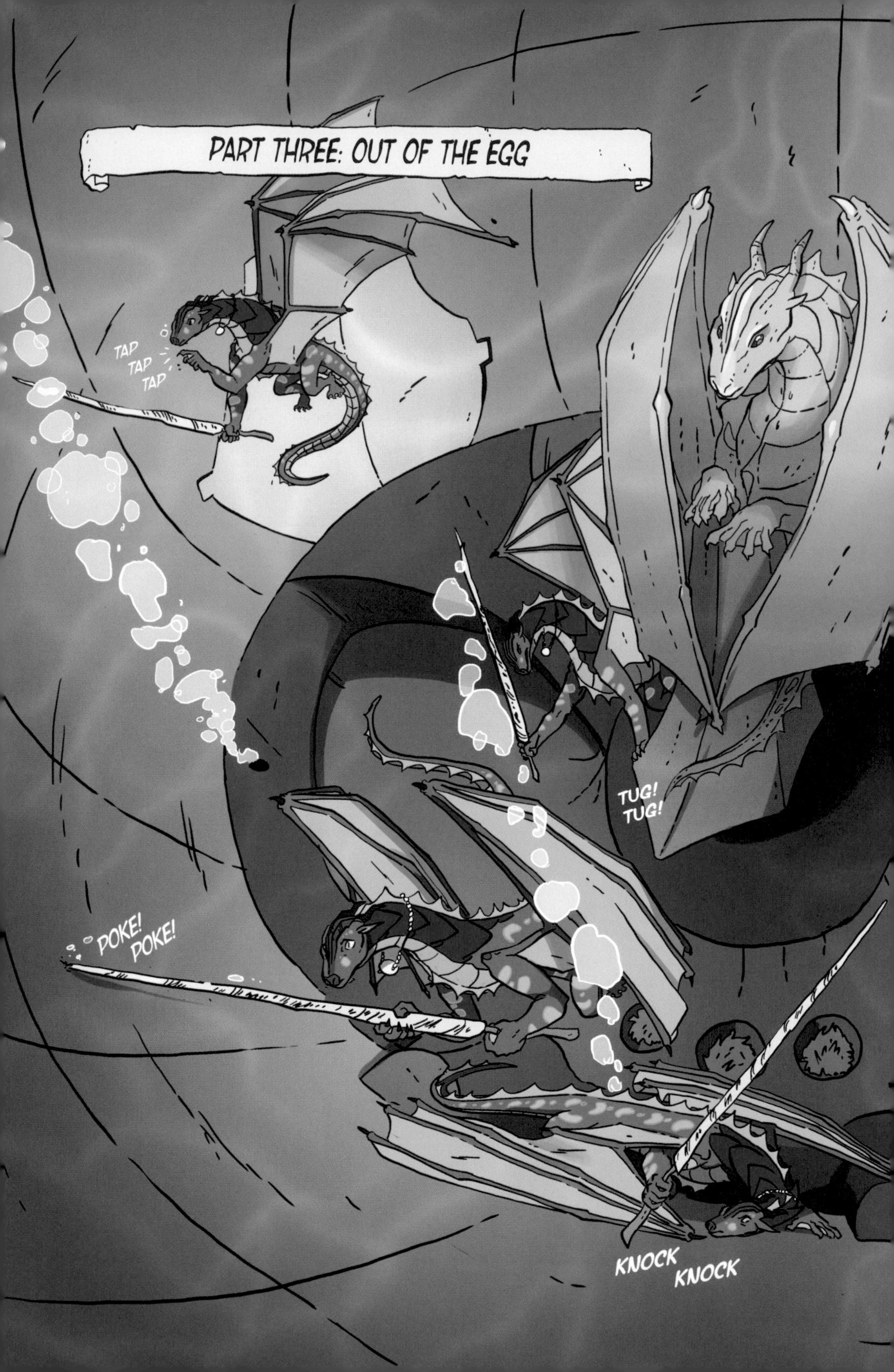
PART THREE: OUT OF THE EGG
TAP
TAP
TAP
TUG!
TUG!
POKE!
POKE!
KNOCK
KNOCK

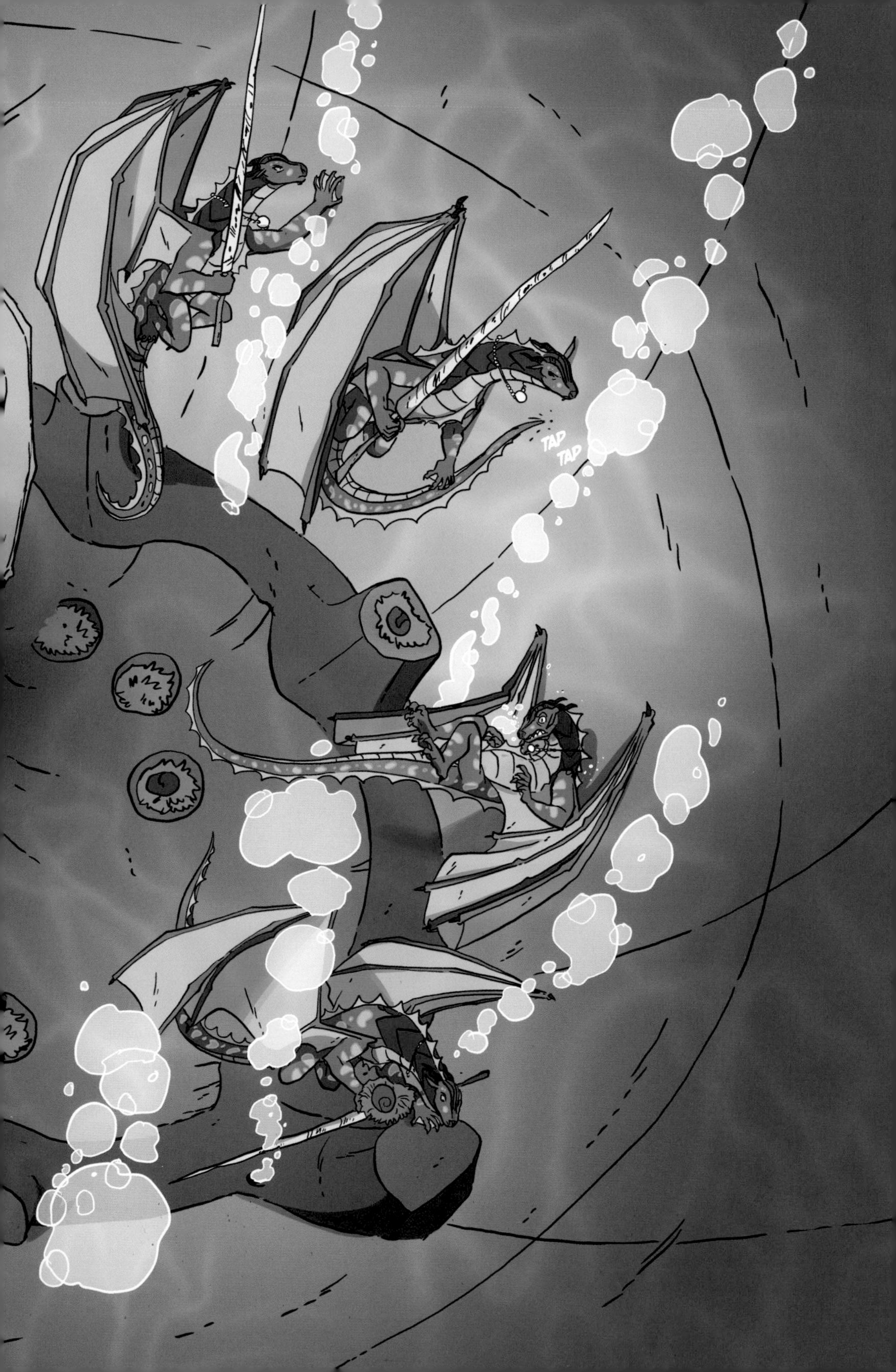
TAP TAP

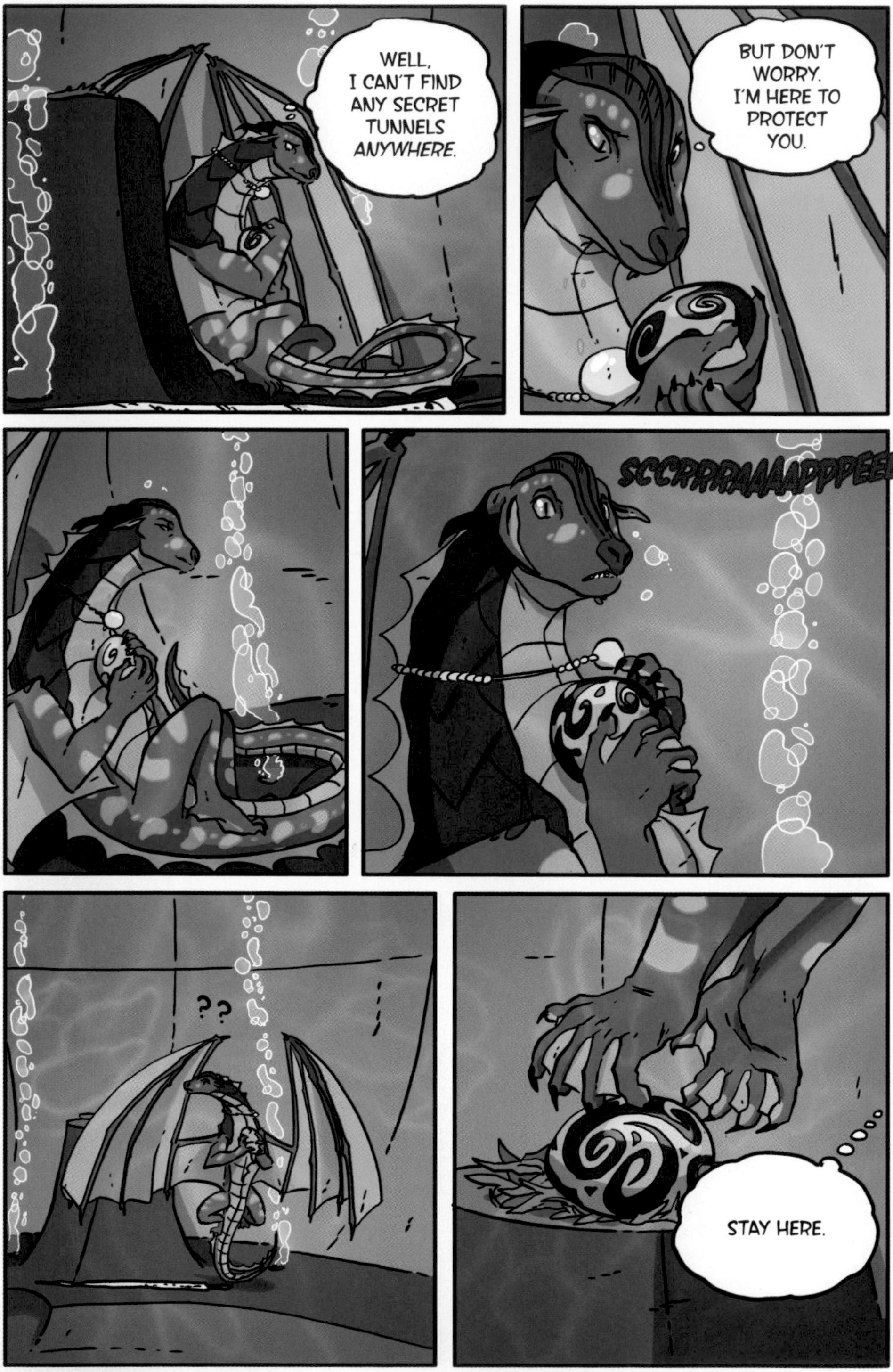
WELL, I CAN'T FIND ANY SECRET TUNNELS *ANYWHERE*.
BUT DON'T WORRY. I'M HERE TO PROTECT YOU.
SCCRRRRAAAAPPPEEE
??
STAY HERE.

SCCRRRRAAAAPPPEEE
SCCRRRRAAAAPPPEEE

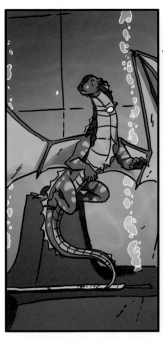

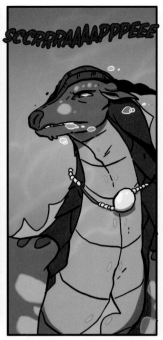

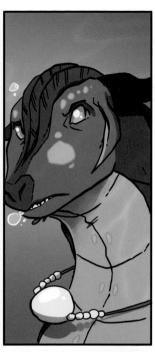

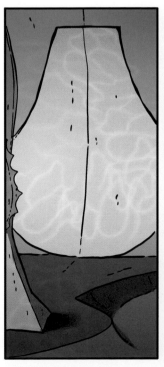

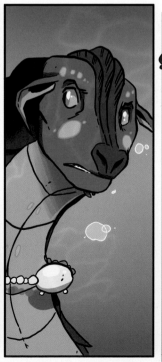

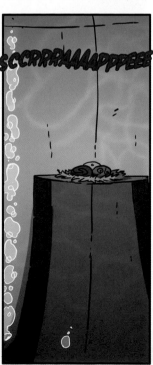

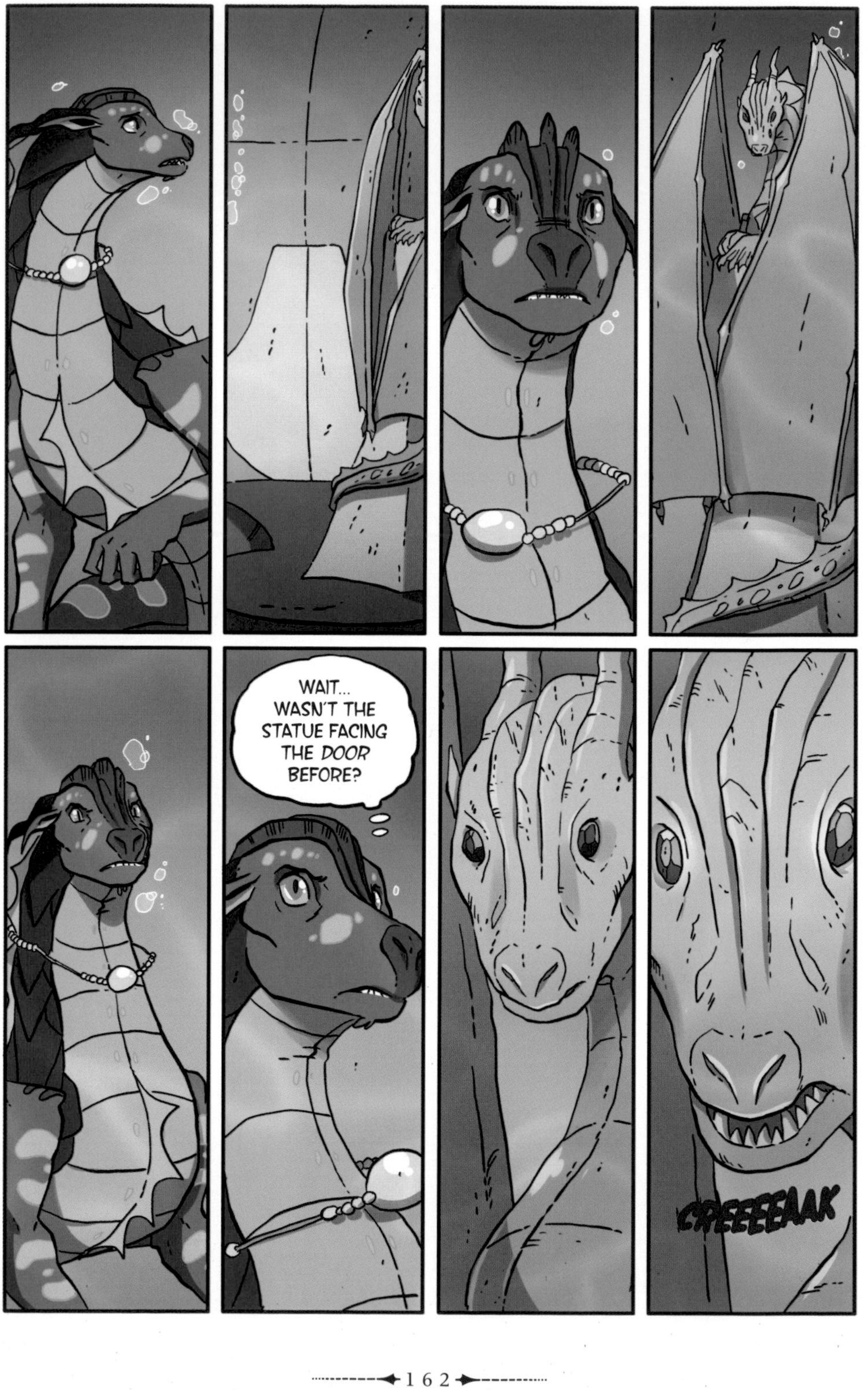
WAIT...
WASN'T THE
STATUE FACING
THE *DOOR*
BEFORE?
CREEEEEAAK

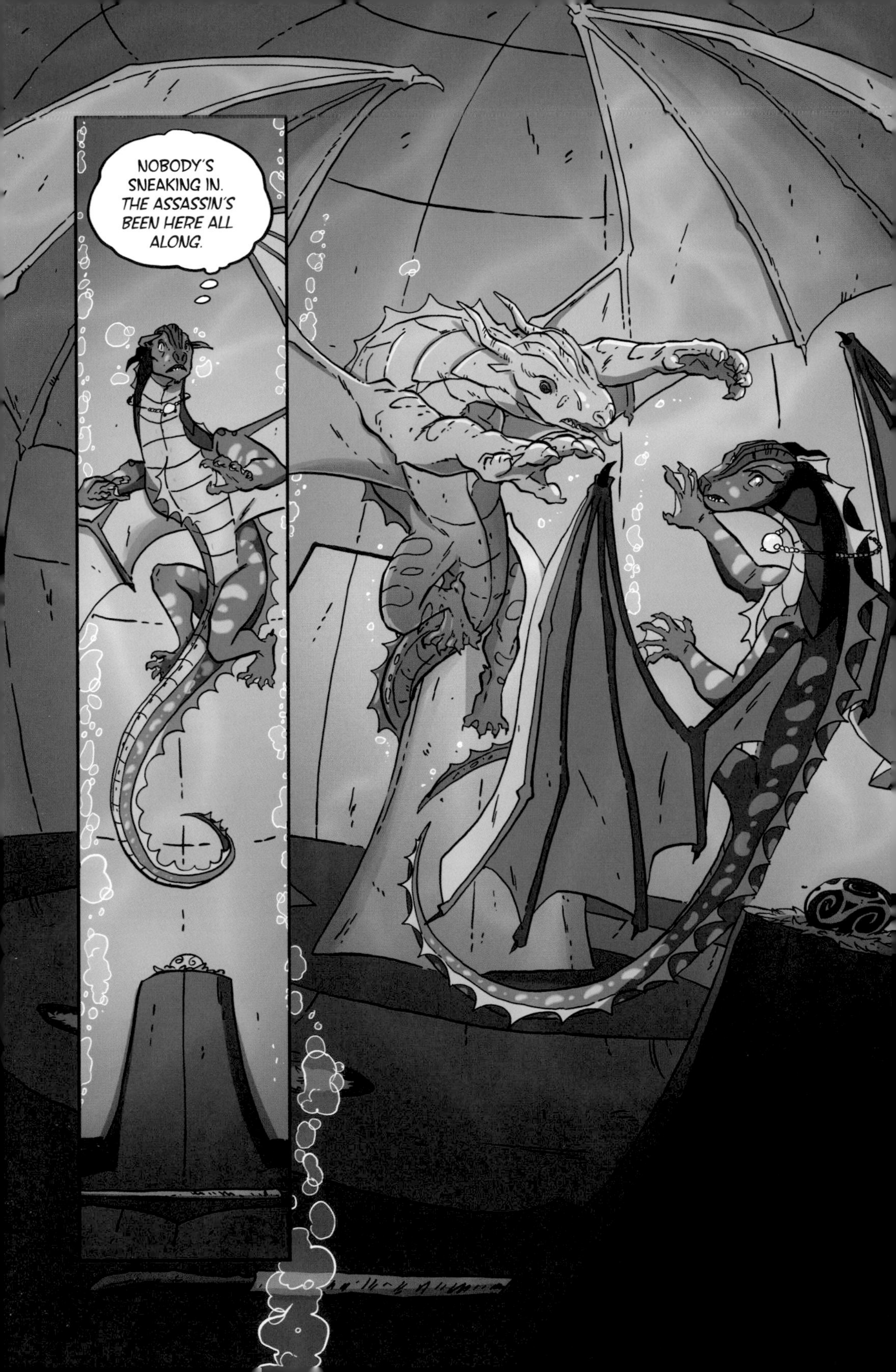
NOBODY'S SNEAKING IN. *THE ASSASSIN'S* BEEN HERE ALL ALONG.

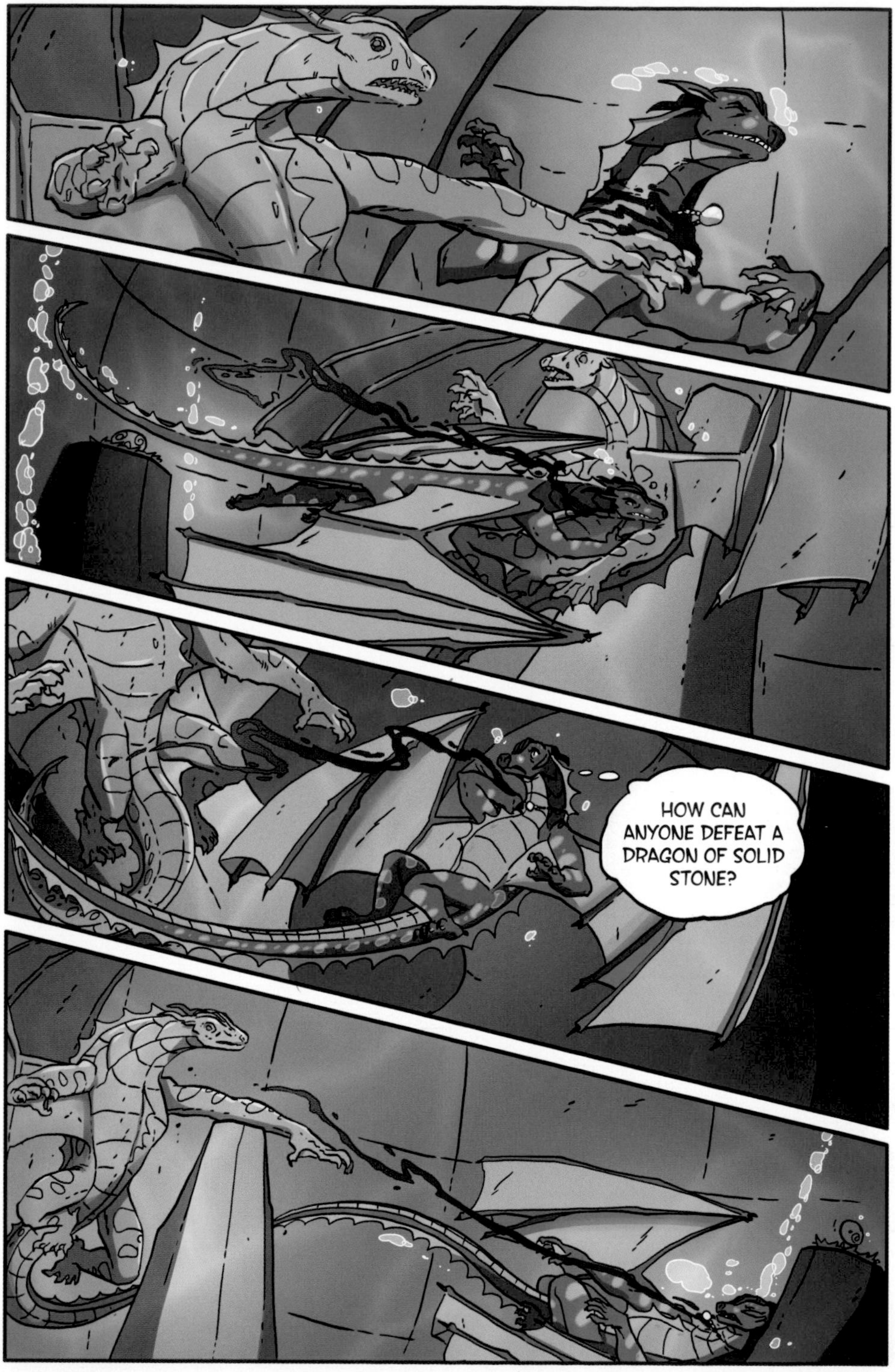
HOW CAN ANYONE DEFEAT A DRAGON OF SOLID STONE?

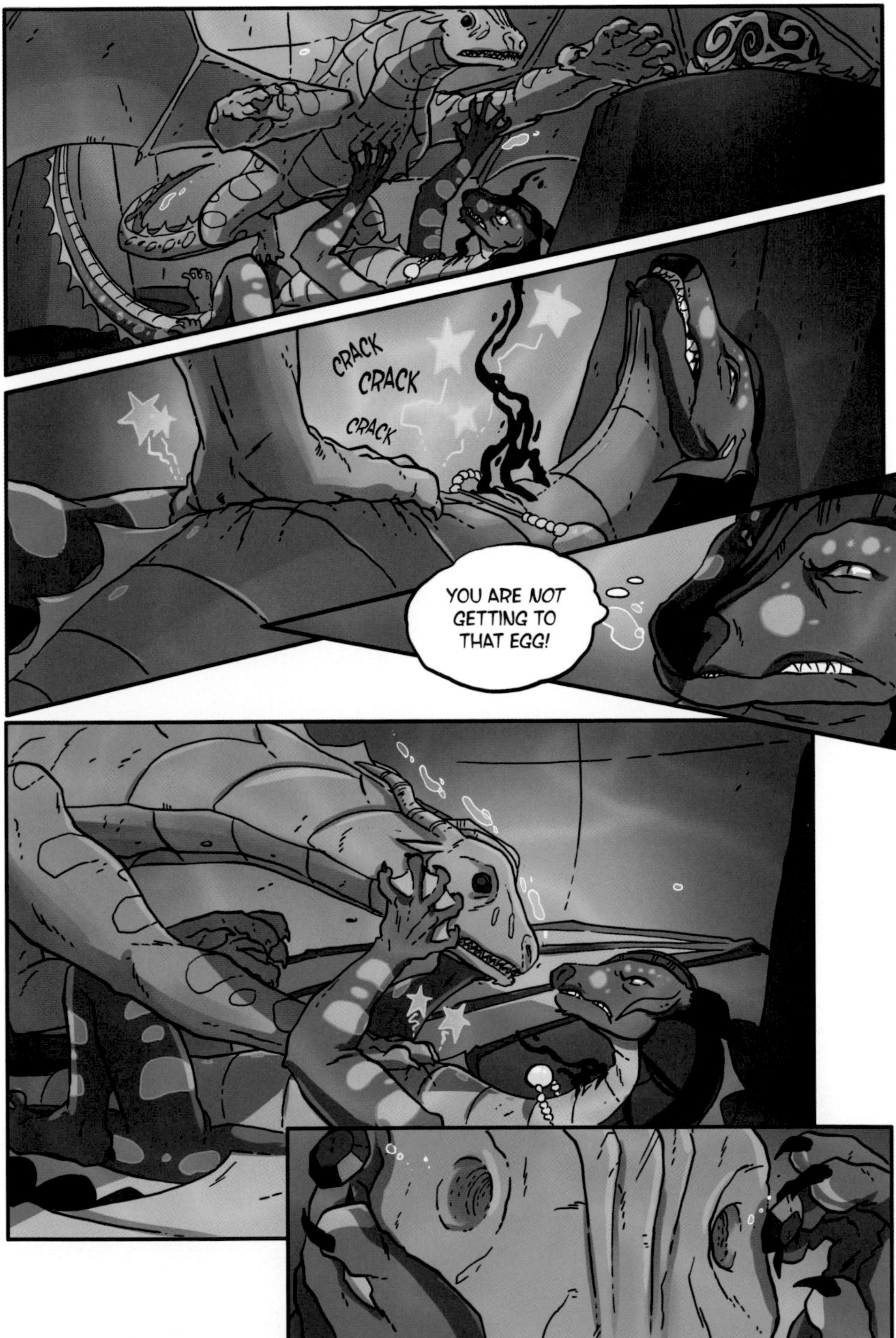
CRACK
CRACK
CRACK
YOU ARE NOT GETTING TO THAT EGG!

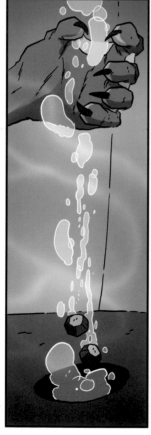

WILL THIS SPEAR EVEN DO ANYTHING AGAINST STONE?

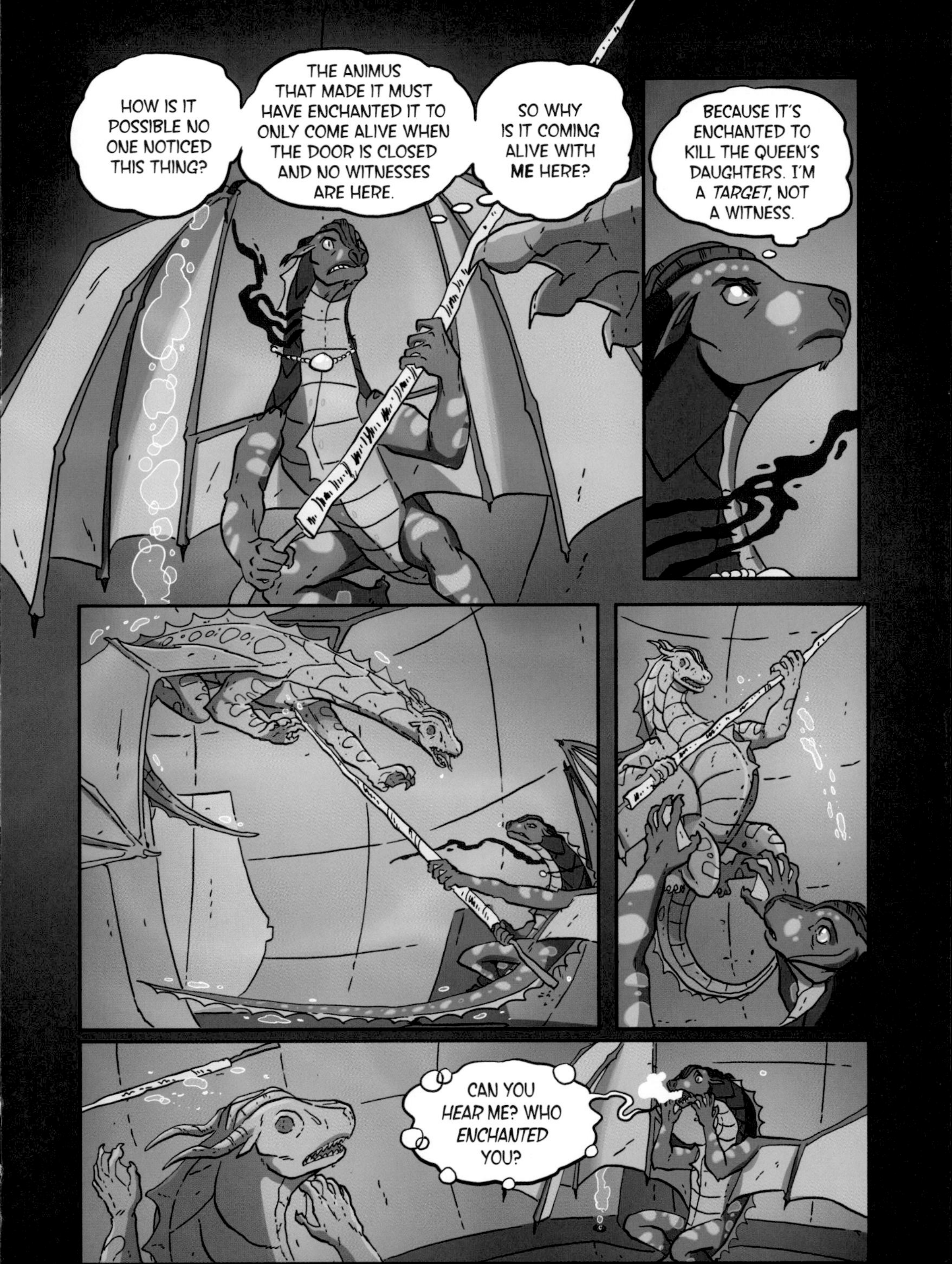
HOW IS IT POSSIBLE NO ONE NOTICED THIS THING?
THE ANIMUS THAT MADE IT MUST HAVE ENCHANTED IT TO ONLY COME ALIVE WHEN THE DOOR IS CLOSED AND NO WITNESSES ARE HERE.
SO WHY IS IT COMING ALIVE WITH **ME** HERE?
BECAUSE IT'S ENCHANTED TO KILL THE QUEEN'S DAUGHTERS. I'M A *TARGET*, NOT A WITNESS.
CAN YOU *HEAR ME*? WHO *ENCHANTED* YOU?

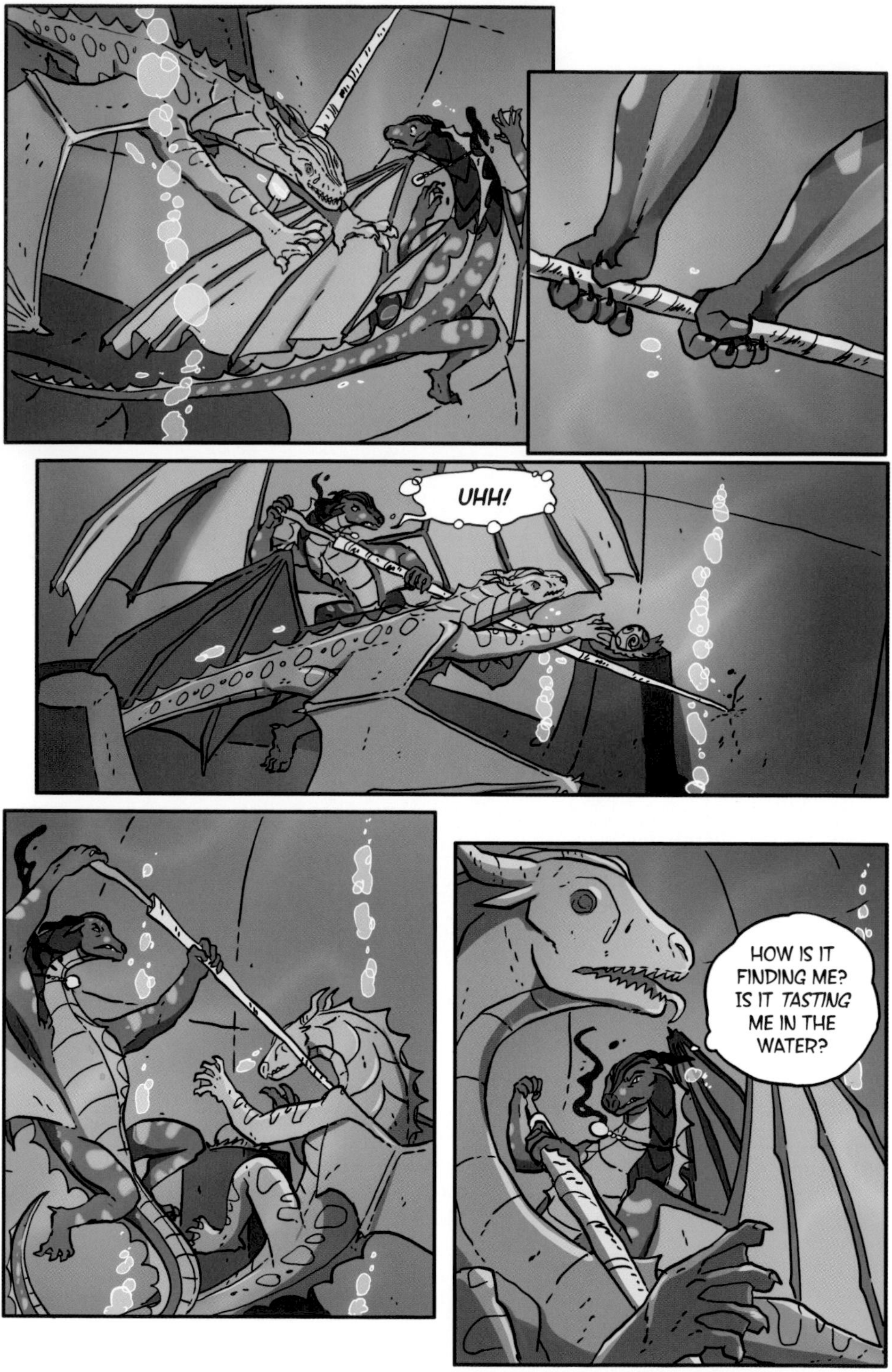
UHH!
HOW IS IT FINDING ME? IS IT *TASTING* ME IN THE WATER?

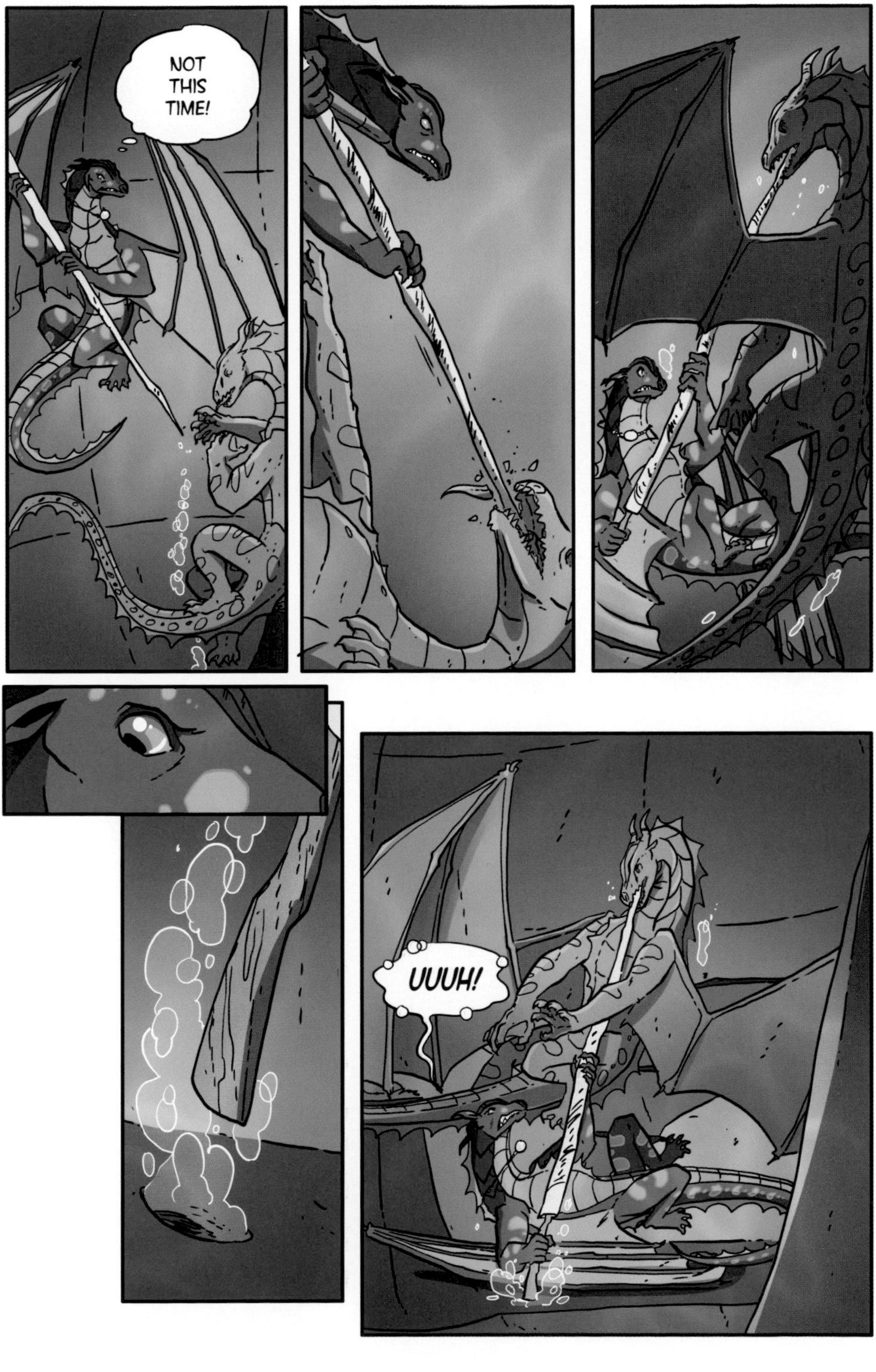
NOT THIS TIME!
UUUH!

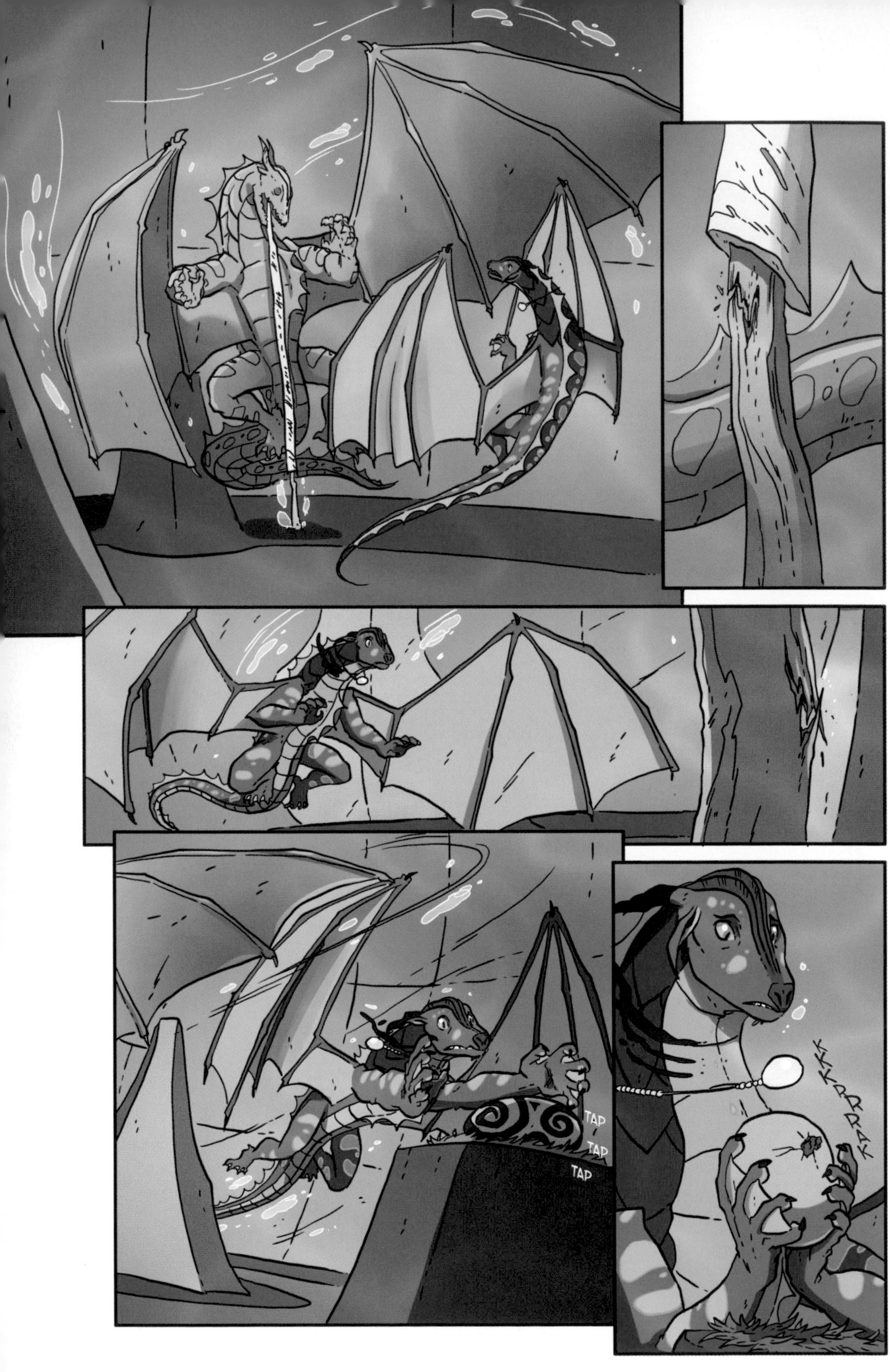
TAP
TAP
TAP
KKKRRRAK

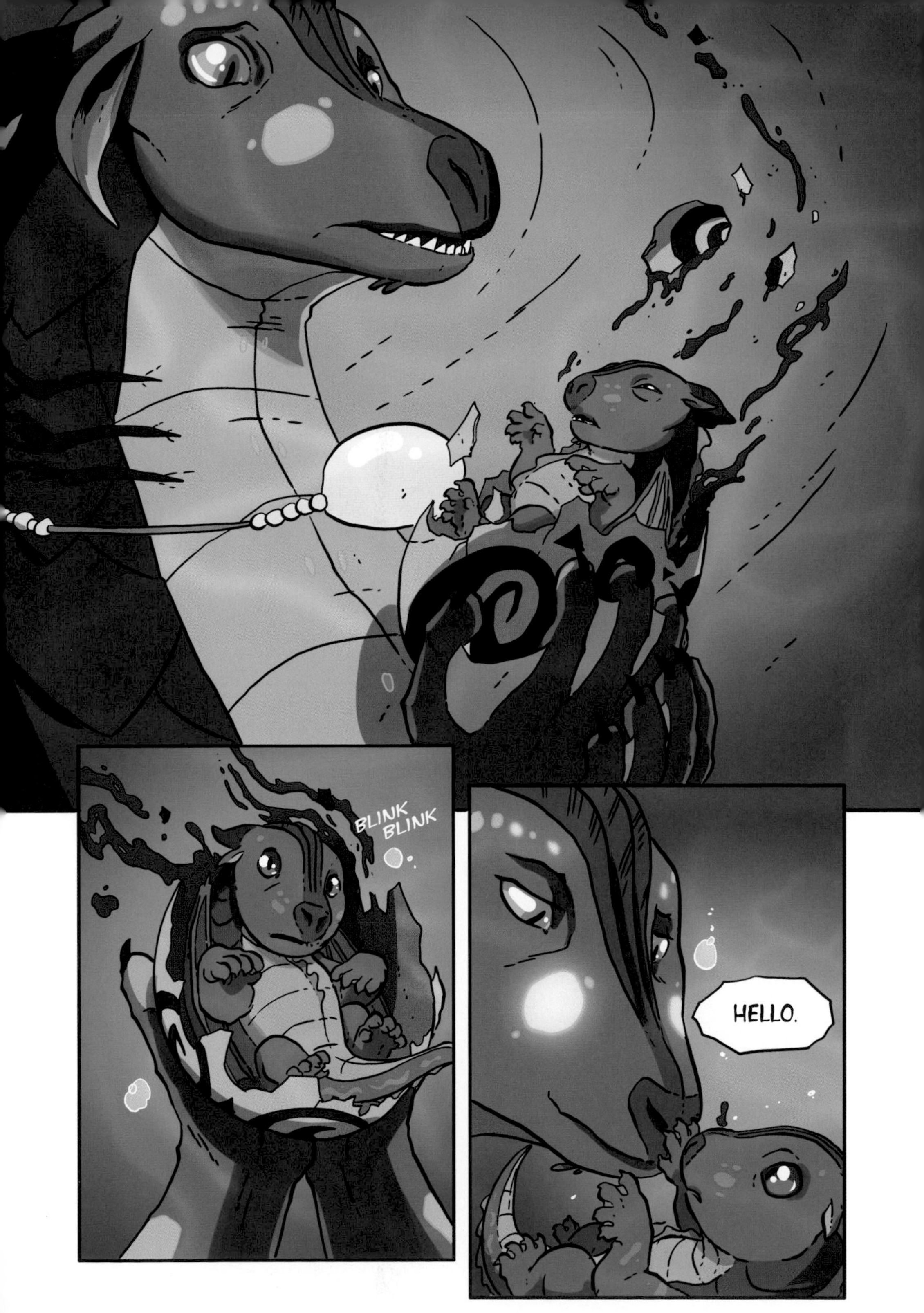
BLINK
BLINK
HELLO.

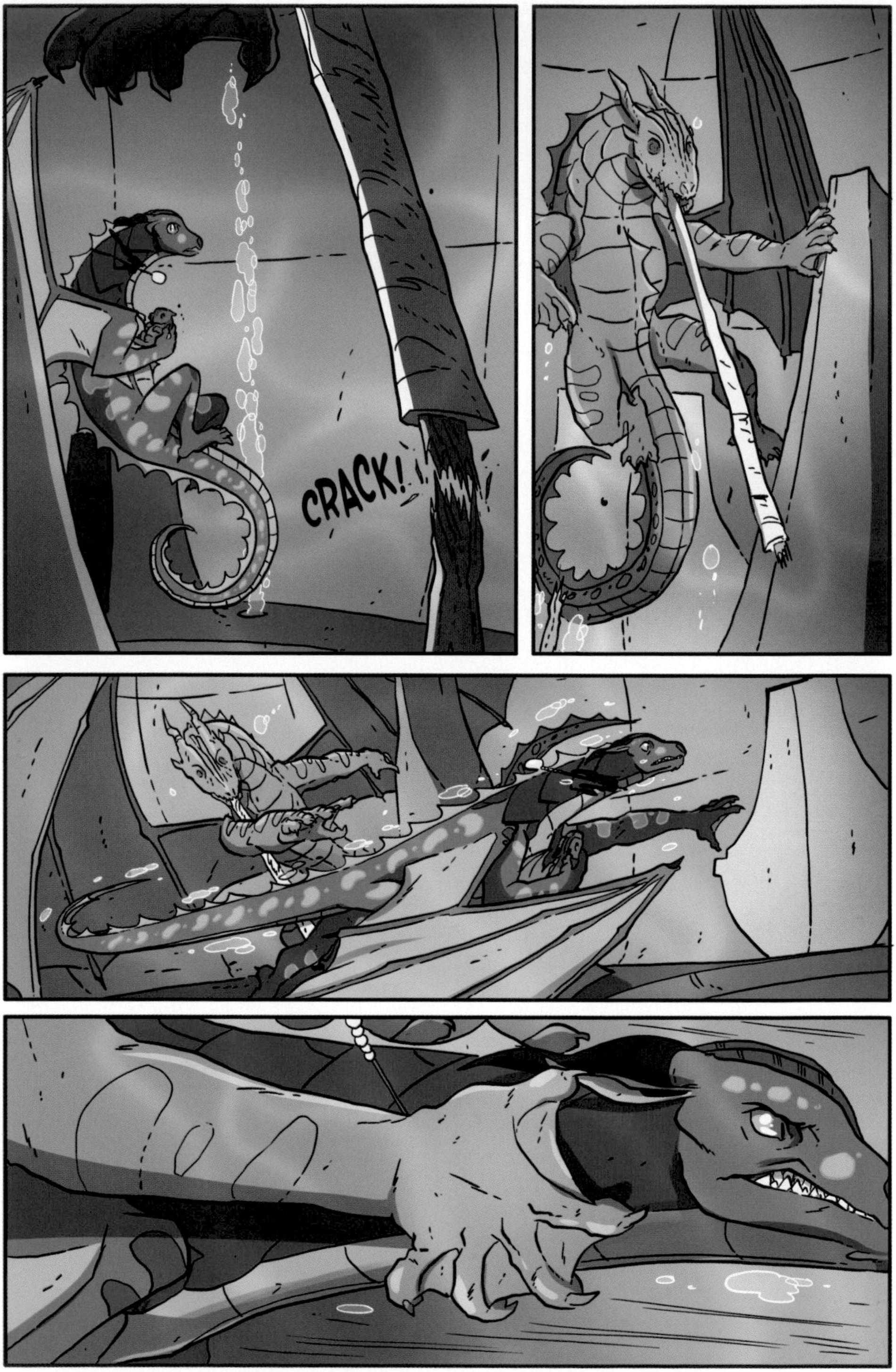
CRACK!

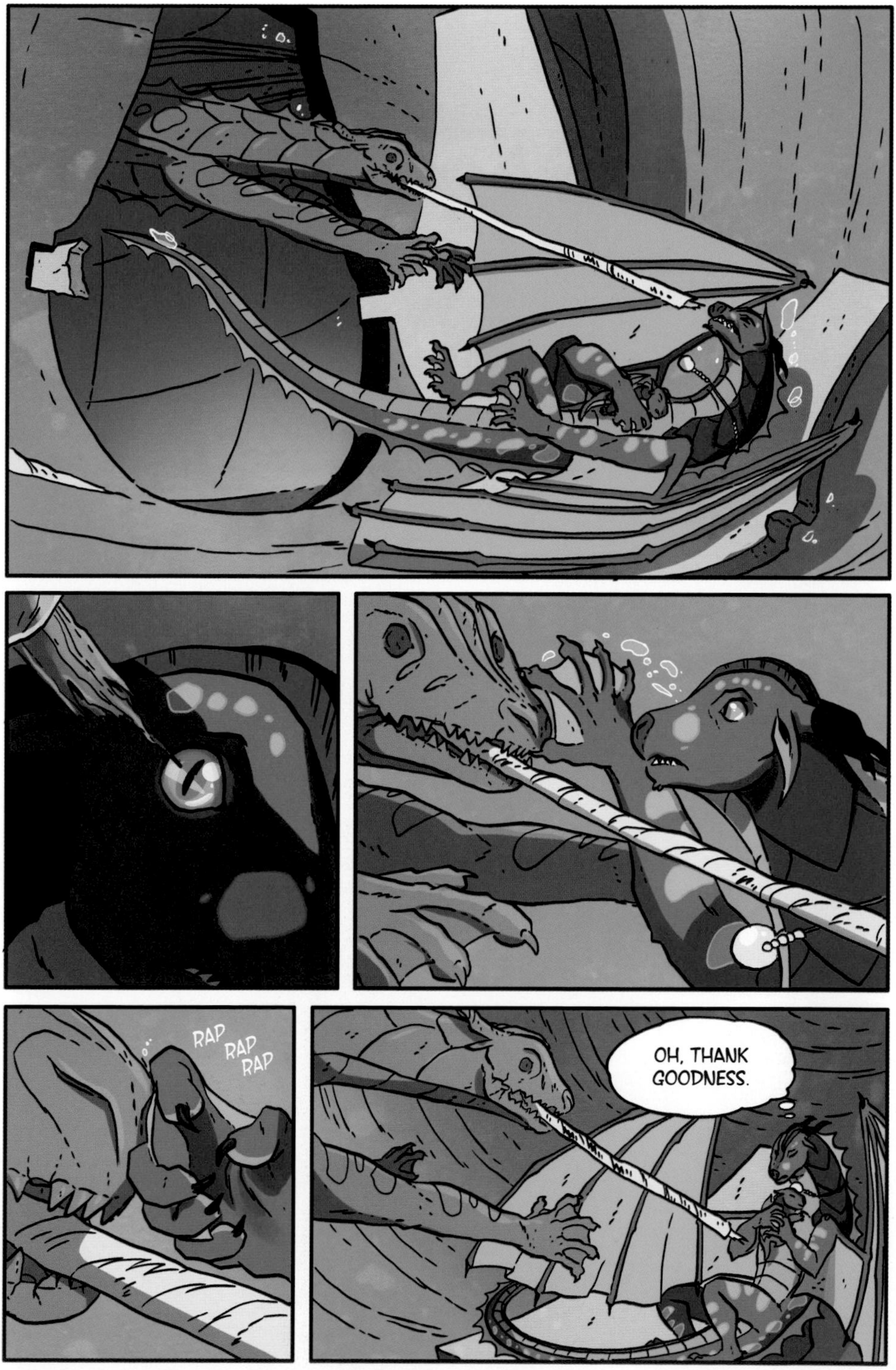
RAP
RAP
RAP
OH, THANK GOODNESS.

ACHOO!

WELL, STOP PUTTING SAND IN YOUR *NOSE*, THEN.

HAVE YOU CHOSEN A NAME FOR HER?

I'M TRYING TO THINK OF THE PERFECT ONE.

MAYBE YOU SHOULD CALL HER *WALRUS*.

SHE'S NOT A *WALRUS*! SHE'S MUCH MORE DIGNIFIED THAN THAT!

VERY. *VERY* DIGNIFIED.

SHE'S AWFULLY CUTE. I THINK SHE HAS YOUR SNOUT, TSUNAMI.

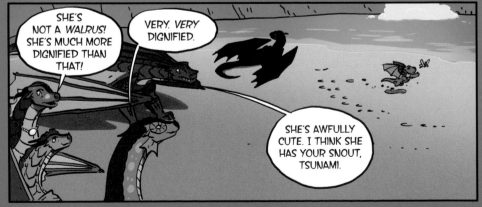

STARFLIGHT, WHAT IS GOING ON WITH YOU?

AND *WHY* ARE YOU LICKING BLISTER'S TALONS?

I AM *NOT*.

YOU REALLY ARE.

I JUST THINK SHE'D BE A GOOD QUEEN.

NO, YOU DON'T. BACK UNDER THE MOUNTAIN, YOU SPECIFICALLY SAID SHE WAS KIND OF EVIL.

BLISTER'S SMART. SHE'S...UH. SHE'S BETTER THAN BURN OR BLAZE.

I DON'T LIKE HER.

REALLY?

SHE CALLED ME *"SWEET"* LIKE THAT'S ALL ANYONE NEEDS TO KNOW ABOUT ME.

BUT YOU *ARE* SWEET.

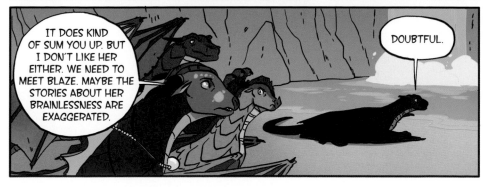

IT DOES KIND OF SUM YOU UP. BUT I DON'T LIKE HER EITHER. WE NEED TO MEET BLAZE. MAYBE THE STORIES ABOUT HER BRAINLESSNESS ARE EXAGGERATED.

DOUBTFUL.

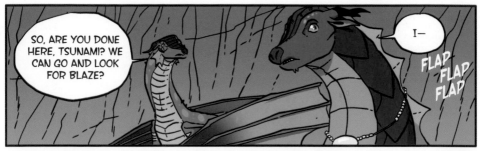

SO, ARE YOU DONE HERE, TSUNAMI? WE CAN GO AND LOOK FOR BLAZE?

I—

FLAP FLAP FLAP

SQUEAK!

HAVE YOU PICKED A NAME?

WHAT DO YOU THINK OF AUKLET?

AN AUKLET IS A KIND OF SEABIRD.

OH. COOL. I MEAN, I KNEW THAT.

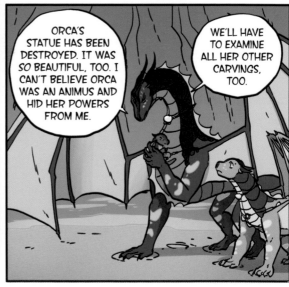

ORCA'S STATUE HAS BEEN DESTROYED. IT WAS *SO* BEAUTIFUL, TOO. I CAN'T BELIEVE ORCA WAS AN ANIMUS AND HID HER POWERS FROM ME.

WE'LL HAVE TO EXAMINE ALL HER OTHER CARVINGS, TOO.

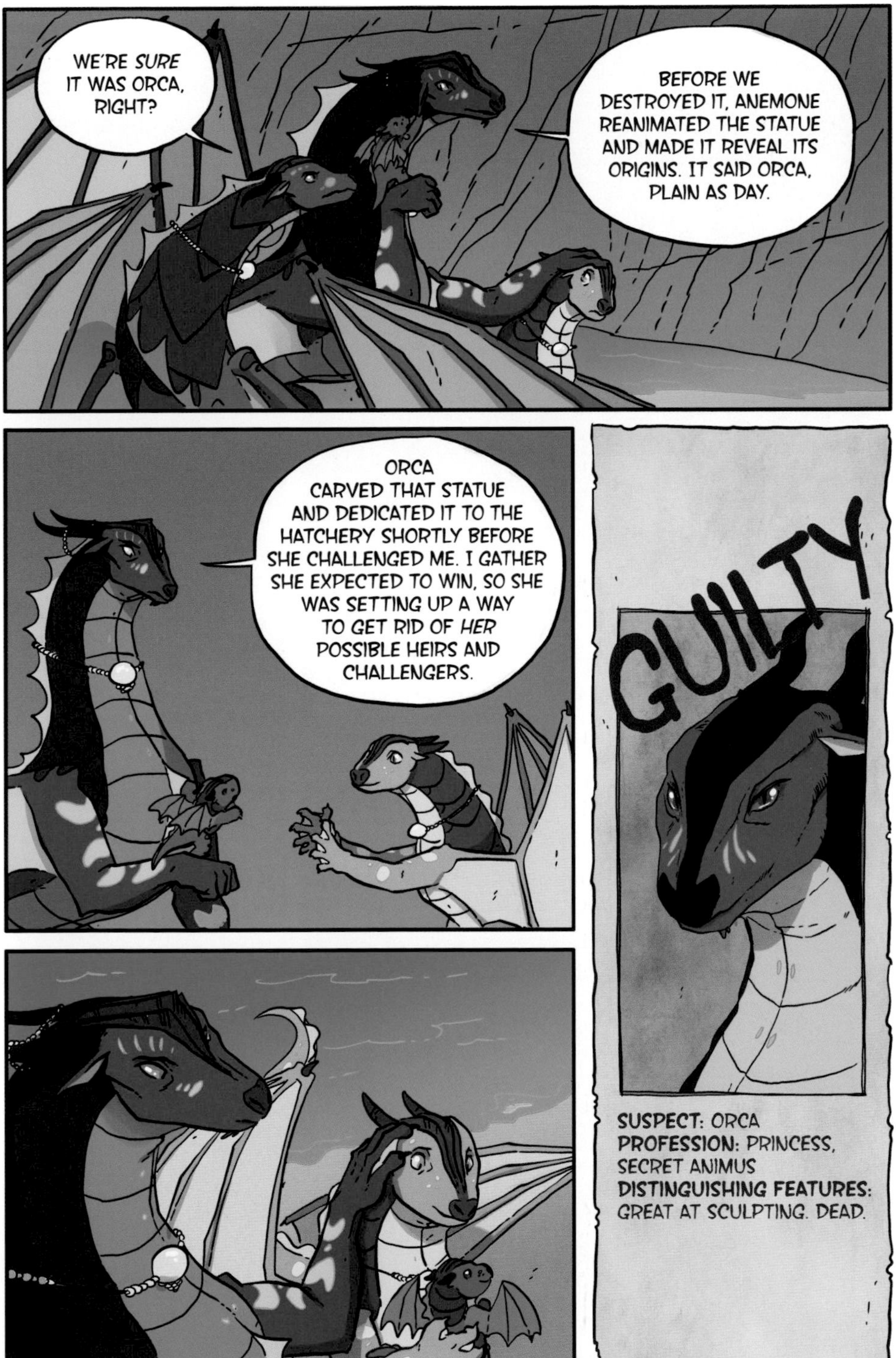
WE'RE *SURE* IT WAS ORCA, RIGHT?
BEFORE WE DESTROYED IT, ANEMONE REANIMATED THE STATUE AND MADE IT REVEAL ITS ORIGINS. IT SAID ORCA, PLAIN AS DAY.
ORCA CARVED THAT STATUE AND DEDICATED IT TO THE HATCHERY SHORTLY BEFORE SHE CHALLENGED ME. I GATHER SHE EXPECTED TO WIN, SO SHE WAS SETTING UP A WAY TO GET RID OF *HER* POSSIBLE HEIRS AND CHALLENGERS.
GUILTY
SUSPECT: ORCA
PROFESSION: PRINCESS, SECRET ANIMUS
DISTINGUISHING FEATURES: GREAT AT SCULPTING. DEAD.

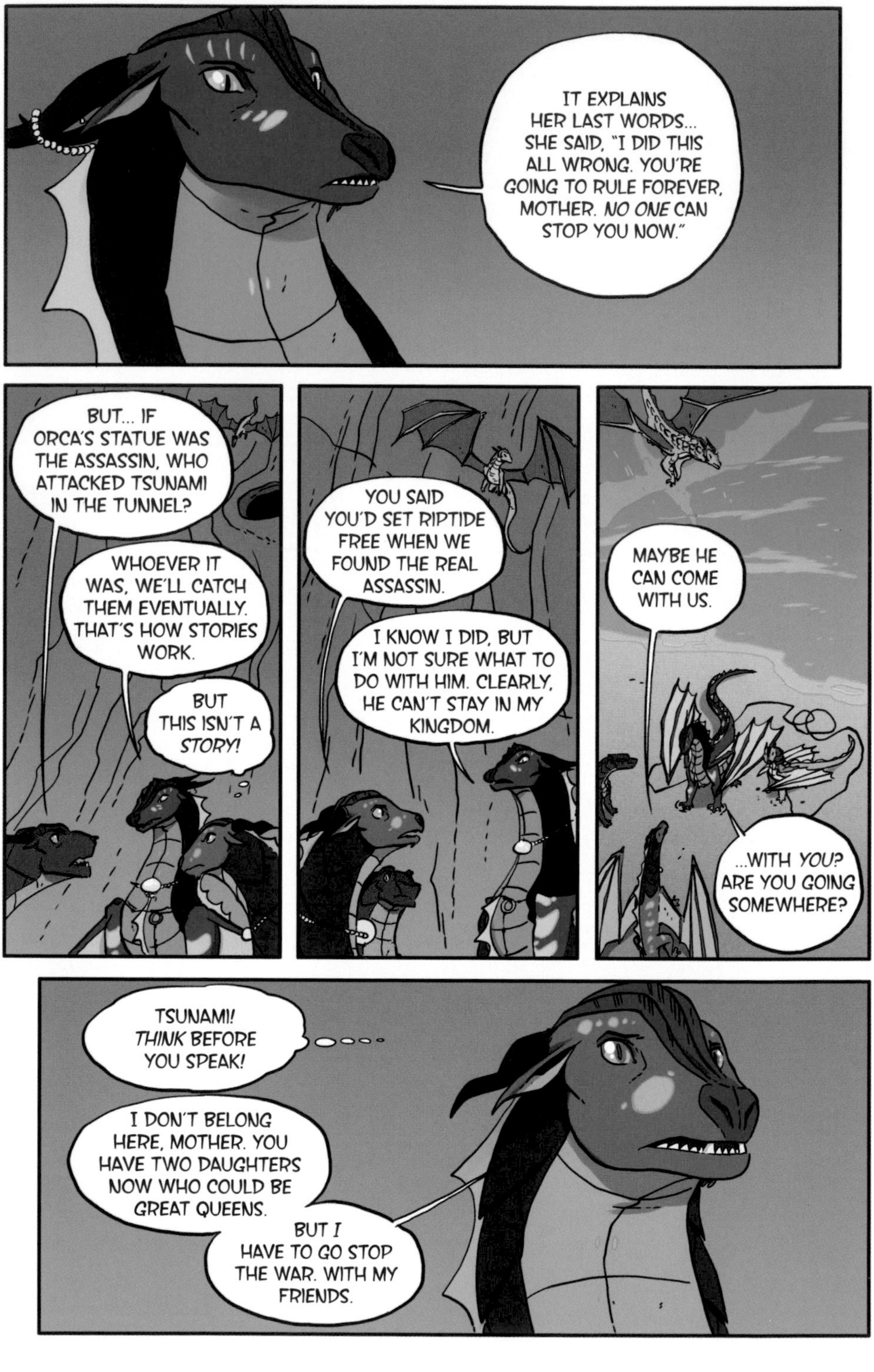
IT EXPLAINS HER LAST WORDS... SHE SAID, "I DID THIS ALL WRONG. YOU'RE GOING TO RULE FOREVER, MOTHER. *NO ONE* CAN STOP YOU NOW."
BUT... IF ORCA'S STATUE WAS THE ASSASSIN, WHO ATTACKED TSUNAMI IN THE TUNNEL?
WHOEVER IT WAS, WE'LL CATCH THEM EVENTUALLY. THAT'S HOW STORIES WORK.
BUT THIS ISN'T A *STORY*!
YOU SAID YOU'D SET RIPTIDE FREE WHEN WE FOUND THE REAL ASSASSIN.
I KNOW I DID, BUT I'M NOT SURE WHAT TO DO WITH HIM. CLEARLY, HE CAN'T STAY IN MY KINGDOM.
MAYBE HE CAN COME WITH US.
...WITH *YOU*? ARE YOU GOING SOMEWHERE?
TSUNAMI! *THINK* BEFORE YOU SPEAK!
I DON'T BELONG HERE, MOTHER. YOU HAVE TWO DAUGHTERS NOW WHO COULD BE GREAT QUEENS.
BUT *I* HAVE TO GO STOP THE WAR. WITH MY FRIENDS.

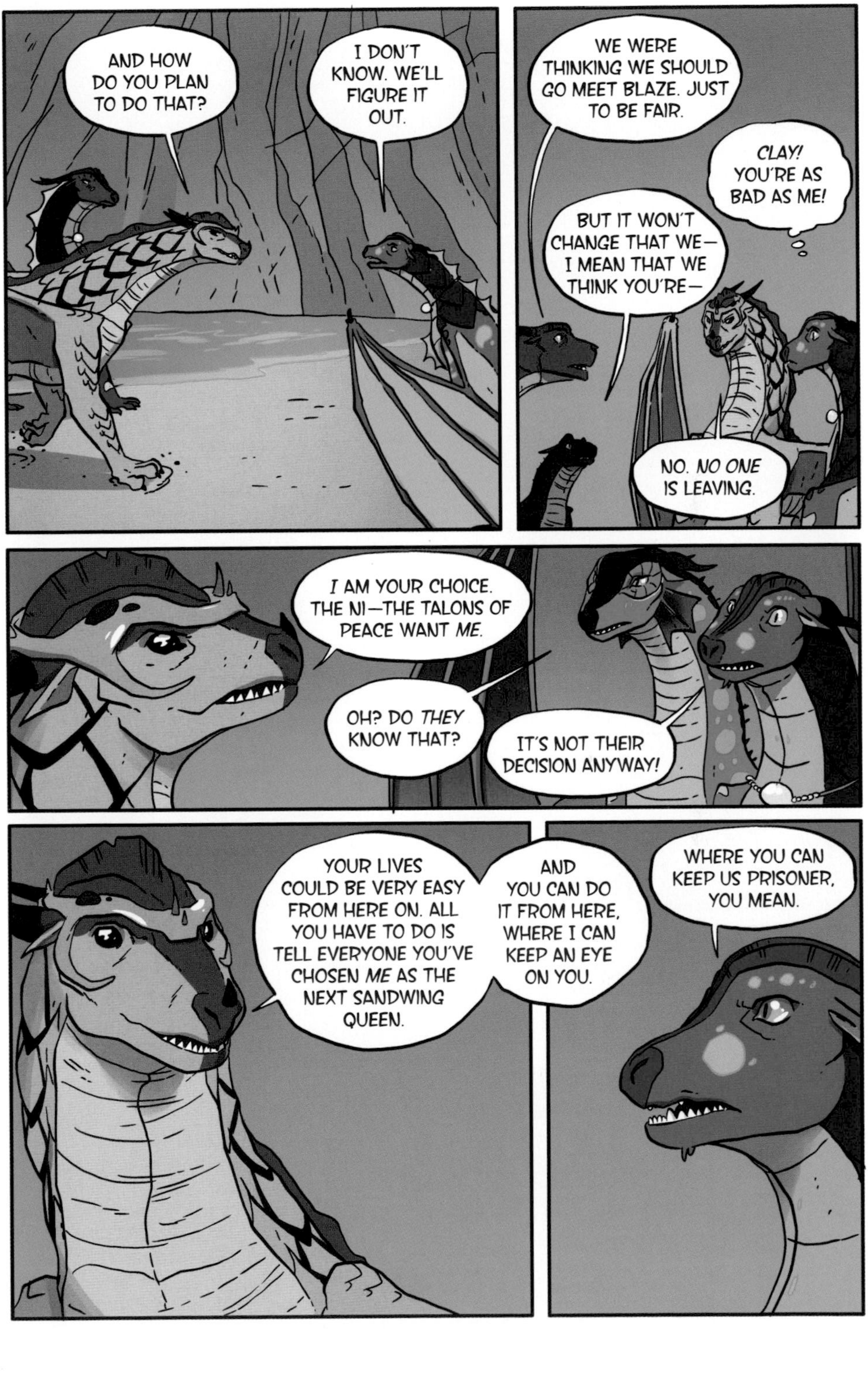
AND HOW DO YOU PLAN TO DO THAT?
I DON'T KNOW. WE'LL FIGURE IT OUT.
WE WERE THINKING WE SHOULD GO MEET BLAZE. JUST TO BE FAIR.
CLAY! YOU'RE AS BAD AS ME!
BUT IT WON'T CHANGE THAT WE— I MEAN THAT WE THINK YOU'RE—
NO. *NO ONE* IS LEAVING.
I AM YOUR CHOICE. THE NI—THE TALONS OF PEACE WANT *ME*.
OH? DO *THEY* KNOW THAT?
IT'S NOT THEIR DECISION ANYWAY!
YOUR LIVES COULD BE VERY EASY FROM HERE ON. ALL YOU HAVE TO DO IS TELL EVERYONE YOU'VE CHOSEN *ME* AS THE NEXT SANDWING QUEEN.
AND YOU CAN DO IT FROM HERE, WHERE I CAN KEEP AN EYE ON YOU.
WHERE YOU CAN KEEP US PRISONER, YOU MEAN.

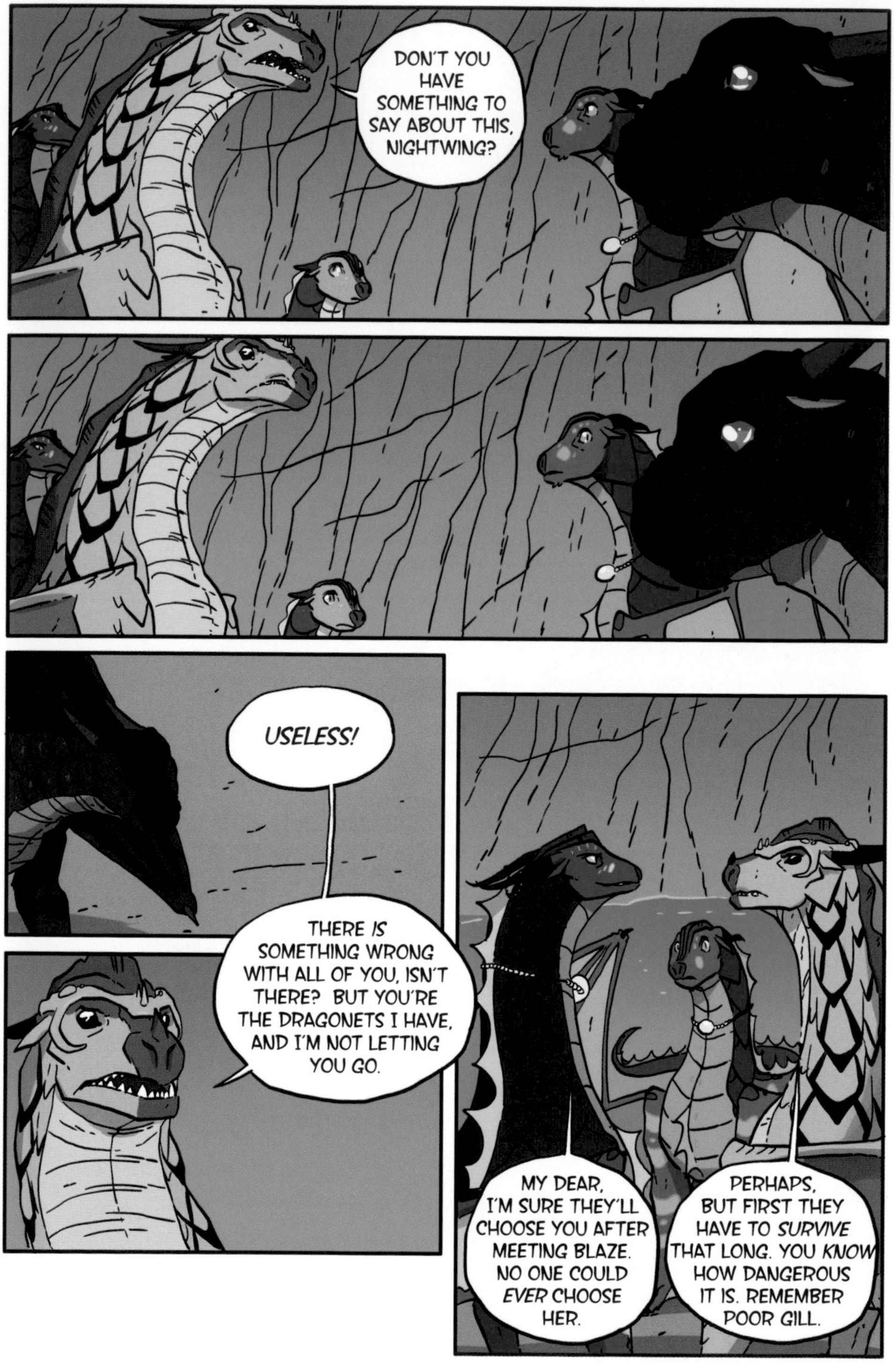
DON'T YOU HAVE SOMETHING TO SAY ABOUT THIS, NIGHTWING?
USELESS!
THERE IS SOMETHING WRONG WITH ALL OF YOU, ISN'T THERE? BUT YOU'RE THE DRAGONETS I HAVE, AND I'M NOT LETTING YOU GO.
MY DEAR, I'M SURE THEY'LL CHOOSE YOU AFTER MEETING BLAZE. NO ONE COULD EVER CHOOSE HER.
PERHAPS, BUT FIRST THEY HAVE TO SURVIVE THAT LONG. YOU KNOW HOW DANGEROUS IT IS. REMEMBER POOR GILL.

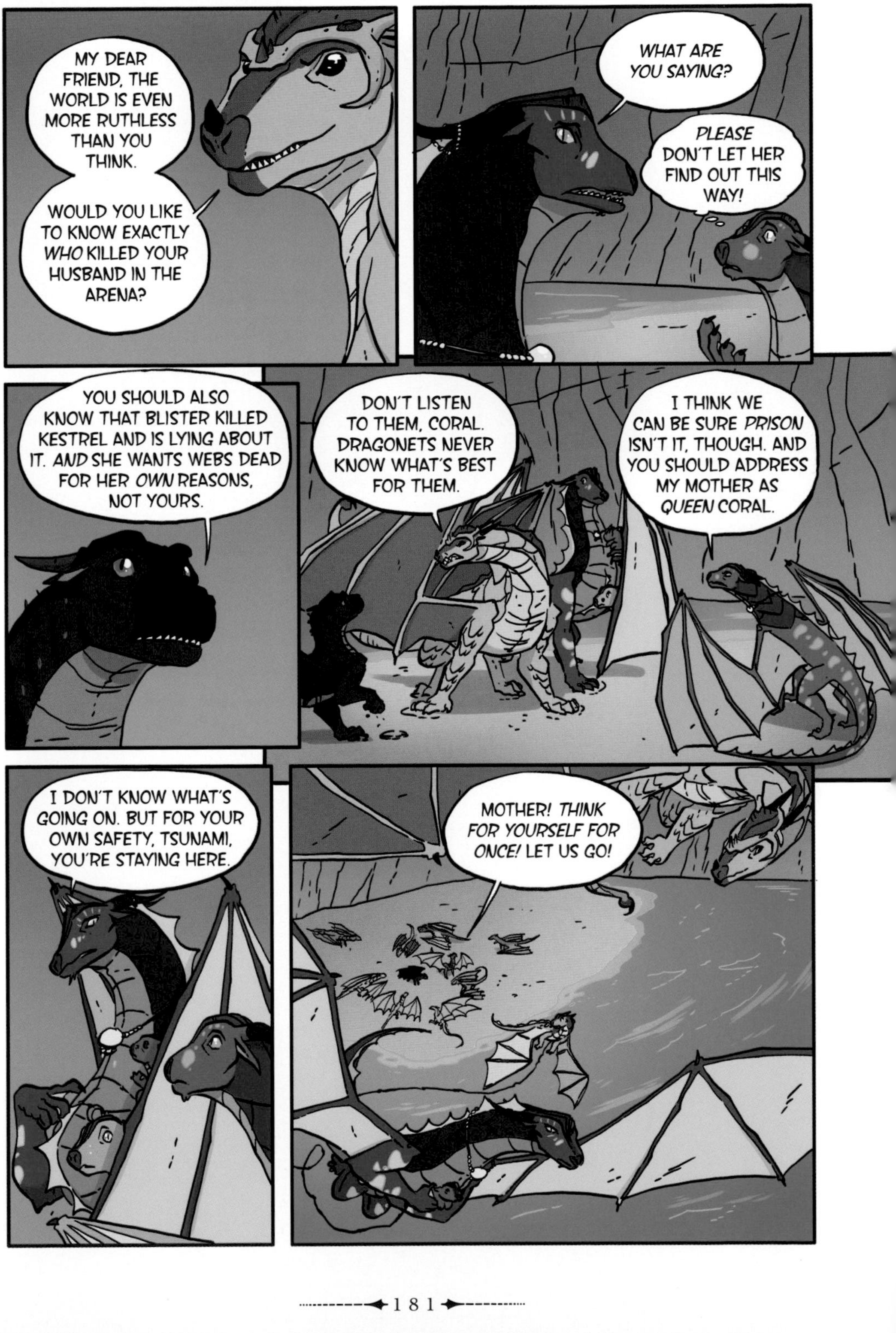

MY DEAR FRIEND, THE WORLD IS EVEN MORE RUTHLESS THAN YOU THINK.
WOULD YOU LIKE TO KNOW EXACTLY *WHO* KILLED YOUR HUSBAND IN THE ARENA?
WHAT ARE YOU SAYING?
PLEASE DON'T LET HER FIND OUT THIS WAY!
YOU SHOULD ALSO KNOW THAT BLISTER KILLED KESTREL AND IS LYING ABOUT IT. *AND* SHE WANTS WEBS DEAD FOR HER *OWN* REASONS, NOT YOURS.
DON'T LISTEN TO THEM, CORAL. DRAGONETS NEVER KNOW WHAT'S BEST FOR THEM.
I THINK WE CAN BE SURE *PRISON* ISN'T IT, THOUGH. AND YOU SHOULD ADDRESS MY MOTHER AS *QUEEN* CORAL.
I DON'T KNOW WHAT'S GOING ON. BUT FOR YOUR OWN SAFETY, TSUNAMI, YOU'RE STAYING HERE.
MOTHER! *THINK FOR YOURSELF FOR ONCE!* LET US GO!

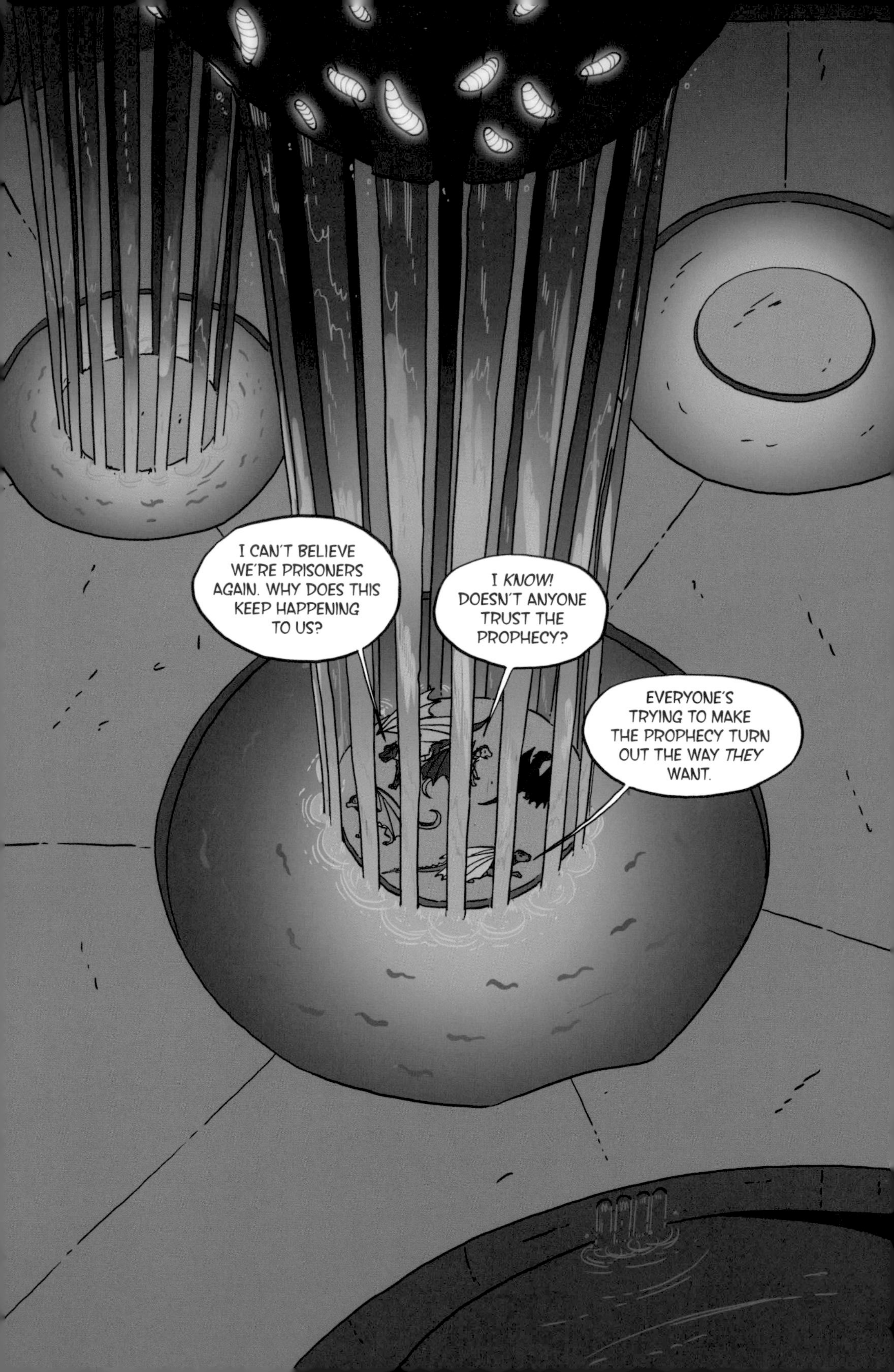
I CAN'T BELIEVE WE'RE PRISONERS AGAIN. WHY DOES THIS KEEP HAPPENING TO US?
I *KNOW!* DOESN'T ANYONE TRUST THE PROPHECY?
EVERYONE'S TRYING TO MAKE THE PROPHECY TURN OUT THE WAY *THEY* WANT.

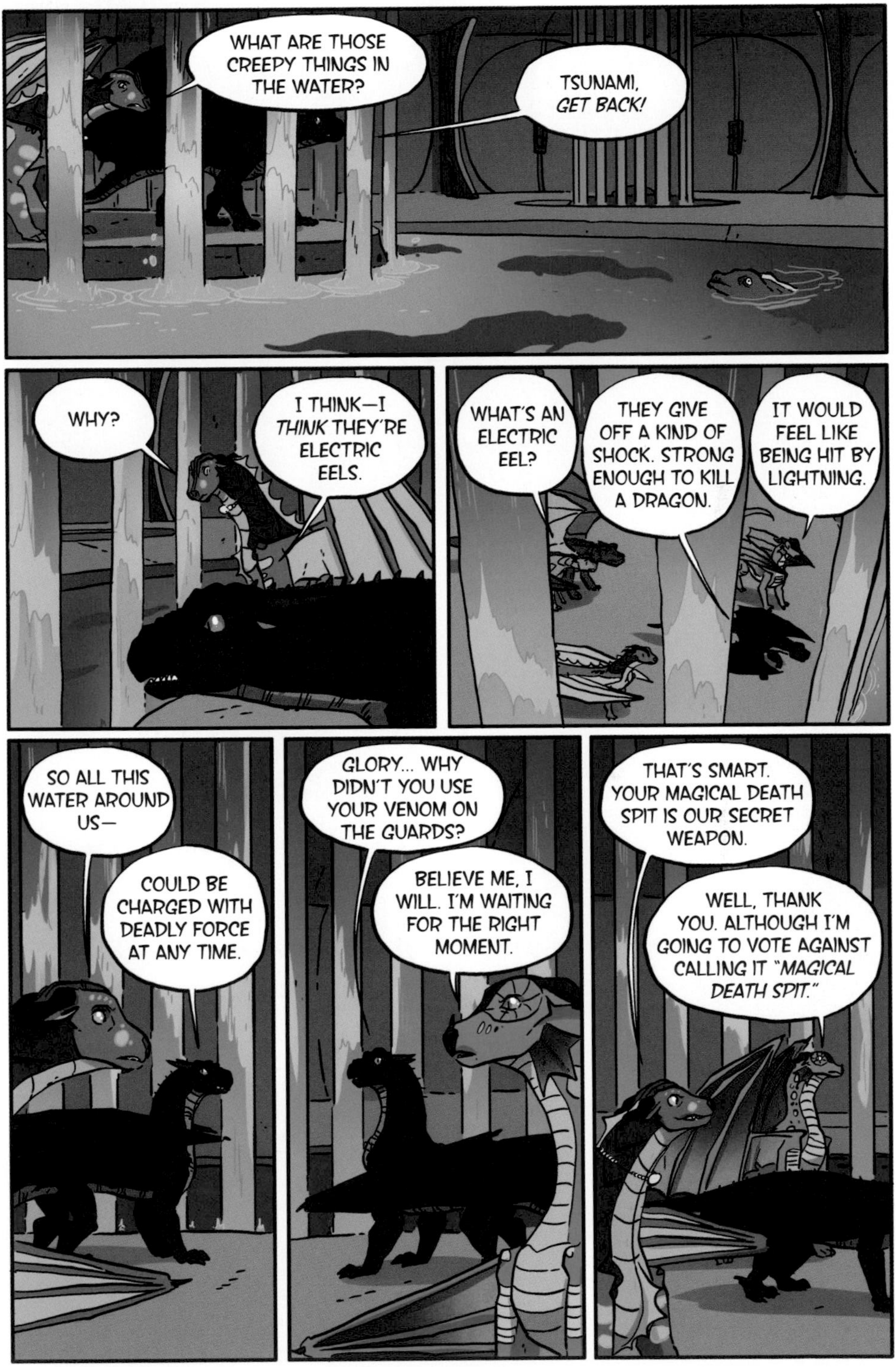
WHAT ARE THOSE CREEPY THINGS IN THE WATER?
TSUNAMI, *GET BACK!*
WHY?
I THINK—I *THINK* THEY'RE ELECTRIC EELS.
WHAT'S AN ELECTRIC EEL?
THEY GIVE OFF A KIND OF SHOCK. STRONG ENOUGH TO KILL A DRAGON.
IT WOULD FEEL LIKE BEING HIT BY LIGHTNING.
SO ALL THIS WATER AROUND US—
COULD BE CHARGED WITH DEADLY FORCE AT ANY TIME.
GLORY... WHY DIDN'T YOU USE YOUR VENOM ON THE GUARDS?
BELIEVE ME, I WILL. I'M WAITING FOR THE RIGHT MOMENT.
THAT'S SMART. YOUR MAGICAL DEATH SPIT IS OUR SECRET WEAPON.
WELL, THANK YOU. ALTHOUGH I'M GOING TO VOTE AGAINST CALLING IT *"MAGICAL DEATH SPIT."*

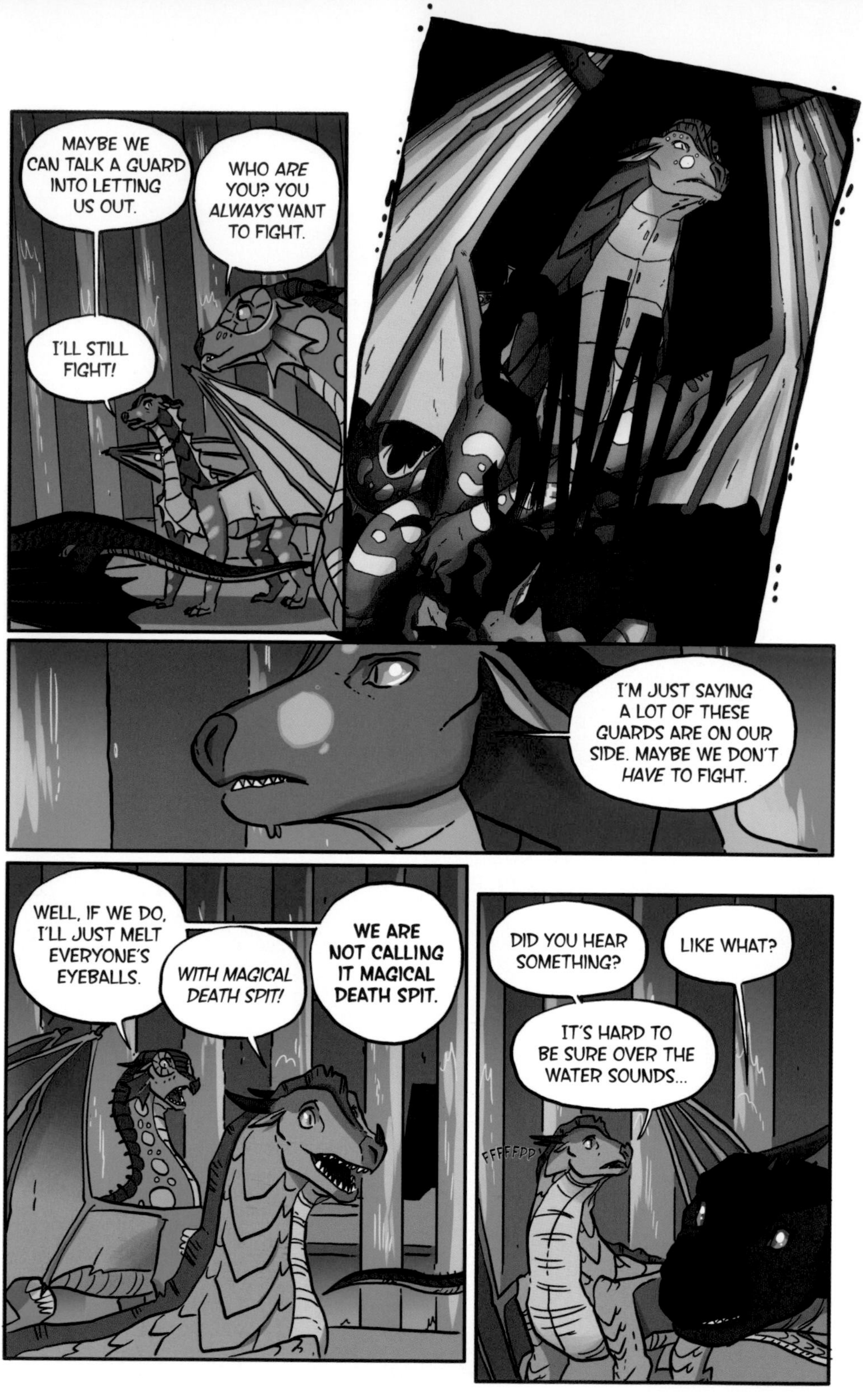

MAYBE WE CAN TALK A GUARD INTO LETTING US OUT.
WHO *ARE* YOU? YOU *ALWAYS* WANT TO FIGHT.
I'LL STILL FIGHT!
I'M JUST SAYING A LOT OF THESE GUARDS ARE ON OUR SIDE. MAYBE WE DON'T *HAVE* TO FIGHT.
WELL, IF WE DO, I'LL JUST MELT EVERYONE'S EYEBALLS.
WITH MAGICAL DEATH SPIT!
WE ARE NOT CALLING IT MAGICAL DEATH SPIT.
DID YOU HEAR SOMETHING?
LIKE WHAT?
IT'S HARD TO BE SURE OVER THE WATER SOUNDS...

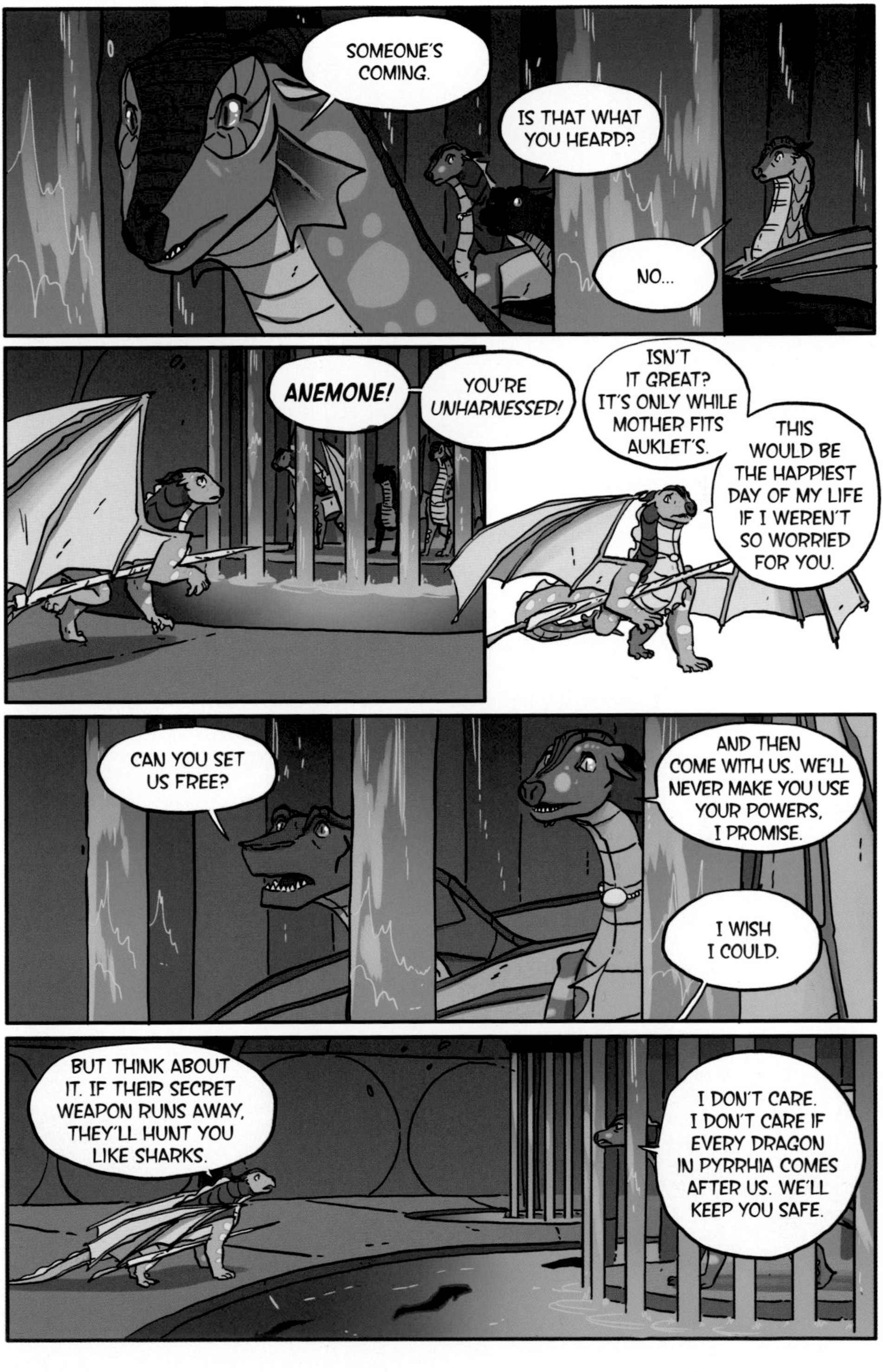
SOMEONE'S COMING.
IS THAT WHAT YOU HEARD?
NO...
ANEMONE!
YOU'RE UNHARNESSED!
ISN'T IT GREAT? IT'S ONLY WHILE MOTHER FITS AUKLET'S.
THIS WOULD BE THE HAPPIEST DAY OF MY LIFE IF I WEREN'T SO WORRIED FOR YOU.
CAN YOU SET US FREE?
AND THEN COME WITH US. WE'LL NEVER MAKE YOU USE YOUR POWERS, I PROMISE.
I WISH I COULD.
BUT THINK ABOUT IT. IF THEIR SECRET WEAPON RUNS AWAY, THEY'LL HUNT YOU LIKE SHARKS.
I DON'T CARE. I DON'T CARE IF EVERY DRAGON IN PYRRHIA COMES AFTER US. WE'LL KEEP YOU SAFE.

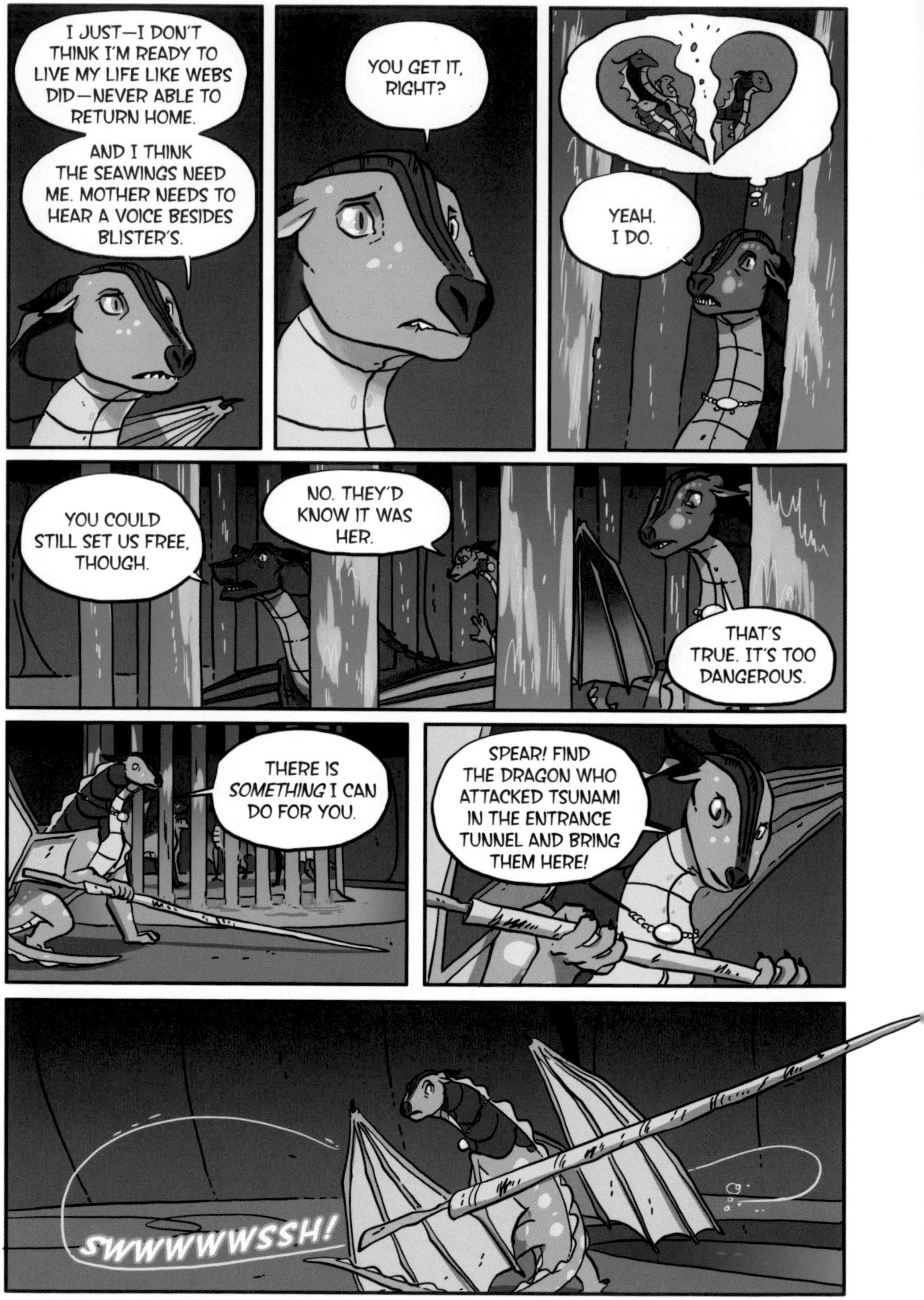
I JUST—I DON'T THINK I'M READY TO LIVE MY LIFE LIKE WEBS DID—NEVER ABLE TO RETURN HOME.
AND I THINK THE SEAWINGS NEED ME. MOTHER NEEDS TO HEAR A VOICE BESIDES BLISTER'S.
YOU GET IT, RIGHT?
YEAH. I DO.
YOU COULD STILL SET US FREE, THOUGH.
NO. THEY'D KNOW IT WAS HER.
THAT'S TRUE. IT'S TOO DANGEROUS.
THERE IS *SOMETHING* I CAN DO FOR YOU.
SPEAR! FIND THE DRAGON WHO ATTACKED TSUNAMI IN THE ENTRANCE TUNNEL AND BRING THEM HERE!
SWWWWWSSH!

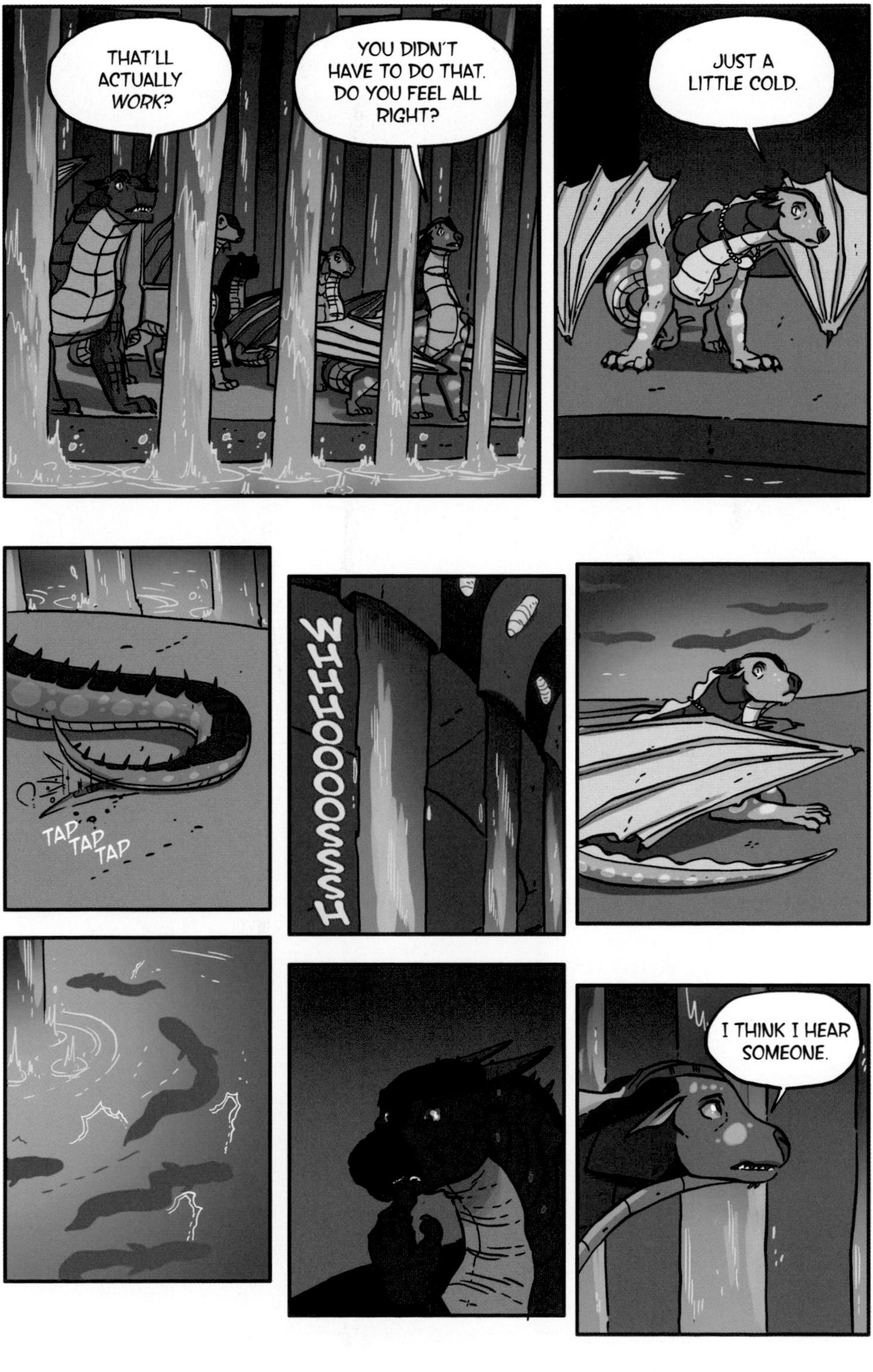

THAT'LL ACTUALLY *WORK?*
YOU DIDN'T HAVE TO DO THAT. DO YOU FEEL ALL RIGHT?
JUST A LITTLE COLD.
TAP TAP TAP
WHHHOOOOSSSH
I THINK I HEAR SOMEONE.

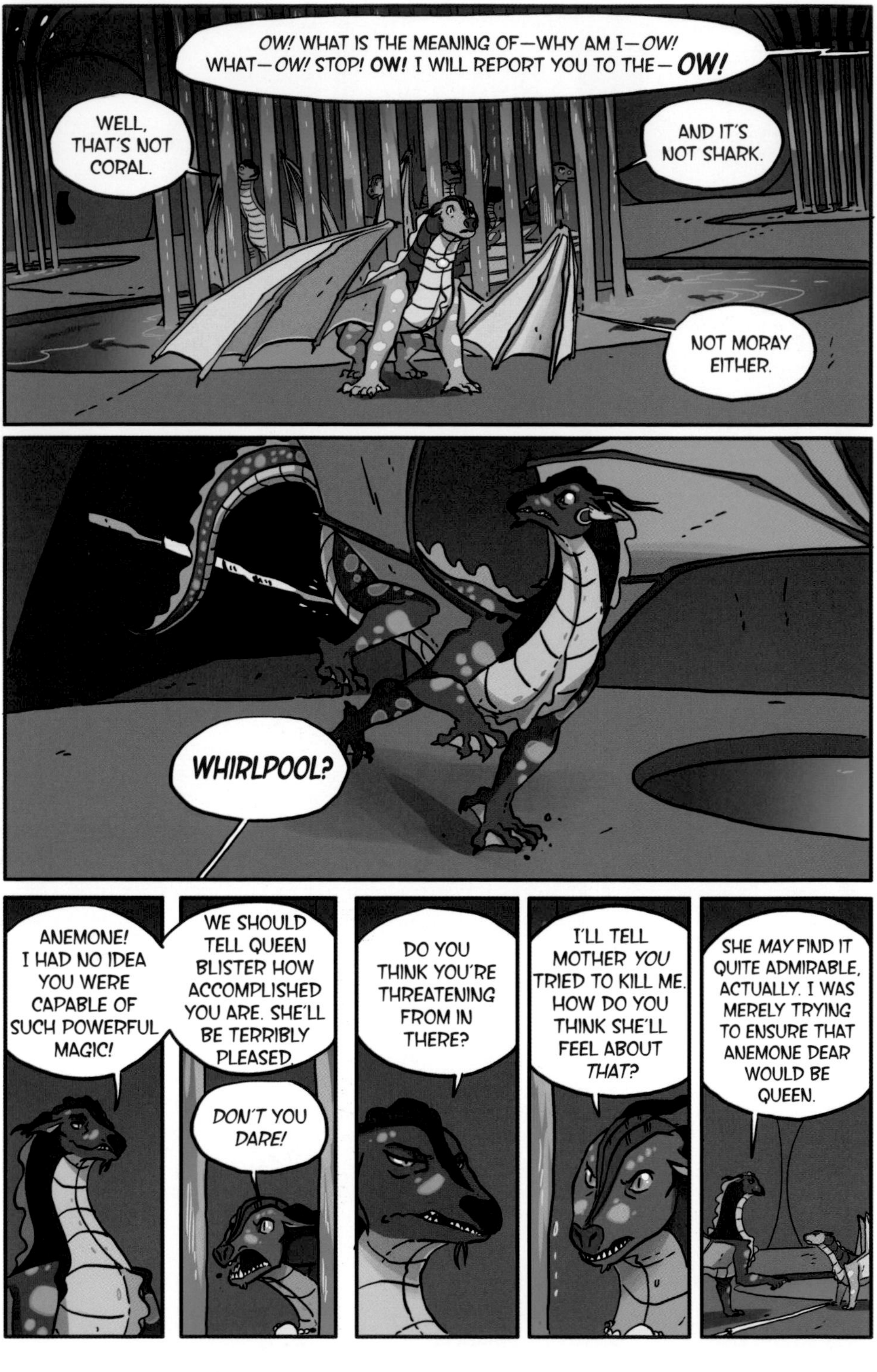

OW! WHAT IS THE MEANING OF—WHY AM I—OW! WHAT—OW! STOP! OW! I WILL REPORT YOU TO THE—OW!
WELL, THAT'S NOT CORAL.
AND IT'S NOT SHARK.
NOT MORAY EITHER.
WHIRLPOOL?
ANEMONE! I HAD NO IDEA YOU WERE CAPABLE OF SUCH POWERFUL MAGIC!
WE SHOULD TELL QUEEN BLISTER HOW ACCOMPLISHED YOU ARE. SHE'LL BE TERRIBLY PLEASED.
DON'T YOU DARE!
DO YOU THINK YOU'RE THREATENING FROM IN THERE?
I'LL TELL MOTHER YOU TRIED TO KILL ME. HOW DO YOU THINK SHE'LL FEEL ABOUT THAT?
SHE MAY FIND IT QUITE ADMIRABLE, ACTUALLY. I WAS MERELY TRYING TO ENSURE THAT ANEMONE DEAR WOULD BE QUEEN.

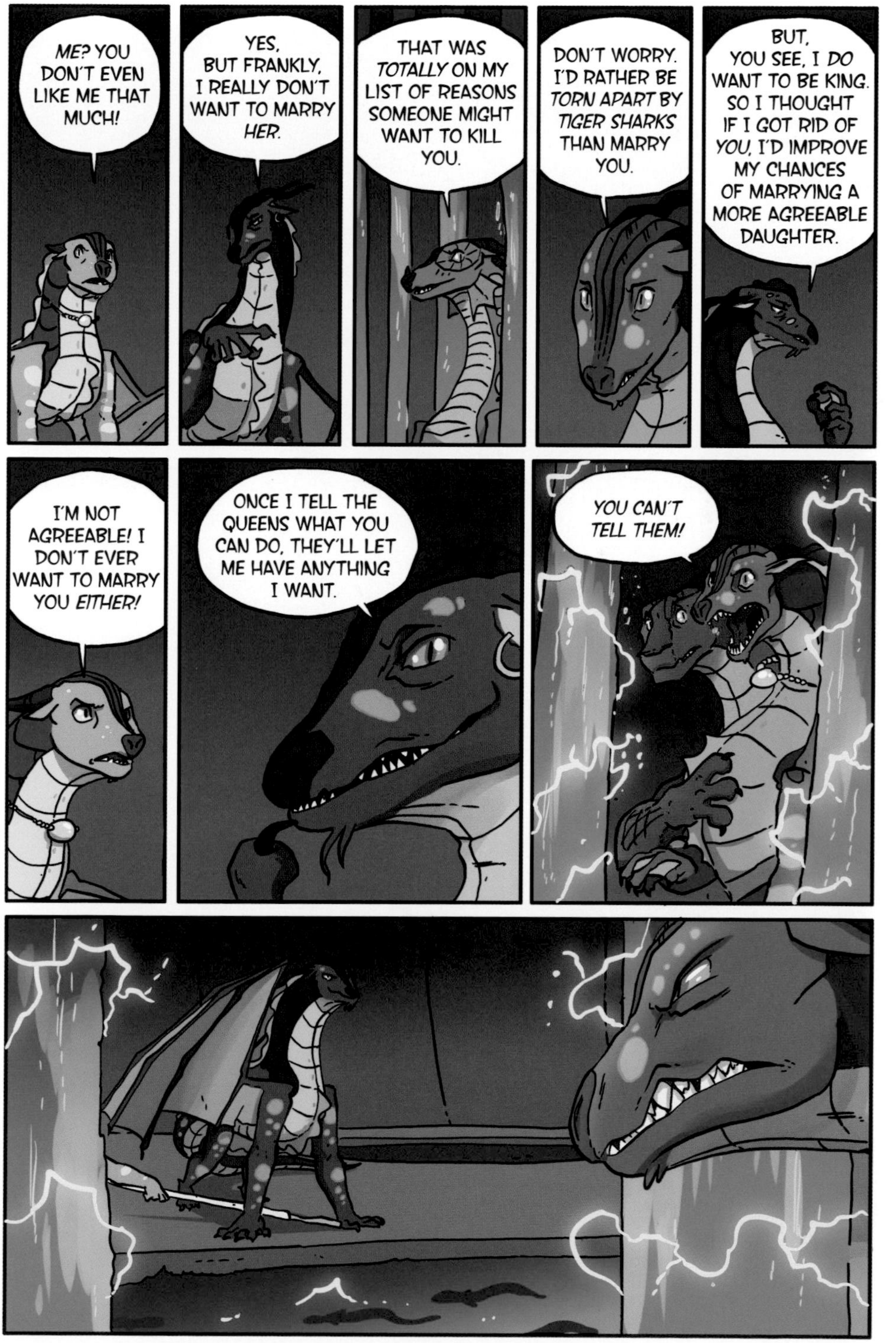
ME? YOU DON'T EVEN LIKE ME THAT MUCH!
YES, BUT FRANKLY, I REALLY DON'T WANT TO MARRY HER.
THAT WAS TOTALLY ON MY LIST OF REASONS SOMEONE MIGHT WANT TO KILL YOU.
DON'T WORRY. I'D RATHER BE TORN APART BY TIGER SHARKS THAN MARRY YOU.
BUT, YOU SEE, I DO WANT TO BE KING. SO I THOUGHT IF I GOT RID OF YOU, I'D IMPROVE MY CHANCES OF MARRYING A MORE AGREEABLE DAUGHTER.
I'M NOT AGREEABLE! I DON'T EVER WANT TO MARRY YOU EITHER!
ONCE I TELL THE QUEENS WHAT YOU CAN DO, THEY'LL LET ME HAVE ANYTHING I WANT.
YOU CAN'T TELL THEM!

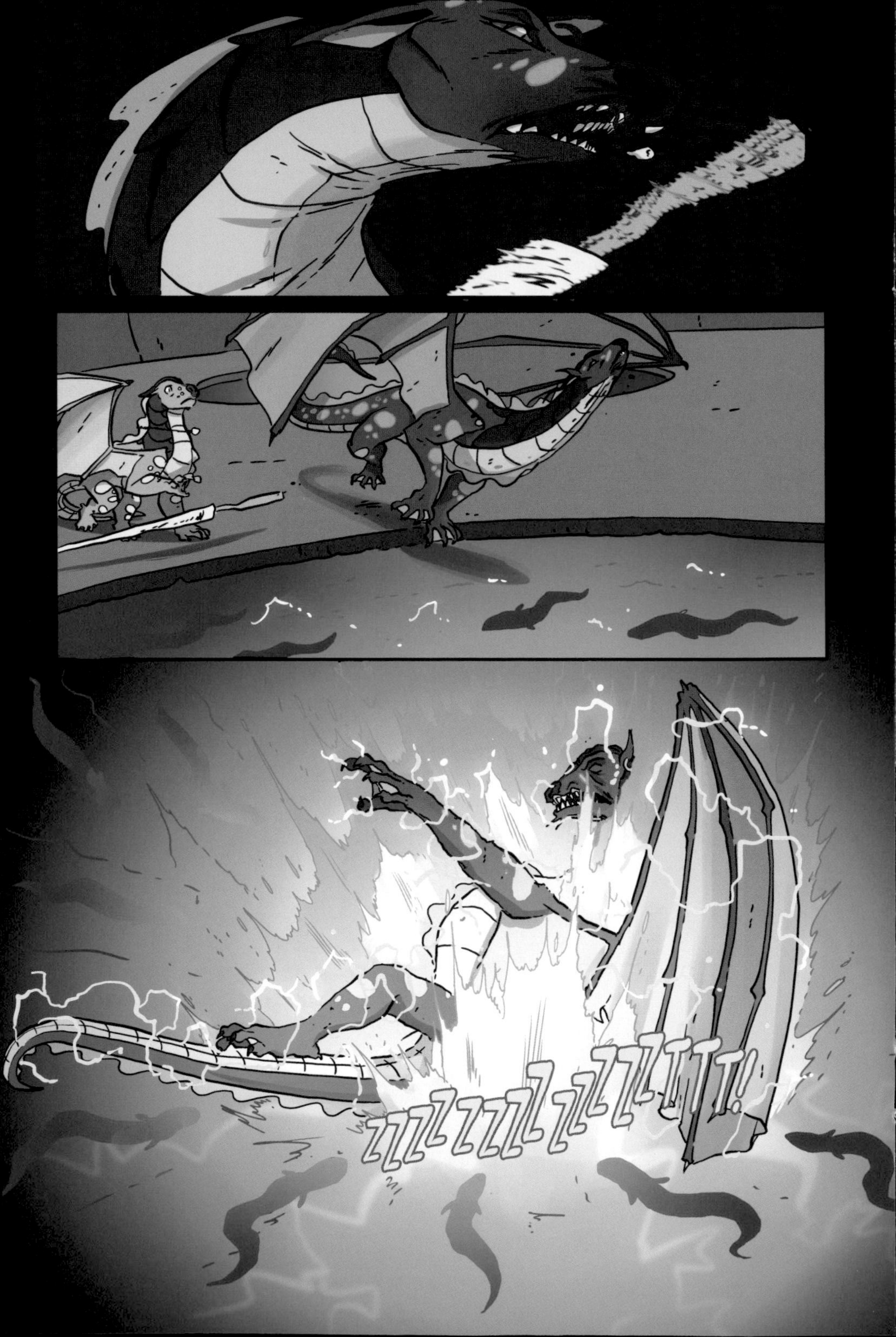
ZZZZZZZZZZZZZZZZZTTTT!

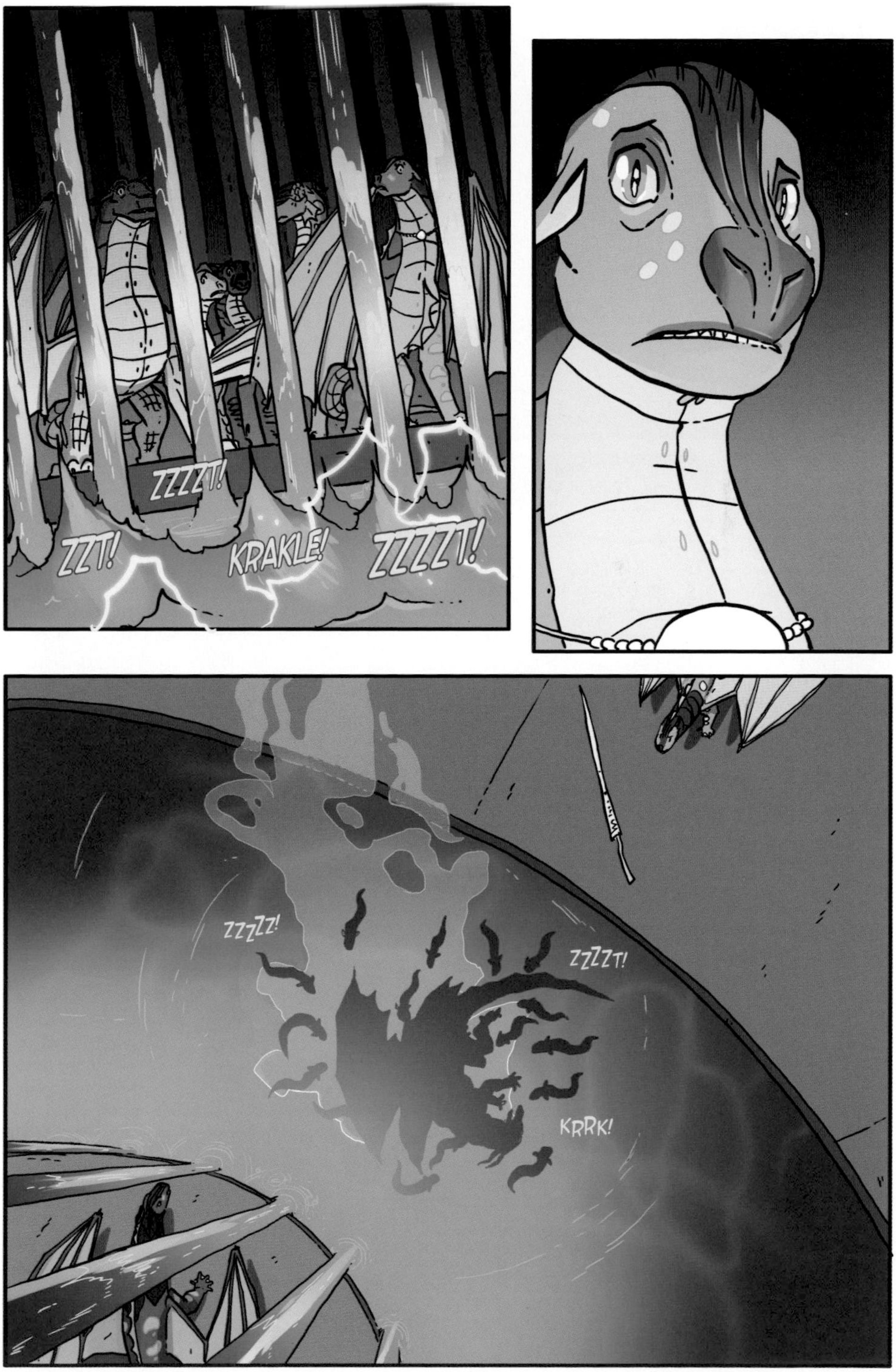
ZZZZT!
ZZT!
KRAKLE!
ZZZZZT!
ZZZZZ!
ZZZZT!
KRRK!

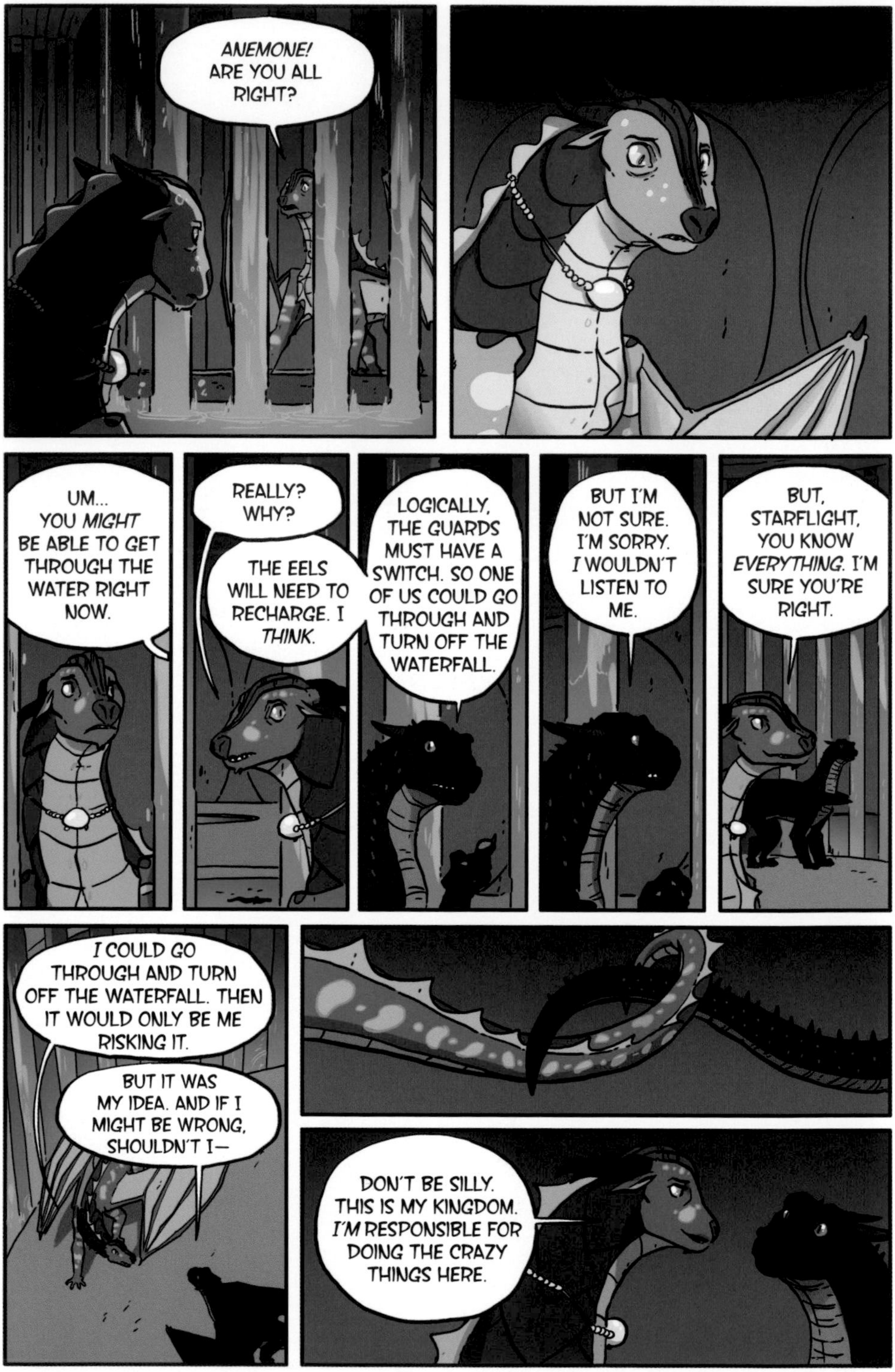
ANEMONE! ARE YOU ALL RIGHT?
UM... YOU MIGHT BE ABLE TO GET THROUGH THE WATER RIGHT NOW.
REALLY? WHY?
THE EELS WILL NEED TO RECHARGE. I THINK.
LOGICALLY, THE GUARDS MUST HAVE A SWITCH. SO ONE OF US COULD GO THROUGH AND TURN OFF THE WATERFALL.
BUT I'M NOT SURE. I'M SORRY. I WOULDN'T LISTEN TO ME.
BUT, STARFLIGHT, YOU KNOW EVERYTHING. I'M SURE YOU'RE RIGHT.
I COULD GO THROUGH AND TURN OFF THE WATERFALL. THEN IT WOULD ONLY BE ME RISKING IT.
BUT IT WAS MY IDEA. AND IF I MIGHT BE WRONG, SHOULDN'T I—
DON'T BE SILLY. THIS IS MY KINGDOM. I'M RESPONSIBLE FOR DOING THE CRAZY THINGS HERE.

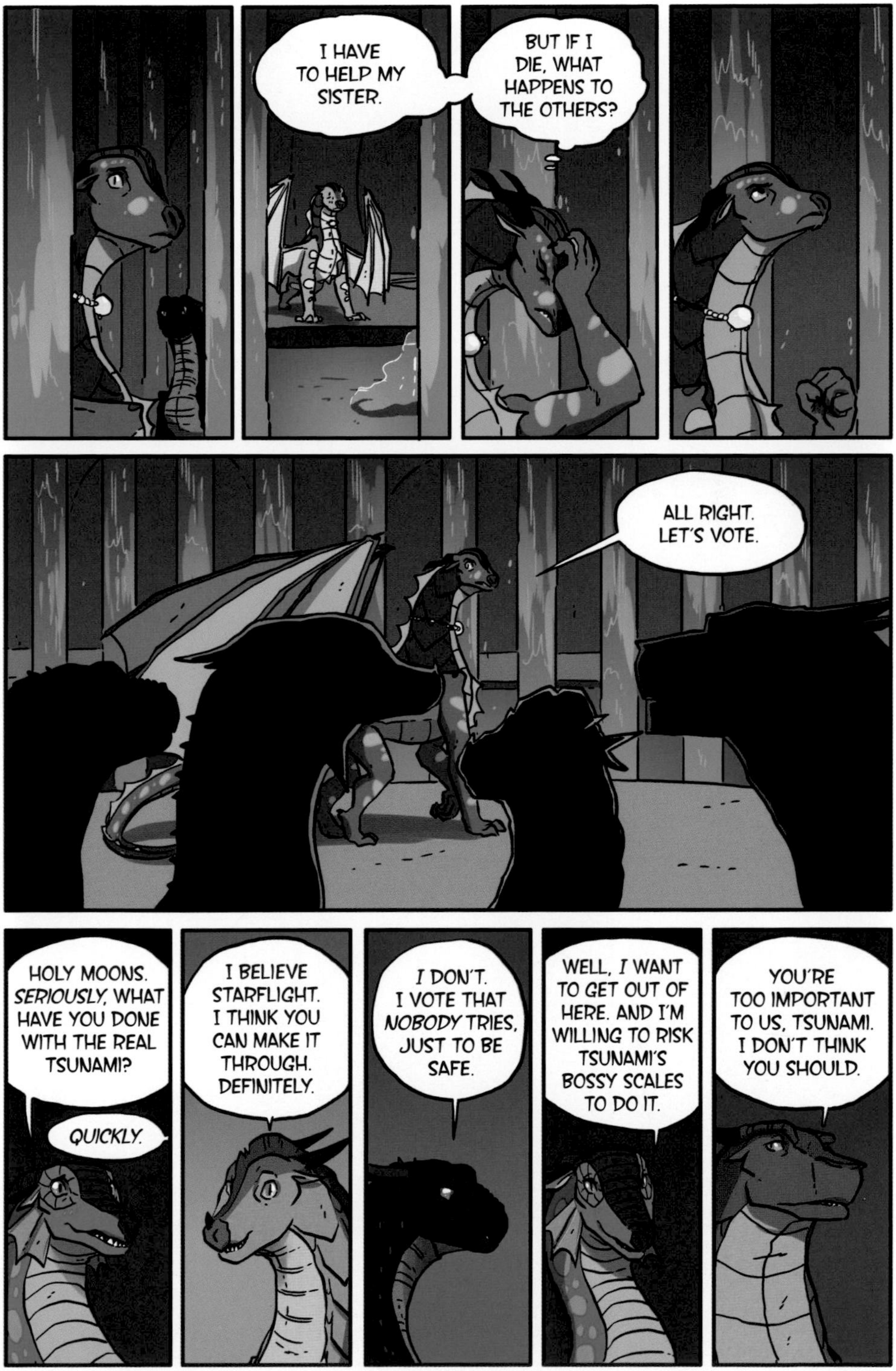
I HAVE TO HELP MY SISTER.
BUT IF I DIE, WHAT HAPPENS TO THE OTHERS?
ALL RIGHT. LET'S VOTE.
HOLY MOONS. *SERIOUSLY,* WHAT HAVE YOU DONE WITH THE REAL TSUNAMI?
QUICKLY.
I BELIEVE STARFLIGHT. I THINK YOU CAN MAKE IT THROUGH. DEFINITELY.
I DON'T. I VOTE THAT *NOBODY* TRIES, JUST TO BE SAFE.
WELL, *I* WANT TO GET OUT OF HERE. AND I'M WILLING TO RISK TSUNAMI'S BOSSY SCALES TO DO IT.
YOU'RE TOO IMPORTANT TO US, TSUNAMI. I DON'T THINK YOU SHOULD.

WELL, *THAT* DOESN'T HELP. SOME COUNCIL YOU GUYS ARE.

BUT I KNOW WHAT I SHOULD DO.

I LISTENED TO THEM. NOW I HAVE TO DECIDE.

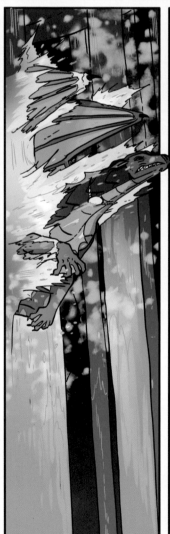

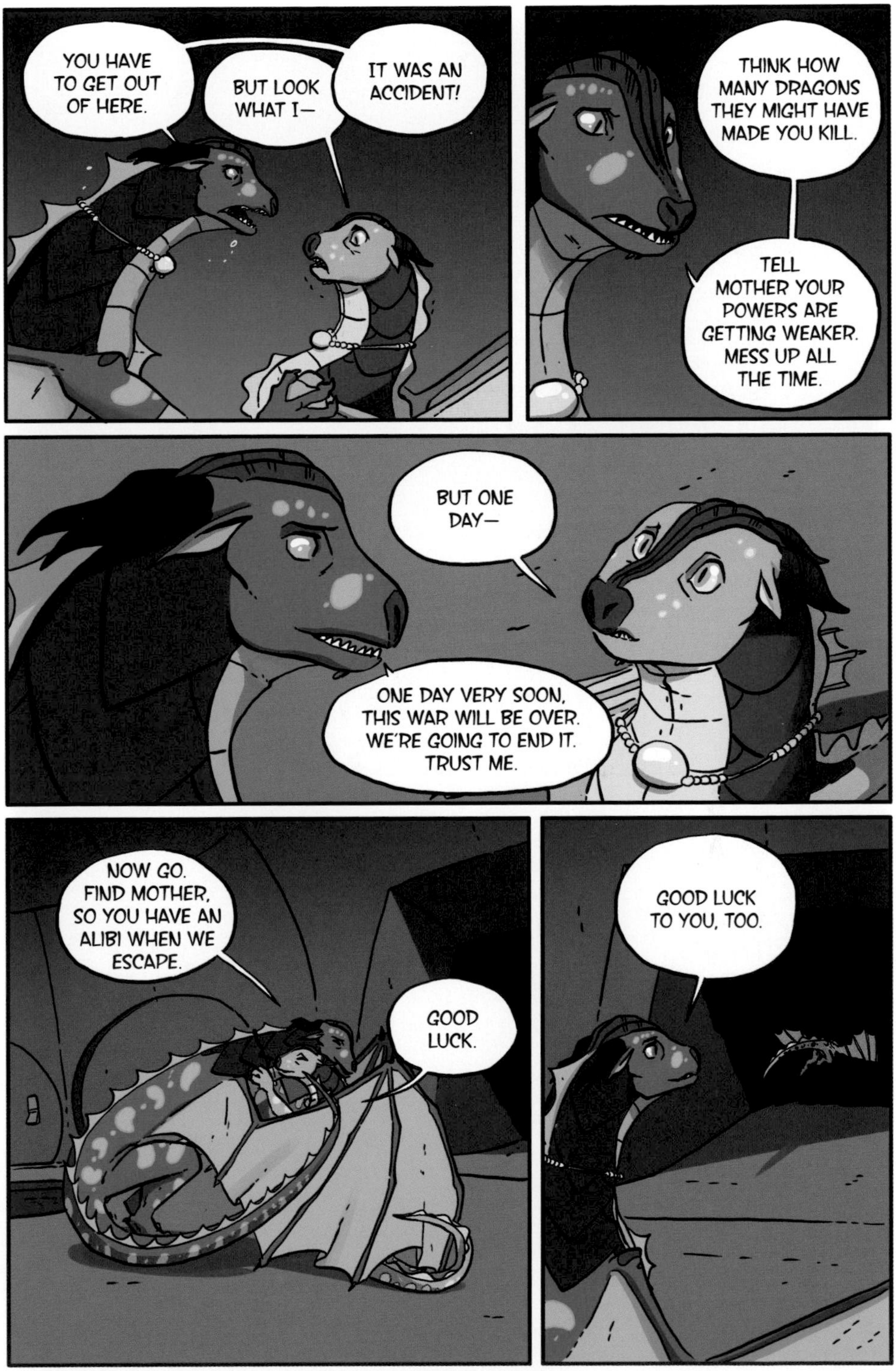
YOU HAVE TO GET OUT OF HERE.
BUT LOOK WHAT I—
IT WAS AN ACCIDENT!
THINK HOW MANY DRAGONS THEY MIGHT HAVE MADE YOU KILL.
TELL MOTHER YOUR POWERS ARE GETTING WEAKER. MESS UP ALL THE TIME.
BUT ONE DAY—
ONE DAY VERY SOON, THIS WAR WILL BE OVER. WE'RE GOING TO END IT. TRUST ME.
NOW GO. FIND MOTHER, SO YOU HAVE AN ALIBI WHEN WE ESCAPE.
GOOD LUCK.
GOOD LUCK TO YOU, TOO.

HEY! *KID!*

YOU COULD
DO THE SAME
THING FOR ME.
SET ME *FREE!*

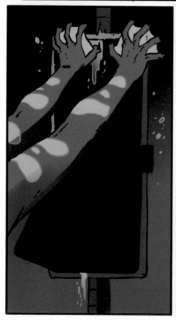

KR
KR
KR
KLANK

WHOOOSH!

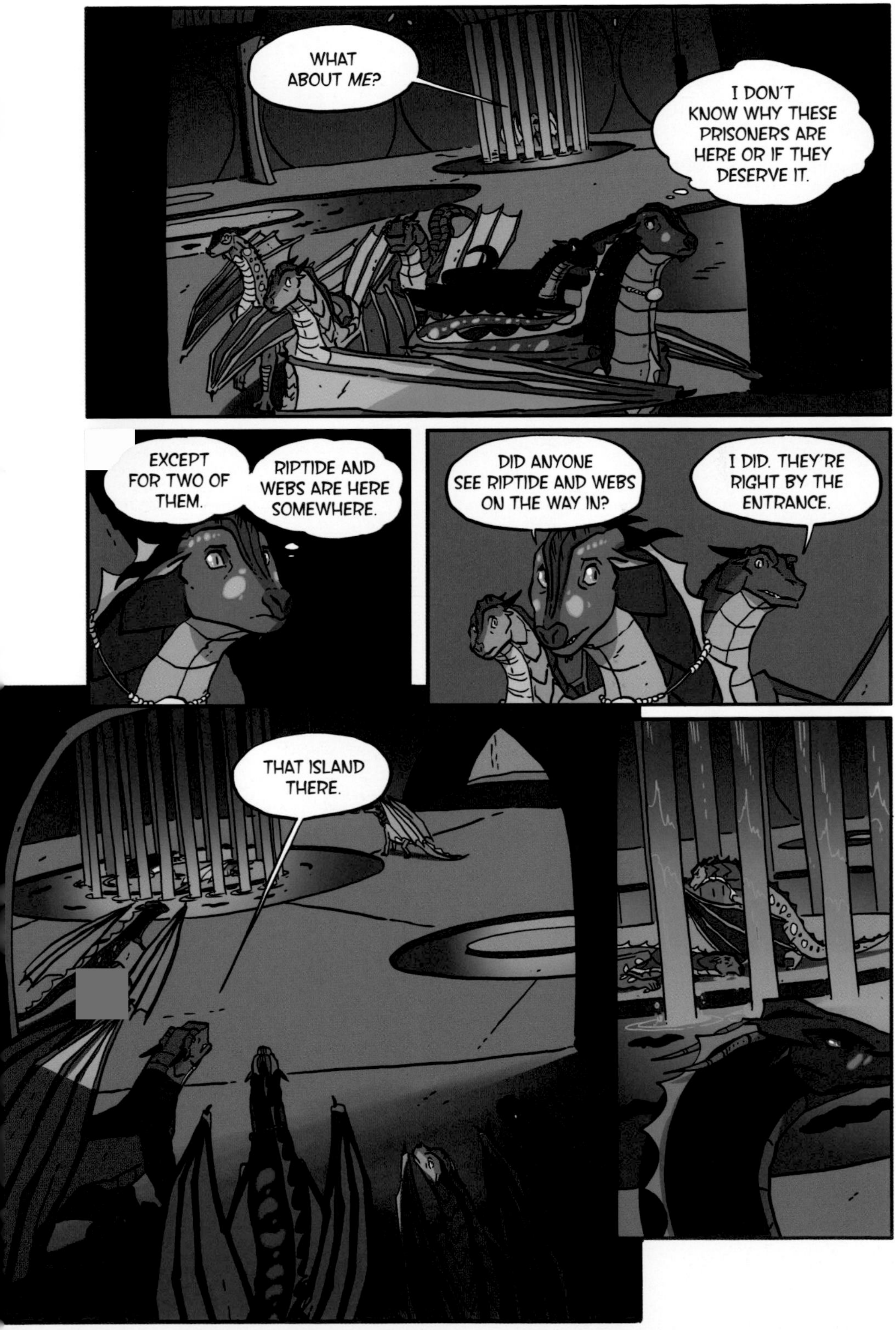
WHAT ABOUT *ME?*
I DON'T KNOW WHY THESE PRISONERS ARE HERE OR IF THEY DESERVE IT.
EXCEPT FOR TWO OF THEM.
RIPTIDE AND WEBS ARE HERE SOMEWHERE.
DID ANYONE SEE RIPTIDE AND WEBS ON THE WAY IN?
I DID. THEY'RE RIGHT BY THE ENTRANCE.
THAT ISLAND THERE.

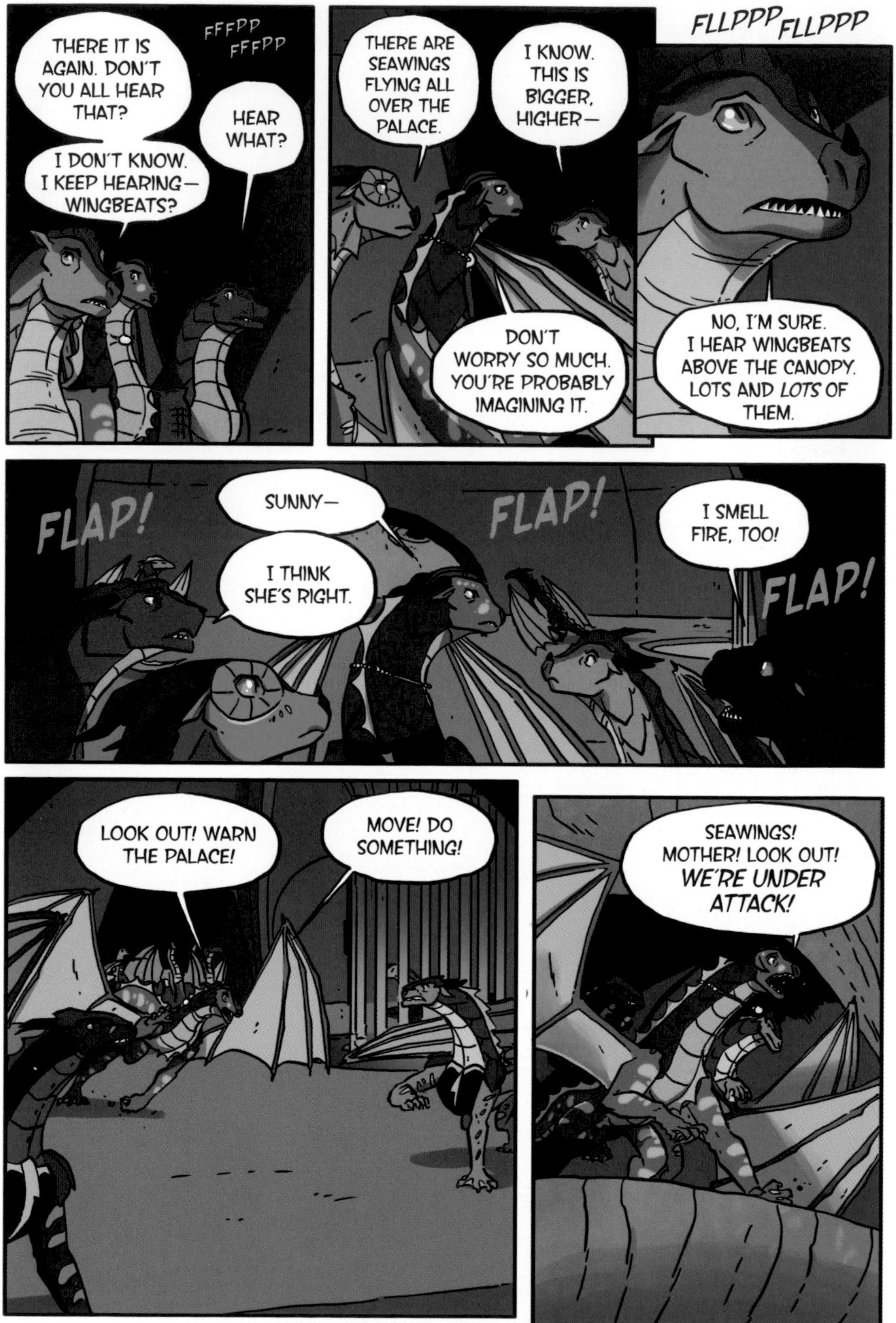
THERE IT IS AGAIN. DON'T YOU ALL HEAR THAT?
FFFPP FFFPP
HEAR WHAT?
I DON'T KNOW. I KEEP HEARING— WINGBEATS?
THERE ARE SEAWINGS FLYING ALL OVER THE PALACE.
I KNOW. THIS IS BIGGER, HIGHER—
DON'T WORRY SO MUCH. YOU'RE PROBABLY IMAGINING IT.
FLLPPP FLLPPP
NO, I'M SURE. I HEAR WINGBEATS ABOVE THE CANOPY. LOTS AND *LOTS* OF THEM.
FLAP!
SUNNY—
I THINK SHE'S RIGHT.
FLAP!
I SMELL FIRE, TOO!
FLAP!
LOOK OUT! WARN THE PALACE!
MOVE! DO SOMETHING!
SEAWINGS! MOTHER! LOOK OUT! *WE'RE UNDER ATTACK!*

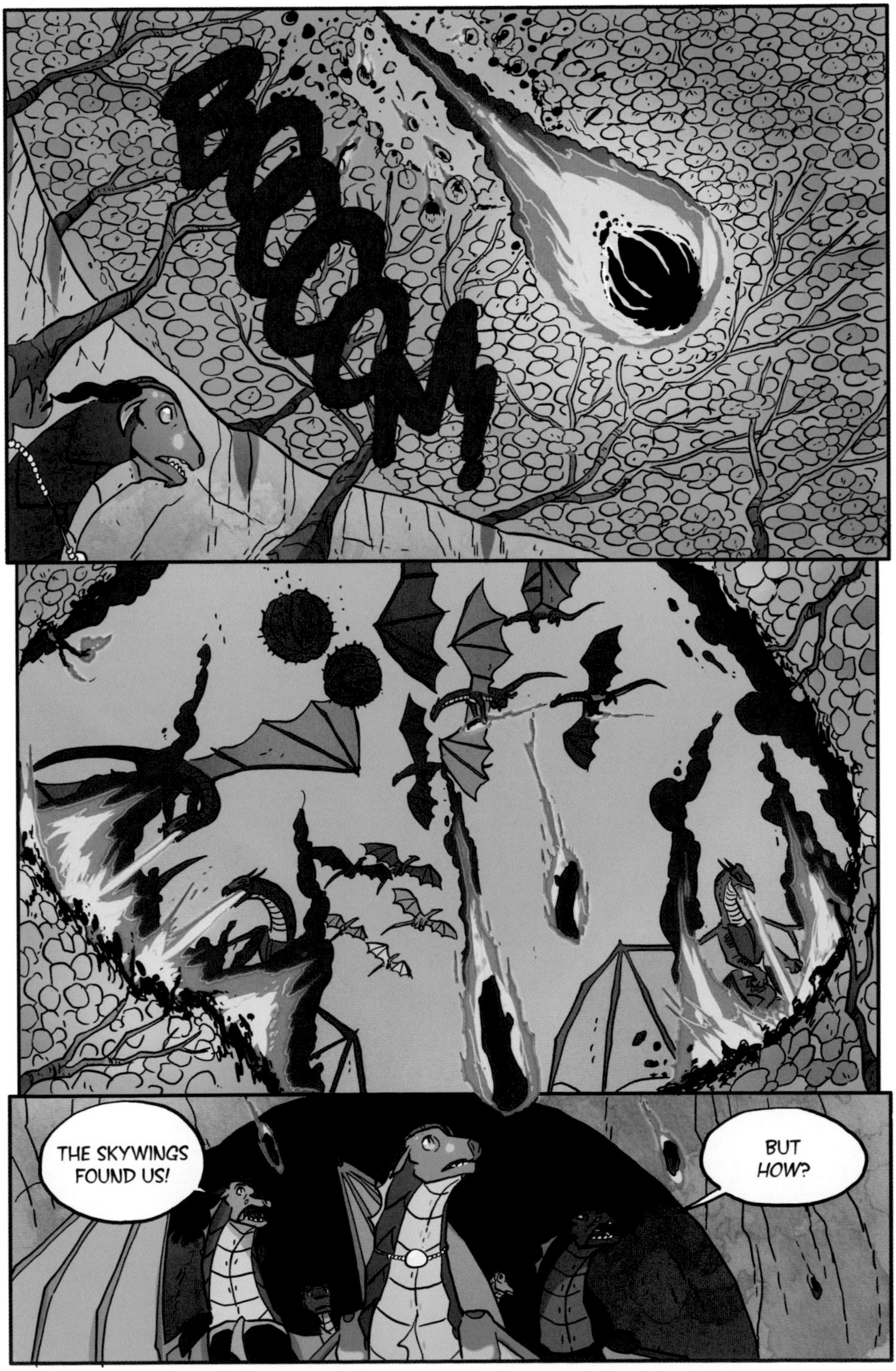
BOOOOM!
THE SKYWINGS FOUND US!
BUT HOW?

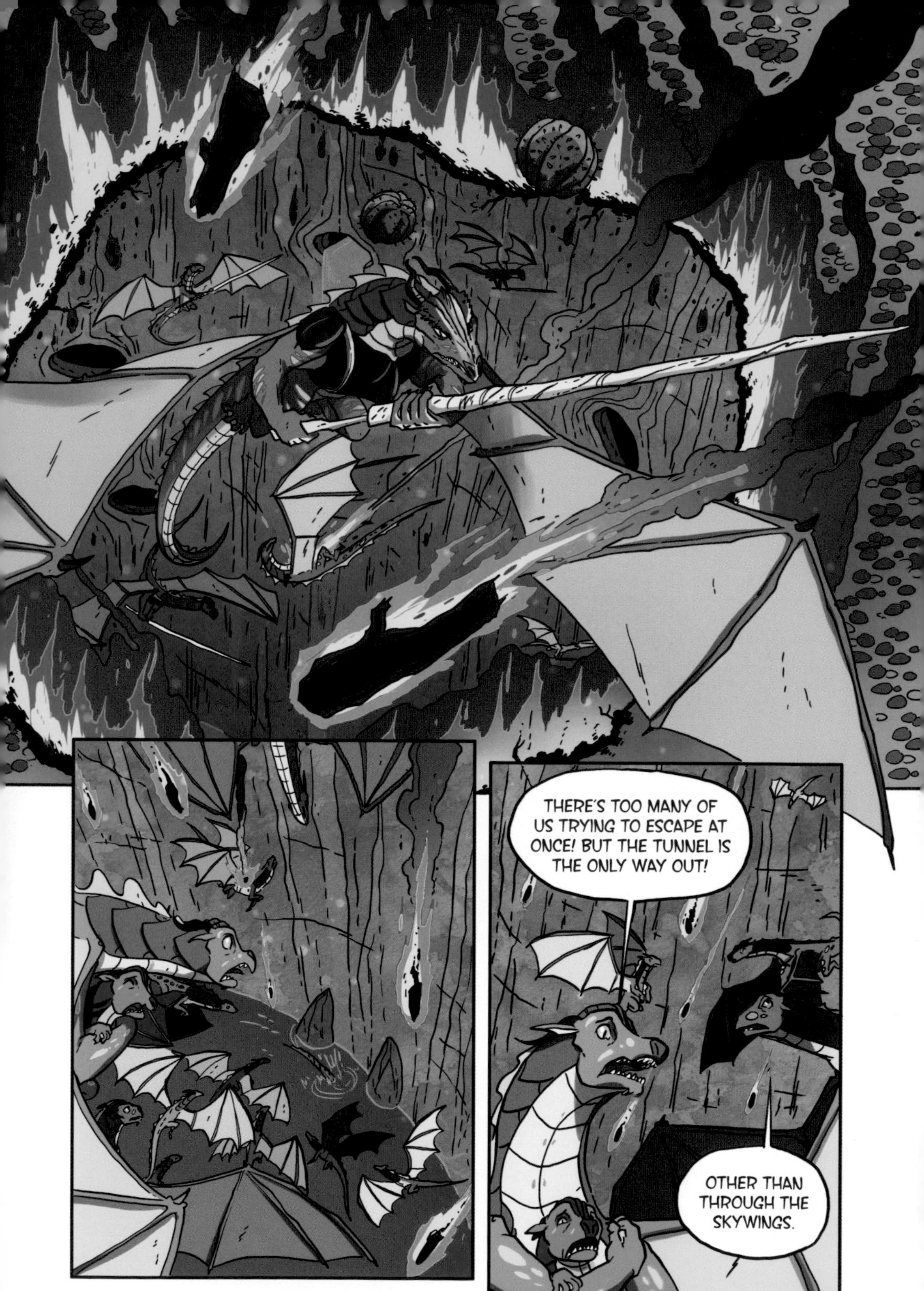
THERE'S TOO MANY OF US TRYING TO ESCAPE AT ONCE! BUT THE TUNNEL IS THE ONLY WAY OUT!
OTHER THAN THROUGH THE SKYWINGS.

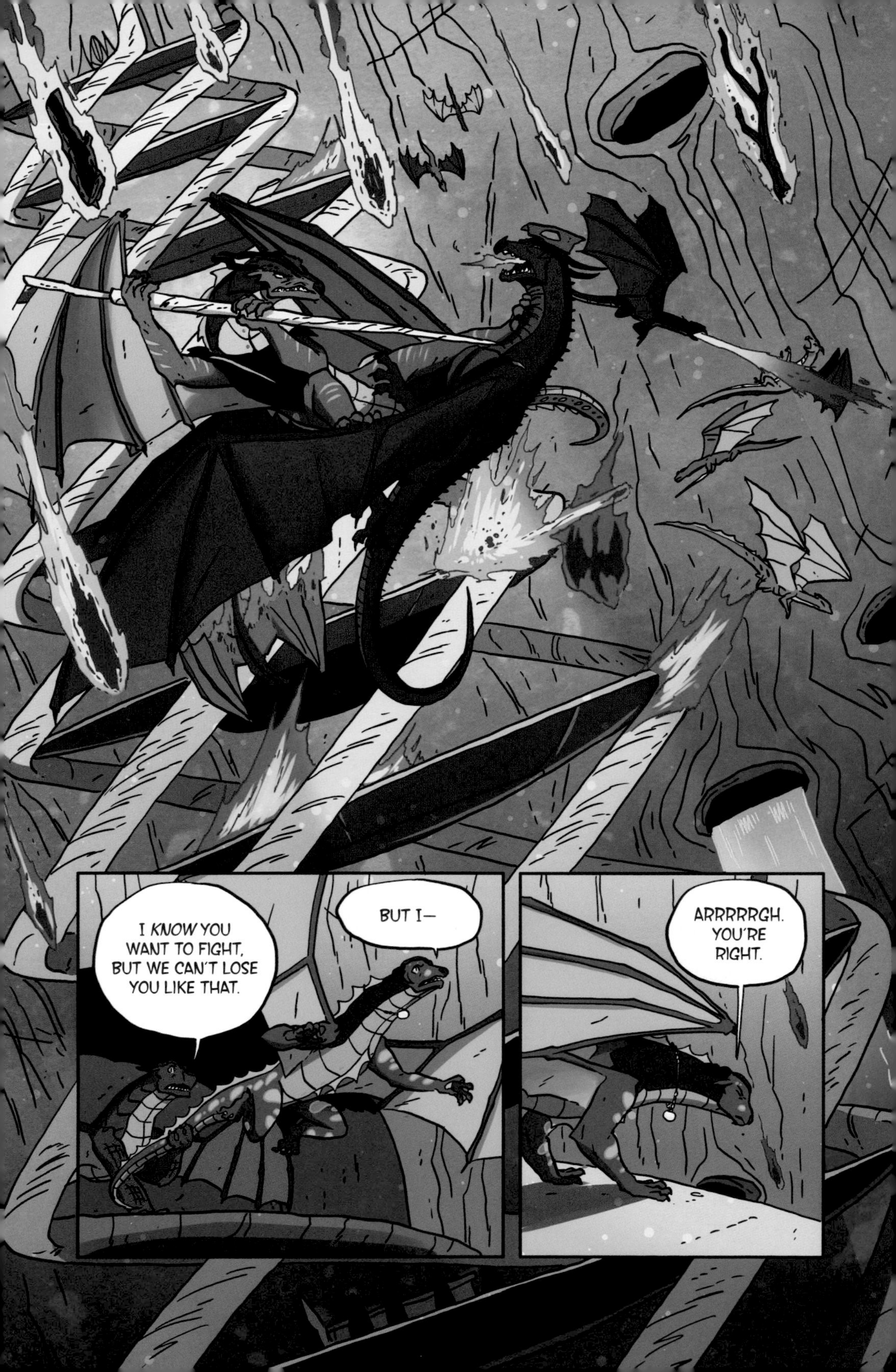
I *KNOW* YOU WANT TO FIGHT, BUT WE CAN'T LOSE YOU LIKE THAT.
BUT I—
ARRRRRGH. YOU'RE RIGHT.

GO! DEFENDING THE PALACE IS MORE IMPORTANT THAN GUARDING PRISONERS.

LET'S GET RIPTIDE AND WEBS OUT.

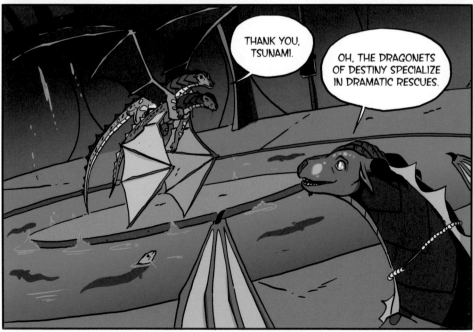

THANK YOU, TSUNAMI.

OH, THE DRAGONETS OF DESTINY SPECIALIZE IN DRAMATIC RESCUES.

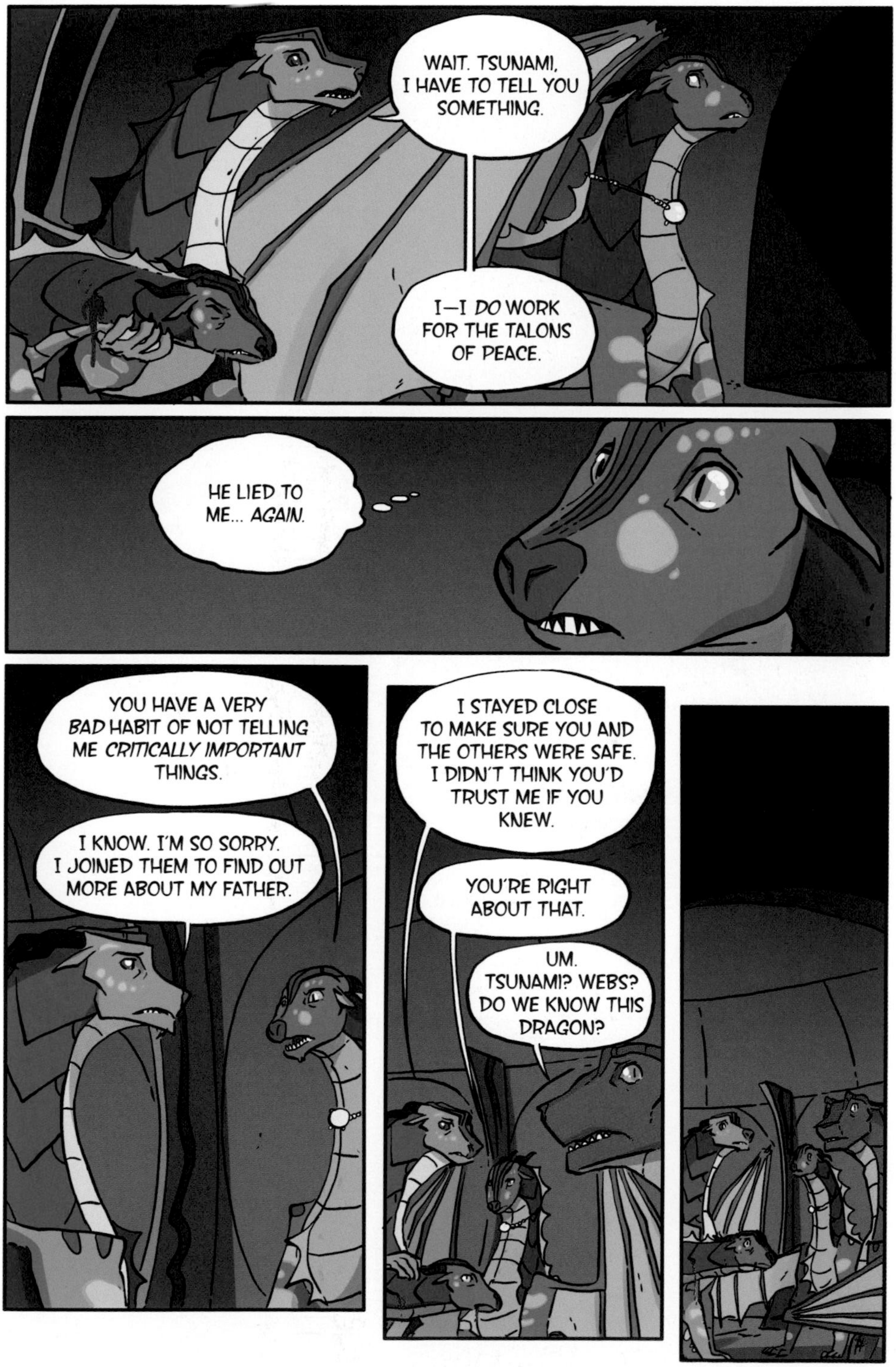
WAIT. TSUNAMI, I HAVE TO TELL YOU SOMETHING.
I—I *DO* WORK FOR THE TALONS OF PEACE.
HE LIED TO ME... *AGAIN.*
YOU HAVE A VERY *BAD* HABIT OF NOT TELLING ME *CRITICALLY IMPORTANT* THINGS.
I KNOW. I'M SO SORRY. I JOINED THEM TO FIND OUT MORE ABOUT MY FATHER.
I STAYED CLOSE TO MAKE SURE YOU AND THE OTHERS WERE SAFE. I DIDN'T THINK YOU'D TRUST ME IF YOU KNEW.
YOU'RE RIGHT ABOUT THAT.
UM. TSUNAMI? WEBS? DO WE KNOW THIS DRAGON?

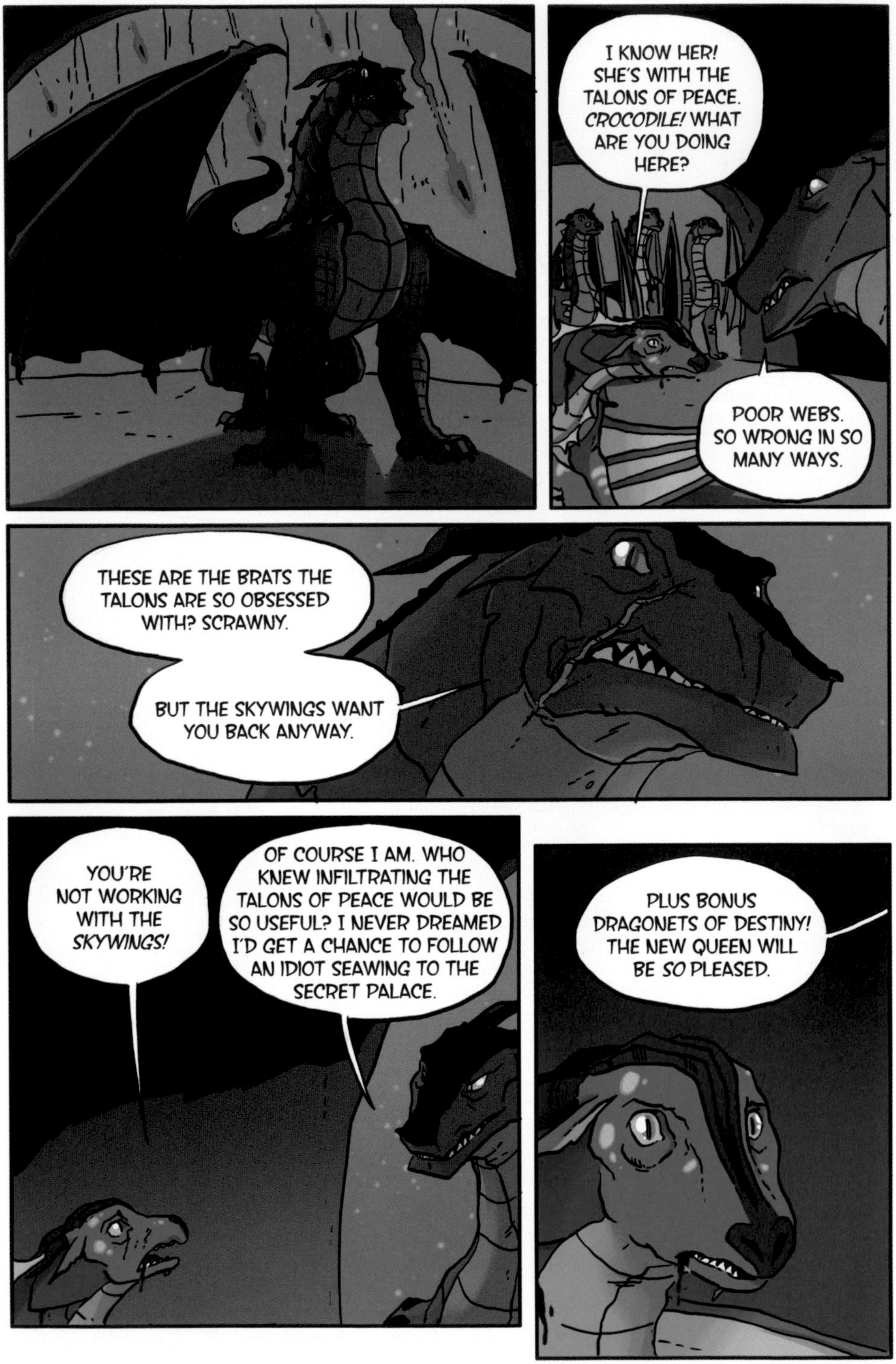
I KNOW HER! SHE'S WITH THE TALONS OF PEACE. *CROCODILE!* WHAT ARE YOU DOING HERE?
POOR WEBS. SO WRONG IN SO MANY WAYS.
THESE ARE THE BRATS THE TALONS ARE SO OBSESSED WITH? SCRAWNY.
BUT THE SKYWINGS WANT YOU BACK ANYWAY.
YOU'RE NOT WORKING WITH THE *SKYWINGS!*
OF COURSE I AM. WHO KNEW INFILTRATING THE TALONS OF PEACE WOULD BE SO USEFUL? I NEVER DREAMED I'D GET A CHANCE TO FOLLOW AN IDIOT SEAWING TO THE SECRET PALACE.
PLUS BONUS DRAGONETS OF DESTINY! THE NEW QUEEN WILL BE *SO* PLEASED.

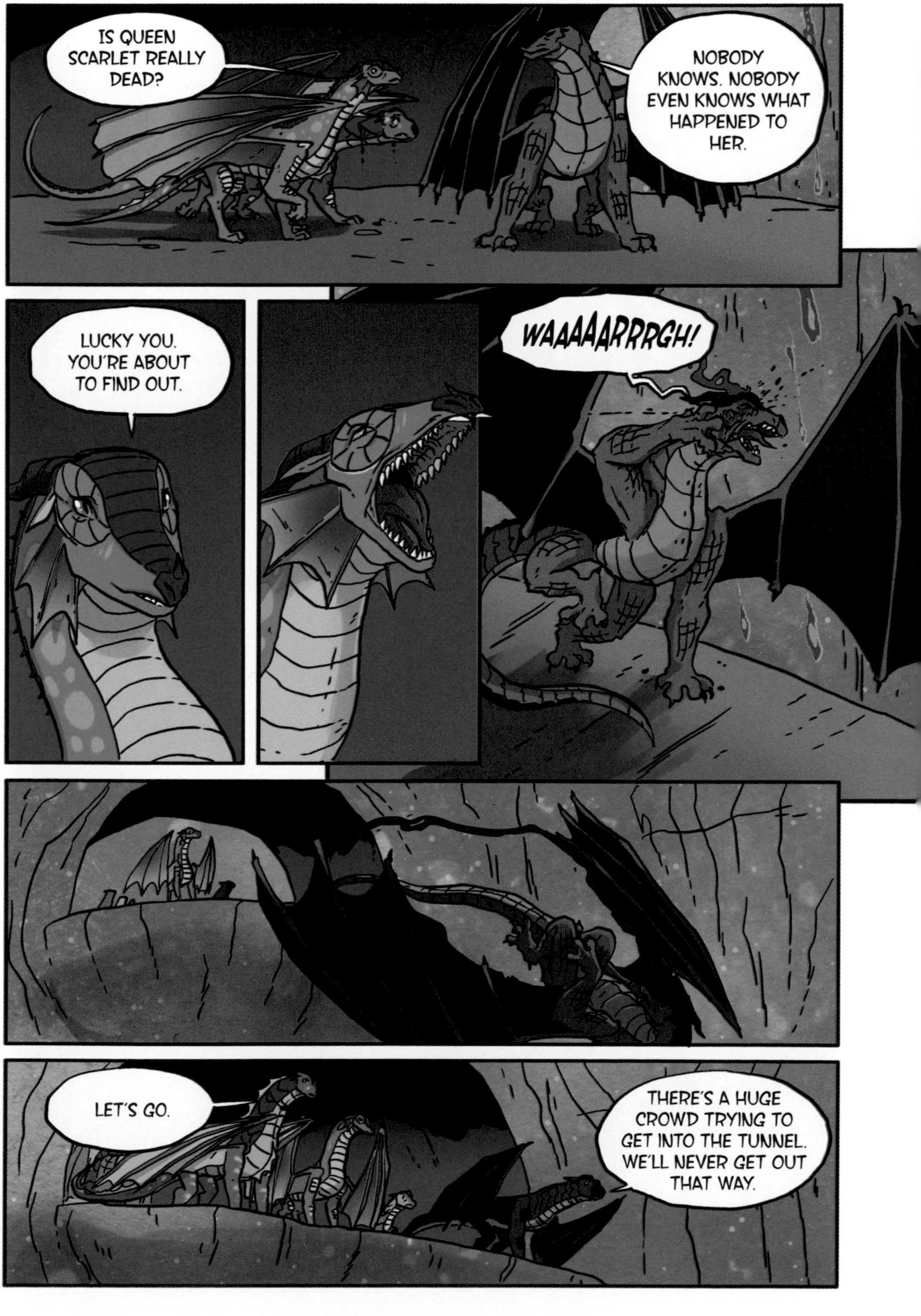
IS QUEEN SCARLET REALLY DEAD?
NOBODY KNOWS. NOBODY EVEN KNOWS WHAT HAPPENED TO HER.
LUCKY YOU. YOU'RE ABOUT TO FIND OUT.
WAAAAARRRGH!
LET'S GO.
THERE'S A HUGE CROWD TRYING TO GET INTO THE TUNNEL. WE'LL NEVER GET OUT THAT WAY.

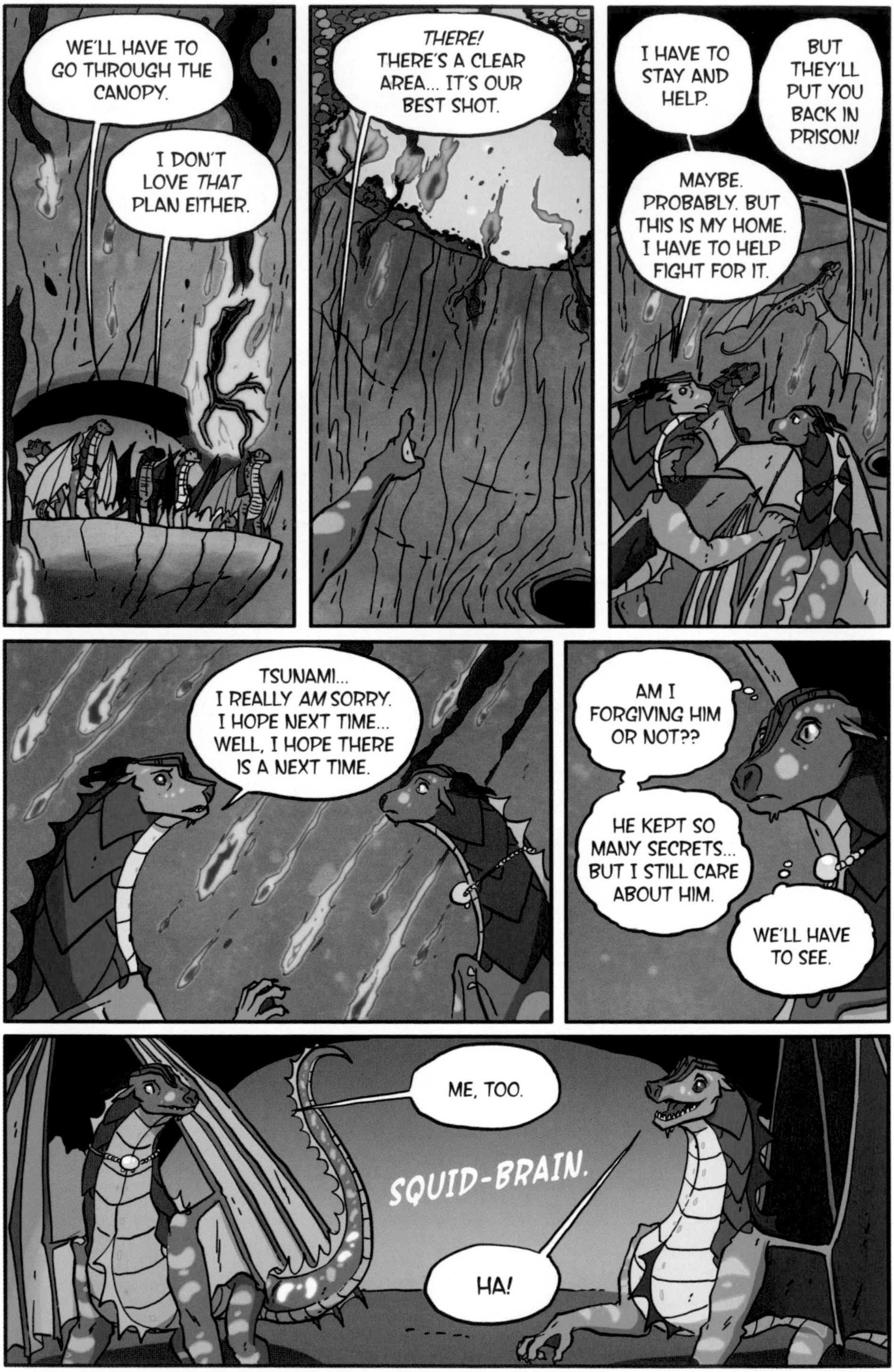
WE'LL HAVE TO GO THROUGH THE CANOPY.
I DON'T LOVE *THAT* PLAN EITHER.
THERE! THERE'S A CLEAR AREA... IT'S OUR BEST SHOT.
I HAVE TO STAY AND HELP.
BUT THEY'LL PUT YOU BACK IN PRISON!
MAYBE. PROBABLY. BUT THIS IS MY HOME. I HAVE TO HELP FIGHT FOR IT.
TSUNAMI... I REALLY *AM* SORRY. I HOPE NEXT TIME... WELL, I HOPE THERE IS A NEXT TIME.
AM I FORGIVING HIM OR NOT??
HE KEPT SO MANY SECRETS... BUT I STILL CARE ABOUT HIM.
WE'LL HAVE TO SEE.
ME, TOO.
SQUID-BRAIN.
HA!

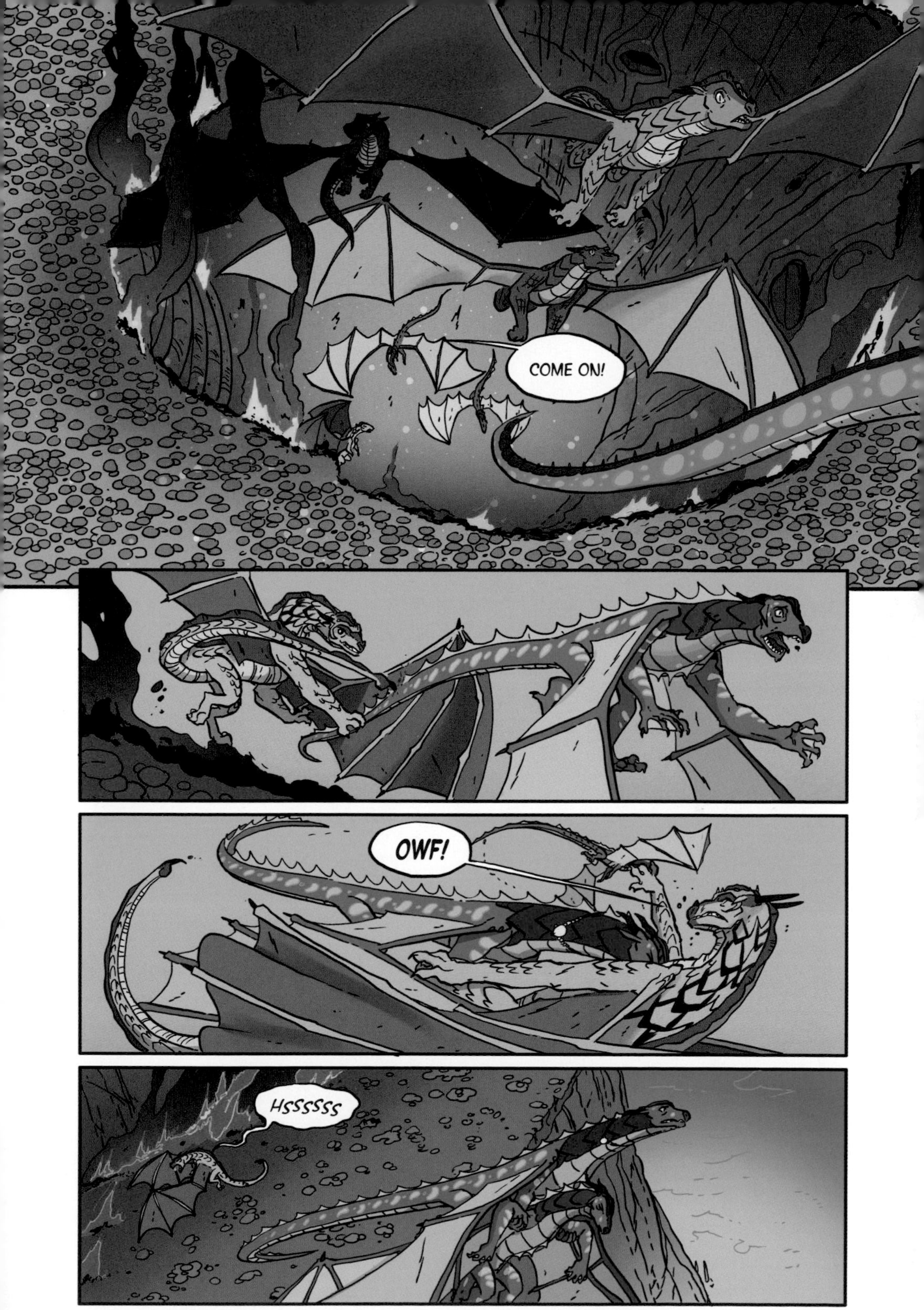
COME ON!
OWF!
HSSSSSS

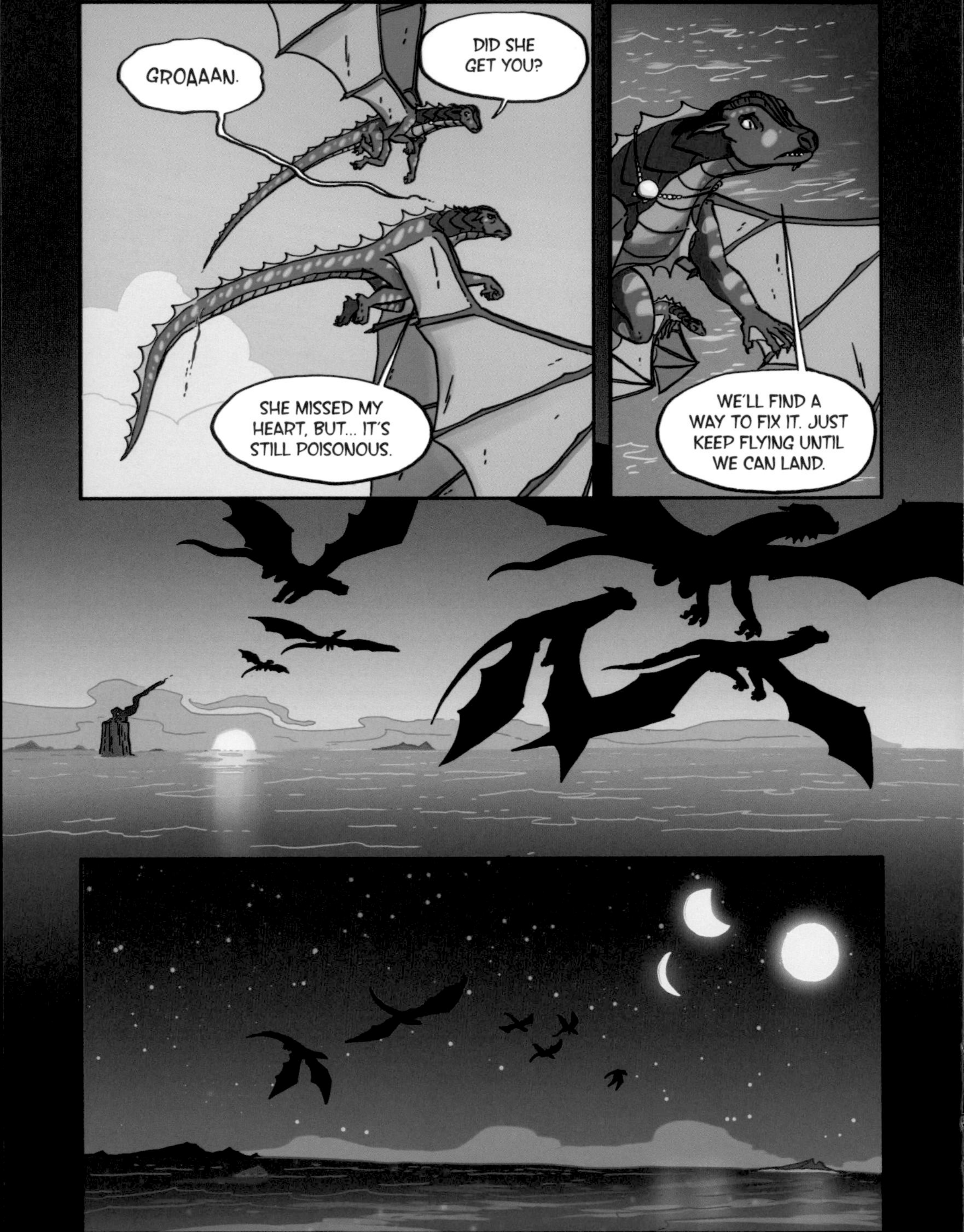
GROAAAN.
DID SHE GET YOU?
SHE MISSED MY HEART, BUT... IT'S STILL POISONOUS.
WE'LL FIND A WAY TO FIX IT. JUST KEEP FLYING UNTIL WE CAN LAND.

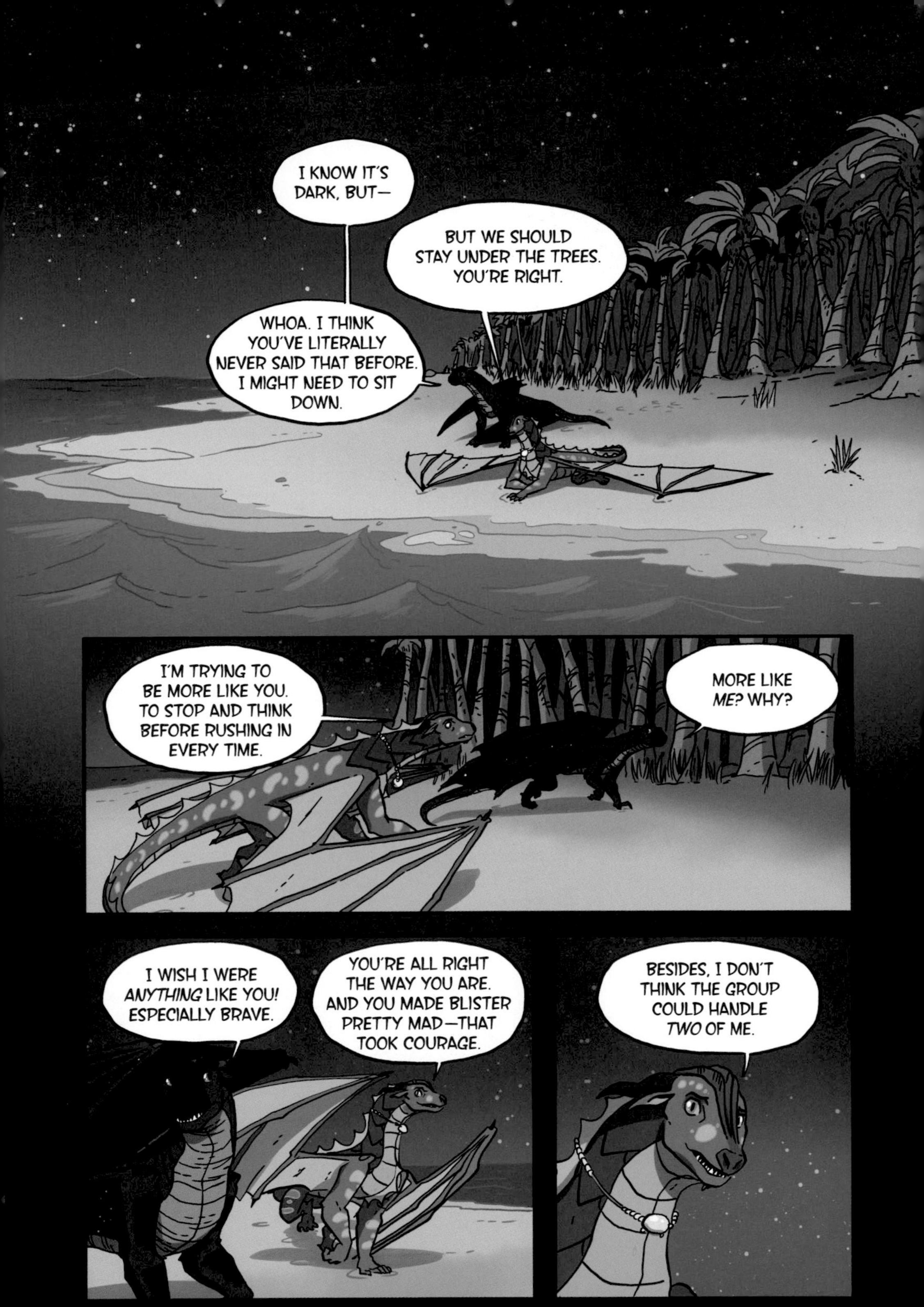
I KNOW IT'S DARK, BUT—
BUT WE SHOULD STAY UNDER THE TREES. YOU'RE RIGHT.
WHOA. I THINK YOU'VE LITERALLY NEVER SAID THAT BEFORE. I MIGHT NEED TO SIT DOWN.
I'M TRYING TO BE MORE LIKE YOU. TO STOP AND THINK BEFORE RUSHING IN EVERY TIME.
MORE LIKE *ME*? WHY?
I WISH I WERE *ANYTHING* LIKE YOU! ESPECIALLY BRAVE.
YOU'RE ALL RIGHT THE WAY YOU ARE. AND YOU MADE BLISTER PRETTY MAD—THAT TOOK COURAGE.
BESIDES, I DON'T THINK THE GROUP COULD HANDLE *TWO* OF ME.

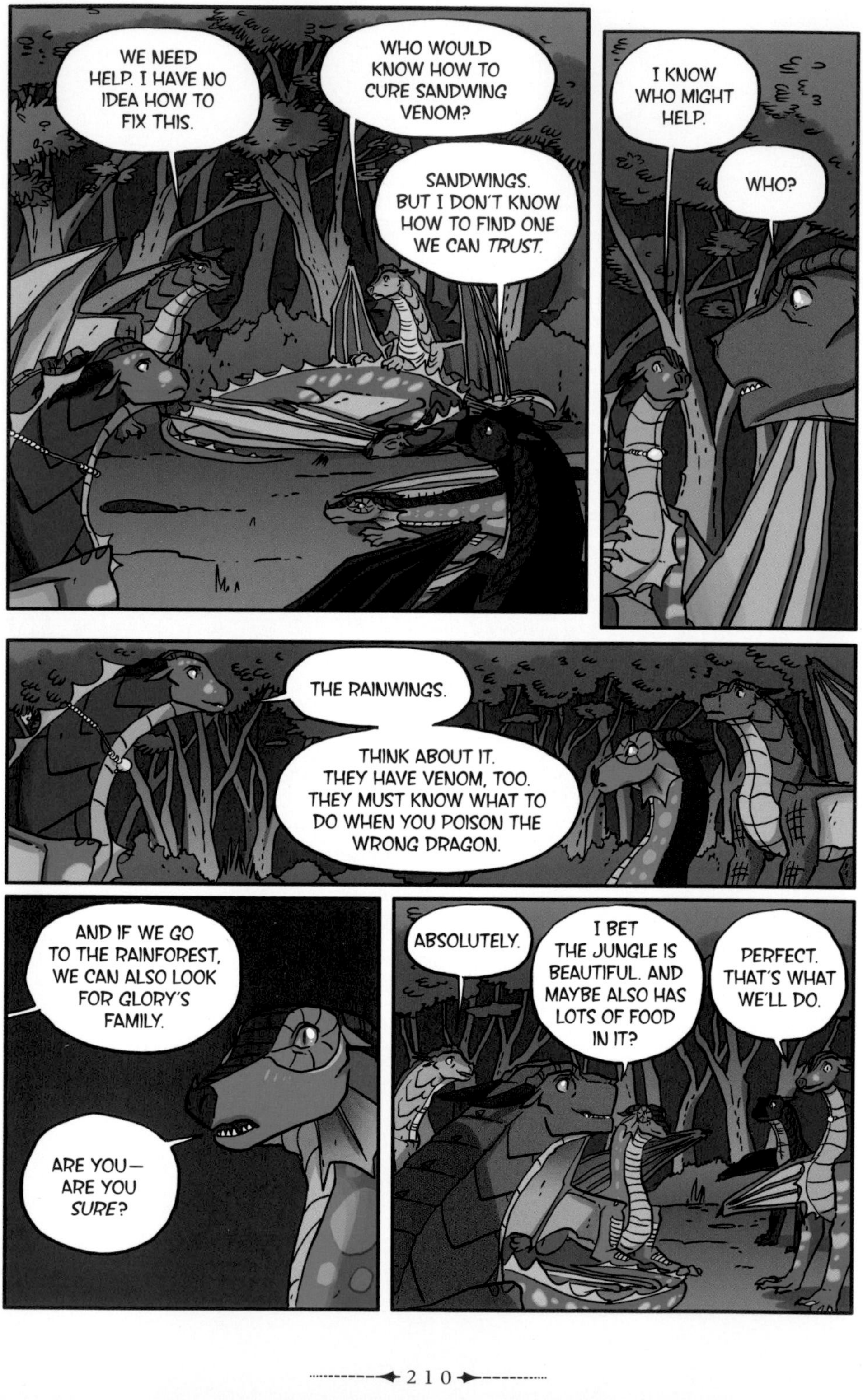
WE NEED HELP. I HAVE NO IDEA HOW TO FIX THIS.
WHO WOULD KNOW HOW TO CURE SANDWING VENOM?
SANDWINGS. BUT I DON'T KNOW HOW TO FIND ONE WE CAN *TRUST*.
I KNOW WHO MIGHT HELP.
WHO?
THE RAINWINGS.
THINK ABOUT IT. THEY HAVE VENOM, TOO. THEY MUST KNOW WHAT TO DO WHEN YOU POISON THE WRONG DRAGON.
AND IF WE GO TO THE RAINFOREST, WE CAN ALSO LOOK FOR GLORY'S FAMILY.
ARE YOU— ARE YOU *SURE*?
ABSOLUTELY.
I BET THE JUNGLE IS BEAUTIFUL. AND MAYBE ALSO HAS LOTS OF FOOD IN IT?
PERFECT. THAT'S WHAT WE'LL DO.

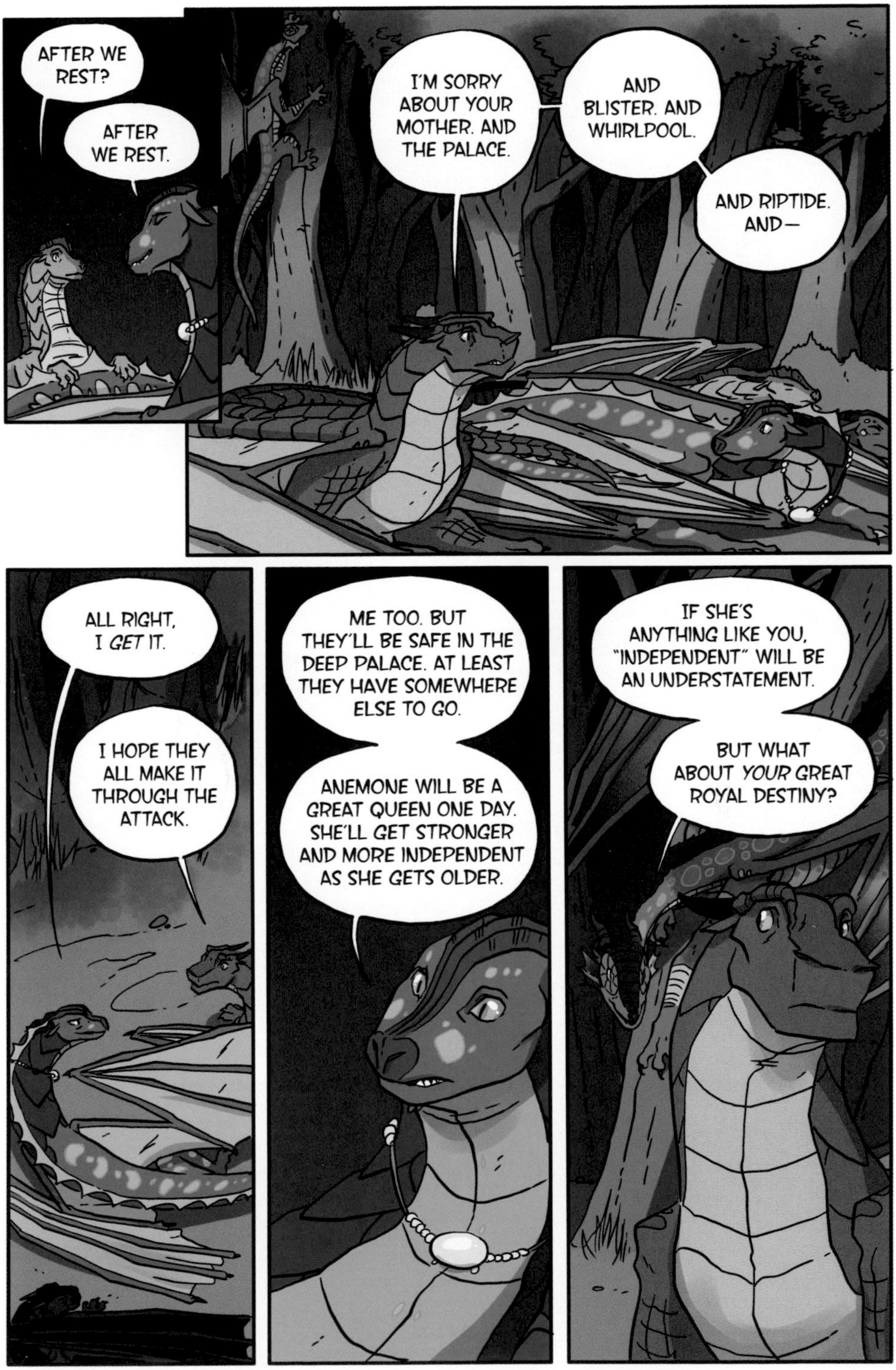
AFTER WE REST?
AFTER WE REST.
I'M SORRY ABOUT YOUR MOTHER. AND THE PALACE.
AND BLISTER. AND WHIRLPOOL.
AND RIPTIDE. AND—
ALL RIGHT, I *GET* IT.
I HOPE THEY ALL MAKE IT THROUGH THE ATTACK.
ME TOO. BUT THEY'LL BE SAFE IN THE DEEP PALACE. AT LEAST THEY HAVE SOMEWHERE ELSE TO GO.
ANEMONE WILL BE A GREAT QUEEN ONE DAY. SHE'LL GET STRONGER AND MORE INDEPENDENT AS SHE GETS OLDER.
IF SHE'S ANYTHING LIKE YOU, "INDEPENDENT" WILL BE AN UNDERSTATEMENT.
BUT WHAT ABOUT *YOUR* GREAT ROYAL DESTINY?

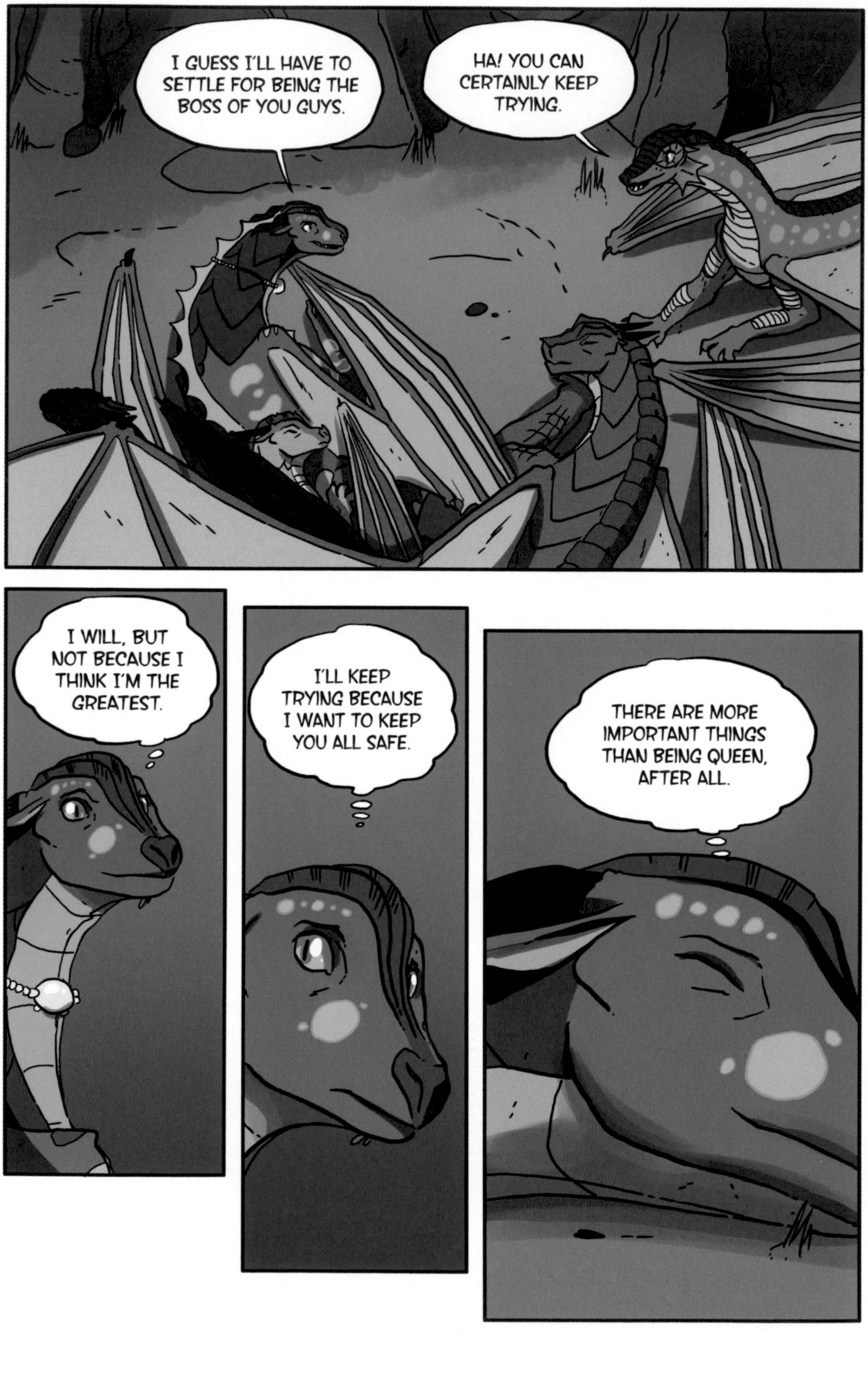
I GUESS I'LL HAVE TO SETTLE FOR BEING THE BOSS OF YOU GUYS.
HA! YOU CAN CERTAINLY KEEP TRYING.
I WILL, BUT NOT BECAUSE I THINK I'M THE GREATEST.
I'LL KEEP TRYING BECAUSE I WANT TO KEEP YOU ALL SAFE.
THERE ARE MORE IMPORTANT THINGS THAN BEING QUEEN, AFTER ALL.

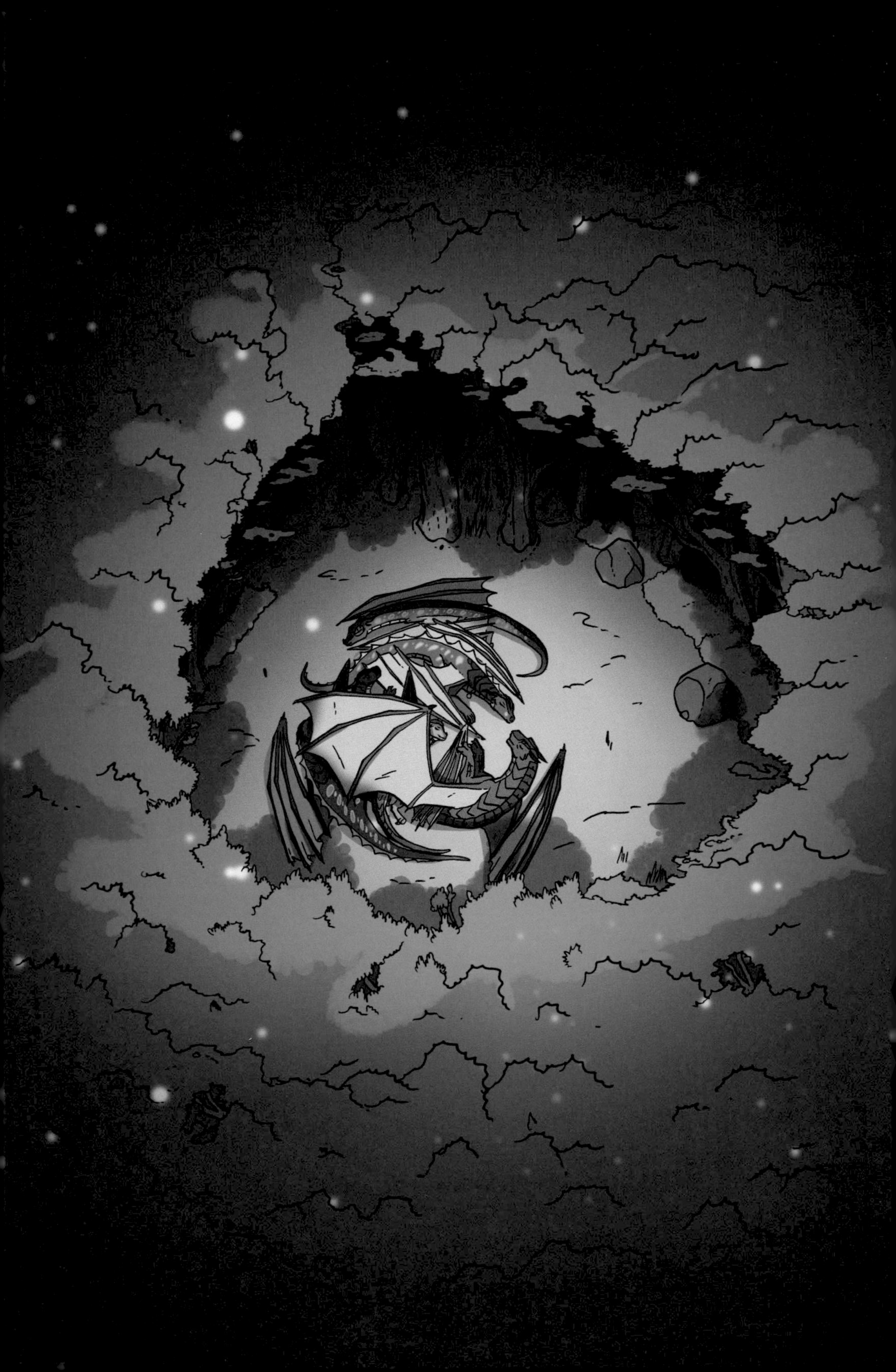

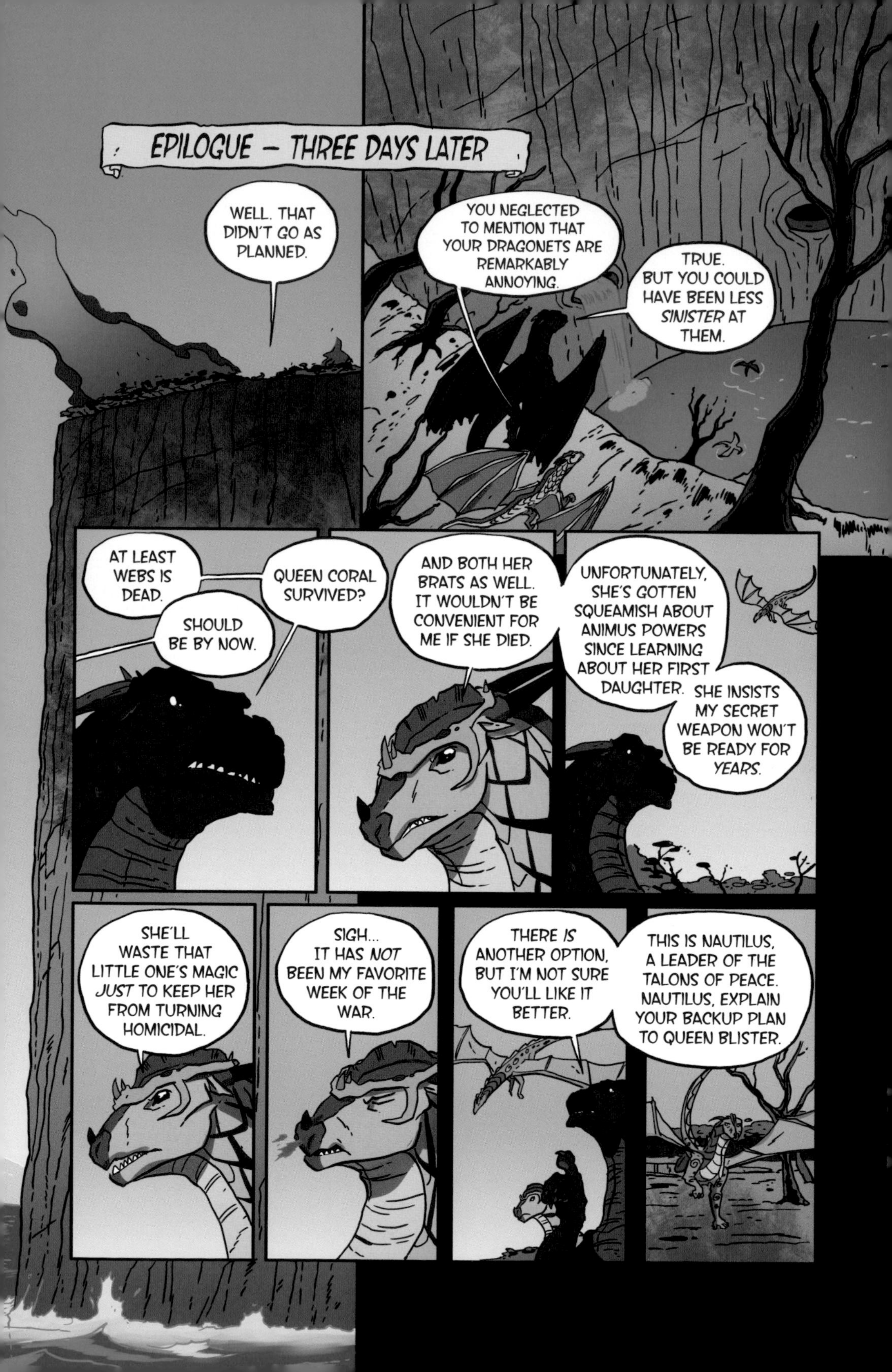
EPILOGUE – THREE DAYS LATER
WELL. THAT DIDN'T GO AS PLANNED.
YOU NEGLECTED TO MENTION THAT YOUR DRAGONETS ARE REMARKABLY ANNOYING.
TRUE. BUT YOU COULD HAVE BEEN LESS SINISTER AT THEM.
AT LEAST WEBS IS DEAD.
SHOULD BE BY NOW.
QUEEN CORAL SURVIVED?
AND BOTH HER BRATS AS WELL. IT WOULDN'T BE CONVENIENT FOR ME IF SHE DIED.
UNFORTUNATELY, SHE'S GOTTEN SQUEAMISH ABOUT ANIMUS POWERS SINCE LEARNING ABOUT HER FIRST DAUGHTER.
SHE INSISTS MY SECRET WEAPON WON'T BE READY FOR YEARS.
SHE'LL WASTE THAT LITTLE ONE'S MAGIC JUST TO KEEP HER FROM TURNING HOMICIDAL.
SIGH... IT HAS NOT BEEN MY FAVORITE WEEK OF THE WAR.
THERE IS ANOTHER OPTION, BUT I'M NOT SURE YOU'LL LIKE IT BETTER.
THIS IS NAUTILUS, A LEADER OF THE TALONS OF PEACE. NAUTILUS, EXPLAIN YOUR BACKUP PLAN TO QUEEN BLISTER.

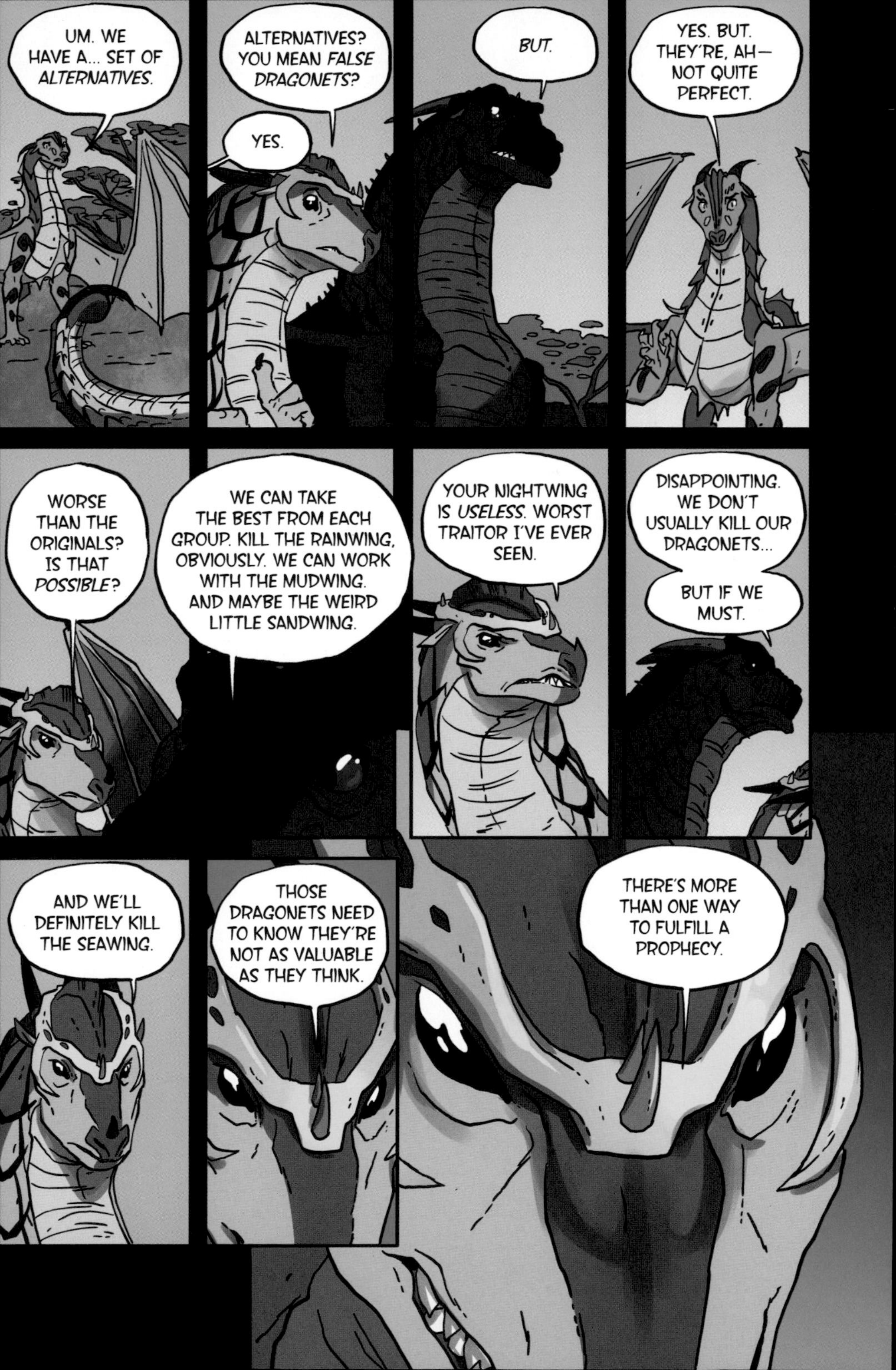
UM. WE HAVE A... SET OF *ALTERNATIVES*.
ALTERNATIVES? YOU MEAN *FALSE DRAGONETS*?
YES.
BUT.
YES. BUT. THEY'RE, AH— NOT QUITE PERFECT.
WORSE THAN THE ORIGINALS? IS THAT *POSSIBLE*?
WE CAN TAKE THE BEST FROM EACH GROUP. KILL THE RAINWING, OBVIOUSLY. WE CAN WORK WITH THE MUDWING. AND MAYBE THE WEIRD LITTLE SANDWING.
YOUR NIGHTWING IS *USELESS*. WORST TRAITOR I'VE EVER SEEN.
DISAPPOINTING. WE DON'T USUALLY KILL OUR DRAGONETS...
BUT IF WE MUST.
AND WE'LL DEFINITELY KILL THE SEAWING.
THOSE DRAGONETS NEED TO KNOW THEY'RE NOT AS VALUABLE AS THEY THINK.
THERE'S MORE THAN ONE WAY TO FULFILL A PROPHECY.

DISCOVER THE EPIC SERIES WHERE IT ALL BEGAN!

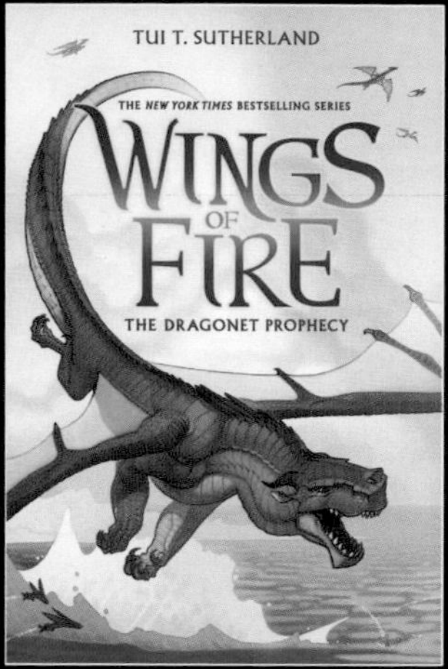
TUI T. SUTHERLAND
THE NEW YORK TIMES BESTSELLING SERIES
WINGS OF FIRE
THE DRAGONET PROPHECY

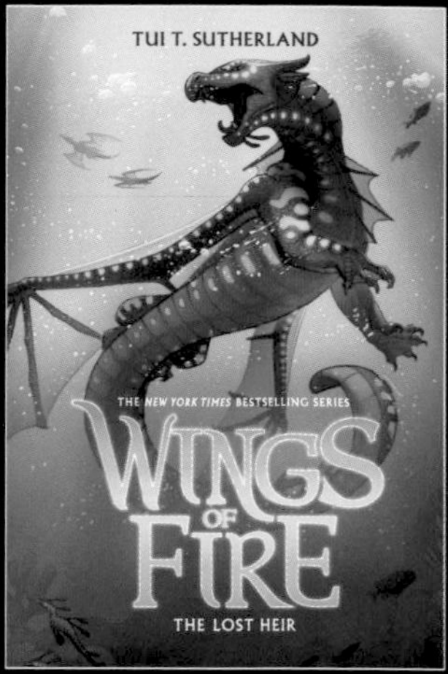
TUI T. SUTHERLAND
THE NEW YORK TIMES BESTSELLING SERIES
WINGS OF FIRE
THE LOST HEIR

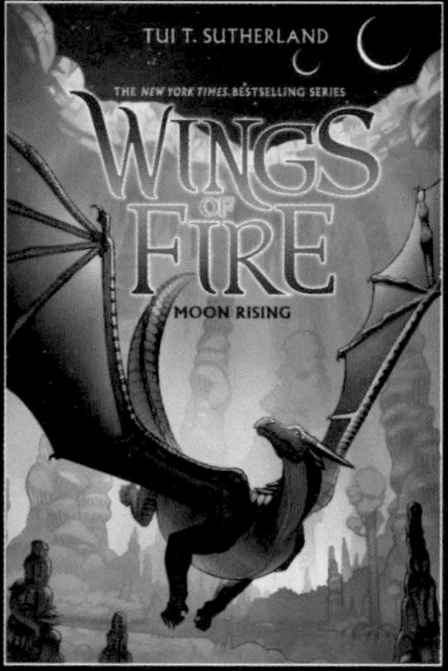
TUI T. SUTHERLAND
THE NEW YORK TIMES BESTSELLING SERIES
WINGS OF FIRE
MOON RISING

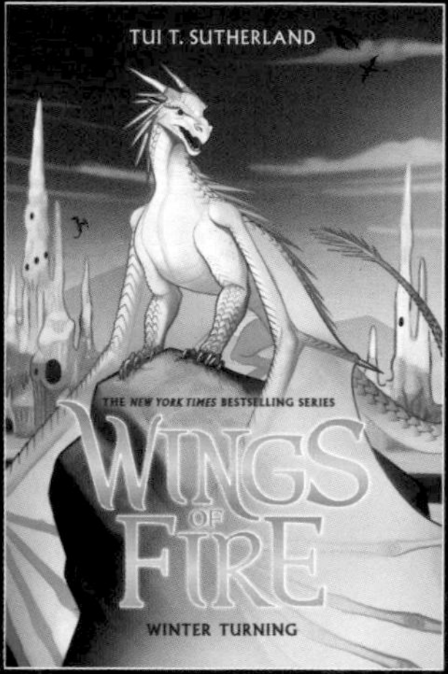
TUI T. SUTHERLAND
THE NEW YORK TIMES BESTSELLING SERIES
WINGS OF FIRE
WINTER TURNING

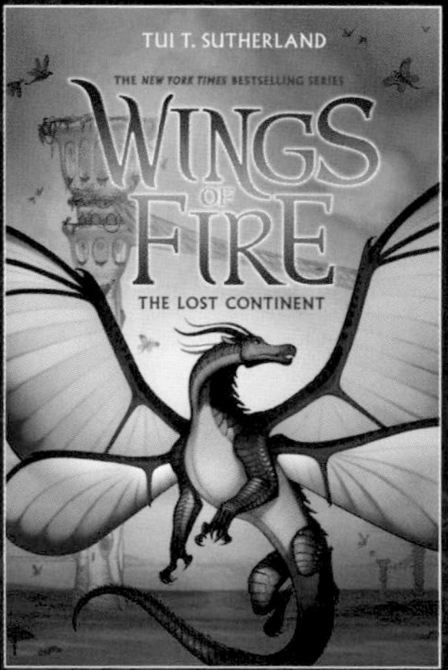
TUI T. SUTHERLAND
THE NEW YORK TIMES BESTSELLING SERIES
WINGS OF FIRE
THE LOST CONTINENT

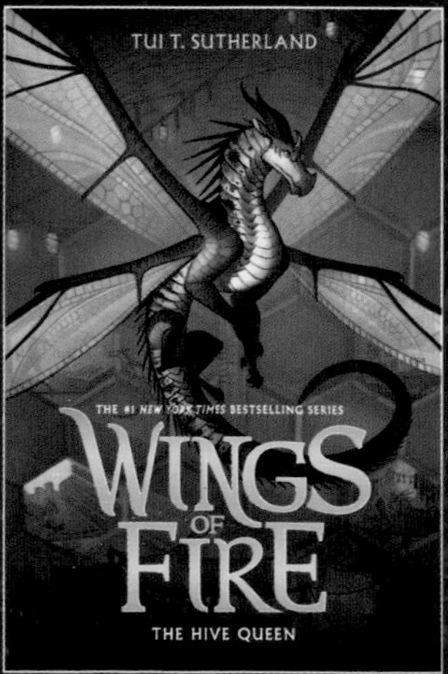
TUI T. SUTHERLAND
THE #1 NEW YORK TIMES BESTSELLING SERIES
WINGS OF FIRE
THE HIVE QUEEN

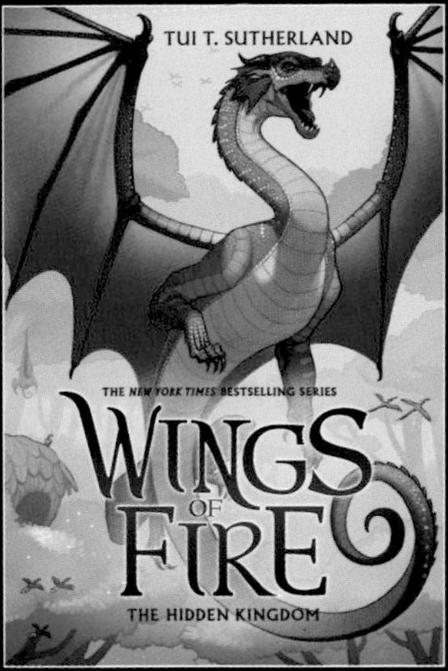
TUI T. SUTHERLAND
THE NEW YORK TIMES BESTSELLING SERIES
WINGS OF FIRE
THE HIDDEN KINGDOM

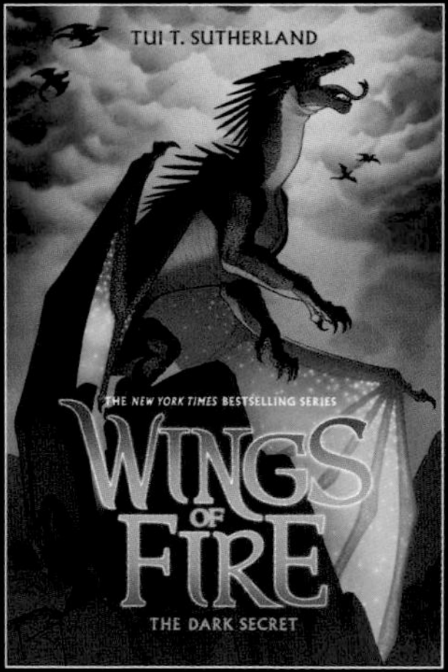
TUI T. SUTHERLAND
THE NEW YORK TIMES BESTSELLING SERIES
WINGS OF FIRE
THE DARK SECRET

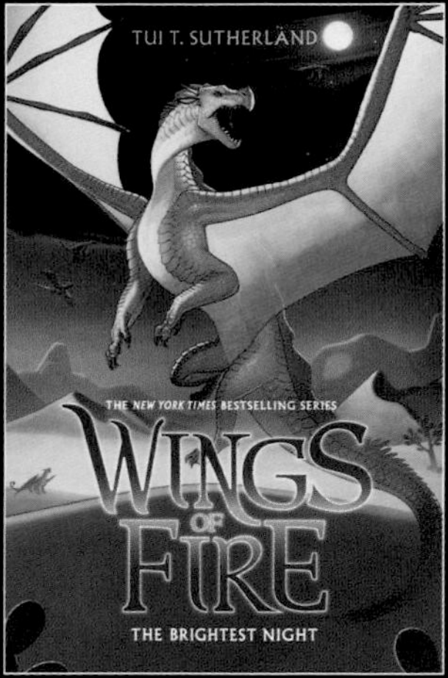
TUI T. SUTHERLAND
THE NEW YORK TIMES BESTSELLING SERIES
WINGS OF FIRE
THE BRIGHTEST NIGHT

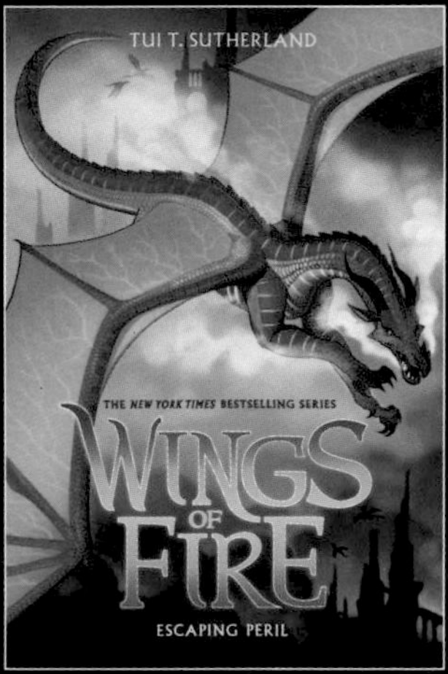
TUI T. SUTHERLAND
THE NEW YORK TIMES BESTSELLING SERIES
WINGS OF FIRE
ESCAPING PERIL

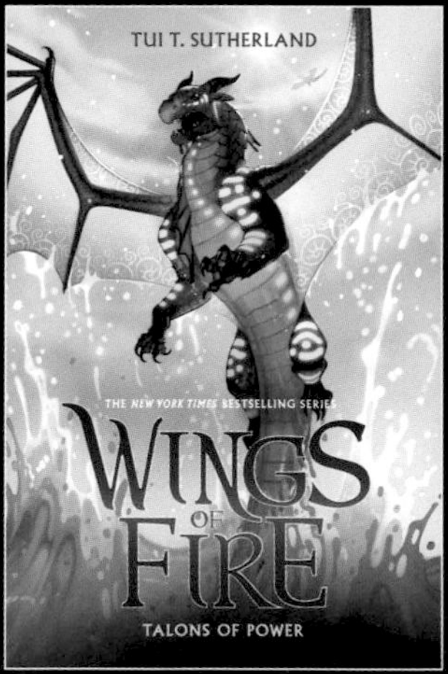
TUI T. SUTHERLAND
THE NEW YORK TIMES BESTSELLING SERIES
WINGS OF FIRE
TALONS OF POWER

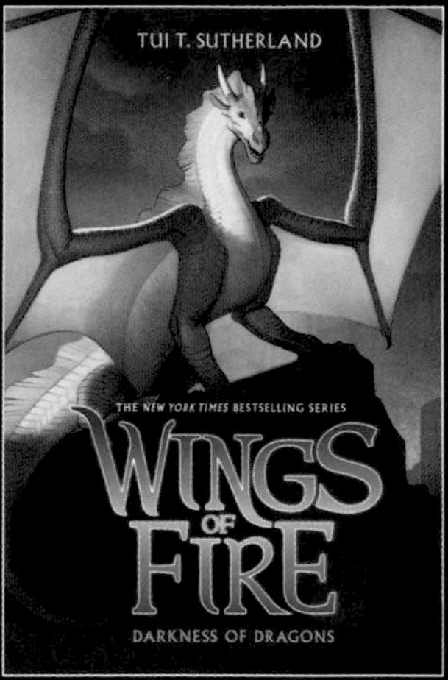
TUI T. SUTHERLAND
THE NEW YORK TIMES BESTSELLING SERIES
WINGS OF FIRE
DARKNESS OF DRAGONS

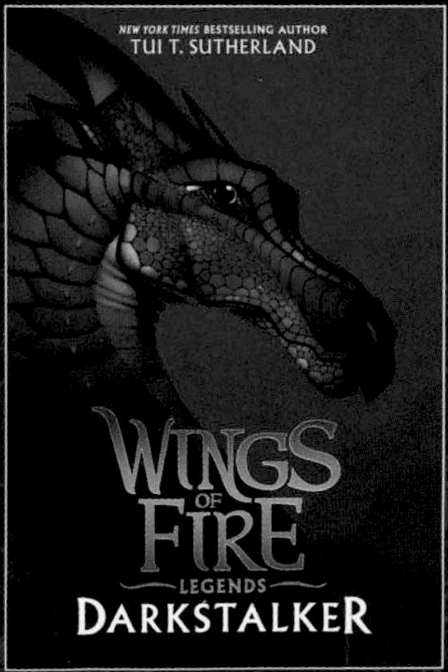
NEW YORK TIMES BESTSELLING AUTHOR
TUI T. SUTHERLAND
WINGS OF FIRE
LEGENDS
DARKSTALKER

PREQUEL

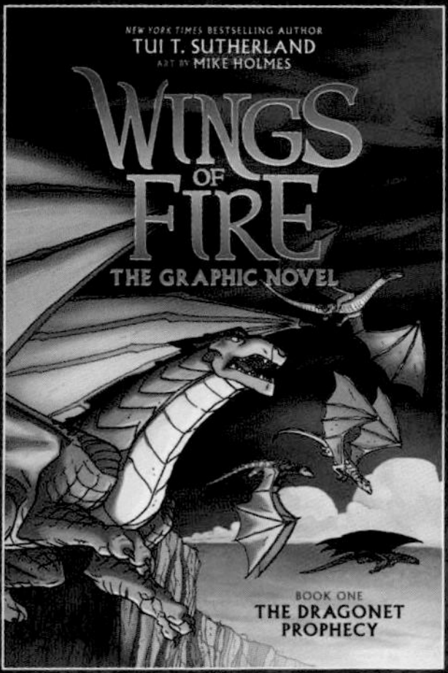
NEW YORK TIMES BESTSELLING AUTHOR
TUI T. SUTHERLAND
ART BY MIKE HOLMES
WINGS OF FIRE
THE GRAPHIC NOVEL
BOOK ONE
THE DRAGONET PROPHECY

GRAPHIC NOVEL

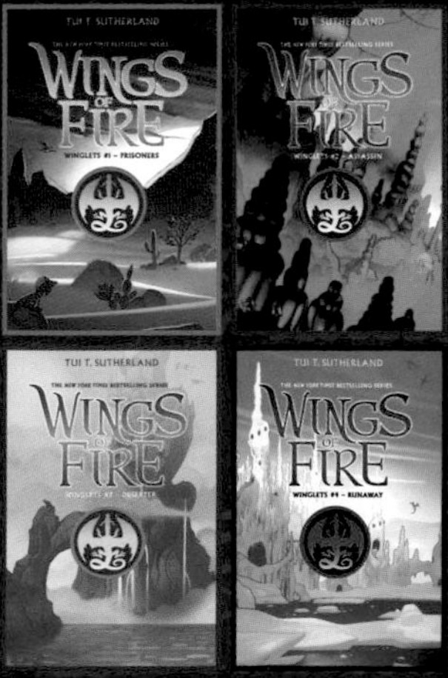
TUI T. SUTHERLAND
WINGS OF FIRE
TUI T. SUTHERLAND
WINGS OF FIRE
TUI T. SUTHERLAND
WINGS OF FIRE
TUI T. SUTHERLAND
WINGS OF FIRE

EBOOK ORIGINALS

TUI T. SUTHERLAND is the author of the *New York Times* and *USA Today* bestselling Wings of Fire series, the Menagerie trilogy, and the Pet Trouble series, as well as a contributing author to the bestselling Spirit Animals and Seekers series (as part of the Erin Hunter team). In 2009, she was a two-day champion on *Jeopardy!* She lives in Massachusetts with her wonderful husband, two awesome sons, and two very patient dogs. To learn more about Tui's books, visit her online at www.tuibooks.com.

BARRY DEUTSCH is an award-winning cartoonist and the creator of the Hereville series of graphic novels, about yet another troll-fighting 11-year-old Orthodox Jewish girl. He lives in Portland, Oregon, with a variable number of cats and fish.

MIKE HOLMES has drawn for the comics series Bravest Warriors and Adventure Time and is the creator of the art project *Mikenesses*. His books include *Secret Coders* (written by Gene Luen Yang), *Animal Crackers: Circus Mayhem* (written by Scott Christian Sava), and the *True Story* collection. He and his wife, Meredith, live in Philadelphia with their son, Oscar, Heidi the dog, and Ella the cat.

MAARTA LAIHO spends her days and nights as a comic colorist, where her work includes the comics series Lumberjanes, Adventure Time, and The Mighty Zodiac. When she's not doing that, she can be found hoarding houseplants and talking to her cat. She lives in the woods of Maine.